THE SHIELD OF
SILENCE

HARRIET T. COMSTOCK

1st WORLD
LIBRARY
Literary Society

The Shield of Silence

Harriet T. Comstock

© 1st World Library, 2007
PO Box 2211
Fairfield, IA 52556
www.1stworldlibrary.com
First Edition

LCCN: 2007901807

Softcover ISBN: 978-1-4218-4274-5
Hardcover ISBN: 978-1-4218-4176-2
eBook ISBN: 978-1-4218-4372-8

Purchase *"The Shield of Silence"*
as a traditional bound book at:
www.1stWorldLibrary.com/purchase.asp?ISBN=978-1-4218-4274-5

1st World Library is a literary, educational organization
dedicated to:

- Creating a free internet library of downloadable ebooks

- Hosting writing competitions and offering book
  publishing scholarships.

1st World Library Literary Society

Giving Back to the World

"If you want to work on the core problem, it's early school literacy."

- James Barksdale, former CEO of Netscape

"No skill is more crucial to the future of a child, or to a democratic and prosperous society, than literacy."

- Los Angeles Times

Literacy... means far more than learning how to read and write... The aim is to transmit... knowledge and promote social participation."

- UNESCO

"Literacy is not a luxury, it is a right and a responsibility. If our world is to meet the challenges of the twenty-first century we must harness the energy and creativity of all our citizens."

- President Bill Clinton

"Parents should be encouraged to read to their children, and teachers should be equipped with all available techniques for teaching literacy, so the varying needs and capacities of individual kids can be taken into account."

- Hugh Mackay

TO MY SON

PHILIP S. COMSTOCK

"We will grasp the hands of men and women; and slowly holding one another's hands we will work our way upwards."

Let us agree at once that—

We are all on the Wheel. The difference lies in our ability to cling or let go. Meredith Thornton and old Becky Adams—let go!

Across the world's heart they fell—the heart of the world may be wide or narrow—and, by the law of attraction, they came to Ridge House and Sister Angela.

Unlike, and separated by every circumstance that, according to the expected, should have kept them apart—they still had the same problem to confront and the solution had its beginning in that pleasant home for Episcopal Sisters which clings so enchantingly along the north side of what is known as Silver Gap, a cleft in the Southern mountains.

To say the solution of these women's problems had its beginnings in Ridge House is true; but that they were ever solved is another matter and this story deals with that.

Meredith Thornton was young and beautiful. Up to the hour that she let go she had lived as they live who are drugged. She had looked on life with her senses blurred and her actions largely controlled by others.

Old Becky, on the other hand, had gripped life with no uncertain hold; she, according to the vernacular of her hills, "had the call to larn," and she learned deeply.

Sister Angela had clung to the Wheel. She had swung well around the circle and she believed she was nearing the end when the strange demand was made upon her.

The demand was made by Meredith Thornton and Becky Adams. Meredith, from her great distance, somewhat prepared Sister Angela by a letter, but Becky, being unable either to read or write, simply took to the trail from her lonely cabin on Thunder Peak and claimed a promise made three years before.

And now, since *The Rock* played a definite part in what happened, it should have a word here.

In a land where nearly all the solid substance is rock—not stone, mind you—*The Rock* held a peculiar position. It dominated the landscape and the imagination of Silver Gap, and the superstition as well. It was a huge, greenish-white mass, a mile to the east of Thunder Peak, and over its smooth face innumerable waterfalls trickled and shone. With this colour and motion, like a mighty Artist, the wind and light played, forming pictures that needed little fancy to discern.

At times cities would be delicately outlined with towers and roofs rising loftily; then again one might see a deep wood with a road winding far and away, luring home-tied feet to wander. And sometimes—not often, to be sure—the Ship would ride at anchor as on a painted sea.

The Ship boded no good to Silver Gap as any one could tell. It had brought the plague and the flood; it brought bad crops and raids on hidden stills; it waited until its evil cargo had done its worst and then it sailed away in the night, bearing its pitiful load of dead, or its burden of fear and hate. Surely there was good and sufficient reason for dreading the appearance of The Ship, and on a certain autumn morning it appeared and soon after the two women, unknown to each other, came to Ridge House and this story began.

Harriet T. Comstock

CHAPTER I

"WAIT AND THY SOUL SHALL SPEAK."

There is, in the human soul, as in the depths of the ocean, a state of eternal calm. Around it the waves of unrest may surge and roar but there peace reigns. In that sanctuary the tides are born and, in their appointed time, swelling and rising, they carry the poor jetsam and flotsam of life before them.

The tide was rising in the soul of Meredith Thornton; she was awake at last. Awake as people are who have lived with their faculties drugged. The condition was partly due to the education and training of the woman, and largely to her own ability in the past to close her senses to any conception of life that differed from her desires. She had always been like that. She loved beauty and music; she loved goodness and happiness; she loved them whom she loved so well that she shut all others out. Consequently, when Life tore her defences away she had no guidance upon which to depend but that which had lain hidden in the secret place of her soul.

As a little child Meredith and her older sister, Doris, lived in New York. Their house had been in the Fletcher family for three generations and stood at the end of a dignified row, opposite a park whose iron gates opened only to those considered worthy of owning a key—the Fletchers had a key!

In the park the little Fletcher girls played—if one could call it play—under the eye of a carefully selected maid whose glance was expected to rest constantly upon them. The anxious father tried to do his double duty conscientiously, for the mother had died at Meredith's birth.

The children often peered through the high fence (it really was more fun than the stupid games directed by their elders) and wondered—at least Doris wondered; Meredith was either amused or shocked; if the latter it was an easy matter to turn aside. This hurt Doris, and to her plea that the thing was there, Meredith returned that she did not believe it, and she did not, either.

Once, shielded by the skirts of an outgoing maid, Doris made her escape and, for two thrilling and enlightening hours, revelled in the company of the Great Unknown who were not deemed worthy of keys.

Doris had found them vital, absorbing, and human; they changed the whole current of her life and thought; she was never the same again, neither was anything else.

The nurse was at once dismissed and Mr. Fletcher placed his daughters in the care of Sister Angela, who was then at the head of a fashionable school for girls—St. Mary's, it was called.

Sister Angela believed in keys but had ideas as to their uses and the good sense to keep them out of sight.

Under her wise and loving rule Doris Fletcher never suspected the hold upon her and, while she did not forget the experience she had once had outside the park, she no longer yearned to repeat it, for the present was wholesomely full. As for Meredith, she felt that all danger was removed—for Doris; for herself, what could shatter her joy? It was only running outside gates that brought trouble.

Just after the Fletcher girls graduated from St. Mary's Sister Angela's health failed.

Harriet T. Comstock

Mr. Fletcher at this time proved his gratitude and affection in a delicate and understanding way. He bought a neglected estate in the South and provided a sufficient sum of money for its restoration and upkeep, and this he put in Sister Angela's care.

"There is need of such work as you can do there," he said; "and it has always been a dream of my life to help those people of the hills. Sister, make my dream come true."

Angela at once got in touch with Father Noble, who was winning his way against great odds in the country surrounding Silver Gap, and offered her services.

"Come and live here," Father Noble replied. "It is all we can do at present. They do not want us," he had a quaint humour, "but we must change that."

Mr. Fletcher did not live long enough to see his dream do more than help prolong Sister Angela's days, for he died a year later leaving, to his daughters, a large fortune, well invested, and no commands as to its use. This faith touched both girls deeply.

"I want to travel and see all the beautiful things in the world," Meredith said when the time for expression came.

"Yes, dear," Doris replied, "and you must learn what life really means."

Naturally at this critical moment both girls turned to Sister Angela, but with the rare insight that had not deserted her, she held them from her, though her heart hungered for them.

"Ridge House is in the making," she wrote. "I am going slow, making no mistakes. I am asking some Sisters who, like me, have fallen by the way, to come here and help me with my scheme, and in the confusion of readjustment, two young girls, who ought to be forming their own plans, would be sadly in the way.

"Go abroad, my dears, take"—here Sister Angela named a woman she could trust to help, not hinder—"and learn to walk alone at last."

Doris accepted the advice and the little party went to Italy.

"Here," she said, "Merry shall have the beauty she craves and she shall learn what life means, as well."

And Meredith's learning began.

They had only been in Italy a month when George Thornton appeared. He was young, handsome, and already so successful in business that older men cast approving eyes upon him. He had chosen, at the outset of his career, to go to the Philippines and accepted an appointment there. He had devoted himself so rigidly to his duties that his health began to show the strain and he was taking his first, well-won, vacation when he met the Fletchers.

Thornton's past had been spent largely with men who, like himself, were making their way among people, and in an environment in which the finer aspects of life were disregarded. He had enjoyed himself, made himself popular, and for the rest he had waited until such a time as his success would make choice possible. When he met Meredith Fletcher he felt the time had come. The girl's exquisite aloofness, her fineness and sweetness, bewitched him. The real meaning of her character did not interest him at all. Here was something that he wanted; the rest would be an easy conquest. Thornton had always got what he wanted and lay siege to Meredith's heart at once.

His approach, while it swept Meredith before it, naturally aroused fear and apprehension in Doris. To Meredith, Thornton was an ideal materialized; to Doris, he was a menace to all that she held sacred. She distrusted him for the very traits

Harriet T. Comstock

that appealed to her sister. But she dared not oppose, for to every inquiry she hurriedly made—and there was need of hurry—she received only favourable reports.

Thornton's own fortune and prospects set aside any fears as to mercenary designs; he had no near relatives, but distant cousins in England were people of refinement and culture and on excellent terms with Thornton. Breathlessly Thornton carried everything before him. Six weeks after he met Meredith he married her.

"Why, you do not know the child," Doris had faltered when the hasty marriage was proposed, "I'm only learning to know her myself. She has never grown up. She sees life as she used to see it through the gates of the park in which she played as a little girl. She has been locked away. It is appalling. I could not believe, unless I knew, that any one could be like Merry."

Of course Thornton did not understand.

"Let me have the key," he jokingly said, "let me lead Merry out. It will be the biggest thing of my life."

And Doris knew that unless the key were given he would break the lock, so Meredith was married in the little American chapel on the hillside and she looked as if she were walking in a love-filled dream as she went out of Doris's life.

Thornton took his wife to the Philippines by way of her New York home. For a week they stayed in it, and it was there that the first sense of loss touched Meredith. The stirring effect of all that she had recently gone through was wearing away, and Doris, and all that Doris meant in the past, haunted the big, quiet house.

"This will never do," thought Thornton, and for the first time he sensed the power the older sister had over the younger. It was already making its way into his kingdom, and Thornton never shared what was his own!

Doris remained abroad for a time, readjusting her life as one does who is maimed. Her devotion to Meredith, she saw now, had been her one passion—to what could she turn?

The letters that presently came from Meredith, while they set much of her fear at rest, made her feel more lonely, nor did they seem to set her free to make permanent plans. She sank into a waiting mood—waiting for letters!

"I'll play around Europe for awhile," she whimsically decided. "I'll buy things for that chapel Sister Angela is planning, and polish my manners. And," here Doris grew grave, "I'll think of David Martin! I wish I could love Davey enough to marry him as I feel he wants me to—and let him blot out this ache for Merry." But that was not to be.

And Meredith wrote her letters to her sister and smiled upon her husband—for after the third month of her marriage that was the best she could do for either of them. All the ideals of her self-blinded life were being swept away in the glaring flame of reality.

Thornton was still infatuated and went to great lengths to prove to his pale, starry-eyed wife her power over him. He was delighted at the impression she made upon the rather hectic but exclusive circle in which he moved; but he dreaded, vaguely to be sure, her hearing, in a gross way, references to his life before she entered it. So quite frankly and a bit sketchily he confided it to her himself.

"Of course that is ended forever," he said; "you have led me from darkness to light, you wonderful child! Why, Merry, you simply have made a new and better man of me—I understand the real value of things now."

But did he?

Merry was looking at him as if she were doubting her senses. Things she had heard in her girlhood, things that floated about

Harriet T. Comstock

in the dark corners of her memory, were pressing close. Dreadful things that had been forced upon her against her will but which she reasoned could never happen to her, or to any of her own.

"You mean," she faltered gropingly at last, "that another woman has—" She could not voice the ugly words and Thornton was obliged to be a little more explicit.

Then he saw his wife retreat—spiritually. He hastened after her as best he could.

"You see, darling," he was frightened, "out here, where a fellow is cut off from home ties and all that, the old code does not hold—how could it? I'm no exception. Why, good Lord! child—" but Meredith was not listening. He saw that and it angered him.

She was hearing words spoken long ago—oh! years and years ago it seemed. Words that had lured her from Doris, from safety, from all the dangerous peace that had been hers.

"Sweetheart," that voice had said, "there is one right woman for every man, but few there be who find her. When one does—then there is no time to be lost. Life is all too short at the best for them. Come, my beloved, come!"

And she had heeded and, forsaking all else, had trusted him.

According to his lights Thornton had sincerely meant those words when he spoke them. He was under the spell, still, as he looked at the small frozen thing before him now.

If he could win her from her absurd, and almost unbelievable, position; if he could, through her love and his, gain her absolutely; make her *his*—what a conquest!

"My precious one, I am yours to do with what you will!" he was saying with all the fervour of his being; but Meredith looked at him from a great distance.

"You were never mine!" was what she said. Then asked:

"Is that—that woman here? Will I ever—meet her?"

Thornton was growing furiously angry.

"Certainly not!" he replied to her last question, incensed at the implied lack of delicacy on his part. Then he added, "Don't be a fool, Merry!"

"No, I won't," she whispered, grimly. "I won't be a fool, whatever else I am. Do you want me to leave you at once, or stay on?"

Thornton stared at her blankly.

"Good God!" he muttered; "what do you mean, stay on?"

"I mean that if I stay it will be because I don't want to hurt you more than I must—and because things don't matter much, either way. I have my own money—but, well, I'll stay on if it will help you in your business."

Then light dawned.

"You will stay on!" Thornton snapped the words out. "You are my wife, and you will stay on!"

"Very well. I will stay," Meredith turned and walked away.

Thornton looked after her and his face softened. Something in him was touched by the spirit under the cold, crude exterior of the girl. It was worth while—he would try to win her!

And that was the best hour in Thornton's life.

Could he have held to it all might have gone well, but

Thornton's successes had been due to dash and daring—the slow, patient method was not his, and against his wife's stern indifference he recoiled after a short time—she bored him; she no longer seemed worth while; not worth the struggle nor the holding to absurd and rigid demands. Still, by her smiling acquiescence, Meredith made things possible that otherwise might not have been so, and she was a charming hostess when occasion demanded.

During the second bleak year of their marriage Meredith accompanied Thornton to England—he was often obliged to go there on prolonged business—but she never repeated the experiment.

While it was comparatively easy to play her difficult role in her home, it was unbearable among her husband's people, who complicated matters by assuming that she must, of necessity, be honoured and uplifted by the alliance she had made.

After the return from England Thornton abandoned his puritanical life and returned to the easy ways of his bachelor days.

Meredith knew perfectly well what was going on, but she had her own income and lived her own detached and barren life, so she clung to what seemed to her the last shred of duty she owed to her marriage ties—she served in her husband's home as hostess, and by her mere presence she avoided betraying him to the scorn of those who could not know all, and so might not judge justly.

Then the crisis came that shocked Meredith into consciousness and forced her to act, for the first time in her life, independently.

Thornton was about to go, again, to England. The day before he sailed he came into his wife's sitting room, where she lay upon a couch, suffering from a severe headache.

She never mentioned her pain or loneliness, and to Thornton's careless glance she appeared as she always did—pale, cold, and self-centred.

"Well, I sail at noon to-morrow!" he said, seating himself astride a chair, folding his arms and settling his chin on them.

"Yes? Is there anything particular that you want me to look after in your absence?"

Meredith barely raised her eyes. Her pain was intense, but Thornton saw only indifference and an unconscious insolence in the words, tone, and languid glance.

Never before in his life had he been balked and defied and resented as he was by the pretty creature before him. The devil rose in him—and generally Thornton rode his devil with courage and control, but suddenly it reared, and he was thrown!

"Do you know," he said—and he looked handsome and powerful in his white clothes; he was splendidly correct in every detail—"there are times when I think you forget that you are my wife."

"I try to." Like all quiet people Meredith could shatter one's poise at times by her daring. She looked so small and defiant as she lay there—so secure!

"Suppose I commanded you to come with me to-morrow? Made my rightful demand after this hellish year—what would you do?"

Thornton's chin projected; his mouth smiled, not pleasantly, and his eyes held Meredith's with a light that frightened her. She sat up.

"Of course I should refuse to go with you," she replied, "and I do not acknowledge any rights of yours except those that I give you. You apparently overlook the fact that—I make

Harriet T. Comstock

no claims."

"Claims?" Thornton laughed, and the sound had a dangerous note that startled Meredith. "Claims? Good Lord! That's quaintly delicious. You don't know men, my dear. It would be a deed of charity to—inform you. Claims, indeed! You drove me, when you might have held me, and you talk claims."

"I did not want to hold you—after I knew that you had never really been mine." Meredith's words were shaken by an emotion beyond Thornton's comprehension; they further aroused the brute in him.

"This comes of locks and bars!" he sneered, recalling Doris's expression, "but, damn it all, unless you were more fool than most girls you might have saved yourself."

To this Meredith made no reply, but she crouched on the couch and gathered her knees in her arms as if clinging to the only support at her disposal.

"See here!" Thornton bent forward and his eyes blazed. "I'm going to give you a last chance. You'll come with me to-morrow and have done with this infernal rot or I'll take the woman with me who has made life possible, in the past, for you and me. What do you say?"

Horror and repulsion grew in Meredith's eyes. She went deadly white and stretched her hands wide as if shielding herself from something defiling.

"Go!" she gasped. "Go with her! By so doing I will not have to explain; I will be free to return—to Doris."

"So!" And now Thornton got up and paced the floor; "having foresworn every duty you owe me, having driven me to what you choose to call wrong, you pack your nice, clean little soul in your bag and go back to pose as—as—what in God's name will you pose as? You!"

Meredith shrank back. She was conscious now of her danger.

"Well, then!" Thornton came close and laughed down upon the shrinking form—her terror further roused the brute in him; all that was decent and fine in him—and both were there—fell into darkness; "you'll pay, by heaven! before you go. You'll—"

"Leave me alone!" Meredith sprang to her feet. "How dare you?"

And again Thornton laughed.

"Dare? You—you little idiot! You'll come with me to-morrow —by God!"

* * * * *

But Meredith did not go with Thornton on the morrow, and if the other took her place she did not seek to know.

The weeks and months dragged on and she was thankful for time to think and plot. It took so much time for one who had never acted before. And then—she knew the worst!

Thornton might return at any time and soon—her child would be born! First terror, then a growing calmness, possessed Meredith. She forgot Thornton in her planning, forgot her own misery and sense of wrong. She did not hate her child as she might have—she learned in the end to consider it as the one opportunity left to her of saving whatever was good in her and Thornton. She clung to that good, she was just, at last, to Thornton as well as herself. Both he and she were victims of ignorance—the little coming child must be saved from that ignorance; the father's and—yes, her own, for Meredith was convinced that she would not live through her ordeal.

Thornton must not have the child—he was unfit for that sacred duty of giving it the chance that had been denied the

Harriet T. Comstock

parents. The new life must have its roots in cleaner and purer soil. Doris must save it. Doris!

Then Meredith wrote three notes. One was to Sister Angela:

> You remember how, as a little girl, you let me come to you and tell you things that I could not tell even to God? I am coming now, Sister—will be there soon after this reaches you; and then—I will tell you!
>
> I want my child to be born with you and Doris near me. I have written to Doris.
>
> And whether I live or die, my husband must not have my child. You must help me.

The second letter was longer, for it contained explanations and reasons. These were stated baldly, briefly, but for that very quality they rang luridly dramatic.

The third note was left on Thornton's desk and simply informed him that she was going to Doris and would never return.

CHAPTER II

"MINDS THAT SWAY THE FUTURE LIKE A TIDE"

Sister Angela read her letter sitting before the fire in the living room at Ridge House.

She read it over and over and then, as was common with her, she clasped the cross that hung from her girdle—and opened her soul. She called it prayer. Meredith became personally near her—the written words had materialized her. With the clairvoyance that had been part of her equipment in dealing with people and events of the past, Angela began slowly to understand.

So actually was she possessed by reality that her face grew grim and deadly pale. She was a woman of experience in the worldly sense, but she was unyielding in her spiritual interpretation of moral codes. She felt the full weight of the tragedy that had overwhelmed a girl of Meredith Thornton's type. She had no inclination, nor was there time now, to consider Thornton's side of this terrible condition. She must act for Meredith and Meredith's child.

Folding the letter, she dropped it into her pocket and sent for Sister Janice, the housekeeper.

Angela gave silent thanks for Janice's temperament.

Janice was so cheerful as often to depress others; so grateful

Harriet T. Comstock

that she gloried in self-abnegation and had no curiosity outside a given command.

"The house must be got ready for visitors," Angela informed Janice. "Two former pupils—and one of them is ill." When she said this Angela paused. How did she know Meredith was ill?

"Shall I open the west wing?" asked Janice, alert as to her duties.

"Open everything. Have the place at its best; but I would like the younger sister, Mrs. Thornton, to have the chamber on the south, the guest chamber."

When Janice had departed, Sister Constance appeared.

In her early days Constance had been a famous nurse and for years afterward the head of a school for nurses. Her eyes brightened now as she listened to her superior. She had long chafed under the strain of inaction. She listened and nodded.

"Everything shall be done as you wish, Sister," she said at last, and Angela knew that it would be.

Lastly, old Jed was called from his outside duties and stood, battered hat in hand, to receive his commands. Jed was old and black and his wool was white as snow; his strong, perfect teeth glittered with gold fillings. How the old man had fallen to this vanity no one knew, but sooner or later all the money he made was converted into fillings.

"They do say," he once explained to Sister Angela, "that 'tain't all gold as glitters, but dis year yaller in my mouth, ma'am, is right sure gold an' it's like layin' up treasure in heaven, for no moth nor rust ain't ever going to distroy anythin' in my mouth. No, ma'am! No corruption, nuther."

Jed, listening to Sister Angela, now, was beaming and shining.

"I want you to go to Stone Hedgeton to-morrow, Uncle Jed. You better start early. You must meet every train until you see a young lady—she will be looking about for someone—and bring her here. In between trains make yourself and the horses comfortable at the tavern. I'm glad you do not drink, Jed."

"Yes-m," pondered Jed, "but I 'spect there might be mo' dan one young lady. I reckon it would be disastering if I fotched the wrong one. Isn't thar something 'bout her discounterments as might be leading, as yo' might say, ma'am?"

"Jed, I rely upon you to bring the right young lady!"

There was no use of further arguing. Jed shuffled off.

Alone, of all the household, little Mary Allan was not taken into Sister Angela's confidence, and this was unfortunate, for Mary ran well in harness, but was apt to go a bit wild if left to her own devices. What people did not confide to Mary she generally found out for herself.

Mary was known to Silver Gap as the "last of them Allans." Her father and mother both died soon after Mary showed signs of persisting—her ten brothers and sisters had refused to live, and when Mary was left to her fate Sister Angela rescued her, and the girl had been trained for entrance into a Sisterhood later on.

She was abnormally keen but discouragingly superstitious; she had moods when the Sisters believed they had overcome her inheritance of reticence and aloofness. She would laugh and chat gaily and appear charmingly young and happy, but without warning she would lapse back to the almost sullen, suspicious attitude that was so disconcerting. Sister Angela demanded justice for Mary and received, in return, a kind of loyalty that was the best the girl had to give.

She regarded, with that strange interpretation of the lonely hills, all outsiders as foreigners. She was receiving benefits from

Harriet T. Comstock

them, her only chance of life, and while she blindly repaid in services, Mary's roots clung to the cabin life; her affections to the fast-decaying hovel from which she had been rescued.

Jed was the only familiar creature left to Mary's inner consciousness. He belonged to the hills—if not of them, and while his birthright made it possible for him to assimilate, he shared with Mary the feeling that he was among strangers.

Jed thought in strains of "quality"; Mary in terms of "outlanders." But both served loyally.

The morning that Jed was to start on his mysterious errand— and he gloried in the mystery—Mary was "minding" bread in the kitchen and "chunking" wood in the stove with a lavish hand. The Sisters were at prayer in the tiny chapel which had been evolved from a small west room; and old Aunt Becky Adams was plodding down the rugged trail from Thunder Peak. Meredith Thornton, too, was nearing her destination and The Ship was on The Rock.

Presently Mary, having tested the state of the golden-brown ovals in the oven—and she could do it to a nicety—came out of the kitchen, followed by a delicious smell of crisping wheat, and sat down upon the step of the porch to watch Jed polishing the harness of Washington and Lincoln—the grave, reliable team upon whom Jed spared no toil.

Mary looked very brief and slim in her scanty blue cotton frock and the apron far too large for her. The hair, tidily caught in a firm little knot, was making brave efforts to escape in wild little curls, and the girl's big eyes had the expression seen in the eyes of an animal that has been trapped but not conquered.

"Uncle Jed," she said in an awed tone, and planting her sharp elbows on her knees in order to prop her serious face, "The Ship is on The Rock."

All the morning Jed had been trying to keep his back to the fact.

"Yo' sure is one triflin' child," he muttered.

"All the same, The Ship is there, Uncle Jed, and that means that something is going to happen. It is going to happen long o' Ridge House—and nothing has happened here before. Things have just gone on—and—on and on—"

The girl's voice trailed vaguely—she was looking at The Ship.

Jed began to have that sensation described by him as "shivers in the spine of his back." Mary was fascinating him. Suddenly she asked:

"Uncle Jed, what are they-all sending you to—fetch?" Mary almost said "fotch."

"How you know, child, I is goin' to fotch—anything?" Jed's spine was affecting his moral fibre.

Mary gave her elfish laugh. She rarely smiled, and her laugh was a mere sound—not harsh, but mirthless.

"I *know!*" she said, "and it came—no matter what it is on The Ship, and I 'low it will go—on The Ship."

"Gawd A'mighty!" Jed burst out, "you make me creep like I had pneumonia fever." With this Jed turned to The Rock and confronted The Ship.

"Gawd!" he murmured, "I sho' am anxious and trubbled."

Then he turned, mounted the step of the creaky carriage, and gave his whip that peculiar twist that only a born master of horses ever can.

It was like Jed to do that which he was ordained to

Harriet T. Comstock

do promptly.

Mary watched him out of sight and then went indoors. She was depressed and nervous; her keen ear had heard much not intended for her to hear, but not enough to control the imagination that was fired by superstition.

"A happening" was looming near. Something grave threatened. The evil crew of The Ship was but biding its time to strike, and Mary thrilled and feared at once.

The bread, as Mary sniffed, was ready to be taken from the oven. The first loaf was poised nicely on the girl's towel-covered hand when a dark, bent old woman drifted, rather than walked, into the sunny kitchen. She came noiselessly like a shadow; she was dirty and in rags; she looked, all but her eyes, as if she might be a hundred years old, but her eyes held so much fire and undying youth that they were terrible set in the crinkled, rust-coloured face.

"I want her!" The words, spoken close to her shoulder caused Mary to drop the loaf and turn in affright.

"I want—her!"

"Gawd! Aunt Becky!" gasped Mary, dropping, like a cloak, the thin veneer of all that Ridge House had done for her. "Gawd! Aunt Becky, I done thought you was—dead and all. I ain't seen you in ages. Won't you set?"

The woman stretched a claw-like hand forth and laid it on the shoulder of the girl.

"Don't you argify with me—Mary Allan. I want her."

There seemed to be no doubt in Mary's mind as to whom Aunt Becky wanted.

"Sister Angela is at prayer, Aunt Becky," she whispered, trying to escape from the clutch upon her shoulder.

"Mary Allan—go tell her I want her. Go!" There was that in Becky's tone that commanded obedience. Mary started to the hall, her feet clattering as she ran toward the chapel on the floor above.

Becky followed, more slowly. She got as far as the opened door of the living room, then she paused, glanced about, and went in.

There are some rooms that repel; others that seem to rush forward with warm welcome. The living room at Ridge House was one that made a stranger feel as if he had long been expected and desired. It was not unfamiliar to the old woman who now entered it. Through the windows she had often held silent and unsuspected vigil. It was her way to know the trails over which she might be called to travel and since that day, three years before, when Sister Angela had met her on the road and made her startling proposition, Becky had subconsciously known that, in due time, she would be compelled to accept what then she had so angrily refused.

On that first encounter Sister Angela had said:

"They tell me that you have a little granddaughter—a very pretty child."

"Yo' mean Zalie?" Becky was on her guard.

"I did not know her name. How old is she?"

"Nigh onter fifteen." The strange eyes were holding Sister Angela's calm gaze—the old woman was awaiting the time to spring.

"It is wrong to keep a young girl on that lonely peak away from everyone, as I am told that you do. Won't you let her come to Ridge House? We will teach her—fit her for some useful work."

Sister Angela at that time did not know her neighbours as well as she later learned to know them. Becky came nearer, and her thin lips curled back from her toothless jaws.

"You-all keep yo' hands off Zalie an' me! I kin larn my gal all she needs to know. All other larnin' would harm her, and no Popish folk ain't going to tech what's mine."

So that was what kept them apart!

Sister Angela drew back. For a moment she did not understand; then she smiled and bent nearer.

"You think us Catholics? We are not; but if we were it would be just the same. We are friendly women who really want to be neighbourly and helpful."

"You all tote a cross!" Becky was interested.

"Yes. We bear the cross—it is a symbol of what we try to do— you need not be afraid of us, and if there is ever a time when you need us—come to Ridge House."

After that Becky had apparently disappeared, but often and often when the night was stormy, or dark, she had walked stealthily down the trail and taken her place by the windows of Ridge House. She knew the sunny, orderly kitchen in which such strange food was prepared; she knew the long, narrow dining room with its quaint carvings and painted words on walls and fireplace; she knew the tiny room where the Sisters knelt and sang. One or two of the tunes ran in Becky's brain like haunting undercurrents; but best of all, Becky knew the living room upon whose generous hearth the fire burned from early autumn until the bloom of dogwood, azalea, and laurel filled the space from which the ashes were reluctantly swept. Every rug and chair and couch was familiar to the burning eyes. The rows of bookshelves, the long, narrow table and—The Picture on the Wall!

To that picture Becky went now. She had never been able to see it distinctly from any window. It was the Good Shepherd. The noble, patient face bent over the child on the man's breast had power to still Becky's distraught mind. She could not understand, but a groping of that part of her that could still feel and suffer reached the underlying suggestion of the artist. Here was someone who was doing what, in a vague and bungling way, Becky herself had always wanted to do—shield the young, helpless thing that belonged to her.

The old face twitched and the soiled, crinkled arms—so empty and yearning—hugged the trembling body. And so Sister Angela found her.

The three years since Angela had seen Becky Adams had taught her much of her people—she called them *her* people, now.

"I am so glad to see you, Aunt Becky," she said, smiling and pointing to a chair by the hearth, quite in an easy way. "Are you tired after your long walk?"

"Sorter." Becky came over to the chair and sank into it. Then she said abruptly: "Zalie's gone!"

The brief statement had power to visualize the young creature as Angela had once seen her: pretty as the flower whose name she bore, a little shy thing with hungry, half-afraid eyes.

"Is she—dead?" Sister Angela's gaze grew deep and sympathetic.

"Not 'zactly—not daid—jes now." Poor Becky, breaking through her own reserve and agony, made a pitiful appeal.

"She has—gone away? With whom?" Sister Angela began to comprehend and she lowered her voice, bending toward Becky.

Harriet T. Comstock

"She ain't gone with any one—she didn't have ter—but she'll fotch up with someone fore long. She's gone to larn—she got the call, same as all her kin—it's the curse!"

Now that the wall of reserve was down the pent waters rushed through and they came on the fanciful, dramatic words peculiar to Becky and her kind. Angela did not interrupt—she waited while the old, stifled voice ran on:

"I had to larn, and I went far and saw sights, and when it was larned I cum back, with Zalie's mother rolled up like she was a bundle. The old cabin was empty 'cept for wild things as found shelter there—me and her settled down and no one found out for some time, and then it didn't matter!

"Zalie's mother, she had to larn and she went with a man as helped her larn powerful quick. He don killed my gal by his ways an' he left her to die. It was a stranger as brought Zalie to me, and then I set myself to the task of keeping her from the curse—but she got the call and she went! I can see her"—here the strange eyes looked as the eyes of a seer look—they were following the girl on the "larnin' way"; the tired voice trailed sadly—"I can see how she went. It was nearing morning and all the moonlight that the night had left was piled like mist down in the Gap. Her head was up and she had her hands out —sorter feelin', feelin', and she would laugh—oh! she would laugh—and then she'd catch the scent, and be off! Oh! my Gawd, my Gawd!"

Becky swayed back and forth and moaned softly as one does who has emptied his soul and waits.

Sister Angela got up and bent over the old woman, her thin white hand on the crouching back.

"When did this happen?" she asked.

"Mos' a year back!"

"And you have only come now to tell me? Why did you wait?"

"Twasn't no use coming before—but now, I 'low she's coming back, same as all us does, after the larnin'! I had a vision las' night—and this morning—I saw The Ship on the Rock—she'll come!"

Again the old woman's eyes were lifted and she peered into the depths of the fire.

"I seed Zalie las' night! She come with hit."

"With what?" Sister Angela had that peculiar pricking sensation of the skin caused by tense nerves.

"With hit. Her young-un! That's what larnin' means to us-all. Hit! After that, nothin' counts one way or 'other. Zalie spoke in her vision—clear like she was in the flesh. She don made me understand that I mus' give hit a chance; break the curse—there is only one way!"

"What way, Becky?" Angela was whispering as if she and the old woman near her were conspiring together.

"Hit mus' go where no one knows—no one ever can know. It's the knowin' that damns us-all. Folks knowin' an' expectin'—an' helpin' the curse. Hit's got to start fresh an' no one knowin'."

Becky's voice was sepulchral.

"You mean," Angela asked, "that if Zalie comes back with a child that you want me to take it, find a home for it—where no one will ever know?"

"You-all don promised to help me," Becky pleaded, for she caught the doubting tone in Angela's voice; "you-all ain't goin' back on that, air yo'?"

The burning eyes fell upon the cross at Angela's side.

"No," she said. "No. Becky, I promise to help you. But suppose Zalie, should she have a child, refused to give it up?"

Becky's face quivered.

"She won't las', Zalie won't." The stricken voice was as confident as if Zalie already lay dead. "Zalie ain't got stayin' powers, she ain't. She don have fever an' what-all—an' she won't las' long—she'll go on The Ship! But if you-all hide hit —so The Ship can't take hit—if you-all give hit hit's chance— then the curse will be broke."

There was pleading, renunciation, and command in the guttural voice:

"Becky, I will promise to help you. If there is a child and you renounce all claim to it, I will find a home for it. It shall have its chance. And now sit here and rest—I am going to bring some food to you."

Sister Angela arose and passed from the room. The doing of the kindly, commonplace thing restored her to her usual calm.

She was not gone long, but when she returned, bearing the tray, Becky had departed and the chair in which she had sat was still swaying.

CHAPTER III

"I BRUSHED ALL OBSTRUCTIONS FROM MY DOORSILL AND STEPPED INTO THE ROAD"

It was just after sunset the following day when Jed turned from the Big Road into the River Road and thanked God that the next five miles could be made before early darkness set in.

Beside him sat Meredith Thornton, white lipped and wide-eyed, and her aristocratic bags rattled around in the space behind.

The smile with which Meredith had faced her past three years lingered still on the set mouth—the smile was for Jed.

"There seem to be more downs than ups on this road," the girl said, in order to cover a groan. "It will be awful after dark."

"Dark or light, ma'am," Jed returned, "it's all the same to me, ma'am. I know dese little ole humps like I know my fingers and toes, ma'am."

"Do—do you always hit the same humps?" Jed was hitting one now, squarely.

"Mostly, ma'am; but I'm studyin' to get there before dark, ma'am. If Washington now, ma'am"—Jed indicated the sleeker of the two horses—"had the ginger, so to speak, ma'am, as Lincoln has got—why, ma'am, the River Road would be flyin' out behind, ma'am, like it war a tail of a kite."

Meredith managed to give a weak laugh and, as the wagon hit another hump, she edged toward Jed. After a few moments he felt her head against his shoulder—from suffering and exhaustion she fell into a brief and troubled sleep.

Like one carved from rock, Jed held his position while a reverent expression grew upon his face.

The glow showed yellow through the western sky, The Gap was growing purplish and dim, and just then, across a foot bridge over the river, a hurrying, bent form appeared. It swayed perilously—Jed heard a muttered curse.

"Gawd A'mighty," he breathed, "it's ole Aunt Becky come back to add to trubble after us-all hopin' she was daid—or something."

Becky was coming toward the road, bending over the bundle she bore; she paused, looked down, and then darted ahead right in the path of the horses. They reared and something snapped.

Meredith awoke and sat up with a cry.

"What is the matter?" she asked. "An accident?"

"'Tain't nothin' so bad as an accident, ma'am," Jed reassured her, "but I don't take no chances with Lincoln's hind hoofs, ma'am, an' somethin' done cracked in dat quarter."

The pause gave Aunt Becky time to reach Ridge House and play her part in the scheme of things.

Panting and well nigh exhausted, the old woman staggered on and was thankful to see at her journey's end that but one light shone in the quiet house. The light was in the living room where Angela sat alone waiting for Meredith Thornton. She had quite forgotten, in her growingly anxious hours, all about poor Becky and her sorrows. So now, when the long window, opening on the west porch, swayed inward, she started up with outstretched arms—and confronted Becky.

"I've brung hit!" Becky staggered to a chair, uninvited, and sat down with her burden, wrapped in a dirty, old quilt, upon her knees.

Angela sat down also—she was speechless and frightened. She watched the old woman unfold the coverings, and she saw the form of a sleeping new-born baby exposed to the heat and light of the fire. She tried to say something, to get control of herself, but she only succeeded in bending nearer the apparition.

"Zalie she cum las' night like I told you she would. She's daid now—Zalie is. I don buried her at sun-up—an' I want it tole —if it ever is tole—that the child was buried long o' Zalie. She done planned while she was a-dying.

"I told her what you-all promised an' she went real content-like after that."

There was sodden despair in Becky's voice.

"Who—is the father of this child?"

The commonplace question, under the strain, sounded trivial —but it was rung from Angela's dismay.

Becky gave a rough laugh.

"Not the agony o' death an' the fear o' hell could wring that out of Zalie," she said. Then: "Yo' ain't goin' back on yo' promise, are yo'?"

Sister Angela rallied. At any moment the wheels on the road might end her time for considering poor Becky.

"You mean," she whispered, "that you renounce—this child; give it to me, now? You mean—that I must find a home for it?"

"Yo' done promised—an' it eased Zalie at the end."

Angela reached for the child—she was calm and self-possessed at last. This was not the first child she had rescued.

"It is—a girl?" she asked, lifting the tiny form.

"Hit's a girl. Give hit a chance."

"I will." Then Angela wrapped the child in the old quilt and turned toward the door.

"Will you wait until I return?" she paused to ask, but Becky, her eyes on that picture of the Good Shepherd, replied:

"No—I don let go!"

With that she passed as noiselessly from the room as if she were but a shadow sinking into the darkness outside.

Angela went upstairs and knocked at Sister Constance's door. Sister Constance was alert at once. Every faculty of hers was trained to respond intelligently to taps on the door in the middle of the night.

"This is—a child—a mountain child," whispered Sister Angela. "It has been left here. Take it into the west wing and tell no one of its presence until we know whether it will be claimed!"

"Very well, Sister." Constance folded the child to her ample breast; the maternal in her gave the training she had received a divine quality. The baby stirred, stretched out its little limbs, and opened its vague, sleep-filled eyes as if at last something worthy of response had appealed to it.

Sister Angela stood in the cold, dark hall listening, and when the door of the west wing chamber closed, she felt, once more, secure. Sister Angela was never able to describe afterward the state of mind that made the happenings of the next few hours seem like flaming pillars against a dead blur of sensation.

There was the sound of wheels. That set every nerve tense.

Meredith was in her arms—clinging, sobbing, and repeating:

"He must never have my child, Sister. Promise, promise!"

"I promise, my darling. I promise." Angela heard herself saying the words as if they proceeded from the lips of a stranger.

"Has Doris come?"

"Not yet. She will be here soon."

"I can trust you and Doris. Doris knows. And now—I let go!"

Where had Sister Angela heard those words before? They went whirling through her brain as if on a mighty wheel.

"I have—let go!"

Then followed terrible hours in the guest chamber with Sister Constance repeating over and over: "It is a perfectly plain case. All is well."

Finally, there was quiet, and then that cry that has power to move the world's heart, a plaintive wail weighted with relinquishment and—acceptance. Meredith's little daughter was born just as the clock below chimed four.

"I will take it to the west wing," Constance said. "Call me if you need me."

But everything seemed settling into calm, and Meredith fell

asleep looking as she used to look in the old days before she had been forced outside the gates. At daylight she opened her eyes.

"Is it morning?" she asked of Sister Angela who sat beside her.

"Yes, dear heart."

"Raise the shade, Sister." Then, as Angela raised it—"Why, how strange! What is that, Sister?"

Angela looked and saw The Ship! In that hour when vitality runs low and with the past horrors of the night still holding her, all the superstition of The Gap claimed her.

"I—I was afraid I would lose the ship." Meredith's mind wandered back to her hurried home-leaving; the dread that the ship that was to bear her from the Philippines might have gone. The mystic Ship upon The Rock was all that was needed to fix her fancy.

"But—I was in time. I *am* in time. The Ship—is waiting. Everything is all right now!—quite all right, Sister?"

Angela went close to the bed.

"My dear one!" she whispered and slipped her arm under Meredith's head.

"It all seems so—plain in the morning, Sister. It is the night that makes us afraid. The night! I cannot remember—what it was—I dreamed."

"Never mind, little girl"—Angela's tears were dropping on the soft, smooth hair that was growing clammy; she felt the cold breath on her face—"never mind, little girl, the dream is past."

"Sister, it was a bad dream. I do not like bad dreams—tell Doris—what is it that I want you to tell Doris?"

"Try to sleep, beloved." Angela knelt.

Meredith slipped back to her childhood—she gave a short, hurting laugh. "Tell her—tell Doris—I did try to learn my lesson—but—"

It was the opening of the door that startled Angela into consciousness. Doris Fletcher stood within the room. Her eyes took in the scene, the pretty face against Sister Angela's bosom; the sunlight lying full across the bed and picking out into a gleam the golden cross that hung to the floor.

"I'm too—late!"

Agony rang in the quiet words.

"And I've travelled day and night! Her letter was forwarded to me."

The letter burned against Doris's bosom like a tangible thing. She crossed the room and sank beside the bed.

They all slipped through the following days as people do who realize that troubles do not come to them, but are overtaken on the way. They seemed always to have been there; some people pass on the other side, but if one's path lies close, then one must go with what courage possible—look hard, feel and groan with the understanding, and pass on as best he can bearing the memory with him.

Father Noble came from many miles back in the hills. Riding his sturdy little horse, his loose black cloak floating like benignant wings bearing him on; his radiant old face shining even in the face of death.

He stayed until the wound in the hillside was covered over Meredith's little form; stayed to see the flowers hide the scar, murmuring again and again: "In the hope of joyful resurrection." His was the task to bridge life and death, and there was no doubt in his beautiful soul.

"And now," he said, after four days, "I must go to Cleaver's Clearing"—the Clearing was twenty hard miles away. "There are children there who never heard of God until I took some toys to them last Christmas. Then they thought that I was God. They are sick now, poor children—bad food; no care— ah! well, they will learn, they will learn."

And the old man rode away.

And still Doris had not seen Meredith's child.

"I cannot, Sister," she had pleaded. "I can think of it only as George Thornton's child."

The hate in Doris's heart was so new and appalling a sensation that it frightened her.

She tried to think of the unseen child with the love that she felt for all children—but that one! She struggled to overcome the sickening aversion that grew, instead of lessened, while the days dragged on. But always the helpless child represented nothing but passion, brutality, suffering, and disgrace. It was *not* a child, a piteous, pleading child—it was the essence of Wrong made visible.

Sister Angela was deeply concerned. The unnatural attitude called forth her old manner of authority. Sitting alone with Doris before the fire in the living room the evening of Meredith's funeral and Father Noble's departure she grew stern and commanding.

"This will never do, my dear," she said. "It cannot be that life has made of you a cruel, unjust woman."

Doris dropped her eyes—they were wonderful eyes, her real and only claim to beauty. Dusky eyes they were, with a light in them of amber.

"How much did Merry tell you?" she asked, faintly, for the older woman looked so frail and pure that it seemed impossible that she knew the worst.

"My dear, she told me—nothing. Her letter said that she wanted to tell me things—things that she could not tell to God"—Angela unconsciously touched her cross—"but there was no time. No time."

"There are things that women cannot tell to God, Sister. Things that they can only tell to some women!"

A bitterness that she could not control shook Doris's voice. She shrank from touching the exquisite detachment of Sister Angela by the truth, and yet she must have as much sympathy as possible and, certainly, cooeperation.

"Sister, this child should never have been born!"

The words reached where former words had failed. A flush touched Angela's white face—it was like sunrise on snow. Then, after a pause:

"Did—Meredith—think that?" A growing sternness gave Doris hope that she might be saved the details that were like poison in her blood.

"Yes. Protected by—by what is law—George Thornton—"

But Angela raised her thin, transparent hand commandingly. It was as if she were staying the torrents of wrong and shame that threatened to deluge all that she had gained by her life of renunciation and repression—and yet in her clear eyes there gleamed the understanding of the depths.

"May God have mercy upon—the child!" was what she said, and by those words she took her stand between past wrong and hope of future justice. "You must take this child, Doris," she said . "All that you know and feel but make the course

Harriet T. Comstock

imperative and inevitable."

"Sister, how can I—feeling as I do?"

"Can you afford not to? Can you leave it—to such a man?"

"But, Sister, you do not know him. If I should conquer my aversion and take the child, if I succeeded in loving it—he would bide his time and claim it. The law that made this horrible thing possible covers his claim to the child."

Angela drooped back in her chair. She looked old and beaten.

"He must not have the child," she murmured. "It's the only chance for the salvation of Meredith's little girl. He *shall* not have it!"

Doris bent toward the fire holding her cold, clasped hands to the heat. Suddenly she turned.

"I am growing nervous," she said, "I thought I heard someone pressing against the window—I thought I saw—a shadow drift outside in the moonlight."

Angela started and sat upright. Every sense was alert—she was remembering her promise to old Becky!

"I wish," she said, haltingly, "I wish I had consulted Father Noble. I have undertaken too much."

"Consulted him about what, Sister?" Doris was touched by the quivering voice and strained eyes; she set her own trouble aside.

Again that pressing sound, and the wind swirling the dead leaves against the house.

"About a little deserted mountain child upstairs. I have promised to find a home for it, but I cannot manage such things any more—I am too old."

The words came plaintively, as if defending against implied neglect.

Doris's eyes grew deep and concerned.

"A deserted child?" she repeated. In the feverish haste and trouble of the past few days the ordinary life of Ridge House had held no part. It seemed to be claiming its rights now, pushing her aside.

Then Sister Angela, her tired face set toward the long window whence came that pressing sound and the swish of the wind, told Becky's story. She told it as she might if Becky were listening, ready at any lapse to correct her, but she carefully refrained from mentioning names.

It eased her mind to turn from Doris's trouble to poor Becky's, and she saw with relief that Doris was listening; was interested.

"It is strange," Sister Angela mused, when the bare telling of the story was over, "how the deep, cruel things in life are met by people in much the same way—the ignorant and the wise, when they touch the inscrutable they let go and turn to a higher power than their own. Meredith felt that her child's chance in life lay in a new and fresh start. The mountain woman's curse, as she termed it, could only be conquered, so she pleaded, by giving her grandchild to those who did not know. It amounts to the same thing.

"Meredith is—gone; the old woman of the hills cannot last long. I wonder, as to the children—I wonder!"

Doris's eyes were burning and her voice shook when she spoke. Her words and tone startled Angela.

"Where is the—the mountain child?" she asked.

Harriet T. Comstock

"Upstairs, my dear. Why, Doris, you are shaking as if you had a chill. You are ill—let me call Sister Constance."

But Doris stayed her as she rose.

"No, no, Sister. I am only trembling because my feet are set on a possible way! I am—I am pushing things aside. Tell me, is this child a girl?"

"Yes."

"How old is it?"

"It was born the night before Meredith's child. It survived against grave dangers—it had no care, really, for twenty-four hours."

"You—you think it will live?"

"Yes."

"Do you think—the grandmother will ever reclaim it?"

"No, my dear. She is very old. I do not know how old, but certainly she cannot last much longer. She is a strange creature, but I am confident she realizes all that she said."

"And she is right—it is the only way." Doris was now speaking more to herself than to Angela. It was as if she were arguing, seeking to convince her conservative self before she stepped out upon a new and perilous path.

"No one knowing! Then the start could be new. It is the knowing, expecting, and suggesting that do the harm. We may call it inheritance, but it may be that we evolve from our knowledge and fears the very thing we would avert if we were left free."

Sister Angela bent forward. She whispered as if she felt the necessity of secrecy.

"What do you mean?"

"Sister, can you not see? Suppose it were possible for me to take Merry's child without the knowledge of its inheritance from the father. Suppose this little mountain child were given its chance among people who did not know."

"The children would reveal themselves, my dear." Angela was defending, she knew not what, but all her nature was up in arms. "It is God's way."

"Or our bungling and lack of faith, Sister, which?"

All the weariness and hopelessness passed from Doris's face; she was eager, her eyes shone. Presently she stood up, her back to the fire, her glance on that far window that opened to the starry night and the narrow, flower-hidden bed on the hill.

"Sister Angela," the words were spoken solemnly as a vow might be taken before God, "I am going to take—both children. But on one condition—I am not to know which is Meredith's."

A log rolling from the irons startled the women—their nerves were strained to the breaking point.

"Impossible!" gasped Angela.

"Why?"

"Your own has claims upon you!"

"None that I am not willing to give—but this is the only way. If, as you say, it is God's way that they reveal themselves, then I lose; if God is with me, I win."

"Dare—you?"

Doris stretched her arms as if pushing aside every obstacle.

"I do," she said. "I am not a daring woman: I am a weak and fearful one—this, though, I dare!"

"But the father—" Angela whispered.

"The—father—" Doris's eyes flamed.

"But he may, as you say, claim the child." Angela hastened breathlessly as one running.

"How could he, if I did not know which child was his?"

The blinding light began to point the way clearer, now, to the older woman.

"It's—unheard of," she murmured, "and yet—"

"I will write to Thornton, offer to take his child," Doris was pleading, rather than explaining. "I think at the first he will agree to the proposal—what else can he do? The shock— remember, he does not even know that a child is expected! Dare we refuse Meredith's child this only and desperate chance —knowing what we do?"

Angela made no reply. She was letting go one after another of her rigid beliefs. Again Doris spoke, again she pleaded:

"I will abide by your decision, Sister, but only after you have gone to the chapel—and seen the way. I will wait here."

Angela rose stiffly, holding to her cross as if it were a physical support. With bowed head she passed from the room and Doris sat down thinking; demanding justice.

A half hour passed before steps were heard in the hall. Doris stood up, her eyes fixed on the door.

Sister Angela entered, and in her arms, wrapped in the same blanket, were two sleeping babies wearing the plain clothing that Ridge House kept in store for emergencies. Doris ran forward; she bent over the small creatures.

"Which?" Nature leaped forth in that one palpitating word—it was the last claim of blood.

"I—forgot—when I brought them to you. We have all— forgot. It *is* the only way—the chance."

Doris took both children in her arms.

"I shall name them Joan and Nancy," she whispered, "for my mother and grandmother. Joan and Nancy—Thornton!"

Then she kissed them, and it was given to her at that moment to forget her bitter hatred.

CHAPTER IV

"JUST AS MUCH OF DOUBT AS BADE US PLANT A SURER FOOT UPON THE SUN-ROAD"

Doris Fletcher had no turning-back in her nature. She never reached a goal but by patient effort to understand, and she was able to close her eyes to by-paths.

Having adopted the children, having foregone her prejudices—good and evil—having set her feet upon the way, she meant to go unfalteringly on, and because doubts would assail her at times, she held the surer to her task.

She remained a month at Ridge House. She wrote to Thornton and in due time his reply came.

Apparently he had written while bewildered and shocked. The old arrogant tone was gone. He accepted what Doris offered and set aside a generous sum of money for his child's expenses.

It was Sister Angela's suggestion that Mary should become the nurse for the children.

"How much does she know, Sister?"

"Nothing—but what we have permitted her to know. The girl, since knowing of the children, has astonished me by her interest in them. Nothing before has so brought her out of her native reserve. I never suspected it—but the girl has maternal instincts that should not be starved."

But Sister Angela was mistaken. Mary knew more than she had been permitted to know.

A closed door to Mary meant seeking access through other channels. Sister Constance had not screened the windows of the west chamber which opened on the roof of the porch and were next to the window of Mary's small chamber. She had forgotten to ward against the startling sound of a baby's cry. But Mary, the night that Becky had left her burden to the care of Sister Angela, had heard that cry and it reached to the hidden depth of the girl's nature. It chilled her, then set her blood racing hotly. She got up and went to the window—it was moonlight in The Gap and the night was full of a rising wind that rattled the vines and set the leaves swirling.

Covering herself with a dark shawl, she crept from her window and, clinging close to the house, reached the west chamber.

Inside, by the light of a candle, Sister Constance sat, hushing to sleep a little child! The sight was burned upon Mary's consciousness as if Fate pressed every detail there so it might not be forgotten. Mary saw the small, puckered face. It was individual and distinct.

She almost slipped from her place on the roof; her breath came so hard that she feared Sister Constance might hear, and she groped her way back.

All next day Mary worked silently but with such haste that Sister Janice took her sharply to task.

"'Tis the ungodly as leaves the dust under the mats, child," she cautioned.

"Yes, Sister." Mary attacked the mats!

"And a burnt loaf cries for forgiveness."

Harriet T. Comstock

"Yes, Sister, but the burnt loaf I will myself eat to the last crust."

"Indeed and you shall—for the carelessness that you show."

Somehow Mary lived through the day with her ears strained and a mighty fear in her heart.

It was nearing morning of the following day—that darkest hour—when the girl arose from her sleepless bed and stole forth again.

It was just then that Sister Constance, her face distorted by grief and the play of candlelight upon it, entered the west chamber with a baby in her arms!

Mary gripped the shutters—she felt faint and weak. Suppose she should slip and fall?

And then she saw two children on the bed and Sister Constance—bent in prayer—her cross pressed to her lips.

All this Mary had seen, but when Sister Angela asked her if she would like to go with Miss Fletcher and care for the children, so great was her curiosity that she, mentally, tore her roots from her home hills; let go her clinging to the deserted cabin where she had been born, and almost eagerly replied: "I'd like it powerful."

So Mary took her place.

Doris Fletcher had her plans well laid.

"I must have myself well in hand," she said to Sister Angela, "before I go to New York. There's the little bungalow in California where father took mother before Merry's birth. It happens to be vacant. I will go there and work out my plans."

It seemed a simple solution. The children throve from the start in the sunshine and climate; the peace and detachment acted like charms, and Mary, stifling her soul's homesickness, grew stern as to face, but marvellously tender and capable in her duties. Doris grew accustomed to her silence and reserve after a time, but she never understood Mary, although she grew to depend upon her absolutely. To friends in New York, especially to Doctor David Martin, Doris wrote often. She was never quite sure how the impression was given that Meredith had left twins; certainly she had not said that, but she had spoken of "the children" without laying stress upon the statement, and while debating just what explanation she would make. After all, it was her own affair. Some day she would confide in David, but there were more important details to claim her attention.

The babies were adorable, but in neither could she trace an expression or suggestion of Meredith. Their childish characteristics gave no clue—they were simply healthy, normal creatures full of the charm that all childhood should have in common. And gradually, as time passed, Doris lost herself in their demanding individualities; she became absorbed. Joan was larger, stronger, seemed older. She had brown eyes of that sunny tint which suggest sunshine. Her hair was brown, almost from the first, with gold glints. She was fair, had little colour unless the warm glow that rose and fell so sweetly in her face could be called colour. Excitement brought the flush, disappointment or a chiding word banished it. At other times Joan had the warm, ivory-tinted skin of health, not delicacy. Nancy was, from the first, frankly blonde. She never changed from the lovely, fair promise of her first year. She was the most feminine creature one could imagine; a doll brought the light to her violet eyes.

"She takes that rather than her milk," Mary explained, then gravely: "She'll take her milk if I hold off the doll."

Nature was never quite sure what to do with Joan. She changed with the years in tint, colouring, and character, but Nancy was fair, fine, and delicately poised from her baby days.

Both children worshipped Doris—Auntie Dorrie, they were taught to call her—and it was amusing to watch their relations to her. To please her, to win her approval, were their highest hopes. Mary clearly preferred Nancy and, for that reason, gave more attention to Joan.

When the children were nearly two Doris wrote to David Martin:

"I am coming home. I am glad that I have always kept the house in commission; I feel that I can trust myself there now."

And so the little family travelled east. Mary in trim uniform (and how she silently hated it) of black, with immaculate cuffs, collars, and cap; the babies perfect in every way and Doris, herself, happier than she had ever been in her life—handsomer, too. Her life had developed normally around the children; she felt a wide and deep interest in everything, and always the sense of high adventure, a daring in her relations to the future.

The old Fletcher house set the standard for the others down the long row. It was brick, with heavy oak, brass-bound doors. The marble steps and white trim were spotless and glistening and behind it lay a deep yard hidden by a tall brick wall. The house had reserved, as the family had, the right, once its civic duty was performed, to develop inwardly along its own lines.

The three generations, in turn, had set their marks upon it. The first Fletcher had been a genial soul given to entertaining, and the dining room, back of the drawing room, gave evidence of the old gentleman's taste. It was a stately and beautiful room and each article of furniture had been made to fit into the space and the need by an artist.

Doris's father was not indifferent to his father's tastes, but he was a student at heart and had a vision as to libraries. He encroached upon the ample space back of the house and had built an oval room through whose leaded panes the peach and plum trees could be seen like traceries on the clear glass. Around the walls of this room the book shelves ranged at just the right height, and above them hung pictures that inspired but did not obtrude. The high, carved chimney with its deep, generous hearth was a benediction.

When Doris had come home from St. Mary's she made known a family trait—she voiced what to her seemed an inspiration but which to the father, at first, seemed madness. Still, he complied and spent many happy hours before his death in what he called "Doris's Daring."

"I want the west wall of the library knocked out, Father," she had said, but Mr. Fletcher only stared.

"We can have the books and pictures in my room—my sunken room. There is enough garden to spare and we can save the roses. We'll drop down from the library by a shallow flight of steps; we'll have a little fountain and about a mile of nice low window seats rambling around the room. I don't want nymphs in the fountain but dear, adorable children tossing water at each other.

"We must have birds in cages, and plants and pictures—it must be a room where we can all take what is dearest to us— and live."

Of course it was an expensive and daring conception, but it was carried out by an inspired young architect, and it was Meredith who had posed for the figures in the fountain.

When Doris returned to New York with her children this room became the soul of the house.

The year after Doris's adoption of the children Sister Angela died suddenly. "She simply fell asleep," Sister Constance wrote.

After that the other Sisters could not feel happy and content in the atmosphere of antagonism that Sister Angela had partially overcome, but with which they had no sympathy. They returned to the Middle West and entered a Sisterhood where their duties and environment were more congenial. Ridge House reverted to the Fletcher estate and Uncle Jed was put in charge.

"I may use it later," Doris explained, "or I may turn it over to Father Noble if he ever needs it."

What this all meant to Mary no one ever knew—she saw, now, no return to her hills, and her longing for them grew as the years passed, and her curiosity flattened in the dull round of duties and commonplace routine. Only one emotion largely controlled her thought and that was a dumb gratitude for what she believed she was receiving. She could not agree that her devoted service gave ample return. She was under obligation, and the feeling was blighting to the girl's independence. Work, the necessity for work, was an accepted state of mind to poor Mary. The luxury and consideration that were hers in her present life took from labour, as far as she mentally considered it, all the essential qualities that gave her independence. She was accepting—so she reflected in that proud detached logic of the hills—from outsiders what no mere bodily labour could repay, certainly not such service as she was giving. Just loving and caring for two little children!

With cautious and suspicious watchfulness through the years Mary regarded Doris Fletcher still as "foreign." Foreign to all that was born and bred in the girl's inheritance of mountain aristocracy, but she had been touched by the justice, the unerring kindness of the woman, who, to Mary's wrong ideals, gave and gave and constantly made it impossible for her to make return.

"Some day," the girl vowed, when her manner was most grim and repelling, "some day I'll do something to pay back!" And then she grew bewildered in the maze of wondering if the "quality" so precious to her understanding might not exist in all places? Might it not be?—but here Mary became lost.

When she recalled, as less and less she did, the unlawful spying of hers on the west chamber of Ridge House, she set her lips in a firm line. She had gone far enough on her upward way to detest the cringing, deceitful methods of her childhood and she sternly sought to right herself, with her burdening conscience, by putting away forever what possible significance lay in the strange coming of that first and second child to Ridge House.

"Were they twins? Were—they?" But Mary always was frightened when she got into her mental depths.

Three or four vital and significant events marked the years intervening between Doris's return to New York and the day when Joan and Nancy entered womanhood.

The first incident seemed slight in itself but proved the truth of the need for caution when one is on a blind trail. With all her good intentions and high hopes Doris was bewildered as to her steps. She who had been the soul of frankness and cheerful friendliness was now reticent and reserved.

"It is poor Meredith's business," friend after friend decided. Where little was known, much was suspected. "The Fletchers cannot easily brook *that* sort of thing."

Just what that "sort" was depended upon the temperament and character of the person speaking.

Then among the first to call after Doris's return was Mrs. Tweksbury, an old and valued family friend, a woman who was worth one's while to gain as friend, for she could be a desperate foe. She had formed all her opinions of Meredith Thornton's tragedy upon what she knew and loved concerning the girl, and what she knew nothing whatever about, concerning Thornton.

To Mrs. Tweksbury he was a black villain who had

murdered—there was no other word for it—an innocent young creature who belonged to that class (Mrs. Tweksbury was frank and clear about "class") not supposed to be subject to the coarser dealings of life.

Mrs. Tweksbury relied absolutely upon what she termed her inherited intuition. This was quite outside feminine intuition. The Tweksbury male intellect had been judicial from the first, and "the constant necessity of knowing men and women," as Mrs. Tweksbury often explained, "had left its mark upon the family."

"*We know!* That is all there is to say. We know!"

So Mrs. Tweksbury "knew" all about everything when she folded Doris in her motherly arms.

"There is no need of a word, my dear," she said, "and you are dealing with the whole thing superbly. Let me see the children. How fortunate that they are twins *and* girls! Girls may inherit from the father, but thank God! nature saves them from the developing along his line. And being *twins* certainly modifies what might otherwise be concentrated."

Doris felt her heart beat fast. She was not prepared to confide in Mrs. Tweksbury, certainly not at present. She loved the old woman for her good qualities, but she shrank from putting herself at the mercy of Mrs. Tweksbury's "inherited intuitions!"

So she said nothing, but sent for the children.

Hidden deep in the old woman's heart were all the denied and suppressed yearnings of a love that had escaped fulfilment—a love that had entered in after her marriage to a man utterly without sympathy with her, but which had been rigidly ignored because of the stern moral fibre that marked her. After the death of all those who had been concerned in her secret romance she had taken upon herself the more or less vicarious guardianship of the son of the man she had loved and foregone.

The boy lived with his mother's people, and Mrs. Tweksbury only visited him occasionally; but her proud, stern old heart knew only one undying passion now—her passion for children.

When Nancy and Joan stood before her, she regarded them with almost tragic, and, at the same time, comic expression. The children were frightened at her twitching, wrinkled face and glanced at Doris, who smiled them into calmness.

In Joan, Mrs. Tweksbury saw resemblance to no one she remembered, so she concluded she must be like the father, physically, whom they must all ignore absolutely. Try as she valiantly did, the old lady felt her quick-beating heart falter before Joan's earnest, searching gaze. It was a relief to turn to Nancy and permit her eyes to dim and soften.

"My dear, my dear," she said to Doris, "how like dear Merry the baby is! Just so, I recall—"

Doris's face grew strained and ashy. "Please," she implored, "please, Aunt Emily—don't!"

"Of course, of course, my child. Very indiscreet of me—but I was taken off my guard." Then—"My dears, will you kiss me?" This to the children keeping their courage up by clinging together.

"No," Joan replied in a tone entirely free from bad manners but weighted with simple truth; "Joan likes to kiss Auntie Dorrie." The inference stiffened Mrs. Tweksbury and caused Doris a qualm.

"And you?" The old lady's tone was pathetic in its appeal to Nancy—her "intuition" was at stake.

Nancy drew nearer. She was fascinated, afraid, but guided by a strange impulse. "Nancy will," she panted, "Nancy will kiss you—two times!"

Mrs. Tweksbury's breath caught in her throat—she strangled but controlled herself and bent as a queen might to the sweet uplifted face at her knee.

After that visit Doris would have had a difficult task in stemming a flood that Mrs. Tweksbury directed, having removed the dam. While she fairly grovelled, emotionally, before Nancy, the old lady defended Joan by stern insistence upon traits of nobility unsuspected by others in the child.

"The wretch of a father," she mentally vowed, "shall not have the child if suggestion can prevent."

Spiritually she fell in line with Doris, and where Mrs. Tweksbury led it were wiser and easier to follow than to blaze new trails.

The second event that marked a new epoch was the coming of George Thornton to claim his own.

CHAPTER V

"AND WHEN IT FAILS, FIGHT AS WE WILL, WE DIE"

George Thornton was a man who believed, or thought he did, in two controlling things in life: Intellect, and the training of intellect, by education and stern attention, to the task at stake.

He had intellect and he had devoted himself to his task, that of worldly success, but he had never recognized nor admitted the necessity of the spiritual in his development, and so it had failed him—and, in a deep, tragic way, he was dying. Had been dying through the years since his devil took the reins, in a mad hour, and rode him.

There had been weeks and months after his leaving Meredith when his soul cried aloud to him but was smothered. He would not heed. He let business and coarse, pleasurable excitement gain power over him, and when they lagged he drank his conscience to sleep.

He knew the danger which lay in the last aid to deaden his pain, so he rarely sought it.

But something new had entered in—something that, in hours when he was obliged to face facts, frightened him, and after months abroad, months in which he nursed his resentment against Meredith and felt his defeat with her, he decided to do the only decent thing left for him to do—apologize and set her free.

Harriet T. Comstock

And then he found her note. The bald, naked statement drove all power to act for the moment from him. Close upon that shock, which he smilingly covered, by explaining on very commonplace grounds, came Doris's letter. The purest elements and the most brutal in many natures lie close. They did in Thornton. Had Meredith been a wiser, a more human and loving woman, she might have helped Thornton to his full stature; but failing him by her helpless insufficiency, she drove him to his shoals.

Had she by the turn of Fortune been obliged, as many women are, to have borne her lot though her heart broke her child might have saved her and the man also—for Thornton had the paternal instincts, though they were unsuspected and wholly dormant.

Again Meredith had defeated him. What could he do with a helpless baby on his hands? What else was there to do but accept Doris's offer? And of course the child was dead to him except by the cold, legal tie that bound them together. That, Thornton grimly held to.

He would press it, too, in his good time!

But Thornton's next few years proved to be a succession of mis-steps with the inevitable results.

He married the woman who could, when she had no actual hold on him, soothe and comfort—not because of his need, but her own. Once, however, she was placed in a secure position, she cast any need of his aside and developed myriads of her own.

If Thornton could not force a social position for her, then he must pay for the luxury of her exile with him. Thornton paid and paid until every faculty he had was strained to the snapping point. Finally he resorted to the last and most dangerous aid he had at his disposal—he drank more than ever before; but even in his extremity he recognized his danger and always caught himself before the worst overcame him.

Business began to show the effect of private troubles, and then Thornton remembered the Fletcher fortune; his child, and the possibilities of making the child a link between money and a growing necessity.

Whatever natural tie there might have been in Thornton's relations with his child had perished. There was merely a legal one now.

And Thornton, having explained this at great length to his wife, and finally getting her to agree to assume a responsibility that he swore should never embarrass her, travelled to New York.

It was a bright, sunny June day when he rang the bell of the Fletcher home and was admitted, by a trim maid, to the small reception room that was a noncommittal link between the hall and the drawing room.

Sitting alone in the quiet place, Thornton was conscious of a silvery *drip, drip* of water. Sound, like smell, has a power to arouse memory and control it. Thornton's thoughts flew back to the week he had spent in this old house with his girl wife. He recalled the sunken room and the fountain with those wonderful figures modelled after Meredith.

Without taking into account the years and happenings that had made him more than a stranger to the family he got up and followed a haunting desire to see the room and the fountain again.

He passed through the drawing room and shrugged his shoulders. It was arrogant, self-assured—he hated that sort of thing. The dining room was better—a fine idea as to colour and furniture; the library, too—Thornton paused and took a comprehensive glance. He liked the library, and the fireplace was perfect. He made a mental note. Then he stepped down

Harriet T. Comstock

into the room with its memory-haunting fountain. He had never seen it in action before, and so clever was the conceit that he drew back, fearing that the tossing sprays would reach him. Then he sat down in a deep chair, crossed his legs, smiled, and looked about.

Here it was that Doris spent much of her time indoors. The window was open and a rose vine was clinging to the frame, rich in bloom. There was a work basket on the low, velvet-cushioned seat—a child's sock lay near it and several ridiculous toys, rigidly propped against the wall, as if on review. Birds sang outside in the plum and peach trees and birds inside, not realizing their bondage, answered merrily—the room was throbbing with life and joy and hope. Thornton smiled, not a pleasant smile, and felt more important than he had felt in many a day; more powerful, too.

"Doris must be over thirty," he mused, "and not of the marrying type. There must be a pretty big pile to back all this." He got quickly to his feet, for Doris appeared just then at the doorway leading to the library. She paused at the top of the stairs—there was a strip of green velvet carpet running down the middle of the marble steps; her white gown came just to her ankles, and the narrow white-shod feet sank lightly into the green carpet as if it were moss.

"I am glad to see that you have made yourself comfortable, George," she said, and smiled her very finest smile. There was no hint of reproof in the tone, but Thornton instantly wondered if it would not have been wiser to have kept to the reception room.

"I hope I have not intruded," he went to the steps and held out his hand, "it *is* home, you know, after all."

This was meant to be conciliatory, but the appeal went astray.

"Let us sit by the window," Doris remarked, "the air is delightful to-day."

And then came the pause during which the path leading to an understanding must be chosen. Doris left the choosing to Thornton. He took the wrong one.

"It brings so much back," he half whispered, "so much!" He was a fairly good actor, but Doris was not appreciative.

"So much that had better be left where it rests," she said. "I have learned that the present needs every energy—the past can take care of itself."

"You have had the real burden." Thornton meant to be magnanimous. "I shall always be grateful for your splendid help at a time when so much was at stake. Your goodness to my child—" For a moment Thornton could not think whether the child was a girl or a boy. He was confused and a bit alarmed.

Doris came to his assistance.

"Meredith's little girl was all that made the first bitter year possible for me. I have done my best, George, my happiest best—she is lovely; the most joyous thing you can imagine. Remembering how much Meredith and I needed each other, I adopted a child at the same time I undertook the care of your baby—the two are inseparable and wonderfully congenial."

Thornton's brow clouded. He could not have described his sensations, but they were similar to those he had once experienced, standing alone in a dense Philippine thicket, and suddenly recalling that he was not popular with the natives. He sensed a menace somewhere.

"You're quite remarkable, Doris," he said, "but was it altogether wise—the adoption, I mean? I suppose you know everything about the—the child, but even so, the break now will be difficult for—for everybody."

Doris gave him a long, steady look.

Harriet T. Comstock

"I know very little about the child I adopted," she said. "The poor waif was deserted, and as to the wrench now, why, life has taught me, also, George, to take what joy one can and be willing to pay for it. We cannot afford to let a great blessing slip because we may have to do without it bye and bye."

"But—inheritance, Doris! You, of all women, to undervalue that! It was a bit risky, but of course while children are so young—" Thornton paused and Doris broke in.

"Inheritance is such a tricky thing," she said, looking out into the flower-filled garden, "it is such a clever masquerader. Often it is like those insects that take upon themselves the colour of the leaf upon which they cling. It isn't what it seems, and when one really knows—why, one can hardly be just, because of the injustice of inheritance."

"Queer reasoning," muttered Thornton. "Why, that—kid's father might be— well, anything!" Why he said "father" would be hard to tell.

"Exactly!" agreed Doris. "But when I did not know, I could be fair and unhampered. It has paid—the child is adorable."

"Shows no—no—evil tendencies?" Thornton grew more and more restive.

"On the contrary—only divine ones."

"We're all lucky." The man sighed, then spoke hurriedly: "I'd like to see my little girl. She is here—of course?"

"Oh! yes. I have never been separated from her. I suppose— you mean to—" Doris paused.

"I mean to relieve you, Doris, and assume my responsibility— now that I dare."

"Your wife—is she willing?" Doris longed to say "worthy" but she knew that the woman was not.

"More than willing." And now Thornton thought that the worst was over.

"I will bring your little girl," Doris said, and went quietly from the room.

Something of the sweetness and strength of the place seemed to go with her. Again Thornton became restless, and it came back to him that his first aversion to Doris Fletcher was connected with this power of hers to overturn, without effort, his peace of mind and self-esteem. But he had outwitted her in marrying her sister—she had antagonized him but he had won then and would win again now! The fountain irritated and annoyed him. He got up and walked about the room.

"A devilish freakish conception," he muttered, gazing at the fountain and kicking at a rare rug on the floor, "a kind of madness runs through the breed, I wager. Too much blood of one sort gets clogged in the human system." And then he listened.

There were childish voices nearing: sweet, piping voices with little gurgles of laughter rippling through. The laugh of happy, healthy childhood.

"She's bringing them both!" thought Thornton, and an ugly scowl came to his brow. He did not know much about children, knew nothing really, except that they were noisy and usually messy—some were better looking than others; gave promise, and he hoped his child would be handsome; it might help her along, and she would need all the help she could muster. Then he heard Doris instructing the children:

"See, Joan, dear, hold Nan by the hand like a big, strong sister, this is going to be another play. Now listen sharp! When we come to the steps you must stand close together and give that pretty courtesy that Mary taught you yesterday. Now, darlings—don't forget!"

There are moments and incidents in life that seem out of all proportion to their apparent significance. Thornton waited for what was about to happen as he might have the verdict were he on trial for his life. He was frightened at he knew not what. Would his child look like Meredith? Would she have those eyes that could find his soul and burn it even while they smiled? Would she look like him; find in him some thing that would help him to forget? He looked up. Doris had planned dramatically. She left the babies alone on the top step and came down to Thornton.

"Aren't they wonderful?" she asked in so calm and ordinary a tone that it was startling.

They were wonderful—even a hard, indifferent man could see that. Slim, vigorous little creatures they were with sturdy brown legs showing above socks and broad-toed sandals. Their short white frocks fell in widening line from the shoulders, giving the effect of lightness, winginess. Both children had lovely hair, curly, bobbed to a comfortable length, and their wide, curious eyes fastened instantly upon Thornton—eyes of purple-blue and eyes of hazel-gold; strange eyes, frankly confronting him but disclosing nothing; eyes of utterly strange children; not a familiar feature or expression to guide him.

"I have called them Joan and Nancy," Doris was saying. "You expressed no preference, you know."

"Which is—is—mine?" Thornton whispered the question that somehow made him flush with shame.

"I do not know!" It was whisper meeting whisper.

"You—what?" Thornton turned blazing eyes upon the woman by his side. Her answer did not seem to shock him so much as it revealed what he had suspected—Doris was playing with him, making him absurd by that infernal power of hers that he had all but forgotten. He recalled, too, with keen resentment her ability to transform a tragic incident into one of humour—or the reverse.

"I do not know. I never have known," Doris was saying. "You see, I was afraid of heredity if I had to deal with it. Without knowing it I could be just to both children; give them the only possible opportunity to overcome handicaps. I thought they might reveal themselves—but so far they have not. They are adorable."

"This is damnable! Someone shall be made to speak—to suffer—or by God!—"

The words were hardly above a whisper, but the tone frightened the children.

"Auntie Dorrie!" they pleaded, and stretched out entreating arms.

"Come, darlings. The play is over and you did it beautifully."

They ran to her, clambered into her lap, and turned doubting eyes upon Thornton.

"You—expect me to—to—take both?" he asked, still in that low, thick tone.

"Certainly not. One is mine. I shall demand my rights, be quite sure of that."

"This is the most outrageous thing I ever heard of!" Thornton was at bay; "the most immoral."

"I have often thought that it might be," Doris returned, her lips against Nancy's fair hair, "but the more you consider it the more you are convinced that it is not. It is simply—unusual." The tone defied understanding. "You must consider what I have done, George, step by step. I did not act rashly. And

Harriet T. Comstock

when we come to actual contact with all the truth confronting us, you and I will have to be very frank. May I send the children away? It is time for their nap." Already Doris's finger was pressing the electric button cunningly set in the coping of the fountain.

"Yes, do. There is much to say," Thornton muttered and, not having heard the bell, was startled at seeing the nurse appear at once. He looked up, and Mary looked at him. The girl felt the atmosphere. Thornton made a distinct impression upon her.

Left alone with Doris, Thornton drew his chair close to hers and waited for her to begin.

"Well," he said, "what have you to say? It would seem as if you might have a great deal, Doris."

"I have nothing to say."

"I suppose you did this to humiliate me—defeat me?" Thornton's lips twitched.

"On the contrary, after the first I gave you very little thought, George. I was concerned in making sure the future of Meredith's child."

"Did you forget that she was also mine?"

"I tried to. After a bit, I did—after the identities of the babies became blurred. If you stop to think and are just, you will understand that I took a desperate chance to accomplish the most good to Meredith's child. That is all that seemed to count. Suppose you could claim your child now, would its future be as secure as it would be with me? Have you really the child's interest at heart—you, who left its mother to—"

"The mother—left me! Don't overlook facts, Doris." Thornton's face flamed angrily.

"Yes. In self-defence she left you!" Doris held him with eyes heavy with misery. "I knew everything necessary to know, George, that enabled me to take this step."

"But not enough to make you pause and consider!" A bitterness rang in the words.

"There are some occasions when one cannot, dare not, consider," said Doris.

Thornton got up and paced the room. Suddenly he turned like a man at bay.

"But the inheritance?" he flung out.

"I told you, George, it was the inheritance that forced me to it."

"I mean—" here Thornton's eyes fell—"I mean the money," he stammered.

"I see!" Doris's voice trembled; then she hastened on: "The money you sent, George, has never been touched. I have waited for this hour."

"And your revenge!" muttered Thornton.

"I had not considered it in that light." A deep contempt throbbed in the words. "When I remember I am not bitter, but I am filled, anew, with a desire to save Meredith's child!"

"At the risk of passing her off as the child of—whom?"

And then Doris smiled—a long, strange smile that burnt its way into Thornton's consciousness.

"It was that doubt that saved, gave hope," she said, and quickly added, "I will tell you all there is to know, and then I request that you spare me another interview until you have come to a decision regarding—your child."

There was pitifully little to tell. A deserted mountain child!

"Who deserted it?" Thornton broke in.

"I did not ask. Sister Angela promised to find a home for it where no one would know of its sad birth—there are people willing to risk that much for a little child. I am!"

"And this—this Sister Angela—" Thornton asked.

"She died the year after."

"And the others?"

"I doubt if they ever knew much, but if they did they forgot—they are like that; besides, I have not heard of them in years."

More and more Thornton realized the hopelessness of personal investigation, and he was not prepared to take outside counsel, certainly not yet.

"The Sisters did fairly well for the outcast in this instance," he sneered, "but we may all have to pay some day. Murder will out, you know!"

"Of course," Doris agreed, wearily; "we all understand that."

"Do you think the children will?" Thornton's eyes were gloomy and grave. "How about the hour when they—know?"

Doris felt the pain in her heart that this possibility always awakened. She raised her glance to the one full of hate and said quietly:

"Who can tell?"

There was a dull pause. Then:

"Well, I guess I have all I want for the present. I'm not out of the game, Doris, just count on me being in it at every deal of the cards. Good-bye—for now."

"Good-bye, George. I will not forget."

Harriet T. Comstock

CHAPTER VI

"THERE ARE TWO ELEMENTS THAT GO TO THE COMPOSITION OF FRIENDSHIP. ONE IS TRUTH; THE OTHER IS TENDERNESS"

After Thornton's departure Doris metaphorically, drew a long breath. She felt that he would make no further move at present—how could he? As one faces a possible surgical operation with the hope that Nature may intervene to make it unnecessary, she turned to her blessed duties with renewed vigour.

Of course, there were hours, there always would be hours, when, alone, or when the children played near her, Doris wondered and speculated but always reached the triumphant conclusion that her love, equal and sincere, for both little girls, had been made possible by her unprejudiced relations with them. And that must count for much.

Every time she was diverted from her chosen path she courageously took stock, as it were, of her gains and possible losses.

For instance, when Mrs. Tweksbury had appeared to discern resemblance between Nancy and Meredith, she wondered if, as often is the case, the impartial observer could discover what familiarity had screened?

But try as she did, at that time, she could not find the slightest physical trace of likeness, and she brought old photographs to her aid. While, on the other hand, the mental and temperamental characteristics of both little girls were such as were common to healthy childhood.

Again it was possible for Doris to face any fact that might present itself—she knew that, by her past course, she had not only secured justice for the children but faith in herself.

Her greatest concern now was the menace of Thornton.

"Think of Nancy," she mused, "sweet, sensitive, and fine, under such influence! And Joan so high-strung and reckless! It would be a hopeless condition!"

Looked upon from this viewpoint Doris grew depressed. While her conscience remained clear as to any real wrong she had done in acting as she had, there were anxious hours spent in imagining that time when, as Thornton said, the girls themselves must know.

When must they know?

Doris had not considered that before to any extent.

Thornton might demand at once that they know the truth. He had a right to that.

Here was a new danger, but as the silence continued the immediate fear of this lessened. And the children were mere babies. They could not possibly understand if they were told, now.

Until such time, then, as they must be told, Doris renewed her efforts in building well the small, healthy minds and bodies.

"When they marry"—this brought a smile—"when they marry! Of course, then, they must know." With that conclusion reached, anxiety was once more lulled to rest.

Gradually the old peaceful days merged into new peaceful days. Doris entered, little by little, into her social duties so long neglected; the children romped and lived joyously in the old house—"just children"—until suddenly a small but significant thing occurred when they were nine years of age that startled Doris into a line of thought that brought about a radical change in all their lives.

She was sitting in the library one stormy day, reading. The tall back of the chair hid her from view, the fire and the book were soothing, and the excuse—that the storm gave her the right to do what she wanted to do, rather than what she, otherwise, might feel she should do—added to her enjoyment.

From above she heard the voices of the children and Mary's quiet intervention now and again.

Then Joan laughed, and the sound struck Doris as if she had never heard it before. What a peculiar laugh it was—for a child! Silver clear, musical, but with a note of defiance, recklessness, and yes, almost abandon.

Joan was teasing Nancy about her dolls—Joan detested dolls, she declared that it was their stupid stare that made her dislike them. She only wanted live things: dogs and cats, not even birds—she was sorry for birds. Nancy's dolls were to her "children," and she was pleading now for an especial favourite and Joan was praying—rather mockingly—that God would let it get smashed because of "the proud nose."

"But God makes children's noses!" Nancy was urging.

"Well! He don't make dolls," Joan insisted, and proceeded with her petition until Nancy's wails brought Mary upon the scene.

Doris listened. She could not hear what Mary said, but presently peace reigned above-stairs and the pelting storm and the book resumed their power.

It might have been a half hour later when she heard soft, stealthy footsteps in the hall. She sat quite still, believing that one of the children was hiding and that the other would be on the trail immediately. The small intruder passed through the library and went into the sunken room.

Doris, herself unseen, looked from behind her shelter and saw that it was Joan, and before she could call to her she was held silent by what the child proceeded to do.

Deftly, quickly she disrobed and stood in her pretty, childish nakedness in the warm room.

For a moment she poised and listened, then she stepped over the rim of the fountain, took the exact attitude of one of the figures, and with rapt, upturned face became rigid.

It was wonderfully lovely, but decidedly startling. Still Doris waited.

The water dripped over the small body; Joan's lips were moving in some weird incantation, and then with the light all gone from her pretty face she came out of the basin, pulled her clothing on as best she could, and flung herself tragically in a deep chair.

For a moment Doris thought the child was crying, but she was not. Her limp little body relaxed and the eyes were sad.

Doris rose and went to the steps.

"Why are you here alone, Joan?" she asked.

Quite simple the reply came:

"I was—trying to make it come true, Auntie Dorrie," this with a suspicious break in the voice.

"What, darling?" Doris came down and took the child in

Harriet T. Comstock

her arms.

"Mary says if you believe anything hard enough you can make it come true. *She* always can! I wanted to play with the fountain girls—I know it would be beautiful—but you have to be *like them.* You have to shut the whole world out—and then you know what they know."

"Why, little girl, do you think the fountain children are happier than you and Nancy?"

With that groping that all mothers feel when they first confront the *individual* in the child they believed they knew Doris asked her question.

"I've used Nancy and me all up!" was Joan's astonishing reply.

"All up?" the two meaningless words were the most that Doris could grasp.

"Yes, Aunt Dorrie. Dolls and Mary's silly stories and Nancy's funny games all over and over and over until they make me—sick!"

Joan actually looked sick, so intense was she.

"Nan is happy always, Aunt Dorrie—she's made like that—but I use things up and then I want something else. Mary said that, honest true, things would come if you believed hard enough. Maybe I cannot believe hard enough—or maybe Mary didn't speak truth. She doesn't always, Aunt Dorrie."

Doris gasped and drew the child closer. It was like being dragged, by the little hand, to an unsuspected danger that she, not the child, understood.

Gradually the inner side of the years was turned out by Doris's careful questions and Joan's quiet simplicity. She revealed so much now that she found that her view of life had a dramatic interest. It appeared, quite innocently, that Nancy could assume any position in order to win her way.

"She always speaks truth, Auntie Dorrie," Joan loyally defended, "but she can make truth out of such queer things; it just *is* truth to Nancy, for she doesn't want to hurt people's feelings. Mary likes Nancy best, for I cannot make truth when I want to. Aunt Dorrie—truth is—a—*a thing*, isn't it?"

"Yes, darling. But we—we see it differently, that is all."

This was comforting to Joan, and she smiled. Then Mary again took the centre of the stage—Mary's interpretations, all coloured with the mystery of her desolate childhood; her old superstitions and power to control by the magic of her imagination. There were certain tales, it seemed, that were held as bribes. Nancy would always succumb to the lures; Joan, only to a few.

"What are they, dear? I love fairy stories, you know."

Doris was keeping her voice cool and calm.

"Why, Mary says there is a Rock on a big mountain that is—bewitched! And everything near it is, too. She says things grow on it and you look at them and they are alive, and you can—can, well, use them! Mary saw a road once and just went up on it—it was a bewitched road, and she got—lost!" Joan's eyes widened. "Mary says she'll have to find her way back somehow, and if Nancy and I are naughty, she'll go and find it at once! Nancy is afraid, but I told Mary I'd follow her!

"And then Mary said that once she just longed and longed for a doll—she had never had one—and she saw The Ship on The Rock and she went up to it—that was before she got lost on the road—and she asked the captain of The Ship for a doll, and he said he would send one to her. And she went home and that very night—that *very* night, Aunt Dorrie, she looked in a room where she heard a funny noise and she saw a live doll!

Harriet T. Comstock

And while she was looking she saw a tall big lady bring in another. You see, when The Rock gets alive, everything is alive and Mary had forgot that—and so the dolls were—were babies. Nancy believes that, but I—tried it on Nancy's dolls—and it isn't true!"

The rain outside beat wildly against the windows; the wind lashed the vines and roared down the chimney.

"Are—you asleep, Aunt Dorrie?" The silence awed Joan.

"No, dear heart. I am just thinking."

And so Doris was—thinking that she was walking in the dark. Her own small flashlight had seemed enough to guide her, and here she discovered that it had only shown her one path, the one she had chosen, and all the other paths—Mary's, Nancy's, and Joan's—had been disregarded.

Suddenly it seemed as dangerous to have too much faith as too little.

"I want you, Joan, dear, to go up and play, now, with Nancy. See if you cannot take all the old games and make a new one. That would be such a pleasant thing to do."

"Must I, Auntie Dorrie? I'd rather stay here close to you. It's a new game. I like it here."

It was hard to send the small, clinging thing away, but Doris was firm.

Once alone, she closed her eyes and let her hands fall, palms upward, on her lap. She felt tired and perplexed. There had come a parting of the ways. Apparently the ninth year was a dangerous year. What must she do? Was Mary more ignorant than she seemed or—more knowing? What had Mary known at Ridge House?

The dull, quiet girl, as Doris recalled her, seemed merely a part of the machinery of the Sisters' Home; she had never taken her into account—but had she been what she seemed? What was she now?

It was appalling—in the doubt as to what was, or was not—to think that so much had been taken for granted.

The children had seemed babies. The mere physical care had been the main consideration, and while that was going on Joan had grown weary of the old games and Nancy had learned to gain her ends by indirect methods.

Clearly, Doris must have help at this juncture.

"I see," she thought on, heavily, "why fathers *and* mothers are none too many where children are concerned."

It was then that she thought of David Martin in a strangely new way—a way that brought a faint colour to her cheeks.

All the afternoon she thought of him while she, having set Mary to other tasks, devoted herself to Nancy and Joan. She read to them, scampered through the house with them, did anything and everything they suggested, until she had subdued the nervous strain and could laugh a bit at her bugbears of the morning. Joan, flushed and towzled, Nancy, sweetly radiant, effaced the menacing images her anxiety had created—but she still needed help. And David Martin was the one, the only one among her friends who seemed adequate to her need.

"I've tried to be a mother," she thought, "but I have taken the father out of their lives—I must supply it."

When the children were in bed and the house quiet, Doris went to the sunken room and, taking up the telephone receiver, called her number. She was calm and at peace. She was prepared to lay the whole matter of the past few years before David Martin, and she was conscious, already, of relief.

Harriet T. Comstock

"I am going to let myself—go!" she thought, her ear waiting for a reply.

It was Martin who answered.

"David, are you quite free for an hour?"

"For the entire evening, Doris. Are the children sick?"

How like Martin that was! What most concerned and interested Doris was first in his thought.

Doris's face twitched.

"It's my friend," she said, slowly, "that I want. Not my physician."

"I'll be there in a half hour."

The soft drip of the rain outside was soothing. So happy did Doris feel that she wondered if her fears would not strike Martin as absurd, and after all, why should she lay her burden of confession upon him in order to ease her perplexity? Along this line she argued with herself while she ordered a tray to be sent up as soon as Doctor Martin arrived.

She gave particular instructions as to the preparation of the dainties Martin enjoyed but which no one but Doris ever set before him.

"I chose the shield of silence," she mused. "Why should I ask another to help me with it now?"

Still, in the end, her honest soul knew that it was not help for herself she was seeking, but guidance for the children whose best interests she must serve.

And then, as one looks back over the path he has travelled while he pauses before going on, Doris Fletcher saw how the love of David Martin had been transformed for her sake into friendship that it might brighten her way. She had never been able to give him what he desired, but so precious was she to him—and full well she knew it—that he had become her friend.

Out of such stuff one of two things is evolved—a resentful man, or the most sacred thing, that can enter a woman's life, a true friend.

Martin had made a success of his profession; his unfulfilled hopes had seemed to broaden his sympathies instead of damming them.

As the clock struck nine Martin appeared at the doorway—a tall, massive figure, the shoulders inclined to droop as though prepared for burdens; the eyes, under shaggy brows, were as tender as a woman's, but the mouth and chin were like iron.

"David, it was good of you to come." Doris met him on the steps and led him to his favourite chair, drawn close to the blazing fire.

"To take any chance leisure of yours is selfish—but I had to!"

Martin took the outstretched hands and still held them as he sat down. After all the silent years the old thrill filled his being.

"This is a great treat," he said in his big, kind voice. "I was just back in the office. I steered two small craft into port this afternoon—I need a vacation."

Doris recalled how this phase of Martin's profession always exhausted him, and she smiled gently into his eyes. Just then the tray she had ordered was sent up. He looked at it and his tired face relaxed; the deep eyes betrayed the boyish delight in the thought that had prompted the act.

"You must need me pretty bad to pay so high!" he said,

watching Doris pour the thick cream into his cup of chocolate.

"I do, David, but really I'm not buying; I'm indulging myself. May I chatter while you eat? There are three kinds of sandwiches on the plate. Take them in turn, they are warranted to blend." Then quite suddenly:

"David, it's about the children. They are over nine. What happens, physiologically, when children—girls—are—are nearly ten?"

"Deviltry, often. At nine they are too old to spank, too young to reason with—it's the dangerous age, at least the outer circle of the dangerous age." Martin tested the second sandwich.

"And the prescription? What do you prescribe for the dangerous age?" Doris felt that it was best to edge toward the vital centre by circuitous routes.

"Barrels and bungholes or what stands for barrels and bungholes—a good school where a mixture of discipline with home ideals prevail. I know of several where giddy little flappers are marvellously licked into shape without danger of breaking. I've felt for some time that your kids needed—well, not love and care, surely, but a practical understanding."

"Why didn't you tell me, David?"

"People never appreciate what they do not pay for. Now that you have offered up this tribute to the animal of me, I know you are ready for the other."

"The other, David?"

"Yes, the best of me. That always belongs to you."

This was daring, and it sent Doris to cover while she caught her breath. David calmly ate on. After the sandwiches there was a bit of fruit cake made from the recipe handed down from the days of Grandfather Fletcher.

"David, do you think mothers, I mean real mothers, have divine intuitions about their children? Intuitions that, well, say, adopted mothers never have?"

"No, I don't. The majority of mothers are vamps. They think they have a strangle hold on their offspring; a right to mould or bully them out of shape. The best school I know is run by a woman who says it takes her a year to shake off the average mother; after that the child becomes an individual and you can get a line on it."

"That's startling, David. It's hard, too, on mothers."

"Oh! I don't know. I often think if mothers could be friends to their children, *real friends*, I mean, and not claim what no human being has a right to claim from another, they'd reap a finer reward. I'd hate to love a person from duty. The fifth commandment is the only one with a promise. It needs it! What is the stuffing in this third sandwich, Doris? It comes mighty near perfection."

"I never give away the tricks of my trade, David! And let me tell you, you are mighty like a sandwich yourself—light and shade in layers; but I reckon you are right about the friend part in mothers. Then, too, I think an adopted mother has this to her credit—she doesn't dare presume."

"No, often she bullies. She thinks she paid for the right. After all, the best any of us can do for a child is to set it free; point out the channels and keep the lights burning!"

"David, you are wonderful. You should have had children." The tears were in Doris's eyes.

"Oh! I don't know—I'd have to have too many other things tacked on. All children are mine now, in a sense."

Harriet T. Comstock

David pushed the tray away and leaned luxuriously back in his chair.

"Now," he said, with his peculiar smile that few rarely saw, "let's have it! The skirmish is over."

Then Doris told him—feeling her way as she poured her confession into the ears of one who trusted her so fully and who asked so little. She saw his startled glance when she, beginning with Meredith's death, struck the high note of the real matter. Martin was not resenting her past reticence, but he was taken off his guard, and that rarely happened to him.

Once, having controlled his emotions, he was placid enough. He noted the outstretched hands in Doris's lap and estimated her weariness and her need of him. After all, those were the big things of the moment. In Martin's thought any act of Doris's could easily be explained and righted. He did not interrupt her, he even saw the humour of her account of the scene with Thornton, years before, when she presented both children to his horrified eyes. Martin shook with laughter, and that trivial act did more to strengthen Doris than anything he could have done. It relieved the tension.

"How did you manage to create the impression, among us all, that these children are twins?" Martin, seeing that Doris had finished with the vital matter, turned to details. "I cannot recall that you ever said so—and there seems to be no reason why they should be twins."

"That's it, David, there never was a reason, really, and I did not intend, at first, to give the impression—I simply said nothing. Things like this grow in silence until they are too big to handle. It was the telling of plain half-truths that did the mischief—and letting the conclusions of others pass. Of course I did not hesitate with George Thornton, he mattered; the others did not seem to count—no one but you, David. I have felt I wronged your faith, somehow."

Martin, at this, began to defend Doris.

"Oh, I don't agree to that. It was entirely your own affair. You wrote to me while you were away about Meredith. I realized how cut up you were, and God knows you had reason to be. Until you needed me, I don't see but what you had a right to act as you saw fit about the children."

"David, I always need you. It is because I need you so much that I have decency to keep my hands off!"

Martin's brows drew close, his mouth looked stern, but he was again controlling the old, undying longing to possess the only woman he had ever loved, and shield her from herself!

Then he gave his prescription:

"Doris, get rid of Mary. Find a proper place for her and forget whatever doubts you may have. Remember only her years of service; she gave the best she had. Then send the children to Miss Phillips'. Of course, you must write to Thornton. Tell him as much or as little as you choose. He's rightfully in the game. We're all three playing with a dummy." How Doris blessed Martin for that "we three!" He had come into the game and, once in, Martin could be depended upon.

"You've run amuck among accepted codes," he was saying with that curious chuckle of his, "and yet, by heaven! you seem to have established a divinely inspired one for the kids."

"You think that, David? You are not trying to comfort me?"

Martin got up. He seemed suddenly in a hurry to be off. He had given what he could to meet Doris's need—given it briefly, concisely, as was his way.

Doris brought his coat and held it for him—her face lifted to his with that yearning in her eyes that always unnerved him. It was the look of one who must offer an empty cup to another

Harriet T. Comstock

who thirsted. Then she spoke, after all the silent years:

"David, I have always loved you, but I am beginning to understand at last about love. I had not the 'call' in my soul. Merry had it, the mountain mother had it—but it never came to me. Without it, I dared not offer to pay the cost of marriage. That would have been unjust to you. I did realize that, but the deeper truth has only come recently. I wonder if you can understand, dear, if I say now, even *now*, that I would be glad for you to marry and be happy—as you should be?"

"Doris, I counted that all up years ago. It did not weigh against you!" Martin's voice was husky.

"Then, David, be my friend and the friend of my little children. For their sakes, I implore your help along the way."

Martin bent and touched his lips to Doris's head which was bowed before him.

"Thank you," he said with infinite tenderness; "you are permitting me to share all that you have, my dear. Good-night."

CHAPTER VII

"TO DO OUR BEST IS ONE PART, BUT TO WASH OUR HANDS SMILINGLY OF THE CONSEQUENCES IS THE NEXT PART, OF ANY SENSIBLE VIRTUE"

In much that frame of mind, Doris arose the day following Martin's call.

By some subtle force the debris of the past seemed to have been disposed of; the misunderstanding on her part and David's.

"It is the 'call' that makes everything possible or tragically wretched," she said, "and one cannot be blamed for being born deficient. Thank God I fitted in, though, when others were called away."

With David's understanding and cooeperation the present could be confronted and the "hand washing of consequences" undertaken.

"I have done my best," Doris felt sure of this, "*my* best, and now I must do a bit of trusting. It has been my one daring adventure. It must not fail."

After many attempts she wrote and dispatched a letter to George Thornton, simply stating that she was about to send the children to school.

Harriet T. Comstock

While waiting for his reply she turned her attention to Mary, for in any case, she decided, the children must be placed in another's care. What Mary felt when Doris explained things to her no one was ever likely to know. The girl's face became blanker; the lines stiffened.

"It was," Doris confided later to Martin, "as if I were wiping the past out as I spoke."

The fact was that Doris was rekindling the past—the past that lay back of the years of plain duty.

"I have not overlooked, Mary," Doris strove to get under the crust of reserve and find something with which to deal emotionally, "the years of devotion to us all. You have made no social ties for yourself; have not taken any pleasures outside —what would you like to do now, Mary?"

"Go home."

"Go—home? Why—where is home, Mary?"

The pathos struck Doris—the pathos of those who, having served others, find themselves stranded at last.

"Down to Silver Gap." As she spoke, Mary was hearing already the sound of the river on the rocks and seeing the spring flowers in the crevices of the hills.

"You mean, go back to Ridge House? You could not stay there alone, Mary, with old Jed."

Mary stared blankly—she was further back than Ridge House.

"I've been saving," she went slowly on, "all the years. I reckon I have most enough to buy the cabin where us-all was born." The tone and words took on the mountain touch. Doris was fascinated.

"You mean your father's old cabin?" she asked.

"Yes. It lies 'cross the river from Ridge House, and when I think of it," a suggestion of radiance broke on Mary's face, "I get a rising in my side. I'm aiming to get it back—"

The girl stopped short—something in her threatened to break loose.

The pause gave Doris a moment to consider. She was baffled by Mary, but she saw clearly that the girl had but one desire.

"Mary," she said, presently, "I have always intended, when the children no longer needed you, to give you some proof of my appreciation of all that you have done for us. You seem to have shown me a way. You shall have the old cabin, if it can be obtained, and it shall be made comfortable for you. It is not so far but what you can have a little oversight of Ridge House, too, and that will mean a great deal to me. I am thinking of opening the house sometime."

Doris got no further for, to her astonishment, Mary rose and came stiffly toward her. When she was near enough she reached out her hands and said:

"God hearing me, 'I'll pay you back some day. I will; I will!"

Doris was embarrassed.

"You have paid everything you owe me, Mary," she returned, quietly. "It is my turn now. I will see about the cabin at once."

Finally a letter came from Thornton. A dictated letter.

He was about to leave for South Africa and would be gone perhaps several years.

He left everything in Doris's capable hands!

Again Doris took breath for the next stretch of the long way.

And Joan and Nancy went to Dondale and Miss Phillips.

It was a hard break for them all and was taken character-istically. Joan, tear-stained and quivering, set her face to the change and excitement with unmistakable delight. Nancy was frightened into silent but smiling acquiescence. She expected, she told Joan, that it would kill her, but she would not make Aunt Dorrie feel any worse than she did by showing what she felt! At this Joan tossed her head and sent two large tears rolling down her cheeks.

"None of us will die, Nan. We all *feel* deathly, but this is—life."

At ten Joan had a distinct comprehension of the difference between living and life. To a certain extent you controlled the former; the latter "got you."

"I—I don't want life," wailed Nancy, "I want Aunt Dorrie."

"But life—wants you!"

Somewhere Joan had heard that, or read it—the old library was no hidden place to her—and she brought it forth now with emphasis.

Nancy made no reply. In that mood Joan would show no mercy. It was when she was suffering the most that Joan could harden and frighten Nancy. She was lashing herself to duty when she sent the whip cracking.

Martin accompanied Doris to Dondale. He was "Uncle David" to the children and part of their happy lives.

"Take—take good care of Aunt Dorrie," Nancy pleaded with him at parting, her poor little face distorted by the effort she was making.

"You bet!" Martin bent and kissed the child. He approved of Nancy. Martin could never patiently endure complications, and Nancy was simple and direct. Joan was another matter. At the last she was in high spirits.

"It's going to be great," she whispered to Doris. "All the girls and the new games and the comings home for holidays and—and everything."

It was after they were alone that Nancy called down extra suffering upon herself.

"Aunt Dorrie will think you did not care, Joan, and Uncle David scowled. You make people think queer things about you."

Joan turned and fixed Nancy with flaming eyes.

"I want Aunt Dorrie to think everything is all right—you didn't! You did not cheat her. I did—for her sake."

"Perhaps," Nancy sometimes struck a high note, unsuspectingly, "perhaps Aunt Dorrie would rather *have* you care."

Joan regarded her intently and then replied:

"Well, then, you're all right, Nan!"

The tone, more than the words, stung Nancy. It hurt her to have any one misunderstand, but it often occurred to her that it hurt more to be understood!

In the train en route to New York Doris sat very quiet, thinking of the two little faces she was leaving—forever! It amounted to that—as every woman knows.

Nothing but their faces held as the miles were dashed past—faces that portrayed the spiritual essence of the old, dear years—faces that would turn, from now on, to others, and take

Harriet T. Comstock

on new expressions, bear the mark of another's impress.

"Well, thank heaven," Doris presently broke out, "I haven't been a vamp mother, David."

Martin came from behind his newspaper.

"And because of that, Doris," he said, "you will have those girls coming back to you. They will want to come." He was thinking of Nancy.

"Yes. I have a sure feeling about that." Then: "How splendid it was of Joan to act as she did! She'd rather we thought her hard than to let us see her pain."

Martin stared. "You mean Nancy?" he asked.

"No. Nan, bless her, cannot disguise herself, but Joan can! Joan will suffer through her strength."

The period, always a dangerous one, the year following school life, became Doris's great concern while the school time progressed in orderly fashion under Miss Phillips's guidance.

"I am keeping my hands off," Doris often confided to Martin. "It is only fair play while the children are at Dondale. You were right—Miss Phillips is a wonderful woman—I have learned to trust her absolutely. She has appreciated what I tried to do for the girls; is building on it; she will return them to me—not different, but—extended! It's the time after, David, that I am planning. That time which is the link between restraint and the finding of one's self."

"I declare," Martin would reply to this, "I wonder that you ever get results, Doris; you harvest while others are sowing."

But deep in us all is the current carrying on and on, and it was hurrying Doris during the years while the girls were at Dondale.

There were the happy vacations, the new interests, the marvel of watching the miracle of evolution from the child to the woman. At times this was breathlessly exciting.

Doris filled her private time with useful and enjoyable hours. She got into closer touch with old friends, saw and heard the best in music and drama, permitted herself the luxury of David Martin's friendship, and shared his confidences about his sister's son in the Far West—a fatherless boy who promised much but often failed in fulfilment.

"Odd, isn't it, Davey," Doris sometimes said, "that you and I, having, somehow, lost what is the commonplace road for most men and women, have been called upon to assume many of the joys and sorrows of that broad highway?"

"We none of us go scot free," Martin returned. "I'm grateful for every decent, common job thrown at me."

And so the years passed and Doris had outlined a vague but comprehensive line of action for the immediate months following the girls' graduation from Dondale.

"I am going to take them abroad," she announced to Martin; "take them over the route that Merry and I took—our last journey together. And, David, in that little Italian town they shall know—about Meredith and Thornton!"

David started, but made no remark.

"And when we return," Doris went on, "I am going to bring the girls out—I hate the term, I'd rather say let them out—just as Merry and I were, in this dear, old house. Mrs. Tweksbury and I have planned rather a brilliant campaign."

And then came that bleak March day—Joan and Nancy were to graduate in June—when the hurrying undercurrent in Doris Fletcher's life brought her to a sharp turn in the stream.

Harriet T. Comstock

She was sitting in the pleasant old room before a freshly made fire; the fountain trickled and splashed, the birds sang, defying the outdoor gloom and chill, and a letter from Miss Phillips lay upon her lap—a letter that had made her smile then frown. She took it up and read it again.

"I am deeply interested in your nieces," so Miss Phillips wrote; "naturally a woman dealing, as I have for years, with youth in the making, is both blunted and sharpened. Young girls fall into types—are comfortably classified and regulated for the most part. Occasionally, however, the rule has its exceptions."

Then Miss Phillips expatiated for a page or so, in her big, forceful handwriting, on Nancy's beauty, sweetness, and charm.

"A fine, feminine creature, my dear Miss Fletcher. A girl I am proud to refer to as one of mine; a girl to carry on the traditions of such a family as yours—a lovely, young American woman!"

This was what brought the smile, but as Doris turned over the sheet the smile departed; a grave expression took its place.

"You and I are progressive women," so the new theme began; "we know the game of life. We know that where we once played straight whist we now play bridge, but we are fully aware that the fundamentals are the same.

"And now I must explain myself. For a young girl with the prospects that Joan has her mental equipment is a handicap rather than an asset. She does everything too well—except the drudgery of the class room, she has managed to endure that, and with credit, but everything else she accomplishes with distinction. She lacks utterly any suggestion of amateurishness!

"I hope you will understand. This would be splendid if she, like Sylvia Reed, for instance, had to look to her wits to solve her life problems; but it will distract her along the path of obvious demands.

"She, I repeat, does everything too well. She dances with inspiration; nothing less. She sings with spirit and originality; she acts almost unbelievably well and she wins, without effort, the admiration and affection of all with whom she comes in contact. I speak thus openly and intimately to you, Miss Fletcher, because, frankly, Joan puzzles me—she always has."

The letter dropped again on Doris's lap. Yes, Doris Fletcher did understand. She saw Joan, not as she was, a tall young creature radiantly facing life, but as a tired little child in this very room stepping' defeated from the fountain, because she could not make her desires come true! She was listening to the old plaint: "I have used the old games—I want something new!"

Yes, Doris understood, and sitting alone, she vowed that Joan should not be defrauded of her own, by misdirected love, prejudice, or luxury.

"She shall have her chance!"

Then it was that something happened. Things—stopped!

For a moment Doris was conscious of making an effort to set them going again. She glanced at the clock—that had stopped! The fountain no longer played; nor did the birds sing!

A black silence presently engulfed the whole world. At last Doris opened her eyes—or had they been open during the eternity when nothing had occurred? She glanced at the clock, a trivial thing against the carving of the wall, but upon whose face Truth sat faithfully. Two hours had passed since she had noticed the clock before!

"But—I have been thinking a long time, planning for the children; reading the letter—" Doris sought to establish a normal state of affairs—she saw the letter lying at her feet, but did not bend to pick it up.

"Only a faint. But I have never fainted before!" she thought on.

She was not frightened, not even excited. She felt as if she had simply come upon something that she had always known was on the road ahead awaiting her. She had come upon it sooner than she had expected to, that was all. She did not want to pass into the silence again if she could help it, so she lay back in the chair quietly, guardedly, and waited.

Then she heard steps. Outside the family only one person came unannounced to the sunken room and gladly, thankfully, Doris turned her eyes and met David Martin's as he paused at the doorway above.

Martin had himself in control before Doris noticed the fear in his eyes. He came slowly to her, sat down beside her and, while simply taking her hand in greeting, let his trained touch fall upon her pulse. It told him the dread secret, but it did not shatter his calm—he even smiled into the pale face and said lightly:

"Well, what have you been trying to do?"

Doris told him, without emotion, what had occurred. She did not remove her hand from his—his touch comforted her; held her to the things she knew and loved and trusted.

"And now, David," she said at last, "I think we have both known that some day this would occur. We are too good friends to be anything but frank—I am not afraid, and it is essential that I should know the truth. The family ogre has caught me—but it has not conquered me yet!"

"Well, Doris—it is the first call!" The man's words hurt like a knife turned upon himself.

"I feared so—and I am forty-nine."

"A mere child, my dear, if we deal honestly with the fact. Your father was fifty-five and might have lived to be seventy if he had stopped in time. Your grandfather—"

"Never mind, David, let's keep to me. How much longer—have I?"

"No man on earth could tell you that, my dear, but I hope—always granting that you will be wise—that you may count on, say, twenty years."

They both smiled. After all, what did it matter?

"And—what do you suggest I should do—as a beginning of the—twenty years?"

"Close this house, Doris, and start another kind of existence—somewhere else."

"Why, David—I must bring the girls out, you know. They must not be told—of this."

"They need be told only what you choose to have them know, but as to the bringing-out farce—that's rot! Those girls will get out by one door or another, never fear. *You* are to be kept in—that's the important thing at present."

"Dear old David!" Doris's eyes dimmed as she looked at the kind face bending over the hands lying limp, now, on her lap. She noticed that there was white on the temple where the dark hair had turned; the heavy shoulders were bent permanently. She longed to do something more for David during the next—twenty years!

"You must not give way, Doris. A change is good for us all." Martin noted the tears in the eyes holding his own, but he did not understand their source.

"I am afraid the girls will be so disappointed," was what Doris said.

"Pampered creatures! It will do them good. But Nancy will love it and Joan can kick the traces if she wants to—that will do her good." Martin leaned back and crossed his legs in the old boyish way.

"What will Nancy love, David?"

"Why, the out-of-door country life. She's that kind. Flowers and animals and quiet."

"Country life?" Doris sat up. "But, David, I could not stand country life, myself. I love to look at the country, listen to it, play with it—but I am a citizen to the core. It is simply impossible. One has to be born with the country in his blood to be part of it."

It was like pleading with the stern expression on Martin's face.

He was not apparently listening, and when he spoke he carried on his own thought:

"Queer how things dovetail. We drop a stitch and then go back and pick it up—now there is that place of yours, down South, Ridge House!"

Doris's face twitched and then, because she was in that state closely bordering upon the unknown, that state open to impressions and suggestions from sources outside the explainable, Silver Gap seemed to open alluringly to her imagination. It *was* like a dropped stitch to be taken up and woven into the pattern!

She suddenly felt that she had always known she must go back. It was like the heart trouble—a thing on her road! Doris smiled and David patted her hands.

"That's the way it strikes me," he said, quite as if he were gaining his inspiration whence hers came. "After you told me about the—the children, you know, Doris, years ago, I went down there and gave the place a look-over. The South always affects me like a—well, a lotus flower—sleeping but filled with wonderful dreams. It gets me! Why, after seeing Ridge House I even went so far as to buy a piece of land known as Blowing Rock Clearing. I've planned, if that scamp of a nephew of mine ever develops into a sawbones, to leave him in charge here and go down South myself and put up a shack on my clearing." Martin was watching Doris now from under his brows; he was talking against the silence that might engulf her again; seeking to hold her to a future that he had been vaguely considering in the past. He thankfully saw her interest growing.

"You did that, David—how like you!"

The tears still came easily to Doris's eyes.

"Oh, well, I have a thrifty streak, and I hated to see a property like Ridge House lie fallow. It's great. The buying of Blowing Rock was pure Yankee sense of a bargain. But you see how it all works out. You'll have the time of your life developing your holdings and, at odd moments, I can start my shack. Look upon the change as an adventure—nothing permanent. In a year or so you may be able to spend most of the time on pavements—though why in God's name you want to is hard to imagine."

Doris was smiling.

"But the girls!" she faltered.

"Forget them. Give them a chance to think of you. Take them abroad—that will be good for you all, but in the autumn, Doris, go South! You must escape next winter."

CHAPTER VIII

"ONE IS ASSURED THAT THERE IS A POWER THAT FIGHTS WITH US AGAINST THE CONFUSION AND EVIL OF THE WORLD"

The warm June sunlight lay over the broad lawns and meadows of Dondale; it touched with luring power the buds to blossom and, by its tricks of magic, girlhood to womanhood.

Only a month ago Joan and Nancy Thornton and those who, with them, were about to leave Miss Phillips's school, had seemed little girls, but now they were changed. There was a gravity when they looked back at the safe, happy years that not even the glory of the future could dispel.

They were eager to go forward but were half afraid.

Joan and Nancy had left the others and walked across the lawn and were sitting on a vine-covered wall under a noble magnolia tree. Nancy was still sweetly fair and she had not outgrown the childish outline of cheek and chin, the pretty droop of the left eyelid, and the quick habit of smiling. She was tall and slim and graceful and bore herself with a touching dignity that was as unconscious as it was distinguished.

Nature had not arrived yet with Joan. She was still in the making, and the best that could be said for her was that she was undergoing the ordeal with bewitching charm.

The dusky hair was filled with life and light; the eyes were yellow-brown and dark-lashed; the skin was creamy and smooth and the features irregular—eyes and mouth a bit prominent in the thin face. Joan was thin, not slim. You were conscious of her bones—but they were pretty bones, and every muscle of her lithe young body was as flexible and strong as a boy's. She could change from awkwardness to grace by a turn of thought. Joan was subject to outside control, while Nancy seemed possessed by innate inheritance. Both girls were in white, and while Nancy's appearance was immaculate, Joan's was suggestive of indifference.

"It is wonderful—this going abroad," Joan was saying while her long, supple fingers wove the stems of daisies into an intricate pattern. "And to go to that little Italian town where mother was married! Nan, I'm going to know all about mother and father this summer."

Nancy's head was lifted slightly, and her cool blue eyes fixed themselves upon Joan. There was no doubt about the colour of Nancy's eyes—they were blue.

"I do hope, Joan," she said, "that you are not going to spoil everything by making Aunt Dorrie uncomfortable. If she has not told us things, it is because she thinks best not to."

"But it's getting on my nerves, Nan. It's ominous. Maybe there is a—a—tragedy in our young lives"—Joan dramatically set her words into comedy—"a dark past. How I would adore that!"

"I would loathe it!" Nancy murmured, "and there couldn't be. I know there is only a deep sadness. I wouldn't hurt Aunt Dorrie by—by unearthing it."

"Nan," here Joan pointed her finger, "do you know a blessed thing about your father? I don't!"

Nancy flushed, but made no reply.

Harriet T. Comstock

"There's where the secret lies—I feel it in my blood!" Joan shuddered and Nancy laughed. "It didn't seem to matter until *now*, but, Nan, we're women at last!"

"Of course," Nancy spoke, "I have thought of that. The best families have such things in them—but they don't talk about them. Now that we are women we must act like women—such women as Aunt Dorrie."

"Nan, you're a snob. A pitiful, beautiful little snob!" Joan wafted a kiss. "Your prettiness saves you. If you had a turned-up nose you'd be an abomination."

"You have no right to call me a snob, Joan!" Nancy's fair face flushed.

"Did I call you a snob, Nan, dear?"

"Yes, you did. It's not being a snob to be true to oneself." Nancy put up her defences.

"I should say not," Joan agreed, but she laughed.

"Just think of all that Aunt Dorrie represents!" Nancy went on. "She's all that her father and her grandfather—"

"And her grandmothers," Joan broke in, "made her! Just think of it! And you and I must carry on the tradition—at least *you* must—I'm afraid I'll have to be a quitter. It makes me too hot."

"You'll never be a quitter, you splendid Joan!" Nancy turned her face to Joan— the old love had grown with the years, "You *are* splendid, Joan—everyone adores you."

But Joan did not seem to hear. Suddenly she said:

"Now do you know, Nan, I hate to go across the ocean this summer. It seems such a waste of time. I am eager to begin."

"Begin what, Joan?"

"Begin to live."

"You funny Joan, what have you been doing since you were born?"

"Waking up, Nan, and stretching and learning to stand alone. I'm ready now to—to walk. I dare say I'll wobble, but—I don't care—I want to begin."

A sense of danger filled Nancy—she often felt afraid of Joan, or *for* Joan, she was not sure which it was.

"I think you'll do nothing that will trouble and disappoint Aunt Dorrie," she said, using the weapon of the weak.

"I think Aunt Dorrie would want me to—to live my life," Joan returned.

"Oh! of course, she'd let you—go. That's Aunt Dorrie's idea of justice. But we have no right to impose on it. People may be willing to suffer, but that's no excuse for making them suffer." Nancy did battle with the fear that was in her—her fear that Joan might escape her, and now, as in the old days, Nancy felt that play lost its keen zest when Joan withdrew.

Joan made no reply. She looked very young with the sunlight flooding over her. Her eyes wide apart, her short upper lip and firm, little round chin were almost childlike when in repose, and her heavy hair rose and fell in charming curves as the breeze stirred it.

"Joan, what do you want to do, really?" Nancy dropped from her perch beside Joan and came close, leaning against the swinging feet as if to stay their restlessness.

"Oh! I don't know—but something real; something like a beginning, not just a carrying on. I want to dig out of me what

Harriet T. Comstock

is in me and—and—offer it for sale!" Joan leaned back perilously and laughed at her own folly and Nancy's shocked face.

"Of course, I may not have anything anybody wants," she went on, "but I'll never be able to settle down and be comfy until I *know*. Having a rich somebody behind you is—is—the limit!" she flung out, defiantly.

"I don't know what you mean, Joan." Nancy was aghast. The fear within her was taking shape; it was like a shrouded figure looming up ready to cast off its disguise.

"Of course you don't, you blessed little snow-child!"—the laugh struck rudely on Nancy's discomfort—"why should you; why should any one in this—this factory where we've all been cut in the same shape? We're all going to be let out of here to—to be married! They've never taken me in."

"Oh, Joan!" Nancy looked about nervously. Of course every girl had this ideal in her brain, but she was not supposed to express it—except vicariously in the charm-lure.

"It's all right, this marrying," Joan went calmly on. "I want to myself, some day, it's splendid and all that—but something in me wants to fly about alone first."

"You're silly, Joan."

"I suppose I am, snow-child. I suppose I'll get frightfully snubbed some day and come back glad enough to trot along with the rest—but oh! it must be sublime to have the chance a boy has. He can have everything—even the try if he *is* rich— and then he knows what he's worth. Why, Nancy, I am going to say something awful now—so hold close. I want to know what my dancing is worth, and my singing, and my making believe. I feel so powerful sometimes and then again—I am weak as—as a shadow!"

"Oh! Joan do be careful—you'll fall over the wall."

Nancy flung her arms about Joan, who had tilted backward as she portrayed her state of weakness.

"You frighten me, Joan, and besides you have no right to disappoint Aunt Dorrie, and if she should hear you talk she'd be shocked!"

"I wonder," mused Joan, "she is so understanding. I wonder. But come, Nan, dear, I must go practise the thing I'm to sing at Commencement, and I have a perfectly new idea for a dance on Class Day."

David Martin and Doris were never to forget the impression Joan made on the two occasions when she stood forth alone, during the Commencement week, like a startling and unique figure, with the background of lovely young girlhood. No one resented her conspicuousness. All gloried in it. They clapped and cheered her on—she was their Joan, the idol of the years which she had made vital and electric by her personality.

She danced on Class Day a wonderful dance that she had originated herself.

Nancy played her accompaniment, keeping her fascinated gaze upon Joan while her fingers touched the keys in accord with every movement.

Lightly, bewilderingly, the gauzy, green-robed figure was wafted here, there, everywhere, under the broad elms, apparently on Nancy's tune. She was a leaf, a petal of a flower, a creature born of light and air.

People forgot they were performing a stilted duty at a school function—they were frankly delighted and appreciative. Joan rose to the homage and, at such moments, she was beautiful with a beauty that did not depend upon feature or colouring.

Harriet T. Comstock

But it was when she sang on Commencement Day that she achieved her triumph.

Martin was watching Doris closely. She had had no return of her March illness; she never spoke of it, nor did he, but for that very reason Martin kept a more rigid guard upon any excitement. There was that in Doris's face which, to his trained eye, was significant. It was as if she had been touched by a passing frost. She had not withered, but she was changed. The time of blight might be soon or distant, but the frost had fallen on the woman's life.

It was when Joan had finished her song that Martin took Doris from the hall.

It happened this way:

The flower-banked platform was empty until the accompanist—it was a young professor, this time, not Nancy—came on.

The audience waited politely; the rows of girlish faces were turned expectantly, and then Joan entered!

Without a trace of self-consciousness she looked at her friends—they were all her friends—with that sweet confidence and understanding of the true artist. The dainty loose gown covered any angle that might have proved unlovely, and Joan was at one of her rarely beautiful moments.

She stood at ease while the first notes were played—she appeared suddenly detached, and then she sang.

It was an old English ballad, quaint and rollicking:

> "I'll sail upon the Dog-star,
> I'll sail upon the Dog-star,
> And then pursue the morning
> And then pursue, and then pursue the morning.

"I'll chase the moon, till it be noon,
I'll chase the moon, till it be noon,
But I'll make her leave her horning.

"I'll climb the frosty mountain,
I'll climb the frosty mountain,
And there I'll coin the weather.

"I'll tear the rainbow from the sky
And tie both ends together."

The ringing girlish voice rose high and true and clear.

"Bravo!" cried a man's voice and then:

"And she'll do it, too!"

It was at this point that Martin took Doris from the room.

In the quiet of the deserted piazza Doris looked up at Martin through tears.

"Joan is feeling her oats." Martin walked to and fro; he had been more moved by the song than he cared to confess.

"The darling!" Doris whispered. Then: "Can't you see what Miss Phillips meant, Davey? The child is talented—she shall never be held back. Wealth can be as cruel and crippling as poverty. Be prepared, David, I mean to let Joan—free."

Martin came close and sat down.

"Go easy, Doris," he cautioned, then asked: "And how about Nancy?"

"David, I'm going to tell Nancy, after we come home from Europe—not all, of course, but enough to make her under-stand—about me! I cannot quite explain, but I am sure I am

Harriet T. Comstock

right in my decision. Nancy, indeed all of us, will, sooner or later, have to let Joan go! I saw that clearly as she sang. I must fill Nancy's life and she must make up to me what I am about to lose. David, is this what mothers feel?"

"Some of them, Doris. The best of them. I'm glad to see you game."

"Oh! yes. I'm glad, too—for Joan's sake. I will be giving Nancy her best and surest happiness—with me, but not Joan. And so, David, Joan must not have the slightest inkling—she must go, when her time comes, unhampered. You, Nancy, and I must contribute that to her future."

Martin saw that Doris was still trembling, she was excited, too, in her controlled way. He was anxious.

"You're seeing things in broad daylight, Doris. Why, my dear, both the girls will be snapped up before any of us catch our breaths. That is what Miss Phillips' is for. Training for fine American wives and mothers. A good job, too."

Doris smiled and shook her head. Then she said suddenly:

"David, the old spectre stalks! It seems as if I ought to know, as if the knowledge were right here, to-day."

"Come, come, now Doris! If you do not quiet down I'm going to pack you off to the hotel. Why, see here, the kids have not revealed themselves. You're lashing yourself about nothing. Can you not reason it out this way—"

Martin sat close to the couch upon which Doris half reclined; he was almost praying that Joan would have a dozen encores— by request, apparently, she was again chasing the rainbow on her Dog-star.

"The inheritance, I mean. For I see it is that that is clutching you. My work brings me close to primitive things—I believe in inheritance down to the roots—but by heaven, we inherit from the ages, not from our next of kin alone. Each son and daughter of us comes into port with load enough to crush us, and if we kept it all we'd go under. We shuffle off a lot. It is the ability to shuffle, the opportunity to shuffle that counts. Why, look here, Doris—"

And Doris was looking, holding with all her strength to the man's words.

"That little mountain woman had more daring and courage, according to what you told me, than poor Merry ever had. She cut a wider circle, got more out of life, I bet, went out of it more satisfied. Her child, with your help, could develop into something mighty worth while for she wouldn't have so much to overcome at the start. On the other hand, Meredith's child would have to blaze her own trail, as far as any guidance from her mother is concerned. Can't you see, that's where inheritance plays the devil with hasty conclusions?"

Doris drew a long breath and sat up. She was seeking to hold to what she could not see.

"David," she whispered, "is it the knowing, or the not knowing? Could I have helped more wisely had I not shirked the truth? In there, a moment ago, it was as if Meredith were demanding. Oh! youth is awful in its possibilities of success or failure."

Martin was seriously alarmed. He had never seen Doris so shaken, but he talked on, seeking by a show of calmness to disarm her fears.

"It's the ability to shuffle off inheritance that counts, Doris. You have given these girls the strength and opportunity—to shuffle. Now, my dear, be sensible. It is up to the girls and they're all right. Hold firm to your own belief, Doris. It's about to be proved."

Harriet T. Comstock

"Hear them." Doris dropped back. "They are still applauding Joan."

The next few months Doris always looked back upon as a connecting stretch of road between what she had but faintly feared and what became assured.

From the day Joan graduated she became the dominant influence in what followed, and Nancy, being non-resistant, was engulfed in the general rush of affairs; was absorbed and smilingly played her part as once she had played Joan's accompaniment.

Joan was not more selfish than the young generally are; she had hours of noble self-renunciation and generosity. Her ego was well developed, but it never drove her cruelly.

Doris justified what happened, when she took time to consider, by her determination to be fair to both girls and then, unconsciously focussing on Joan because Joan was always in evidence. The girl's vitality and joyousness were unfailing. Everything was of interest, and she seemed to gather the flowers of life not so much for her own enjoyment as for the glory of shedding them on others. That is what disarmed people—this lavishness of the girl. She gave spice to life, and that has its value. If Nancy ever knew the natural desire to shine in her own light, not Joan's, she smilingly hid it—not even Doris suspected it.

After Nancy was made to understand her aunt's state of health—and it was, in the end, Martin who informed her—she rose superbly to what offered, poor child, an opportunity peculiarly her own. To her was given the sacred duty of watching the one she loved best in the world; of warding off anything that threatened her peace and comfort. Here were power and authority and, though no one suspected, she would rule in her narrow, detached kingdom. Nothing should defeat her. They should all look to her!

Almost fiercely Nancy undertook her silent task. She smiled, she learned new subtleties; she soon became the pretty barrier between Doris and any troubling thing.

With her half-afraid glance fixed upon the dazzling Joan, it was small wonder that Doris fell into the trap set for her by Martin and Nancy.

She took the girls abroad—or was it Joan that led the way? She considered, after reaching the little Italian town from which she had seen Meredith depart, how best to speak of Thornton. She got so far as the telling of Meredith's wedding in the unchanged chapel on the hill when Joan startled her by asking quite as a matter of course:

"Is our father still alive?"

Nancy turned pale and shrank before the question, but she saw that the cool tone had controlled the situation. Doris looked relieved instead of shocked.

"We've often talked of it, Nan and I," Joan proceeded; "it did not seem very vital one way or the other until now."

"As far as I know," Doris was surprised at her own calmness, "he is still alive."

"I'm glad of that," Joan remarked, and there was a glint in her eyes. "I'd hate to have him dead—just now."

Quite without reason Doris laughed. After all, what she had conjured up as a ghost was turning into a human possibility. It was never to frighten her in the future. Joan had felled the spectre by her first stroke.

Then Nancy spoke:

"I never want to hear his name again," she said, firmly, relentlessly.

Harriet T. Comstock

Doris looked at her in amazement. Later she confided to Joan her surprise.

"I did not know the child had such sternness."

Joan shrugged her shoulders and smiled.

"Nan is like a rock underneath, Aunt Dorrie," she said. "I suppose it is—what shall I say?—blood! It is concentrated in Nan. She's like you. Disgrace, or what seemed like disgrace, would kill her—it would make me fight!"

And after that conversation all inclination to confide further in the girls as to their relationship or lack of it deserted Doris.

She saw a new cause for caution and went back to the stand she had taken when the children were babies—but with far less courage.

"When they marry, of course, it must be told."

Doris returned to New York in September, and after a fortnight in which she closed the old house and made arrangements for the servants, she was so exhausted that she gladly turned her face southward.

Nancy, already, was her mainstay. The girl had apparently got under the burden, and held it secure on her firm, young shoulders. She developed initiative and the healing touch. No one disputed her where Doris was concerned, and Martin grimly accepted her as the most necessary thing in the hope that lay in Ridge House.

Their appearance there was marked by two incidents that Doris alone heeded.

First was the effect Nancy had upon Jed.

The man stared at the girl as if he saw a ghost. Like the very old, his real sensations lay in the past. Nancy stirred him strangely. The emotion was like a warm ray of sunlight striking in a dark place. Doris watched him with interest and concern; but Jed had no words with which to enlighten her. He only smiled wider, more often, and took to following Nancy like a wavering, distorted shadow.

The second incident was Mary.

From her cabin across the river she had manipulated the arrangements at Ridge House so perfectly that the machinery was oiled and running when the family arrived.

Mary was more reserved, more self-contained than she had ever been, but again, as Martin said to Doris, she must be judged by what she did, not by what she suggested, and she had accomplished marvels not only at the old place, but in her cabin across The Gap. In her once-deserted home Mary had contrived to resurrect all the ideals that had perished with her forebears. The rooms shone and glittered; the garden throve; and Mary spun and wove and designed and made money. She was respected, feared, and secretly believed to be "low-down mean," but calmly she went her way.

What she knew lay buried in her stern reserve, and she saw a great deal.

She saw at once what had occurred since she left her years of service. Mary no longer served—she ruled.

She saw that Joan, as she had given promise of doing, was controlling the forces of her small world. Doing it as once she had done it in the nursery, with a radiant witchery that had gained its ends with all but Mary herself!

While Mary's eyelids drew together, she focussed through the narrow slits upon Joan and with a hot, deep resolve she took up cudgels for Nancy.

Harriet T. Comstock

And she bided her time.

Back and forth from her cabin to the big house she walked daily, and to Mary's cabin Nancy, presently, went—for comfort and inspiration, though she did not realize it.

Often, unknown to others, the two would sit near the fire, making a vivid picture. Mary in her plaid cotton gown, bent over her folded arms, swaying to and fro, making few comments but conscious of being understood. Nancy, fair and lovely, speaking more openly to the plain, silent woman near her than she had ever spoken to any earthly being and feeling, under her sweet unconsciousness, the underlying confidence.

"Of course," she once whispered to Mary, "I would love all the things that Joan loves and wants, but my duty to Aunt Dorrie is bigger than they, Mary. I am sure if Joan saw things as I do, she would act as I am acting. But we are keeping Joan from knowing."

"Why?" The sharp word startled Nancy—was Mary disapproving?

"Aunt Dorrie and Uncle David think best, Mary."

Mary touched upon the hidden hardness in Nancy's softness and retreated.

And during that red-and-gold autumn, their first in The Gap, Doris was soothed strangely to a state of perfect relaxation—a state not pleasing to Joan, and rather puzzling to David Martin, who postponed a proposed trip to the West until he felt sure of Doris's health. It seemed that, having dropped the old life, Doris was not merely willing to step into a new one— she was drifting in. Without resistance she floated. She would lie for a whole afternoon on the porch watching the play of colour on The Rock. She smiled, recalling, rather vaguely to be sure, the superstitions concerning The Rock.

It was all delightfully restful and beautiful and not a care in the world!

Mary and Nancy saw to every detail. Joan was frankly interested in every phase of the experience. "It might be," mused Doris from her pillows, "that having left everything to that Power that does control, I am to have my heart's deep desire—keep both Joan and Nancy!"

Harriet T. Comstock

CHAPTER IX

"I COUNT LIFE JUST A STUFF TO TRY THE SOUL'S STRENGTH ON. LEARN, NOR COUNT THE PANG; DARE, NEVER GRUDGE THE THROE"

No one but Mary, apparently, saw what was to happen. It was the old nursery problem re-acted.

Joan had tired of her game, had used all the material at hand, and was burning to be on the adventurous trail.

The old restlessness and defiance were singing in the girl's blood; mockery rang in her voice and that wonderful laugh of hers. She was about to smash into the safe joyousness of things as they were! She threatened Nancy's toys. And Mary, alone, took heed. Joan herself was unconscious. She always was of her changing mood; she simply realized that she was lost; somehow, astray.

And Nancy, looking mutely in Mary's eyes, seemed to say:

"It will all be so lonely; so terrible with Joan gone!"

That was it. The old fear of, or for, Joan had materialized—it was Life with Joan left out!

"And why should one have so much and the other so little?" asked Mary of that deep knowledge in her busy brain. "Why shouldn't they share alike—and twins at that!"

Then Mary stopped short in her thinking. Her own words took her back, back to a dark night—she was peering, aided by a dim light from within, at a baby lying in the arms of—

Mary drew her breath sharp; her thin, flat bosom heaved and her fingers clutched her gown.

David Martin had so far classified his perplexity concerning Doris as to name it "Southern fever."

"Hookworm?" Joan broke in gleefully.

Martin frowned but did not reply.

"Doris," he turned to the couch, "I must go out West." She understood. Martin never spoke openly about his family affairs. Until he was surer of that nephew of his he kept him in the background.

"Yes, David." Doris smiled up at him.

"I want you to promise me that you will take more exercise!" Martin said.

"Why, certainly, David, but I thought you wanted me to—to rest."

"I do—but you are rested. I do not want you to enjoy resting. It's dangerous."

"Oh! bully for you, Uncle David," Joan broke in, delightedly, "Aunt Dorrie is just plain flopping and Nan and Mary are abetting her."

For some reason Martin turned to Joan, not Nancy who was standing patiently by.

"Joan, get your aunt on horseback—lead up to it, of course—and go slow."

"But—Uncle David—" Nancy drew near. Her kingdom was threatened.

"My dear," Martin always melted to Nancy, "after Joan gets her on horseback, *you* ride with her."

And so Doris got off her couch, rather dazedly, as one thinking his legs have been shot off finds them still attached to him.

She had been actually letting go! She, of all people, and just when there was so much to do—so long as she had strength to do it!

It was December when Martin started for the West and Joan's restlessness gained power.

Christmas rather eased the situation, for with it Father Noble appeared.

He startled Doris as Uncle Jed had, by his persistence.

"They cannot be as old as they look," she concluded, and gladly entered into all the plans for carrying sunshine and joy into the deep places of the hills.

"Dear me, dear me!" explained Father Noble, whose memory of her was so blurred that Doris did not venture to refer to it in detail; "I thought when the Sisters went away this beautiful old house would fall into disuse. It is a great happiness to feel its welcome once more."

Then the old man raised his hat from his silvered head and, standing so in the doorway, besought a blessing "on them who waited but to do His will."

Joan and Nancy rode with him back into the clearings; they revelled in it all and carried out every suggestion offered. They learned, through Father Noble's interpretation, to ignore the stolid indifference of the people; they played for, not with, the shy children, and distributed marvellous toys that were limply held in small hands that were yet to learn the blessed sense of ownership.

"When you are gone," Father Noble explained and chuckled delightedly, "they will watch the trails for your coming back. They never forget; they are worth the saving—but one must have faith and patience."

Then January settled down in The Gap. The short days were full of clouds and shadows; the river ran sullenly, and with greater need for sympathy Joan made ready to demolish Nancy's toys. She came into the living room one morning in her riding togs. She was splashed with mud and her face was dull except for the wide, burning eyes.

Nancy was weaving at the window—Mary had taught her, and she gave the impression, sitting there, of having looms in her blood.

Around the fire lay four hound puppies—they had taken the place of dolls in Nancy's affections. As Joan entered the dogs raised their absurd heads and with their flappy ears and padded paws patted the floor in welcome.

"Where is Aunt Dorrie?" asked Joan, poising herself on the arm of a deep chair.

"In the chapel," Nancy replied, bent over the snarl she had made of woof and warp.

"I wish Aunt Dorrie would have that room sealed!" Joan spoke ill-naturedly; "I know it's haunted. If we don't look out the ghosts will ooze over the whole house. Ooh!"

Nancy did not answer but set the treadle to its duty. The clacking noise emphasized Joan's nervousness.

"Aunt Dorrie doesn't know what to do here—that's why she

takes to the chapel. That's why everyone takes to chapels."

Nancy broke her thread and Joan laughed.

"I wonder why Aunt Dorrie came here like a dear, silly old pioneer?" The laugh still persisted in the mocking words.

"It's—it's quite the thing," Nancy said, fatuously, "to have country places. I think it's wonderful."

"You may not be able to help being a snob, Nan, but don't be a prig." Joan's words struck hurtingly. Then suddenly her mood changed.

"Forgive me, snow-child," she whispered, going close to Nancy. "I'm a beast. Isn't it queer to be conscious, now and then, of the beast in you?"

"Please don't, Joan, dear. Please don't talk and act so." Nancy's eyes were blinded by tears.

"Very well, then, I will be good." Joan flung herself in a chair and presently asked curiously:

"Nan, what are you going to do when you've done all the things down here millions of times?"

"There will always be new duties," Nancy ventured.

"Duties! Oh! Nan, surely you're too young to play with duties—you'll hurt yourself." The mockery again entered in.

Just then Jed stumbled into the room with an armful of wood. His bleared eyes clung to Nancy's face and he nearly fell over a rug.

When he went out Joan seemed to follow him. She spoke musingly as if voicing her thoughts:

"It's terrible for anything as old as that to be running around," she said. "It isn't decent. He ought to be tucked up in his nice little grave. He looks as if he'd been forgotten."

"Joan, you are wicked—you make me afraid!" Nancy came from the loom and crouched by Joan.

"Snow-child, again forgive me!" Joan bent and drew Nancy's fair head to her knee. "But oh! I am so—so utterly lost."

"Joan, what is it? What is the matter?"

"I don't know, Nan." Joan was looking into the fire—seeking; seeking. "Things that quiet you and Aunt Dorrie just drive me on to the rocks. I feel as if I'd be wrecked if I didn't steer well out into the open. And when I get as far as that, I know that I couldn't find my way out even if—if everything let go of me. I suppose I would sink. This isn't my place, Nan, but I don't know where my place is! I feel sure I have a place, everyone has—but where is mine?"

There was desperation in the words, the desperation of helpless youth. No perspective, no light or shade, but terrible vision.

"Joan, darling, why can you not wait until you see the way?" Nancy was prepared now for battle.

"That's it, Nan. I can't. All I can do is to push off the rocks—then I'll have to sink or swim. This is killing me!"

Joan flung her head back as if she were choking.

And just then Mary came into the room.

A gray shawl, home-spun—it was made from the wool of Mary's own sheep—was clutched over her thin body; a huge quilted hood—Mary herself had quilted it—half hid her dark, expressionless face.

Harriet T. Comstock

"I met the postman," she announced, "as I came along. He give me this!"

Mary held a letter out to Joan and passed from the room.

The moment, while Joan glanced at the letter, had power to grip Nancy's imagination and fill it with a vision.

As sure as she ever saw anything, she saw Joan going away! Going away as she had never gone before. Going to a Far Country.

"Whom is the letter from?" she faltered, and Joan tore open the envelope while her eyes drank in the words.

"It is from Sylvia Reed, Nan. Her dream has come true. She has her studio—she wants me!"

"Joan, you will not go—you must not!" All that Nancy dared to put in her plea she put in it then.

"Why not?" asked Joan impressed. "Why not, Nan?"

"Aunt Dorrie—" Nancy's words ended in a sob.

"Aunt Dorrie shall decide."

And with that Joan, her face radiant, her breath coming quick, walked from the room and on, on to the little chapel upstairs.

Doris was sitting by the window. The day was going to be clear at its close, and a rift in the sullen clouds showed the gold behind; the light lay in a straight line across the chapel floor.

Doris was not in a depressed mood. She often sat for an hour in the quiet place. She took her tenderest treasures of thought there. She had been thinking that afternoon of David Martin. How wise he was! What a friend! How he understood her! How unworthy she was of the richness that flooded her life!

It was then that Joan came in. She did not go close to Doris—the physical touch was not the first impulse with either of them.

"Aunt Dorrie, I have a letter from Sylvia Reed."

Instantly Doris was stirred as Nancy had been. Mentally she braced. She recalled vividly Sylvia Reed, Joan's particular friend at Miss Phillips's. The girl had genius where Joan had talent. She had inherited enough to take her comfortably through school, had a small income besides, but she would have to work and win her way to the success she promised. Sylvia's ambition was only equalled by her belief in herself and her eagerness to prove it to others. She was a few years older than Joan, and a girl of remarkable character and sweetness.

"She wants me, Aunt Dorrie. She wants me to come to her. She has a studio in New York; not down in that part of the city which Uncle David doesn't like, the place where he says folks show off with the window shades up. Sylvia is in the safe uptown where the *real* thing is!"

The eagerness in Joan's hurrying voice made Doris smile. The girl was trying to clear all obstacles away before coming to the point. That was her way.

"Why, Aunt Dorrie, Sylvia has two orders for book covers, already, besides twelve hundred a year!"

The letter had been packed with ammunition and Joan was using it recklessly.

"Just listen, Aunt Dorrie."

And Joan spread the letter on her knee; her hands were trembling as she patted it open.

"This is what Sylvia says:

The Studio is perfect—north side full of windows; south side full of fireplace; your room and mine on the east; stars and sunlight on tap from the windows. We are on top of the city and nothing hinders our view. We walk up and none come but those worthy of us—come, Joan, you always said that you would.

Your future will be blasted unless you break away from your rich relatives. Nothing is such a curse as that which prevents you proving yourself; you remember about the poem which dealt with proving your soul?—how you spouted it. I know that you are gifted, child, but the world doesn't. If we fail, you at least can, after you pay proper respects to my remains, go back to that adorable aunt of yours and flop in the lap of luxury—but make the attempt to reach glory first.

I suppose Nan will raise a ladylike dust—but come! Come empty-handed—it's the only honest way. Come prepared to eat your bread by the sweat of your brow—or go hungry.

I bet your aunt will see the squareness of this offer if you put it right. Come!

The light broadened outside—the little chapel was flooded with the golden glow.

Even while her heart sank and grew heavy, Doris was moved with an almost terrible understanding of the girl across the room. She wanted to push her on her way instead of holding her back, and at the same time she was striving to clutch her as she went her way.

Yes, that was it. Joan was already started; nothing could hold her back—but still the battle waged, while Doris smiled tremblingly.

"I know, Aunt Dorrie, I know. It hurts—but—but—oh! listen, dear. This seems my chance; perhaps it isn't—but I can never know until I try. Dearie—I will do just what you say. I will, and I will think you right. I want so much to try and find out what is in me that I—I cannot see clear."

For a moment Doris could not see the girl across the room. The sunlight fell full on her, and hid her, rather than revealed her.

"I'll try to be worthy of your faith in me, darling. Go on." Doris spoke quietly.

They did not come together physically, these two. They felt no need of the affectionate human contact; it was more one soul reaching out to another with courage and honesty.

Doris listened, following closely. People and places became visualized as Joan spoke. Sylvia Reed with her strong, purposeful face and eyes of a young prophet; the new nest of genius where the brave creature, believing in herself, waited for another in whom she trusted and for whom she held a deep-founded affection. Doris felt her way in silence—relinquishing, loving, fearing, but never blinded. She knew the moment's pain of disappointment caused by the realization that with all her love and riches she had not, for the time being, anything to offer this untried soul that could lure it from its vision.

Presently she heard herself speaking as if a third person were in the room:

"If this means anything it means that it must be met in the spirit with which Sylvia is meeting it. She has risked all; is willing to pay the price—are you?"

"Yes, Aunt Dorrie."

"You know, darling, that it would be easier for me to lavish everything on you?"

"Yes, Aunt Dorrie."

124 Harriet T. Comstock

"You understand that if I leave you free to meet this chance in its only true way—the hard, struggling way—it is not because I desire to sicken you of it and so regain you for Nancy and me?"

"Oh! yes, Aunt Dorrie, I do understand that."

"I'm sure you do, child, or you would not be here. And so I set you free, little Joan, I wish you luck and success, but if you find the chance is not your chance, my darling, will you come as frankly to me as you have come to-night?"

"Yes—yes, Aunt Dorrie, and you are—well—there is no word for you, but I feel as if you were my mother and I'd just—found you! You'll never seem quite the same, Aunt Dorrie—though that always seemed good enough. Why"—And here Joan slipped to her feet and danced lightly in the sunny room tossing her hair and swaying gracefully—"why, I'm free to fail even if I must—fail or succeed—and you understand and love me and don't begrudge me my freedom—you are setting me free and not even disapproving."

The dance in that sanctuary did not seem incongruous; Doris watched the motion as she might a figment loose in the sunlight. It was as much a prayer of thanks as any ever uttered in the peaceful place.

CHAPTER X

"HOPES AND DISAPPOINTMENTS,
AND MUCH NEED OF PHILOSOPHY"

A week later Joan started for New York, a closely packed suitcase in her hand, a closely packed trunk in the baggage car ahead, and some hurting memories to bear her company on the way.

Memories of Nancy's tears.

How Nancy could cry—once the barriers were down!

And worse than Nancy's tears were Doris's smiles.

Joan understood the psychology of smiles—as she remembered, her proud head was lowered and she was surprised to find that *she* was shedding tears.

"But it's all part of the price of freedom!" At last Joan dried her eyes. "And I'm willing to pay."

So Joan travelled alone up to town, and it was a wet, slippery night when she raised the knocker on Sylvia Reed's green-painted door and let it fall.

The door opened at once and disclosed the battle-ground of young genius. The old room was dim, for Sylvia had been toasting bacon and bread by the open fire and she needed no

Harriet T. Comstock

more light than the coals gave. Sylvia wore a smock and her hair was down her back. She looked about twelve until she fixed her eyes upon you, then she looked old; too old for a girl of twenty-four.

"Joan! Joan!" was all she said as she drew Joan in. Then, after a struggle, "Do you mind if I—sob?"

"No, I'm going to do it myself." And Joan proceeded to do so and remembered Nancy.

"I'm so—happy!" she gulped. "I was never so happy in my life. I feel as if I'd got hatched, broken through the shell!"

"You have," cried Sylvia, unevenly. "We're going to—to conquer everything! Come in your room, Joan, shed as much as you like. I expected you this morning. I have only bacon and eggs—shall we go out to eat?"

"Go out? Heavens, no! And I adore bacon and eggs. Sylvia, I have edged into glory!"

"You have, Joan—edged in, that's about it."

After the meal before the fire they cleared things away, and then they talked far into the night. Sylvia had already laid emphasis upon her small order.

"And really, Joan, that's great," she explained; "many a girl has to wait longer. Some day I'm going to be hung in the best exhibitions in town, but as a starter a magazine is nothing to be sneered at. I'm modelling, too—I have a duck of an idea for a frieze—only I'm not telling anybody about that—it's too ambitious. What are you going to do, Joan?" This sudden question made Joan stare.

"I—I don't know," she replied, frankly, but with no shade of despondency. "I'll take a look around to-morrow and, then pack my little wares in my basket and peddle them, as you have done. If anybody wants a dancer—here I am! Anybody want funny little songs sung?—here's your girl! I seem to have only samples. I can be adaptable. That's my big asset." They both laughed, but Sylvia soon grew serious. Her short service in reality had already sobered her. It was one thing for the gifted young girl of a fashionable school to watch the impression she made by her wits upon people who were paying high for just such exhibitions, and quite another to convince buyers of goods that they were what you believed them to be.

"The public is a tightwad," was what she muttered presently, "unless you're willing to compromise or—prove it to them."

"I—I don't know what you mean," Joan replied. She was groping after the thing that had made Sylvia's eyes grow old.

"Well, all you need to know, Joan, my lamb, is to prove it to them—never compromise!" Sylvia was herself again. Too well she knew the value of starting out with one's shield bright and shining even if one had to come home *on* it, all rusted with one's life blood.

Things were not yet very tragic for Sylvia, and her shield was in good condition, but she had an imagination and a keen sense of self-protection.

"We're going to be the happiest pair in town," she whispered to Joan later that night as she bent over the tired girl; "and was there ever such a spot to live in? See, I'm going to raise your shade high, for the night is splendid and—the stars! Go to sleep with the stars watching you, old girl, and you're all right."

Joan slept heavily, dreamlessly, and awoke to—more bacon and eggs with hot rolls and coffee added.

"I'm going to float about a bit to-day," she said, and her feet were fairly dancing. "I've only known New York before holding to Aunt Dorrie's hand or my nurse's. Today I'm going to go back alone and then—catch up with myself."

Suddenly she began to sing her old graduation song:

"I'll sail upon the Dog-star
I'll sail upon the Dog-star;
I'll chase the moon, till it be noon,
But I'll make her leave her horning.

"I'll climb the frosty mountain
And there I'll coin the weather.
I'll tear the rainbow from the sky
And tie both ends together."

Sylvia leaned back, clapping and laughing. This was as it should be. Fun, youth, gaiety. She went to her easel in the north room, humming Joan's old ballad, and never did better work in her life than she did that day.

Joan sallied forth equally happy and her past, thank heaven, had been brief enough and rosy enough to make the tying of the ends nothing but a joyous task. She rode downtown on top of a bus. The crisp air stung and rallied her. She longed to sing from the swaying vehicle—she felt as if she were on top of the world and that it was keeping time to the tune she wanted to sing. She looked so lovely that the conductor grinned delightedly as he remarked:

"Snappy weather, miss!" and Joan nodded in friendly fashion and agreed. She walked to the old home, standing with drawn blinds by the little, close-locked park. It looked stately and reserved as one of the family might have done. It smilingly held its tongue.

"I'd like to see the sunken room and the fountain," Joan thought. "I cannot imagine it with the fountain and the birds still. They will never be still for me!"

She was a bit surprised to feel how far she had travelled from the Joan who was part of Nancy and the sunken room. It was quite shocking to find that she was not missing Nancy. She wondered if she were heartless and selfish? But after all, how could one be missed from a life in which she had never, could never, have part? And full well Joan realized that in this big venture of hers the old, except as a stepping-stone, was separated forever.

"If I become famous"—and Joan, tripping along, felt as if fame were as possible for her as the luncheon she was now feeling the need of—"if I become famous then they will understand, but even then my life and theirs will be different."

This point of view made Joan feel important, tragic, but desolate.

"I'm hungry," she thought, seriously, and made her way to a restaurant, where once she had gone with Doris while on a wonderful shopping expedition. The place was little changed; it had passed into other hands, but the menu proudly proclaimed the same enticing dishes.

Joan ordered what once had seemed the food of the gods, but to her now it was as chaff.

Across the table, made dim by her misty eyes, she seemed to see Doris smiling fondly, faithfully, at her. Doris's power over people was largely due to that faith she had in them.

"And I will be all you want me to be, Aunt Dorrie!" Joan promised that while she choked down the food. "I feel as if I were in the bear's house," she mused, whimsically. "I'm half afraid that I'll be pounced upon."

And so she paid her bill and went back, via the bus, to Sylvia. She ran up the long flights of stairs and burst in upon Sylvia with the announcement that "nothing would count if you didn't have someone to come home and tell it to." And then she forgot her glooms while they prepared an evening meal

Harriet T. Comstock

more conservative than bacon and eggs.

"Yes, my beloved," Sylvia returned as she plunged a wicked-looking little knife into the heart of a grapefruit: "And that accounts for half the marriages in life." Sylvia was refraining, just then, from telling of her own engagement. She wanted and needed Joan for the present—her secret would keep.

"You funny old Syl," Joan flung back over her shoulder as she drew the curtain over the closet that screened the housekeeping skeletons from the wonderful studio. "We won't have to resort to marriage, anyway. We've solved the eternal question!"

"Exactly! And now give those chops a twist. Thank the Lord, we both love them crisp."

The experiment in a few days had Joan by the throat. So utterly had she thrown herself into it, so almost unbelievably had Doris Fletcher permitted her to do so, that it took on all the attributes of reality and demanded nothing less than obedience to its laws, or surrender to defeat.

Doris had given Joan, when she came North, a check for five hundred dollars. Upon reaching Sylvia she had, after paying her expenses, that, and fifty dollars in cash left.

It had seemed boundless wealth for the first few days and continued to seem so until the necessity for bringing the check into action faced the girl.

"I must find something to do!" she vowed as she made her way to the bank where she had deposited the check. "No more fooling around."

Sylvia made no suggestions; never appeared to be anything but satisfied with things as they were. The companionship, the feeling of *home* that Joan had introduced into her life, were deep joys to the girl who, like many women who know not the art of making a home, are soul-sick for the blessings of one.

"I'd work till my last tube ran dry," she thought to herself, standing at the wide north window, "if I could keep her singing and dancing about and—getting meals!"

Joan did not interfere with Sylvia's profession—she gave it new meaning—but Sylvia realized that Joan was interfering with her own. Still, Sylvia was never one to usurp the rights of a Higher Power, and at twenty-four she was intensely, shame-facedly religious and absolutely lacking in desire to shape the ends of others.

"The thing that's meant for her will slap her in the face soon," Sylvia comforted herself. "And she's such a wonder!"

But if Sylvia refrained from nudging Joan on her course, even to the extent of opening her eyes to sign-posts, others were not so obliging. Into Sylvia's studio youth, in its various forms of expression, floated naturally. Sylvia attracted women more than men, but her girl friends brought their male comrades with them and everybody was welcome to anything that Sylvia had. Fortunately most of the young people were honestly striving to earn their living; they were sweetly, proudly unafraid, but when they relaxed and played they made Joan's eyes widen, until she discovered that they often dressed their ideas, as they did themselves, rather startlingly while adhering, privately, to a respectability that they refused to make public.

They were, on the whole, a joyous lot belonging to that new class which causes older and more conservative folk to hold their breath as people do who watch children walking near a precipice and dare not call out for fear of worse danger.

The women attracted and interested Joan immensely. The men amazed her.

"You see," she confided to Sylvia, "the men seem like a new sex—neither men nor women."

Sylvia stood off regarding her work—she smiled happily

Harriet T. Comstock

and replied:

"They are, dear lamb. The girls will all, eventually, put on; fill up"—Sylvia added a dab of clay to a doubtful curve—"but men, when they chip off from the approved design, look like nothing on earth but daubs!"

"Yes," Joan added, "that's what I mean." Then, with a thoughtful puckering of the brows, "the girls will be women, somehow, but what will become of these—this new sex, Syl?"

Sylvia was tense as she eyed her work. She answered vaguely:

"Some of them will crawl up, and *do* things and justify themselves, the others will—"

"Will what, Syl?"—for Sylvia was moving like a panther upon her prey—her prey being the small figure on the pedestal.

"Do this—or have it done for them!" and at this the offending clay was dashed to atoms.

"Failure!" breathed Sylvia—"mess!"

Then with characteristic quickness she began a new design. Joan watched her and caught a sudden insight. She realized what it was that marked Sylvia for success. Presently she asked musingly:

"Does any one ever marry these—these men, Syl?"

"Heavens, no! They only play with them; don't get confused on that line, lamb."

"Don't worry about me, Syl. I don't even want to play with them. Syl, I do not think I shall ever marry. I'm like Aunt Dorrie, but if I ever should marry it would be something to help one grip life, not something to—to—well, haul along!"

Sylvia turned and eyed Joan.

"My pet lamb," she remarked, "you are all right! Make sure that no one side-tracks you—give them half, but no more. And, Joan, run along now, child, and get dinner."

A few days later Sylvia broke into Joan's revery by the smouldering fire. It was a gray, cold day and Joan's spirits were at low tide.

She had not been successful in any venture as yet, and so vivid was her imagination, so sincere her determination to play fair, that starvation and early death seemed the most likely objects on her mental horizon. She had eliminated Doris and Nancy as life-preservers—they figured only as blessed memories in a past that was not yet regretted but which was fast fading into a black present.

"Joan, my darling, suppose you come to the rescue. My model has gone back on me—let me see you dance! My model had sand bags on her feet yesterday, anyhow, and my beautiful figure looks as if it had the beginnings of paralysis."

Joan sprang up. Instantly she was aglow and trembling with delight.

"Here, take this balloon," ordered Sylvia, "it is still gassy enough to float—it's a bubble, you know."

Through the room Joan floated after the elusive ball. Sylvia watched her with a light breaking over her own face.

"Great, great!" she cried from her corner, "go it, Joan, you're the real thing!"

Joan was not listening. What her eyes saw were the figures in the fountain of the sunken room. She was one of them again— the story was coming true! It was no longer a golden balloon she was touching, fondling, reaching for, tossing—it was

Harriet T. Comstock

sparkling water, and birds seemed singing in the big north studio.

At last it was over. On Sylvia's canvas the figure appeared to have undergone a marvellous change by a few rapid and bewitched strokes. The sand-bag impression had been removed— the figure was alive!

"Syl, dear, you are wonderful!"

Joan came and stood close. "What have you done to it?"

"Put you in it. Or," here Sylvia tossed her palette aside and caught Joan by the shoulders, "you've put yourself in me. I've a line on your opportunity, Joan, it came to me like a flash of inspiration. I hope you are game."

"I'm game, all right," Joan returned, quietly. She was thinking of her next visit to the bank.

"Dress your prettiest, my lamb. Look success from head to foot and then go to the address I'll give you. I have a friend, Elspeth Gordon, who is opening a tea room. She may not think you necessary to her scheme of things, she's Scotch and terribly thrifty, with a dash of nearness, but you tell her that *I* say you'll be the making of her."

Joan laughed and darted away to array herself in her best.

"What am I supposed to do there?" she asked. Her brightness and gaiety had returned.

"Oh! any one of your accomplishments. Of course it was merely a matter of making things jibe. Elspeth only telephoned about the tea room this morning."

"You mean I am to wait on tables or cook?" asked Joan, somewhat daunted.

"Lord, child, no! Here, wait. On second thought, I'll go with you. I might have known you couldn't put it over. Watch me!"

Sylvia was worth watching as she pulled her tam o' shanter over her head, her face all aglow.

"I've undervalued your 'samples,' as you call them, my lamb," she chatted on. "Of course you must take lessons and be a legitimate something some day—a singer, I fancy, but in the meantime we must utilize what we have."

On the way through the frosty streets Sylvia grew more mystifying.

"It's putting the *punch* in these days that counts, Joan. You are to be—the punch. Eats are all right in their way, but folks do not live by bread alone; they flourish—or tea rooms do—on punch."

Joan, running along beside Sylvia, accepted the rambling talk without question. Her acquaintance with tea rooms was limited, but she had caught Sylvia's mood.

"Just imagine," Sylvia was a bit breathless; "a cold, dreary afternoon outside—a warm, bright tea room with enchanting tables drawn close to an open fire, and someone—you, my lamb—singing a ballad, when there is a lull—in the offings! Why, Elspeth is as good as *made* if she has the wit to grab you—and Elspeth is no fool."

Joan began to see the opening ahead.

"Oh!" she drawled—the word lasted a half block and ended in a mocking laugh.

"Could I dance in costume?" she asked, tossing her head, "or tell fortunes as I used to at school? Do you remember, Syl, how I went to the kitchen door, once, and took the maids all in, and then Miss Tibbetts came down to see what was going on, and I read her palm—and—" but here Joan stopped short physically. "What's the matter, Syl?" she said.

"Why, of course!" Sylvia was regarding Joan impartially. "They might object to having you break in on their silly tea-talk, the police might raid the place if you danced—but palm reading! Oh! my dear, you've struck it in the dark. Hurry!"

And hurry they did, arriving at the Bonny Brier Bush a few minutes later in rather a breathless but radiant state.

The proprietress, Elspeth Gordon, was a tall, slender woman, no longer young, but carrying herself with a dignity that amounted almost to majesty. She was gowned in crisp lavender linen with immaculate white collars and cuffs and was standing in the middle of her Big Experiment, as she termed it, when Joan and Sylvia burst in.

"All ready but the opening of the door—legitimately," she said, smiling on Sylvia and bowing cordially to Joan. "Doesn't it look inviting?" She gave a broad glance to the sweet, orderly room: the small tables, glass covered; the rose-chintz covers and draperies; the clear fire on the broad, old-fashioned hearth, and the blossoming rose bushes on the window sills.

"It certainly does," Sylvia replied with enthusiasm.

"I've put everything I own into this venture," Elspeth went on; "if I fail, I'm done for."

For all her years of discretion and her plain common sense, Elspeth Gordon's mouth and tone betrayed the artistic temperament. Upon that Sylvia was banking.

"I have a splendid cook—a Scotch woman. I'm going to specialize on scones, and oat cakes, and such things, but oh! it is the opening of the door and the awful days of waiting until the public finds out!"

"Exactly!" Sylvia nodded and Joan stared. "You'll have to lure the public, Elspeth, there's no doubt about that. Tea rooms are no novelty these days. You'll have to tease it with a bait, and the rest is easy.

"Now, my dear, here's your bait!" With this, Sylvia turned so sharply upon Joan that Elspeth started nervously and regarded her guest as she might have a tempting worm: something possibly necessary, but which she hesitated to touch.

"She can read—palms!"

"Oh! Syl—" Joan panted, but Sylvia scowled her to silence.

"She can read palms," she repeated, holding Elspeth by her firm tone; "a little more reading up, a bit of experience, and she'll work wonders. She doesn't know it, but she's psychic— of course this is going to be fun; not real. Just a lure. We'll have Joan in a long white robe—a girl I know can design it. We'll have a filmy veil over the lower part of her face— mystery, you know. Look at her eyes, Elspeth, aren't they great? Give that 'into-the-future' stare, Joan!"

Joan rose to the fun of it all. She grasped the possibilities, but Elspeth faltered.

"I don't want to be—ridiculous," she said, slowly. "I'm quite serious, and my food is going to be above question."

"Of course! And if you think Joan will make you ridiculous, you've got another guess coming, Elspeth. Now, when do you open?"

"I have planned to open day after to-morrow." Elspeth spoke hesitatingly, keeping her cool, businesslike glance on Joan.

"All right," Sylvia was tapping her fingers restlessly; "that's Thursday. I'll get a girl I know to work on the costume to-night; we'll buy books on palmistry on our way home. We'll give you just four days to lure your public with scones, and then if you don't call Joan up, she'll start a tea room herself across the way."

This made them all laugh, but there was an earnestness in their eyes.

And on Sunday night Elspeth spoke over the telephone.

"Could you come to-morrow at two, Miss Thornton?"

Joan, sitting close to the telephone, winked at Sylvia. They had all been sitting up nights working, reading, and praying for that question.

"I think so," was the reply in quite an unmoved and businesslike tone.

"And remember, Joan," Sylvia cautioned later, "this is but a means to fit you for a profession!"

"I'll remember," Joan twinkled, "in the meantime, I am going to enjoy myself."

CHAPTER XI

"LET US LIVE HAPPILY,
FREE FROM CARE AMONG THE BUSY"

There was one of Sylvia's friends who, from the first, caught and held Joan's imagination. That was Patricia Leigh.

Patricia rarely got further than the imagination—after that she was idealized or suspected according to the person dealing with her.

Joan idealized Patricia—"Pat," she was always called.

The girl was fair and delicately frail, but never ill. She wrote verse, when moved to do so, and did it excellently, and she never thought of it as poetry.

When she was not moved to verse—and she had a good market for it—she designed the most astonishing garments for her friends. She could, at any time, have secured a fine position in this line and was frequently turning away offers. When the designing palled upon Pat she fell back upon her personal charm and enjoyed herself!

Patricia had, outwardly, a blood-curdling philosophy which she frankly avowed she believed in, absolutely, though Sylvia warned Joan that it was "bunk!"

What really was the case was this: Patricia was an adept at

Harriet T. Comstock

playing with fire. Lightly she tossed the flame from hand to hand; gaily she laughed, but at the critical moment Patricia ran!

She revelled in portraying the fire danger, but she covered her retreats by masterful silence.

"My code is this," she would proclaim: "In passing, snatch! You can discard at leisure."

There was no doubt but that Patricia did more than her share of snatching. When she played, she played wildly, but she was a coward when pay time came.

But who was there to show Patricia in her true light? Her good qualities, and they were many, pleaded for her. She was too little and sweet to be held to brutal exactions, and she was such a gay, blithesome creature, at her maddest, that when she ran one felt more like commending her speed than hurling epithets of scorn at her.

"If she wasn't a thousand times better than she makes herself out to be," Sylvia confided to Joan, "I'd never let her into my studio; but Pat is golden at heart, and she ought to be spanked for acting as she does."

"Hasn't she any family?" asked Joan. "No one whom she may —hurt?"

"That's it, my lamb, she hasn't. Mother died when she was four years old; father, an actor, but devoted to her, and insisted upon trotting her around with him. She was confided to the care of cheap boarding-house women; she ran away from school once and travelled miles alone to get to her father, and when he died—Pat was eighteen then—she began her career, as she calls it. Snatch and skip!"

"Poor, dear, little Pat!" said Joan, and her eyes filled.

"There, now!" Sylvia exclaimed, "she's caught your imagination."

That was true, and by the magic Joan began to see life as Patricia said *she* saw it: a place of detached opportunities and no obligations.

"I believe," Patricia would say, looking her divinest, "that in developing ourselves we most serve others. We relieve others of our responsibilities; we express ourselves and have no gnawing ambitions to sour us. Self-sacrifice is folly—it makes others mean and selfish, others who may not hold a candle to us for usefulness. Now"—and here Patricia, smoking her cigarette, would look impishly at Sylvia, quite forgetting Joan—"take, for instance, Teddy Burke!"

"Pat!" Sylvia was in arms, "I will not hear of your actions with Mr. Burke. They're disgraceful. You should be ashamed of them."

"On the other hand," Patricia always looked like a young saint, rather a wild one, to be sure, when she spoke of Burke, "I'm proud of my defiance of stupid limitations and fogyish ideals. Here is a man, a corker, Joan, with a wife who, acting upon tribal instinct, never dreams that she may be set aside. She travels the world over, foot loose, but with her little paw dug deep in her husband's purse. Here are two ducks of kiddies living with governesses and nurses over on a Jersey estate and pining for the higher female touch. Here am I with a batch of verses going quite innocently into Mr. Burke's office—he's an editor, you know—and he buys my stuff and howls for more. I grow white and thin providing more, and in weak moments show my beautiful inner soul to him. He, being a gentleman and an understanding one, asks me out to Jersey, and those children just cram into the hungry corners of my life. They play with me; they—they"—here a subtle touch of truth struck through Patricia's ironic tones—"they *teach* me to play. Haven't I a right to snatch—what was snatched from me?"

Harriet T. Comstock

Sylvia cried out: "Rot!" But Joan made no reply.

Often would Sylvia, deeply serious, urge Patricia to turn her talents to designing.

"Verses only take you near danger, Pat, dear," she would say; "and look at the things you can make for people! Why, dear, you bring out all their good points."

"You would have me stick my precious little soul full of needles and pins? Oh! you black-hearted creature. Not on your life, Syl! Designing is my job—it gets enough for me to fly on—but I mean to fly! And as I fly, I pause to sip and feed, but fly I must."

For Joan, Patricia felt a strange attraction. The child that was so persistent in Joan appealed to Patricia while it irritated her.

"She'll get hurt if she doesn't grow up!" the girl thought, and began at once rather crude forcing measures.

"A professional woman," she imparted to Joan, "is a different breed from the household pet—you must learn to scrimmage for yourself and take what helps your profession. You cannot stop and nurse the *you* of you. One's Art is the thing. Now love helps—love the whole world, Joan, it keeps you young. Play with it, but don't make the mistake of letting it take you in. The thing that threatens Sylvia is her—Plain John!"

Joan and Patricia laughed now. Sylvia's love affair was tenderly old-fashioned. Her man was on the Pacific Coast, making ready for her; she was going to keep right on with her work— her John had planned her studio before he had the house!

"'Love and fly!' is my motto," Patricia rambled on; "fly while the flying is good. Get your wings clipped, and where are you? Sylvia will have children and they will mess up her studio and her career—and look at her promise!" It was Patricia that had forced Sylvia's engagement into the open.

In some vague way Patricia felt that she was educating Joan, not weakening her foundations; but gradually Joan succumbed to the philosophy of snatch-and-fly, and the Brier Bush gave ample opportunity for her to practise it.

From the first she was a success. In her loose, flowing robe of white—Patricia had wrought that with inspiration—she was a witching figure. The filmy veil over the lower part of her face did but emphasize the beauty and size of her golden eyes. The lovely bronze hair was coiled gracefully around the little head, and after a week or so the gravity with which she read palms gave the play a real touch of interest.

People dropped in, sipped tea, and paid well to play with the pretty disguised young creature who was "guessing so cleverly." They departed and sent, or brought, others. The Brier Bush became popular and successful; Elspeth Gordon secured for it a most respectable standing.

"Why, Miss Gordon is the granddaughter of a bishop!" it was whispered, "and take my word for it that little priestess there with her is either a professional, finding the game lucrative, or a society girl out on a lark behind a screen."

Most people believed the latter conjecture was true and then the Brier Bush became fashionable.

Joan reaped what seemed to her a harvest, for Elspeth was as just as she was canny.

"After a year," Joan promised Sylvia, "I will begin to study music seriously. Why, I have decided to specialize, Syl— English and Scotch ballads"; and then off she rippled on her "Dog-star"—the song was a favourite in the studio; so was the Bubble Dance.

*   *   *   *   *

And about this time Joan's letters to Ridge House made the

Harriet T. Comstock

hearts there lighter.

"A job!" Nancy repeated, reading the announcement of Joan's success.

"I thought only workingmen had jobs. And in a restaurant, too! Aunt Dorrie, I don't think you ought to let Joan do such things."

"Joan is earning her living," Doris said, calmly, though her heart beat quicker. "These fad things are often successes, financially, and I can trust Joan perfectly."

Christmas was a disappointment.

"I cannot leave this year, Aunt Dorrie," Joan wrote; "this is our busy time. Next year I will be free and studying music."

Doctor Martin was to have been back from the West, but was detained, so Nancy and Doris again helped Father Noble with his hill people, and Mary came over to Ridge House and decorated the rooms to surprise them when they came back from the longest trip of all.

Doris had discarded, largely, her couch. With her inward anxiety about Joan to be controlled, she was more at ease in action and it was good for her.

Nancy's devotion was taken for granted, as was her happiness. What more could Nancy want?

It was Mary who resented this.

"'Tain't fair!" she muttered as she went about her self-imposed tasks, "'tain't fair." And scowlingly Mary still bided her time.

Early in the new year David Martin returned from the West bearing about him the impression of battle crowned by victory.

He was jovial and boyishly delighted with Doris's improvement.

"I haven't long to stay," he confided to her, "but I had to see how things were going here before I settled down in New York. Nancy looks fine! She's happy, too." This to Nancy, who was fondling the pups by the fire.

"Well, then, how about Joan?"

Doris, her hands folded in her lap, did not reply.

At this Martin took to striding up and down the long, sunny room. The thought of Nancy rested him; Joan always irritated him.

"When is she coming back?" he asked suddenly.

"She's got—" Nancy hesitated at the word; "she's got a job. She won't come home until she's lost that."

Martin turned on Doris a perplexed and awakened face.

"What's this?" His voice had the ring of the primitive male.

"Well, you know Joan is with Sylvia Reed, David. You remember that girl who painted so beautifully at Dondale? Sylvia has a studio, now, and is regularly launched. She's doing extremely good work. Nan, show Doctor Martin that magazine cover that Sylvia did."

David took the magazine indifferently from the obedient Nancy and dropped it at once.

"Who's looking after them?" he inquired, leaping, in his deadly rigid way, over much debatable ground.

"They're looking after themselves, David." Doris metaphorically got into position for a severe bout.

"You don't mean," Martin came close and glowered over Doris, "you cannot possibly mean that Joan is going in for that loose, smudgy stunt that some girls are doing down in that part of town known as Every Man's Land?"

Nancy ran to the window and bent over her loom. She was always frightened when David Martin looked as if he were going to perform an operation.

"Certainly not," Doris replied; "the girls have a place uptown in a perfectly respectable quarter. Joan shares the expense. This is very real and fine, David. And you are not going to blame me for permitting Joan to do this—it was the only thing to be done. The girl has a right to her life and the use of her talents; this was an opening that we could not ignore. Sylvia Reed is older than Joan."

"How much?" David's voice was like steel.

"Four years." In spite of her anxiety, Doris had to laugh.

"Is this a joke, Doris?" Martin was confused.

"Why, no, David, it isn't."

"Were you mad, Doris? Why, don't you know that many girls are simply crooked while they call themselves emancipated? I am amazed at you. How did you dare! Have you thought what an injustice you've done the girl? Keeping her in cotton wool, feeding her on specialized food, and then letting her loose among—among garbage pails?"

Nancy fled from the room. The operation was on!

Doris got up and linked her arm in David's—they paced the floor slowly, getting control of themselves as they went. Presently Doris spoke:

"You see, dear, I have always held certain beliefs—I have

always been willing to test them—and pay."

"But dare you let Joan pay?" Martin was calm now.

"Not for mine, but for her own—yes. Aren't you going to let this boy of yours try his own flight, David?"

"That's different."

"It won't be always, David, dear—someone must make the break—our dear young things in the big cities are breasting the waves, David. I glory in them, and even while I tremble, I urge them on. You should have seen Joan when she came to me with her great desire burning and throbbing. Why, it would have been murder to kill in her what I saw in her eyes then. It was her *Right* demanding to be free."

"It's the maddest thing I ever heard of!" Martin broke in. "I wonder if you have counted the cost, Doris?"

"Yes, David, through many long days and wakeful nights. I have shuddered and felt that it was different for Joan; that *she* should have been kept in—in bondage. It would have been bondage for her. But, David, the only thing I dared *not* do was to keep freedom from the child."

"And suppose"—Martin's face grew grimmer—"suppose she goes under?"

"She will come to me—she promised. I am prepared to go as far as I can with my girls on their way; not mine. That was part of my bargain with God when I took them."

"You're a very strange and risky woman, Doris."

"And you are going to be fair, David, dear. Now tell me about your boy."

Instantly Martin was taken off guard. He smiled broadly and

Harriet T. Comstock

patted Doris's hand, which lay upon his arm.

"Bud's coming out on top!" he said—Clive Cameron was always Bud to Martin. "I've kept closemouthed about the boy," he went on, forgetting Joan; "he's meant a lot to me, but I've always recognized the possibility of failure with him and felt the least I could do, if things came to the worst, was to leave an exit for him to slip out of, unnoticed. He's always kept us guessing—my sister and I. He never knew his father. From a silent, observing child he ran into a stormy, vivid youth that often threatened disaster if not positive annihilation—but he's of the breed that dashes to the edge, grinds his teeth, plants his feet, and looks over!—then, breathing hard, draws back. After a while I got to banking on that balking trick of his. Once I got used to the fact that the boy meant to know life—not abuse it—I knew a few easy years while he plodded or, at times, plunged, through college.

"He couldn't settle, though, on a job, and that upset us at last. He ran the gamut of professions in his mind—but none of them appealed to him. When he was nineteen he suddenly took an interest in his father—we'd never told him much about him. Cameron wasn't a bad chap—he simply hadn't character enough to *be* bad—he was a floater! When Bud got that into his system, it sobered him more than if he'd been told his father was a scamp. A year later the boy came to me and said: 'Uncle David, if you don't think I'd queer your profession—I'm going to make a try at it.'"

Martin's face beamed and then he went on:

"That was a big day for me, Doris, but even when the chap went into it, I kept quiet. I feared he might balk. But he hasn't! He's big stuff—that boy of mine. He confided everything to me this time. Certain phases of the work almost drove him off—dissecting and, well, the grimmer aspects! Often, he told me, he had to put up a stiff fight with himself before he could enter a dissecting room—but that does one of two things, Doris: makes a doctor human or a brute. It has humanized

Bud. He'll be through now, in a year or so, and I'm going to throw him neck and crop into my practice. I'll stand by for awhile, but I have great faith in my boy!"

Doris looked up at the grave, happy face above her own.

For a moment a sensation she had never experienced before touched her—it was like jealousy!

"How he would have adored a son of his own," she thought, "and what a father he would have been!"

She faltered before speaking, then she said quietly:

"If—if I have deprived you of much, David, at least I have not killed the soul of you."

"I'm learning as I go along, my dear," Martin replied.

"We're not all developed in the same way."

"And, David," Doris trembled as she spoke, "as you feel for your boy, so I feel for my Joan. You must trust me."

"That is different," Martin stiffened.

"It is the same."

Harriet T. Comstock

CHAPTER XII

"IN ALL DIRECTIONS GULFS
AND YAWNING ABYSSES"

That was what David Martin felt was encompassing Joan. He wanted to take a hand in her affairs, but before he left Ridge House Doris made him promise that unless she changed her mind, he would not even call upon Joan.

"If she knows that you have your eye on her, David, much of what I hope for will be threatened. You have quite a dreadful eye, dear man, and Joan is sensitive. She may look you up—I will write to her about you. If she doesn't, she does not want you to—well, Davey, meddle! And she has a perfect right to her freedom. She is self-supporting now!"

Doris could but show her pride in Joan's cleverness.

"Very well, Doris. I wash my hands of the matter, but I think it sheer madness!"

With that Martin returned to town and waited, hopefully, for a summons from Joan. It did not come!

He did go so far, one evening, as to walk on the block where the studio was, but he got no satisfaction from that except the proof of its respectability.

"I cannot look back just now!" Joan had thought when

considering Martin, "and Uncle David would tell me things about Aunt Dorrie and Nancy that would rumple all my calm, and I dare not risk it."

In this she was wise—for there were times when, the novelty and freedom of self-support worn off, the temptation to return to the waiting flesh-pots was very great. At such moments of weakness Patricia rallied her.

"Don't be one of the women who are ready to sell their birthrights for a meal ticket," Patricia urged, looking her daintiest and saintliest.

"But what *is* one's birthright?" Joan asked.

"The self-expression of—yourself," Patricia smiled serenely.

This always reinstated Joan in her old resolve.

"To come to town and cut capers at the Brier Bush," she confided to Sylvia, once Patricia was off the scene, "is poor proof of anything. Syl, I'm going to get to work seriously soon with my music."

"We'll get a piano," practical Sylvia suggested; "there is no need to grow rusty while you're making money."

And so they secured the piano, and the studio had another charm.

The Brier Bush, in the meantime, was waxing great in popularity and financial success. Elspeth Gordon from her position of assurance gave it a unique touch. No one could take liberties with her tea room. Presently delicious luncheons were added to the scheme, and, while Joan's part was regarded with amused complacency, the excellent food and service commanded respect.

At first women came largely to the pretty, attractive rooms;

Harriet T. Comstock

then, occasionally, men, rather timidly, presented themselves, but finding themselves taken for granted and the food above reproach, they appeared in numbers and enjoyed it.

And then one rather gloomy, early spring day Mrs. Tweksbury came upon the scene.

Joan knew her at once, although the old face was more wrinkled and delicate.

Of course Mrs. Tweksbury had not the slightest inkling concerning Joan's movements, and she looked upon the veiled young creature moving about the tea room with a cool, calm stare of amused disapproval.

"Quite a faddish thing you're making of your venture," she said to Elspeth Gordon, for of course with a bishop for a grandfather Miss Gordon was taken for granted. Elspeth smiled her most dignified smile and replied graciously:

"Just a bit of amusement, Mrs. Tweksbury. It helps digestion and, incidentally, helps business."

"But the—the young woman, Miss Gordon—is she a professional?"

"Have you tested her, Mrs. Tweksbury?"

"Oh! no, my dear Miss Gordon." Mrs. Tweksbury had beautiful old hands and she turned the palms up while she considered them.

"Suppose you judge for yourself, Mrs. Tweksbury." Elspeth was charmingly easy in her manner.

"Who is she?" bluntly asked the old lady.

"Ah!" And here Elspeth recoiled. "My palmist and my best recipes are sacred to me, Mrs. Tweksbury. But may I call my little seer to you?"

Mrs. Tweksbury consented, and when Joan looked at the pink, soft palm a spirit of mischief possessed her.

Skirting as near as she dared to the facts in her possession, she gently, but startlingly, took the owner of the hand at a disadvantage.

At first Mrs. Tweksbury was confirmed in her idea that the girl before her was a society girl—her general knowledge could be explained by that, but suddenly Joan became more daring— she vividly recalled much that she had heard Doris say in defence of the old woman whom Nancy and she feared and often ridiculed.

It took but a twist to change a private incident into a blurred but amazing suggestion.

Mrs. Tweksbury was frankly and angrily impressed.

When passing from the room Miss Gordon spoke to her:

"Do you believe in my Veiled Lady?" she asked.

"Certainly not, Miss Gordon, but I'm—afraid of her! You had better guard her somewhat—or she'll be taken seriously."

"We'll never see *her* again!" prophesied Joan, chuckling over her victory with the old lady; "I've evened up for Nan and me!" she thought, and then the incident passed from her mind.

But not so easily did the matter go from the confused thoughts of Mrs. Tweksbury.

"I dare say," she finally concluded, "that if one could tear the veil from the face of that impudent little minx one would discover the smartest of the objectionable Smart Set. The girl should be curbed—how dare she!"—here Emily Tweksbury flushed a rich mahogany red as she recalled some of the cleverly concealed details of, what seemed to her, the most private affairs.

"Outrageous!" she snorted, and vowed that she deserved all that she had received for supporting the new-fangled nonsense that was spreading like a new social evil in the heart of all she held sacred.

Patricia Leigh had not been so interested in years as she was in Joan's affairs at the Brier Bush. They smacked of high adventure and thrilled the girl.

To Sylvia they were rather grovelling means to a legitimate end. She scowled at Joan's vivid description of her experiences and warned her to trust not too fully to her veil.

"But it's a splendid lark!" Patricia burst in, defensively; "it's Art spelled in capitals. Joan, take my advice and get points about the swells and scare them stiff!"

"Pat, you should be ashamed!" Sylvia scowled darkly.

"Yes?" purred Patricia. Then: "I see the finish of Plain John's romance, my sinister Syl, if you don't limber up your spine. Genius, love, and unbending virtue never pull together."

And then—it was when March was dreariest and drippiest— Kenneth Raymond strode—that was the only word to describe his long-legged advance—into the Brier Bush for luncheon with Mrs. Tweksbury.

He had listened to variations of Mrs. Tweksbury's first visit to the tea room with varying degrees of impatience.

He hated tea rooms; he had little interest in young women, and particularly disapproved of the type bordering on license; but he had consented to go in order to lay the old lady's growing nervousness concerning the details of her first visit.

"My dear," Mrs. Tweksbury had said to Raymond, "the more I think of it the more I am puzzled."

"Exactly," Raymond replied; "the more you think of it the more puzzles you introduce. Undoubtedly the young woman is a girl playing outside her legitimate preserves. She's taking an unfair advantage. They always do. Presuming on sex and social position. Unless the girl is an outlaw, she'll confine her antics to the safe outer edge."

In this mood Raymond strode into the Brier Bush with Mrs. Tweksbury at his heels. They took a table near the fireplace and, rather arrogantly, Raymond looked about.

"No one was going to take him in!" was what his stern young eyes and dominant chin proclaimed.

He was of that type of man that gives the impression of being handsome without any of the damaging features so often included. He was handsome because he was strong, well set up, and completely unconscious of himself.

He was always willing to pay the right price for what he wanted, but he meant to get good value! He was lavish with what was his own, as Mrs. Tweksbury almost tearfully asserted, but about that he never spoke and always frowned down any reference to it.

He expected the usual thing at the Brier Bush, and was just enough to show some appreciation when he did not find it.

The rooms were unique and charming. Elspeth Gordon was impressive as she walked about among her guests. She might permit them to be amused; help, indeed, to give them a cheery hour in the busy day, but not for a moment would she admit what could be questionable in her scheme.

That being proved, Raymond critically attacked the bill of fare. Its promise was like the atmosphere of the place, honest and wholesome.

No man is proof against such dishes as were presently set before him. Raymond was so engrossed by their merit and so surprised by it that he forgot the main thing that had brought him to the Brier Bush until he felt Mrs. Tweksbury's foot firmly and insistently pressing his. He looked up.

Joan was passing their table and very slightly she inclined her head toward it.

Her eyes were what startled Raymond. If eyes in themselves have no expression, then the soul, looking through, has full play.

All Joan's youth and ignorance and unconscious wisdom shone forth. Mrs. Tweksbury amused her, but the man at the table disturbed her. She misinterpreted the calm glance he fixed upon her. It was a disapproving glance, to be sure, and Joan shrank from that, but she felt that he was cruelly misjudging her and was so sure of himself that he dared to do it—without even knowing!

This she resented with a flash of her wonderful eyes.

What Raymond really meant was—doubt. Not of her, but himself.

"Saucy witch!" whispered Mrs. Tweksbury; "Ken, test her, for my sake!" Again the foot under the table steered Raymond's thoughts.

He found himself smiling up at Joan and, rising, offered her the third chair at his table.

She sat down quite indifferently, but graciously, and spread out her pretty hands. Joan's hands were lovely—Raymond was susceptible to hands. To him they indicated fineness or the reverse. Art could do much for hands, but Nature could do more.

Quite as graciously and simply as Joan had done Raymond spread his own hands forth with the remark: "At your mercy, Sibyl."

Now Joan, through much study of books and with a certain intuition that stood her in good stead, had cleverly conquered her tricks. For what they were worth, she offered them charmingly, seriously, and with impressiveness.

Then, too, from much guessing, with astonishing results, she had grown to half believe in what she was doing. Patricia aided her in this. Patricia had a superstitious streak and took to fads as she took to her verse—on her flying trips.

"You are a business man," Joan began, fixing her splendid eyes on the frankly upturned hands—she was comparing them with the hands of the Third Sex, those studio-haunting men whose hands, like their linen and morals, were too often off-colour.

"An honest business man!" Joan thought that, but did not voice it.

"You will succeed—if—" This she spoke aloud and then looked up. She was ready now to punish her prey for that look of doubt in his eyes.

"If—what?" Raymond was conscious of the "feel" of the hand which held his—Joan's other hand was lying open beside his on the table.

"If—" and now Joan traced delicately a line in his palm—a faint, wavering line running hither and thither among the more strongly marked ones; "if you strengthen this line," she said. "You are too sure of—of your inherited traits. This line indicates individuality; it will rule in the end, but you are making personality your god now. That is unwise. As a well-trained servant it is wonderful, but as a master it will run you

Harriet T. Comstock

off your best course."

How Patricia would have gloried could she have heard her words mouthed by Joan!

Raymond stared. He felt Mrs. Tweksbury's foot on his and, mentally, clung to it as a familiar and safe landmark.

"Just what difference lies between individuality and personality?" he asked so seriously that Joan's mouth twitched under her life-saving veil. She brought Patricia's philosophy into more active action.

"The difference is the meaning of life. One comes into this consciousness with his individuality—or soul, or whatever one cares to call it—intact. It accepts or repudiates what the personality—that is intellect—learns through the five senses. If it is *truth*, then it becomes part of the individuality—if it is untruth, it is discarded. Individuality is never in doubt—it *knows*. It is not bound by foolish laws evolved from the five-sensed personality; it will, in the end, have its way. You will have to listen more to your individuality; be controlled less by your personality. The latter is too fully developed"—at this broad slash Raymond coloured in spite of himself—"the former has been pitifully ignored."

The pause that followed was made normal only by the pressure on Raymond's foot.

Presently he said, boldly:

"You have the same line in your own hand, Sibyl!"

Joan started and looked down. She had not considered a home thrust possible. Instinctively her long, slim fingers clutched the secret of her palm.

"I am not reading my own lines," she said, quietly; "I am learning from them, however!"

Then she rose with dignity and passed to another table where a broad, flat, commonplace hand lay ready.

"Well?" Mrs. Tweksbury pounced into the arena like a released gladiator. "What do you make of it, Ken?"

Raymond laughed. He saw that Mrs. Tweksbury was more impressed than she cared to acknowledge.

"I don't know what she told you, Aunt Emily," he said, taking up the check beside his plate, "but it was rather cleverly concealed rot, as far as I am concerned. Drivel; faddy drivel, but the girl's a lady, or whatever that word stands for. I half believe the child takes herself seriously—she has wonderful eyes. She should wear blinders—it isn't fair to leave them outside the veil. Comical little beggar!"

"But, Ken," Emily Tweksbury followed her companion from the room, "you are like that—you really are! You just take life by the throat and you are sure of yourself in a way that frightens me."

"Oh, come, Aunt Emily, that girl has caught you by her nonsense. See here, let us do a bit of sleuthing! I bet the sibyl often is at dinners where we go—and I'm not so sure but what I would know those hands of hers anywhere—they were not ordinary hands. Two can play at her little game."

This seemed to offer some inducement to Mrs. Tweksbury and she brightened.

"Her walk, too, Ken. Did you notice that?"

"Yes—I did, by Jove! Longer strides than most girls take and a swing from the hips like a graceful dance motion. Yes, that walk should be a dead give-away."

"And her eyes, Ken, she *has* eyes!"

Harriet T. Comstock

"Yes," rather musingly, "she has eyes!"

"Ken, we mustn't give further countenance to this silly, faddy place."

This with conviction.

"Why should we, Aunt Emily? I only went at your request, you know."

"Of course. The girl got on my nerves." Mrs. Tweksbury could smile now.

"Well, I'm going to get on hers!" Raymond set his jaw.

Two days later Kenneth Raymond went to the Brier Bush again for luncheon. This time Mrs. Tweksbury did not accompany him.

He took a table at the far end of the room near the windows— he wanted light. He ordered his luncheon, read his paper, and to all intents and purposes gave the impression of a business man who, having discovered a place of good food, repaired to it with confidence. Of course Elspeth Gordon did not remember him—why should she? But Joan did—and why should she? She was reading the palms of a hilarious group near the table at which Raymond sat reading the stock reports; she was in a gale of high spirits but, when she was aware of Raymond's glance, she paused and caught her breath.

"Anything bad in my hand?" asked the girl whose palm Joan was scanning.

"Oh, no! Something splendid. You are never to make mistakes, because your caution is stronger than your desire," Joan murmured.

"I think *that* is stupid," the girl returned; "no fun in that kind of thing."

Joan prolonged each reading at the safe, jolly table; she planned, when she was done, to ignore the man near her and go in the opposite direction, but while she planned she was aware that she would do no such thing. The bird and the snake know this force, so do the moon and the tides.

And at last Joan got up and turned toward Raymond. As she passed his table—he was busy with his soup then—her head was high and her eyes fixed upon Miss Gordon at the other end of the room. She was estimating her chances of reaching Elspeth with the limited self-control at her command. Then she heard words and paused without turning her head.

"I wish you would stop a moment. I have a question to ask you."

Joan had a sudden fear that if she did not stop the question would be shouted.

"Very well," she said, quietly, and sat down opposite Raymond.

She clasped her pretty hands before her and—waited.

It is not easy to laugh away the moments in life that we cannot account for—they often seem the only moments of tremendous import; they are the channels which, once entered, give access to wide experiences. Joan felt her breath coming hard; she was frightened. Raymond pushed his plate aside and, leaning forward a bit over his clasped hands, said casually:

"Just how much of this rot do you believe?"

"None of it."

"Why do you do it?"

"I am earning my bread and butter and—dessert."

"Especially—the dessert?"

"No. Especially bread and butter. It is only a bit of fun, you know—this reading of the palms. Miss Gordon thinks it—it aids digestion," Joan was speaking hardly above a whisper.

"She does, eh?" Raymond had an insane desire to snatch the shielding veil from the face across the table. He wondered what would happen if he did?

"I wish," he said instead, "I wish you'd cut it out, you know."

"What—my bread and butter?"

"No—this tomfoolery. I don't believe you have to earn your living. I'd lay a wager that you are doing it as a stunt to vary the monotony of a dull existence, but there are other and better ways of doing that, you know."

Raymond was deadly earnest and did not stop to consider the absurdity of his words and tones.

"What ways?" asked Joan, and Raymond detected the suggestion of a smile behind the vapoury veil.

"I don't think I need to tell you that," he said.

"Perhaps not—but after consideration I've chosen this way. I like it." Joan was getting control of herself, and in proportion to her gain Raymond lost.

"I suppose you think me an impudent ass," he ventured.

"I'm—thinking of something else," Joan answered.

"What, for instance?"

"That line—in your hand."

"I thought you said this was only fun; that you did not believe in it?" Raymond frowned as he saw his next course advancing toward him.

"There are exceptions," and Joan helped him arrange his dishes.

"Some day, if you are interested, come and I'll tell you more about that line in your hand." She rose with quiet grace and moved away.

"Oh! I say—" Raymond followed her with his eyes—"why not to-day?"

"There are others," Joan tossed back and was gone.

That night she went to Patricia Leigh's. Patricia had had a busy and prosperous day. She had written some verses that she felt were good—they had a tang that always gave Patricia the belief in their quality; she had sold two other small things. She was, therefore, at her flightiest, and greeted Joan with delight.

"I'm so glad Syl is not tagging on, Joan," she said. "Syl is the best they make, but she does somehow get under the skin and make people feel themselves 'seconds'."

Joan sank into a chair.

"Syl is writing reams to her John," she explained. "I doubt if she noticed my leaving. She probably thinks I'm still singing."

And then Joan told Patricia about the man who, for some unknown reason, had made himself permanent in her interest.

"I wish I knew about him," she murmured; "I cannot recall any one in the least like him in Mrs. Tweksbury's life. I don't want to ask Aunt Doris—besides, he may just be a chance acquaintance of Mrs. Tweksbury's. I hardly think that, though—for she looks volumes at him and he sort of appropriates her."

Harriet T. Comstock

Patricia was frankly interested—she was flying, and at such moments her bird's-eye view was a wide and sympathetic one.

Joan, too, in this mood was bewitching.

"All Joan needs," thought Patricia, "is to discover her sex appeal; get it on a leash and take it out walking. She's like a marionette now—hopping about, doing stunts, but not conscious of her performance."

"Lamb!" Patricia lighted a fresh cigarette, "a week from to-night you breeze in here and what I do not know about your young man, by that time, will not count for or against him."

"But, Pat, do be careful!" Joan was frightened by what she had set in motion.

"Careful, lamb? Why, if carefulness wasn't my keynote, I'd be—well! I wouldn't be here."

CHAPTER XIII

"JOYOUS WE LAUNCH OUT ON TRACKLESS SEAS CAROLLING FREE, SINGING OUR SONGS"

A week from that night Joan again eluded Sylvia. She did it by not going to the studio for dinner. She felt deceitful and mean, but there were heights—or were they depths?—that Sylvia could not reach, and intuitively Joan felt that Sylvia would disapprove of what she was now doing.

Patricia was not in when Joan reached her rooms—they were small, dim rooms and rather cluttered.

Sitting alone, waiting, Joan thought of Patricia more intimately than she often did. She recalled what Sylvia had told of her; remembered the warnings, and her eyes dimmed.

"Poor old Pat!" she mused, "she's like a pretty bird—just lighting on things, or"—and here Joan thought she had struck on something rather expressive—"or like a lovely, bright cloud casting a shadow. No matter what colour the cloud is, the shadow's dark. Dear old Pat! Well—I see the colour."

This was satisfying and brought up her feeling about Patricia, which had been depressed.

And just then Patricia tripped in, humming and rippling and stumbling over a rug as she felt her way in the gloom—Joan had not turned on the lights. Presently she stopped short and

Harriet T. Comstock

asked sharply:

"Who is here?"

Joan bubbled over and Patricia gave a relieved laugh.

"Lordy!" she gasped, "you gave me a bad minute. I thought—"

"What, Pat?" Joan touched the switch.

"I—I thought—it might be someone else. I haven't had a thing to eat since breakfast," Patricia announced, dropping on a couch and pulling the cushions into all the crevices surrounding her thin, weary little body.

"I'll get the nicest little meal for you in a jiffy!" Joan sprang to her feet. "Is there anything *to* fix?" she added, quickly.

"There's always something"—Patricia closed her eyes—"eggs and milk and—and canned horrors." Then, with a radiant smile:

"I've been on the trail of your man, Joan, and it was some trail."

"Pat, darling," Joan hung over the couch, "you take a couple of winks. I'm going out to get—a steak."

"A what?" Patricia regarded Joan gravely. "A brand-new steak for me? Joan, you must be mad!"

"Pat, lie down and dream a minute or two. A steak, fried potatoes, a vegetable, and dessert with coffee, cheese, crackers —and—and—" Joan was putting on her hat while she spoke and Patricia was sniffing adorably.

A half hour later Joan crept noiselessly back, her arms full of bundles. Patricia lay fast asleep on the couch.

Sleep does revealing things, and in spite of her hurry, Joan stopped and looked at the girl lying in the full glare of the electric light.

She was like a weary child. All the hard lines on the thin face were obliterated; the soft hair fell in cunning curls about the neck and ears; the long lashes rested delicately on the fair skin.

All the world stains were covered by the sweet presence of Patricia's youth, which had stolen forth in slumber time.

Then it was that Joan discovered that she was crying. Big tears were rolling down her cheeks, and in her heart was growing a new, vital emotion—a selfless, nameless, urging tide of protection for something weak and helpless.

When the meal was prepared Joan kissed Patricia awake.

The girl sat up and gazed dazedly at the small table drawn to the couch, at the candles burning on it, at the covered dishes from which crept the most bewildering smells.

"The god of the famishing—bless you!" whispered Patricia and fell to the joy of the meal with the abandon of the starved.

She ate and drank and smoked. She let Joan wait upon her and dispose of the debris. She even directed Joan to the closet where her kimono and slippers were; she let Joan undress her and put them on.

"How thin you are, Pat lovey!" Here Joan kissed a white shoulder.

"A mere bag of bones, Joan lamb, but they are easy to carry around."

"And such ducks of feet, Pat, I never saw such cunning feet. They do not look big enough to be of use."

"They'll carry me as far as I have to go, Joan, and take it from me, I'm not keen for a prolonged trip. It's too much trouble to keep yourself alive to want to spin it out."

"Oh, Pat! Hasn't my dinner done you any good?" Joan smoothed the soft, fluffy curls tenderly.

"Why, you old darling," Patricia broke forth, "you've given me a glimpse of what would make it worth while—the trip, I mean. That's the trouble. I get the glimpse, acquire the taste, and then I wake up to—sawdust. Oh! good God, Joan."

Joan rose and turned off the lights; she left the candles burning and sat down on a stool by Patricia.

After a while Patricia reached for her cigarettes and spoke as if several big things had not occurred. She gurgled as a mischievous child might who had stolen jam and escaped detection.

"Your man, Joan," she began puffing away, "is named Kenneth Raymond. In tracking him I resorted first to Hannah Leland, society editor of *Froth*. Hannah stores up items about the upper crust as a squirrel does nuts. Her articles always have background; she's let in everywhere because folks are afraid to shut her out. She can see more through keyholes than others do through barn doors, and her scent is—phenomenal!"

Joan hugged her knees and looked grave.

"I—I hate to snoop, Pat," she whispered.

"You don't have to—I got Hannah's snoops for you. They're innocent enough—really, they're the soundest of sound little nuts.

"Mrs. Tweksbury had a romance! Don't grin, Joan. She didn't always look like a squaw in front of a tobacco shop—they say she was rather a stunner. She married Tweksbury before she got the bit in her mouth—afterward she clutched it good and proper and trotted the course according to the rules.

"Then came Raymond—this man's father. He somehow got it over to Mrs. Tweksbury—the real thing, you know, and she reached and got it over to *him*, that it was up to them to— keep it clean. Gee! Joan, her past sounds like a tract with all the sobs left out and a lot of iron put in.

"Raymond, in a year or two, married a woman who lived only long enough to produce this man upon whose trail we're scouting. This Kenneth was a measly little offspring and his mother's people undertook to give him a chance to live. He picked up and he and his father became pals—Hannah rooted out a picture of them riding horseback. Then the father was thrown from his horse and killed right before the eyes of the boy, and that put him back years—he barely escaped. I don't believe he would have, from accounts, if Mrs. Tweksbury hadn't butted in at that point and made it a matter of honour to the boy to—to—carry on!

"Well, once he mounted *that* horse he rode it as he did all others—hard and grim. He never played in all his life. He's been making good. Society he loathes; women do not exist for him, outside of Mrs. Tweksbury. I bet he knows *her* past and is paying back for his dad—he's like that.

"Well, when I'd got everything Hannah had in her safe I had a burning desire to have a look at Mr. Kenneth Raymond myself. So this afternoon I went to his office—"

"Pat!" cried Joan. "Oh! Pat, how could you?"

"Easiest thing in the world, my lamb. You see, the chance of viewing a human being—with one fortune in his pocket and another coming to him when Mrs. Tweksbury lets go— actually on a job holding it down like grim death—was a sight to gladden the heart of a tramp like me. I sallied down to Wall Street and had some fun.

"I found his building without a moment's delay and I casually asked the elevator boy where Mr. Raymond's office was, and the little chap grew effusive—either Mr. Raymond is lavish with tips, or the human touch, for his goings and comings are meat to that kid.

"He told me I had better hustle, for at four-thirty every day Mr. Raymond beat it! The boy was an artist in word-painting. He described my man as a real toff, none of your little yappers. He's going to haul in the pile and playing honest-to-God—fair, too!"

Joan burst out laughing. Patricia mimicked the ribald manner of the boy deliciously.

Patricia nodded her thanks and went on:

"Well, I hung around his corridor for ten minutes, Joan; and at four-thirty exactly his door opened and I had timed myself so perfectly that he tumbled over me and nearly knocked me down.

"He has better manners than you might expect from such a deadly prompt person. He steadied me and looked positively concerned when he realized what a pretty, helpless little thing I am!" Patricia gave a wicked wink and lighted her fifth cigarette.

"I told him I was looking for — and I made up a preposterous name; and he puckered his lofty brow and said he couldn't recall any such name in the building, and then I told him I had about concluded that I had the wrong address, and he offered to look the name up for me, but I sighed and said that it was too late. My man always left his office at three-forty-five and that I would have to come again.

"We went down in the elevator together, the boy winking all the way down at me—and—that's all, Joan, except that you've got to go careful with Mr. Kenneth Raymond. You don't want to hurt that fairy godmother of his; she hasn't had many things of her own in life, and I do insist that while one is grabbing it's better to grab where there is a flock than pick a ewe-lamb. Besides, this Kenneth Raymond hasn't begun to understand himself—he's been too busy understanding life. Have a heart, Joan!"

Joan looked up sedately.

"Isn't it queer, Pat, but now that I know him he doesn't seem interesting in the least. He's priggish and conceited; he's a poser, too. It is too bad, Pat, for you to tire yourself out and get such a—a dry stick for your pains."

Patricia regarded Joan for a full minute and then she remarked:

"You had better go home and get to bed, child. And look here—I give you this advice free: a fire lighted by an idiot can do as much damage as any other kind of a fire."

"Thanks, Pat. I'll remember that when I—play around dry sticks. Good-night, you old, funny Pat, and thank you."

Joan bent and kissed the top of Patricia's head.

After that evening with Patricia Joan clung to Sylvia with unusual tenacity. She also went to see a well-known teacher of music and got his opinion of her voice.

"Your voice needs nearly everything to be done for it that can be done to a voice," the professor frankly told her, "but you *have* a voice, beyond doubt. You have feeling, too, almost too much of it; it is feeling uncontrolled, perhaps not understood.

"If you are willing to give years to it you will be a singer."

The man thought that he was killing hope in the girl before him, but to his surprise she raised her eyes seriously to him and said:

Harriet T. Comstock

"I am a working girl, but I am saving for the chance of doing what you suggest. I will begin next winter. I think I know that I shall never be great, but I believe I will sing some day."

The man bowed her out with deep respect.

When Joan told of her interview Sylvia was delighted, and Patricia, who had happened in for a cup of tea, looked relieved.

"Of course you'll sing, Joan," she said, enthusiastically, "and if you don't turn your talent to account you'll bring the wrath of God down upon you. That Brier Bush is well enough to start you—but you're pretty well through with it, I fancy."

Patricia was arraigning herself with Sylvia for reasons best known to herself. She had the air of a very discreet young woman.

Long did Joan lie awake that night on her narrow bed. She had raised the shade, and the stars were splendid in the blue-black sky.

She was happier, sadder, than she had ever been in her life before—more confused.

She wanted Doris and Nancy and the shelter and care; she wanted her own broad path and the thrill that her own sense of power gave her. She wanted to cling close to Sylvia; she was afraid of Patricia but felt the girl's influence in her deepest depths.

In short, Joan was waking to the meaning of life, and it had taken very little to awaken her, for her time had come.

Three days later Kenneth Raymond ate his luncheon at the Brier Bush and spoke no word to Joan. The following day he nodded to her, and the day after that he said, in a low voice as she passed:

"I want to have you read my palm again."

"Once is enough," Joan replied.

"I have forgotten what you said," Raymond broke in; "besides, I have another reason. You've set me on a line of thought— you've got to clear the track."

"Oh, very well." And Joan sat down and took the broad hand in hers.

"I've read a lot of stuff since I saw you first," Raymond began. "There is something in this palmistry."

"I just take the words and play with them," Joan replied. "I truly do not know whether there is anything in it—or not. It is only fun here."

"Look at me!"

This Joan refused to do.

"There is that line in my hand like yours"—Raymond was in dead earnest—"what—does it mean?"

"I told you what it means," Joan faltered.

"Do you want me to read your palm?" Raymond bent farther across the table.

"Yes, if you can!" Joan was on her mettle. She instantly spread her hands to the bent gaze and prayed that no one would take the tables near by. It was late; the rush was over and Elspeth Gordon, for the moment, had left the room.

"You're not what you appear," Raymond began.

"Who *is*?" Joan flung this out defiantly.

Harriet T. Comstock

"You're daring a good deal—to taste life. You're testing your line; making it prove itself—*I* haven't dared!"

Joan did not speak, and her small hands were as quiet as little dead hands in the strong ones which held them.

"Does it pay—the daring, the testing?" Raymond's eyes, dark and unfaltering, tried to pierce the veil.

"Yes—I think so."

"You make me want to try—do you dare me?"

"It does not interest me at all what you do." Joan was like ice now. "You evidently misunderstand our play here. Let go of my hands!"

"I haven't finished yet. You've got to hear me out."

"Let go of my hands!"

"All right—but will you stay here?"

"I'll stay until I want to go."

"Very well. I know I'm a good deal of a fool—but sometimes a slight thing turns the stream. I thought it was all rot—a play that you'd made up—this line business." Raymond spoke hurriedly. "Of course I'd heard of it, but I never gave it a thought. Just for sport, after that first day, I got bushels of books and I've been sitting up nights reading. There's something in it!"

Joan laughed. The man looked like an excited boy who had started a toy engine going.

"See here! They say your left hand is what you start with; your right hand what you have made of yourself—that line that you have and I have is in my right hand—is yours in both?"

Joan tried not to look—but ended in looking.

"No," she replied. "I reckon it only comes in the right hand with anybody."

"No, it doesn't; the lady I was with the other day hadn't it in either hand!"

"Isn't she lucky?" Joan laughed.

"No, she isn't!" Raymond spoke solemnly. "Only the people who have it—are."

"I'm going now." Joan got up; and so did Raymond.

"See here," he said, bluntly. "I've never had a bit of adventure in my life—I'm a stick. I don't know what you will think of me; I don't care much; but you've started something in me; it's nothing I'm ashamed of, either, and you needn't be afraid. But won't you talk to me some time—about—well, this stunt and some other things?"

"Certainly not!" Joan drew back and added: "and I am not in the least afraid."

CHAPTER XIV

"BUT AFTER IT COMES OUR LIVES ARE CHANGED"

And just when winter was turning to spring in the southern hills something happened to Nancy.

The winter at Ridge House had revealed many things. It had been lonely, and it had brought conviction about Joan's absence. The girl was not coming back to them, that must be an accepted fact. She would, undoubtedly, when she became adjusted, return on visits—but they must not expect her as a fixture, for she was succeeding! This realization had caused Doris many silent hours of thought, but never once had she known bitterness or a sense of injustice. Joan had as much right as any other human soul to her own development. Doris was glad that Joan had never known what Nancy knew about the need for coming to The Gap. The knowing would have held Joan back. With Nancy it was different. Nancy was not held from anything she wanted.

David Martin spent as much time as he could at Ridge House. He came to the hard conclusion, at length, that Doris, in her new environment, had reached her high-water mark. Detached from strain and care, living quietly, and largely in the open, she had responded almost at once—to her limit, and there she remained. How long this improved state would hold was the main thing to be considered; nothing more comforting could be looked for.

"Then, what next?" thought David, and his jaw grew grim.

And Nancy, with a winter far too quiet and uneventful even for her, had contrived to do some thinking for herself. Not for the world would the girl have accepted Joan's choice. The safe and sheltered life was wholly to her taste, but she wanted others to fall into line. Like many another, she was not content to hold her own views, she was unhappy unless she was approved and imitated. She wanted the spice and thrill of Joan in her life; Joan was part of it all—the rightful part. With this Nancy took to self-pity in order to establish her claim.

"Why should I be taken for granted and be obliged to give up all the fun and brightness while Joan does as she pleases?"

Doctor Martin, even Doris, expected Nancy to come when she was called and go to bed when the clock struck ten, while Joan could follow her own sweet will.

At this point Nancy re-read Joan's letters—all letters from Joan were common property. If ever there was innocent jugglery Joan's letters were. They were vivid and interesting; they carried one along on a stream as clear as crystal, but they arrived at nothing.

The studio was left to the imagination of the reader. Doris saw it as a safe and artistic home for earnest young girlhood; Nancy saw it as an open sesame to fun, rather wilder than school bats, but with the same delicious tang. Doctor Martin viewed the place as most dangerous, and those young people gathered there as perilous offsprings of a much-deplored departure from conservative youth.

"Fancy Joan helping in a restaurant!" groaned Nancy when Joan had particularized about her "job." "Joan, of all people!"

"It will be good practice," Doris remarked in reply. "When Joan marries, she will have had some experience."

"Marry?" David Martin broke in—he was on one of his flying visits. "If anything could unfit a girl for marriage, the thing Joan is doing is that."

"Very well," Doris said, quietly; "marriage isn't everything, David."

Doris was beginning to defend Joan, and it hurt her to be obliged to do so. She did not regret the relinquishing of the girl, but she had hoped, in her deepest love, that the experiment might either prove a failure or that it might carry Joan to a peak—not a dead level. It was beginning to seem that the sacrifice on her part meant simply separating Joan from her—not giving Joan to anything worth while.

There were moments, rather vague, elusive ones, to be sure, when Doris turned from Joan and contemplated Nancy.

"The child is perfectly content and happy," she thought; "but ought she to be so—at her age? Nancy should marry—she will, of course, some day.—" Then Doris wondered whom Nancy could marry.

"Next winter I may be able to go to New York," she comforted herself; "or I'll send Nancy to Emily Tweksbury; the child shall have her life chance."

But with Doris the inevitable was happening: she was sliding gracefully down the inclined plane which others had arranged for her. She was making no effort, because none was required of her. The peace and comfort of the old house in restoring comparative health had placed its mark upon her. It was wonderful to lie on the porch and watch the beauty of The Gap change from season to season. The sound of the river was always in her ears, and there was a dramatic appeal in kneeling at the altar in the tiny chapel to pray for them whom she loved so tenderly.

And Nancy was so sweet and companionable! Poor little

Nancy! She was playing Doris's minor accompaniment as once she had played Joan's more vivid one. But the youth in her was surging and rebelling—not against love and service, but inequality.

"Joan should bear half, anyway!"

Just what it was that Joan should share Nancy could not have told, she simply knew that she wanted Joan—wanted what Joan represented.

With the passing of winter and the early coming of spring Nancy and Doris reacted to the charm of The Gap. The shut-in days were past. Almost before one could hope for it, the dogwood and laurel and azalea burst into bloom and the windows and doors were flung back in welcome to spring.

The grounds around Ridge House needed much attention, and Doris contrived to make Uncle Jed believe that he was the gardener. Nancy, surrounded by dogs, no longer pups, wandered on the Little Road and timidly took to the trails. It was quite exciting to go a little farther each day into the mysterious gloom that was pierced by the golden sunlight. Gradually the girl felt the joy of the mountaineer; vaguely the emotion took shape.

What lay just around the curve ahead? What could one see from that mysterious top? Was there a "top"? If one went on, overcoming obstacles, what might there not be? These ambitions were quite outside the by-paths once or twice taken with Father Noble.

Doris was glad to see the light and colour in Nancy's pretty face; she was grateful, but inclined to be anxious when Nancy wandered far.

"Is it quite safe?" she questioned Jed.

"Dat chile is as safe as she is with Gawd," Jed reverently

Harriet T. Comstock

replied—and perhaps she was, for God's ways are often like the trails of the high places—hidden until one treads them.

Nancy, by May, had lost all fear of the solitude, and with seeking eyes she wandered farther and higher day by day. She brought back wonderful flowers and ferns to Ridge House; she grew eloquent about the "lost cabins" as she called them, secreted from any gaze but that which, like hers, sought them out. She took gifts to the old people and timid children.

"It's such fun, Aunt Dorrie," she explained, "to win the baby things. At first they are so frightened. They run and hide— they never cry or scream, and bye and bye they come to meet me; they bring me little treasures, the darlings! One gave me a tiny chicken just hatched."

But beyond the last cabin that Nancy conquered was a hard, rocky trail that led, apparently, to the sharp crest called by Uncle Jed Thunder Peak.

"Does any one live on Thunder Peak?" asked Nancy of Jed.

The old man wrinkled his brow. He had not thought of Becky Adams for years; at best the woman had been but a landmark, and landmarks had a habit of disappearing.

"No, there ain't no reason for folks to live on Thunder Peak. It's a right sorry place for living."

Jed found comfort, now he came to think of it, in knowing that Becky had departed.

"Whar?" he asked himself, when Nancy, followed by two of her dogs, went away; "whar dat old Aunt Becky disappeared to?" Then he pulled himself together and went to deliver the message Nancy had confided to him.

"Tell Aunt Doris I'm going for a long walk and not to worry if I'm not home for luncheon."

Jed repeated this message over and over aloud. He fumbled it, corrected it, and then finally gripped it long enough to speak the words automatically to Doris and Doctor Martin.

"That old fellow," Martin said, looking keenly after him, "is going to go all to pieces some day like the one-hoss shay. He looks about a hundred. I wonder how old he is?"

Doris smiled.

"I imagine," she said, "that he is not as old as he looks. He told me that his grandfather was married in short trousers and never lived to get in long ones. They begin life so early and just shuffle through it."

"You find that thing in the South more than anywhere else." Martin was nodding understandingly. "It's like a dream—more like looking at life than living it. I suppose when they die they wake up and stretch and have a laugh at what they feared and passed through in their sleep."

"We will all do that, more or less, Davey."

"More or less—yes!" Then suddenly:

"Doris, I think you can plan on three months in New York next winter. My boy is coming on from the West. I'm going to take my shingle down and hang his up."

"Really, David? Take yours *down*?" Doris looked dubious.

"Yes. I'll stay around with him, but I'm going to put my shack on the map right under Blowing Rock. I've brought the plans to show you."

Martin took them from his pocket and sat down beside Doris, and while they became absorbed, Nancy was climbing her way up Thunder Trail.

Before she realized that she had come so far, she was in the open, the sunlight almost blinding her. She started back and screwed her eyes to make sure that she saw aright. Not only was she out of the woods but she was on the edge of a trim garden plot; there was a dilapidated cabin just beyond it, and an ancient creature standing in the doorway.

At first Nancy could not make out whether it was a man or a woman. She had never seen any one so old, and the eyes in the shrunken face were like burning holes—caverns with fire in them!

Nancy was too stunned to move or speak. Her knowledge of the hills forbade the usual fear, but a supernatural terror seized her and she waited for the old woman—she decided it was a woman—to make the first advance. This the woman presently did. She turned, and with trembling haste took up a rusty spade by the door; she shuffled toward a corner of the opening and began to dig at a mound that was covered with loose earth. Weakly, fearfully, the claw-like hands worked while Nancy stood fascinated and bewildered. Finally the old woman came toward her and there was a tragic pathos on the wrinkled face that tended to quiet the girl's rising fear. The cracked voice was pleading:

"How did yo' get out?" The words came anxiously and with difficulty, like the words of a deaf mute that had been taught to speak mechanically.

Nancy smiled weakly and looked silently at the speaker.

"Been tryin' to find hit?" the strained voice went on. "Yo' better lie still, Zalie—yo' larned enough, chile!"

And then, because the rigid girl did not speak, the old woman drew nearer.

Nancy, believing herself in the presence of a harmlessly insane creature, rallied her courage and sought to soothe, not excite, the woman.

"I'm lost," she faltered. "I am sorry to have disturbed you; I am going now."

She half turned, keeping her eyes on her companion.

"Come—set a bit," pleaded the crackling voice; "come warm yo'self before I tuck yo' up again. How cold yo' little hands are! Po' little Zalie, jes' naturally—tryin' to find hit."

There are limits of fear beyond which, for self-preservation, a kind of calm strength lies that suggests ways of safety. Nancy did not run or cry out, she did not withdraw her icy hands from the brown, claw-like fingers that held them; she even smiled a faint, ghastly smile that reassured the old woman. Her eyes softened; her voice almost crooned.

"Us-all is safe—no one comes nigh—it's comfortin' ter tech yo', Zalie, an' hit is well placed. Through all the years I done wanted to tell yo'; I've said it by yo' grave many's the time, chile—" Becky waited a moment. She looked cautiously about the sun-lighted place and peered into the gloom of the forest-edge, then she looked again at Nancy, while her thin hand pointed to the mound under the tree across the bit of open. Nancy shuddered.

"What is—that?" she gasped.

"Yo' little grave, Zalie—yo' little bed. I 'tend it loving and proper; I take a look-in onct so often—but yo' is cute, like yo' was when yo' stole out in the moonshine to larn. You done got out yo' grave when I wasn't watching. Come, now, let me put yo' back!"

The old woman turned, and in that instant Nancy fled like a spirit. Noiselessly, swiftly she disappeared. She heard the crackling voice behind her:

Harriet T. Comstock

"Jes' creep back by yourself, eh, Zalie?" And then came the sound of metal patting down the loose earth on the mound by the solemn trees.

Nancy could never tell what occurred on her descent from Thunder Peak. When she reached The Gap, she found that her dogs had strayed from her: they had either dropped behind or run before. She was not exhausted. She felt strong and calm. The adventure was assuming a thrilling proportion now she was at a safe distance. But she had no intention of telling Doris. Oddly enough, she felt the need of keeping it secret. She shivered as she recalled the touch of the claw-fingers and the sound of the dry, hard voice. She had a growing sense of uncleanness, now that the shock was wearing off. It almost seemed that a poison had been left upon her that was eating its way into depths of her being. She was afraid that someone would know; she trembled when old Jed remarked:

"Dis yere little ole pup don slink back like he seed a hant and he had burrs stickin' to his sorry-lookin' hide—seems he was off the scent. No 'count!"

Jed gave the hound a push with his foot, but he had set Nancy's nerves tingling.

"I lost the scent myself," she said, striving for calmness. And then relying upon the old man's simplicity she asked, pointing across The Gap:

"What did you say was the name of that peak, Uncle Jed?" She wanted to make very sure!

The old man raised his bleary eyes and looked troubled. He was conscious of something stirring in the dark of his mind.

"Thunder," he replied, then he laughed, and the gold in his few remaining teeth glistened. Cackling and shuffling along beside Nancy, he muttered—his mind again on old Becky:

"Her—as was—or her as is! Maybe she ain't a *was*—'pears like she can't be an *is*." Then he grew calmer and faced Nancy. "Stay away from Thunder, chile. 'Tain't safe, Thunder ain't— only fer hants."

"I'll stay away, Uncle Jed," Nancy promised fervently, and tried to laugh off the foolish, superstitious fear that the old man's words had aroused.

Jed went off muttering—he was strangely disturbed.

As the first impression of her adventure wore off Nancy was surprised to find that a new fear and restlessness oppressed her. It was like the after effects of a blow that had stunned her.

She slept badly—a terrific electric storm swept through The Gap and there seemed, to the frightened girl in the west chamber, noises never heard before. Creaking steps in the hall; calls in the wind and sharp summons as the branches of the trees lashed the windows and the blazing lightning shattered the darkness with blinding flashes.

Nancy crept downstairs the next morning pale and shaken. She rallied, however, when she saw Doris.

Doris was greatly affected by electric storms and was lying on a couch by the hearth. Doctor Martin was sitting beside her, and the little breakfast tray, laid for the three, was drawn close.

They ate the meal quietly, and then Martin took up a book to read aloud while Nancy went to her loom.

She huddled over it—there was no other word to describe her crouching, lax attitude; her face was drawn and haggard. Doris watched her; she was not listening to Martin. Suddenly she felt a kind of shock as she realized that she was thinking of Nancy as an old woman!

As the spring holds all the promise of autumn in its delicate

Harriet T. Comstock

shading, so youth often depicts the time on ahead when line and colour will take on the aspect of age.

It was startling. Doris almost cried aloud. Nancy old! Nancy lean and shrivelled with her pretty back bent to—the burden of life!

Then Doris laughed nervously, and Martin started. The book he was reading from was no laughing matter.

"Forgive me, David—I was not listening; I was—planning. You know how agile a mind can be after—a bad headache?" This was not convincing to Martin and he scowled.

"What were you planning?" he asked, and Nancy at her wheel turned her head.

"Nancy's winter in town. She must have loads of pretty things, and I will open the old house—perhaps we can lure Joan also, and have the time of our lives. How would you like that Nan, girl?"

The tone was pleading, almost imploring. Doris had a sense of having wronged the girl, somehow.

"Oh, Aunt Dorrie, I should love it!" Nancy came across the room, all suggestion of age gone. "That is—if it will not harm you, dear."

"I think it would do you both good," Martin spoke earnestly; "I begin to realize what you once said, Doris. One has to have the country in his blood to be of the country. You must have change and"—turning to Nancy—"give this child a chance to—to show off."

He reached out and pinched Nancy's pale cheek.

"Run out," he commanded, suddenly; "run out into the sunshine and forget the storm. You're exactly like your aunt—

conquer it, conquer it, child, while conquering is part of the programme."

Nancy managed a smile, leaned and kissed Doris, waved a salute to Martin, and fled from the room.

"David, somehow I've hurt that girl." Doris spoke wearily.

"How?" Martin questioned.

Doris looked up and shook her head.

"How have I, Davey? I cannot tell."

"She's not hurt—but she's in line to be sacrificed if we don't look out. I'm the guilty one—I thought only of you."

And then the two planned for the winter.

Nancy took her dogs and went for a walk—a safe and near walk. The colour crept into her pale face, but her eyes had a furtive look and every noise in the bushes set her trembling. She had a conscious feeling of wanting to get away—far, far away. The Gap frightened her; she remembered old stories about it. Suddenly she looked up at The Rock and her breath almost stopped.

Fascinated, she stared; her eyes seemed to be following an invisible finger—The Ship was on The Rock!

Try as she might, Nancy could eat but little lunch. The small table was on the porch. Doris had recovered from her headache and was particularly gay—the planning for Nancy had done more for her than it had for Nancy herself.

"You had better go to your room and lie down," Martin suggested, eyeing the girl.

"Yes, I will, Uncle David."

But once in the dim quiet of the west wing chamber fresh memories assailed her.

This was the room, she recalled, into which Mary had seen—how absurd it was!—the dolls turned to babies. Such foolish, childish memories to cling and grip! How much better to be like Joan and laugh away the idle tales! Joan had always laughed—she was laughing now somewhere, looking her gayest and forgetting troubling things.

Then Nancy cried, not bitterly or enviously, but because she was tired of playing Joan's accompaniment!

Presently she got up and bathed.

"I'm going to Mary's!" she suddenly thought, and then felt as if she had been getting ready to go all day. She felt deceitful, sly, in spite of her constant reiteration that it had just occurred to her.

She left the house unseen; she hid behind a bush when she saw the hounds raise their heads from the sunny porch—she wanted to go alone to the cabin across the river.

It was three o'clock when she reached it, and she had hurried along the short trail, too. Mary was not in sight, but the living-room door was open and Nancy stood looking in with a baffling sense of unreality; the place looked different; almost as if she had never seen it before. She mentally took note of the furniture as though checking the pieces off.

The big bed, gay with patchwork quilts—Nancy knew all the patterns: Sunrise on the Peaks; Drunkard's Path; the Rainbow—Mary was making up for all that her forebears had neglected to do. Early and late she spun and wrought—she piled her bed high with the results of her labours; she covered the floor with marvellous rugs; she filled her chest of drawers with linen—Nancy glanced at the chest and fancied that she smelt the lavender that was spread on the folded treasures.

How the candlesticks shone; how sweet and clean it was, how safe!

Nancy stepped inside and sat down. The logs were laid ready for the lighting on the cracked but dustless hearth.

And then, quite unconsciously, the girl began to croon an old song, swaying back and forth, her arms folded and her eyes peaceful and waiting.

Mary, returning from her garden planting, stood by the door, unnoticed, and grimly took in the scene.

What it was that disturbed and angered her she could not have told, but she could not see Nancy sitting so—and—and—looking as she looked!

Mary strode across the room, causing Nancy to start nervously.

"What ails yo'?" Mary asked, "you look powerful sorry."

"I'm—I'm frightened, Mary."

Oddly enough, it was easy to speak frankly to the stern, plain woman across the hearth. And it was easy for Mary, after her first glance, to be ready with anything that could comfort the girl near her.

"What frightened yo'—the storm? I thought 'bout you."

"Yes—the storm, but—Mary, who lives on Thunder Peak?"

Some people are unnerved by surprise; Mary was always steadied.

"There ain't any one," she said, quietly, and leaned over to light the fire; the afternoon was growing chilly.

"Who used to live there, Mary? There is a cabin there."

Harriet T. Comstock

Mary did not flinch, but she was feeling her way, always a little ahead of Nancy.

"There was an old woman lived there—long ago; she died."

"Are you sure, Mary?"

"I'm right certain. She plumb broke down when she was ninety, and that was years back."

"Mary, there's a grave there!"

"Yes; when folks die they just naturally have a grave." A cold, icy light flickered in Mary's eyes; she reached and took up another log and carefully placed it.

"Mary, I went to Thunder Peak, I was following the trail. I came suddenly into the open and I saw an old woman. She touched me"—here Nancy shuddered. "She—she seemed to—to think she knew me. She called me a queer name. I cannot remember it. I was terribly frightened. Are you *quite*, quite sure the old woman died, Mary?"

"She died, she surely died. Old women ain't such precious sights among the hills. Like as not it was someone from Huckleberry Bald, t'other side of Thunder, as has taken over the deserted cabin and just wants to frighten folks, like you, off. They are mighty cute, those old women on Bald. They want their own place, and—and they sometimes shoot at any one that comes nigh."

The voice and words were cool and even. Nancy drew a long breath.

"Oh, Mary," she said, "you just take all the fear away. I kept feeling that old hand on my arm as if it were dragging me; the feeling is gone now. Jed said"—here Nancy wavered—"he said the place was haunted."

"Jed was a born fool and yo' can't do much with that kind. They grows more fool-like at the end."

Nancy laughed.

"I'm just a silly myself," she said rising and stretching her pretty arms over her head as if awakening from sleep. Then:

"Mary, I'm going to New York next winter. Going to have—a wonderful time."

And now Mary looked up and her eyes brightened.

"At last," she muttered; "you're to have your chance!"

"My—chance, Mary?"

"Your chance—same as Miss Joan."

And a moment later Mary was watching Nancy as she went singing down the river road.

"Gawd!" she muttered, and her yellowish skin paled. "Gawd! What has she come back for?—what?" and Mary's eyes lifted to Thunder Peak. Later she made ready for a long walk—she knew the trail to Thunder Peak would be hard after the storm.

CHAPTER XV

"EVERY HEART VIBRATES TO THAT IRON STRING"

And Mary's was vibrating to the iron as she plodded up the trail.

There had been much damage done by the storm. Trees were lying across the muddy path; there were washed-out spots, making it necessary to go out of one's way. But Mary did not notice the obstacles further than to make a wide detour. She was thinking, thinking—patching her bits of knowledge together with surmises provided by her vivid imagination.

Beginning with the day when old Becky, looking for Sister Angela, had stolen into the kitchen at Ridge House and demanded "her," Mary patiently fitted her scraps into a pattern as she patched her wonderful quilts.

"Yes; no!" Then a stolid nodding of the head.

The sunset, bye and bye, and then the early shadows, crept up the trail behind the lonely woman plodding along; they seemed to swallow her, and only her quick breathing marked her going.

"I can pay—at last!" She paused and spoke the words aloud.

"Pay back!"

Through the years since her return to The Gap she had saved and saved to return to Doris Fletcher the money advanced to buy the cabin.

Mary had never accepted it as a gift; the cabin could never be really hers until, by the labour of her hands, she had redeemed it.

What matter that her people called her "close" and mean? She knew what she was about, but in her slow, silent way she had learned, while she laboured apart, to feel an undying gratitude to the woman who had made everything possible for her.

And now she was taking her place beside them who had been her friends. No longer were they "foreigners." Surely Mary had come to realize that quality was not confined to places; it was in the heart and soul, and if anything threatened it, why, then—Here Mary drew herself up and raised her face to the stars.

She had tears in her eyes, but her mouth drew in a hard line. She felt a burning curiosity rising in her consciousness. What did it all mean? What had it meant back in Ridge House long ago?

But as the burning rose higher and fiercer Mary battled with it.

It was their secret! They must keep it—even from her! So would she pay though they might never know; *must* never know! She would prove herself worthy of the trust they had placed in her; she would even the score and hold danger, whatever the danger was, back. That should be her part to play!

When Mary reached the clearing on Thunder Peak she stood where Nancy had stood the day before and took in the scene.

Two or three times, after her return to The Gap, she had gone to The Peak and searched among the dirt and rubbish for any trace of old Becky. She had come to believe, at last, that the woman was dead—she had never been seen after the death of Sister Angela.

It was years now since Mary had given a thought to the deserted garden and cabin—the clearing was at the trail's end and no one ever took it, for it led nowhere.

But now, to Mary's astonished eyes, the garden appeared almost as well planted as her own, and from the chimney of the tumble-down cabin a lazy curl of smoke rose. Under the dark pine clump the outlines of a narrow mound could be plainly seen, and beside it lay a spade and a spray of withered azaleas.

Mary's throat was dry and painful. People to whom tears are possible never know the agony, but Mary was used to it.

Presently she walked across the open that lay between the edge of the forest and the cabin and stood by the threshold.

The door hung by one hinge, and through the gap Mary saw old Becky! She had hoped against hope that what she had told Nancy might be true, but she was prepared for the worst.

It seemed incredible that this poor, wretched skeleton by the hearth could be Becky—but Mary knew that it was. Back from her wandering the pitiful creature had come—home!

She had come as Mary herself had come—because the call of the hills never dies, but grows with absence.

"Aunt Becky!"

The crone by the hearth paused in her stirring of corn-meal in a pan, but did not turn.

"Aunt Becky!" And then the old woman staggered to her feet and faced Mary.

Not yet was the fire dead in the deep sockets—from out the caverns the last sparks of life were making the eyes terrible.

"Yo'—Mary Allan!" Contempt, more than fear, rang in the tones. "What yo' spyin' on me for, Mary Allan?"

Mary went inside. She was relieved by the fact that Becky knew her—she had feared that she would find no response. She did not intend to question or argue; she meant to control the situation from the start.

"Hit's in the grave 'long o' Zalie!" Becky was on her defence. "Zalie"—here the befogged brain went under a cloud—"Zalie she come a-looking—but hit's in the grave! I tell yo'-all, hit's in the grave!"

The trembling creature wavered in the firelight. She was filled with fear—but of what, who could tell?

Mary's face underwent a marvellous change—it grew tender, wistful.

"Set, Aunt Becky," she said, compassionately, and gently pushed the woman into a deep rocker covered over with a dirty quilt; "set and don't be frightened. I ain't come to hurt yo'—I've come to help."

Becky seemed to shrink.

"Hit's in—" she began, but Mary silenced her.

"No hit ain't in the grave! Zalie she knows it—an' I know it!"

"Where is hit—then?" A cunning crept into Becky's cavernous eyes. "Where is hit?"

"Aunt Becky, no one must know! You want it—that way." Inspiration guided Mary, or was it, perhaps, that iron strain, the strong human strain of her kind that led her true? "Zalie,

Harriet T. Comstock

she done come back; not to look for hit, but to keep you from hit!"

The stroke told. Becky shrank farther in the chair.

"Gawd!" she moaned—"it's that lonely! An' the longin' hurts powerful sharp."

Mary's face twitched. Did she not know?

"But hit!"—she whispered—"don't you love hit strong enough, Aunt Becky, to let hit alone, where hit's happy, not knowing?"

There was something majestic about Mary as she kept her eyes upon the old woman while she pleaded with her.

The past came creeping up on the two women by the ashy hearth—it gave Becky strength; it blinded Mary. In the old woman's memory a picture flashed—the picture that once had hung on the wall of Ridge House!

She folded her bony arms over her bosom and panted:

"Yes—I love hit—well enough!" The last hold was loosening. Then:

"It's powerful lonesome—and the cold and hunger bite cruel hard—"

"Aunt Becky, listen to me!" The woman turned her eyes to the speaker, but her thoughts were far, far away.

"I'll come to you, Gawd hearing me; I'll ward off the cold and hunger. I'll come day after day—if you'll leave hit—where it can't ever know."

Suddenly Becky's face grew sharp and cunning; all that was tender and human in her faded—self-preservation rose supreme.

"I'll leave hit, Mary Allen," she cackled, "but if yo' tell that hit ain't in the grave 'long o' Zalie all the devils o' hell will watch out for yo' soul!"

Mary was not listening. She rose and mechanically moved about the disordered room. Like a sleep walker she set the rickety furniture in place; she began to gather scraps of food together—hunting, hunting in corners and cupboards. She made some black coffee—rank and evil-smelling it was—and finally she set the strange meal before the old woman.

Becky eyed the repast as one might who fancied that she dreamed. Cautiously she touched the food with her lean fingers, then she clutched it and ate ravenously, desperately fearing that it might disappear.

Mary looked on in divine pity, swaying to and fro, never speaking nor going near.

She was thinking; thinking on ahead. She would make the cabin clean and whole; she would wash and clothe the poor creature now eating like a hungry wolf; she would feed her. Becky should become—hers!

Then Mary's mouth relaxed. She was appropriating, adjusting. Something of her very own at last! Something that would wait for her, watch for her, depend upon her. Something to work for and live for; something upon whom she might pour forth the hidden riches that had all but perished in her soul.

It was midnight when Mary groped her way from the cabin. Becky was asleep on the miserable bed in the corner; she was breathing softly and evenly like a baby.

Outside, the moonlight lay full upon the open spaces and on the little grave under the pine clump. Mary stood, before entering the woods, and raised her head.

Harriet T. Comstock

"I'm paying—I'm paying back what—I owe," she murmured, and all the wretched company of her early childhood seemed to hold out imploring hands to her. Her father, her mother, the line of miserable brothers and sisters who never had their chance!

Sister Angela came, too, her cross gleaming, her eyes kind and just. Doris Fletcher and her blessed giving; giving of the marvellous chance at last! And lastly, Nancy, with her beautiful face, Nancy who must not be cheated, Nancy who—trusted her! Nancy who *might* be—but no! Mary ran on. She would not know! She must not!

And so it was that the last of the Allans redeemed the debt and silently found peace for her proud heart.

She was released! She had proven herself, though no one must ever know. It was the not knowing that would mark her highest success.

On the morrow Mary went to Ridge House quite her usual reserved self.

Nancy met her with the brightest of smiles.

"Doctor Martin has gone away, Mary," she explained, "and now I will be terribly busy, but next winter—oh! next winter, Mary, Joan will be with us in the dear old house. A letter came to-day—she is going to take lessons from a very great teacher. Do you remember how Joan could sing, Mary? I shall play for her again and be so happy. It's wonderful how happy one can be, Mary, when one isn't afraid and just goes singing ahead. I cannot sing like Joan, but I can scare away fears!"

Mary regarded the girl with a hungry craving in her eyes over which the lids were drawn to a slit. There was a fierce intentness in the gaze: the look of the runner who has almost reached the goal but hears his pursuers close.

CHAPTER XVI

"AND THEY PLANTED THEIR FEET
ON THE 'SUN ROAD'"

If the spring has a direct and concentrated effect upon a young man's fancy, it must have equal effect upon a young woman's, else the man's would perish and come to look upon the spring as the lean part of the year. Joan had meant all she said when, in the strength and virtue of her youth, she had drawn herself away from Kenneth Raymond and proudly remarked:

"Certainly not! And I am not afraid."

Both statements were sincere and should have brought her peace and satisfaction. They did neither.

Raymond had, apparently, taken her at her word, and sought other places in which to appease his hunger, and Joan turned to Patricia, for Sylvia was called out of town.

That dream of a frieze that had long smouldered in Sylvia's soul had broken bounds and a rich man, erecting a summer home on the Massachusetts coast, having seen some of Sylvia's work, had invited her down to "talk over" the frieze idea.

"And he'll let me do it!" Sylvia had confided breathlessly to Joan as she packed her suitcase. "I can always tell when a thing is going to come true. Now if I had shown him sketches he might not have taken me—but when I can *talk* my pictures all along the walls of his big, sunny room it will be another matter.

"Blue background"—Sylvia was forgetting Joan as she rambled on, punching and jamming her clothing into the case—"and a bit of a story running through the frieze—a kind of sea-nymph search for the Holy Grail—stretching from the door back *to* the door. Can't you see it, Joan?"

Joan could not. She was seeing something else. Something daily becoming visualized. A seeking, yearning desire issuing from her soul and trying to find—what?

"You'll have Pat here?" suddenly asked Sylvia. "I'd rather have someone besides Pat, but the others are either away or worse than Pat. You're good for Pat if she isn't for you. You sort of stiffen her up—she told me so. Pat needs whalebone. When her purse gets flat her morals dwindle; mine always get scared stiff. I'll write twice a week, Joan, my lamb, Sunday and Wednesday. I'll be back before long."

And off Sylvia went with her heavy bag and her light heart, and Joan called Patricia up on the telephone.

"All right," Patricia responded, "but if I get homesick for these rooms, I must be free to come."

"Of course," Joan agreed.

Patricia was in a dangerous mood and Joan was vividly alive to impressions.

Patricia was writing verses as a bird carols—just letting them pour out. She was selling them, too, and running out to New Jersey to talk over with Mr. Burke the publication of a book.

"I cannot see," Patricia had said to Sylvia, "why one should feel it necessary to stick to hot, smelly offices when a library, looking out over acres of country, is at one's disposal."

"Is Mrs. Burke there?"

Sylvia had a terrible way of stepping on toes when she was making her point.

"Certainly!" Patricia flung back—it happened that the lady was there for a brief time—"though," Patricia went on, "she doesn't sit on the arm of my chair while styles of paper are considered. You're low-minded, Syl."

Patricia looked so high-minded just then that everyone laughed at Sylvia's expense.

And Joan, because she was young as the year was, kept remembering the eyes, and feeling the touch of Kenneth Raymond. There were no words to explain her mood, but she remembered the sound of his voice—and she wanted to see him again!

She believed her emotions were grounded upon the fact that she knew a good deal about Raymond—more than he suspected. He was of Aunt Doris's safe and clean world. He was only dipping into a pool outside of his own legitimate preserves to touch, as he thought, a lily that should not be there!

Raymond had suggested this to Joan. He fancied, from his conservative limitations, that the Brier Bush was rather a dubious pool!

"If he only knew!" Joan thought, and was glad that he did not. How humdrum it all would have been had he known! As it was, the wonderful feeling she had was laid upon a very safe foundation—not even Aunt Doris or Sylvia could object—and she would tell them all about it some day, and it would be part of the free, happy life and a proof that no harm can come where one understands the situation and has high motives.

But Raymond did not come to the Brier Bush, and so Joan had to conclude that he had not that unnamable emotion

Harriet T. Comstock

which was taking her appetite away, and he was forgetting, perhaps, all about that line that ran in the palms of both of them!

As a matter of fact, Raymond was trying very diligently to do just that thing. He worked hard and paid extra attention to Mrs. Tweksbury.

"My boy!" Emily Tweksbury urged, "come up to Maine with me for the summer, you look peaked."

Raymond laughed.

"How about business?" he said.

"Of course," Mrs. Tweksbury replied, "no one appreciates more than I do, Ken, your moral fibre. It's a big thing for you to create a business if for no other reason than to give employment to less fortunate young men; but you have other responsibilities. Your position, your fortune, they make demands. I'm not one to underestimate the leisure class; I know the old joke about tramps being the only leisure class in America; it's a silly joke, but it ought to make us think. After a bit, if we don't look out, the leisure class, here, will be all women. They'll dominate art and poetry and society—and I must say I like a good *team*. I never cared for too much of any one thing. Ken?"

"Yes, Aunt Emily."

"I want you to marry and have—a place."

"A place, Aunt Emily?" Raymond looked puzzled.

"Yes. Make a stand for American aristocracy—though of course you must call it by another name. You're a clean, splendid chap—I know all about you. I've watched apart and prayed over you in my closet. You see your father and I made a ghastly mess of our lives, but we kept to the code—for your sake. We left your path clear, thank God!"

"Yes, Aunt Emily—I've thanked God for that, too, in what stands for *my* closet."

"What stands for your closet, Ken? I've always wanted to know what takes the place of women's sanctuaries in the lives of men."

Raymond plunged his hands into his pockets—he and Mrs. Tweksbury had just finished breakfast, and the dining room of the old-fashioned house opened, as it should, to the east.

"Oh! I don't know that I can tell you, Aunt Emily," Raymond fidgeted. "Fellows are beginning to think a bit more about the clean places in women's lives. I reckon that we haven't so much an idea about sanctuaries of ours as that we are cultivating an honest-to-God determination to keep from making wrecks of women's shrines. I know this sounds blithering, but, you see, a decent chap wants to ask some girl to give him a better thing than forgiveness when the time comes. He wants to cut out the excuse business. He doesn't want women like you to be ashamed of him—when they come where they have to call things by their right names."

"Ken, I don't believe you're in good form. You'd much better come up to Maine!"

Emily Tweksbury looked as if she wanted to cry; her expression was so comical that Raymond laughed aloud.

"I'll come in August," he said at last. "I'll take the whole month and frivol with you."

Mrs. Tweksbury was, however, not through with what she had to say. She looked at the big, handsome fellow across the room and he seemed suddenly to become very young and helpless, very much needing guidance, and yet she knew how he would resent any such interference in his life.

"What's on your mind, Aunt Emily?"

Harriet T. Comstock

Raymond had turned the tables—he smiled down upon the old lady with the masterful tenderness of youth.

"Let's have it, dear."

Mrs. Tweksbury resorted to subterfuge.

"Well, having you off my hands," she said, smiling as if she really meant what she said, "I am thinking of Doris Fletcher!"

"Do I know her?" Raymond tried to think.

"No. She left New York just about the time you came to me. She's a wonderful woman, always was. Has a passion for helping others live their lives—she's never had time to live her own."

"Bad business." Raymond shook his head.

"Oh! I don't know, boy. The older I grow the more inclined I am to believe that it is only by helping others live that one lives himself."

This was trite and did not get anywhere, so Mrs. Tweksbury plunged a trifle.

"Doris Fletcher is going to bring her niece out next winter; wants me to help launch her."

Raymond made no response to this. He was not apt to be suspicious, but he waited.

"She has twin nieces. Her younger sister died at their birth— she made a sad marriage, poor girl, and the father of her children seems to have been blotted off the map. The Fletchers were always silent and proud. I greatly fear one of the twins takes after her obliterated parent, for Doris rarely mentions her—it is always Nancy who is on exhibition; the other girl is doing that abominable thing—securing her economic freedom, whatever that may mean. Doris has tried to make me understand, but how girls as rich as those girls are going to be can want to go out and support themselves I do not understand—it's thieving. Nothing less. Taking bread from women who haven't money."

Mrs. Tweksbury sniffed scornfully and Raymond laughed. He wasn't interested.

Mrs. Tweksbury saw she was losing ground and made a third attempt.

"But this Nancy seems another matter. I remember her, off and on. I was often away when the Fletchers were home, and the girls were at school a good many years, but this Nancy is the sort of child that one doesn't forget. She's lovely—very fair—and exquisite. Her poor mother was always charming, and I imagine Doris Fletcher means to see that Nancy gets into no such snarl as poor Meredith's—Meredith was Doris's sister. Ken—!"

"Yes'm!" Raymond was looking at his watch.

"I wish you'd lend a hand next winter with this Nancy Thornton."

Raymond gave a guffaw and came around to Mrs. Tweksbury.

"You're about as opaque," he said, "as crystal. Of course I'll lend a hand, Aunt Emily—*lend* one, but don't count upon anything more. I—I do not want to marry—at least not for many years. My father and mother did not leave a keen desire in me for marriage."

"Oh! Ken, can't you forget?"

"I haven't yet, Aunt Emily, but I'm not a conceited ass; your Miss Nancy would probably think me a dub; girls don't fly at my head, but I'm safe as a watchdog and errand boy—so I'll fit in, Aunt Emily."

He bent and kissed her.

A week later the old house was draped and covered with ghostly linen and every homelike touch eliminated according to the sacred rites of the old regime; and man, that most domestic of all animals, was left to the contemplation of a smothered ideal—the ideal of home.

Mrs. Tweksbury, with two servants, started by motor for Maine.

"I may not be progressive in some ways," she proudly declared, "but a motor car keeps one from much that is best avoided— crowds, noise, and confusion. And I always insist that I am progressive where progress is worth while."

But, alone in the still house, Raymond felt as if a linen cover also enshrouded him—he lost his appetite and took to lying at night with his hands clasped under his head—thinking! Thinking, he called it—but he was only drifting. He was abdicating thought. He got so that he could see himself as if detached from himself—

"And a dub of a chap, too, I look to myself," he reflected, ambiguously. "I wonder just what stuff is in me, anyway? I've been trained to the limit, and I have a decent idea about most things, but I wonder if I could pull it off, if I were up against it like some other fellows who have rowed their own boats? Having had Dad and Aunt Emily in my blood, has given me a twist, and the money has tied the knot. I don't know really what's in me—in the rough—and there *is* a rough in every fellow—maybe it's sand and maybe it's plain dirt."

This was all as wild and vague as anything Patricia or Joan could evolve. It came of the season and the everlasting youth of life.

"I'm going to talk over the rot with that little white thing down at the Brier Bush," Raymond declared one night to that self of his that stood off on inspection; "what's the harm? She's got the occult bug, and I'm keen about it just now. No one will be the worse for me having the talk—she's all right and that veil of hers leaves us a lot freer to speak out than face to face would." And then Raymond switched on the lights and read certain books that held him rigid until he heard the milkman in the street below.

In those nights Raymond learned to know that sounds have shades, as objects have. Below, following, encompassing there were vague, haunting echoes. Even the rattling of milk cans had them; the steps of the watchman; the wind of early morning that stirs the darkness!

And then in the end Raymond did quite another thing from what he had planned. He left the office one day at four-thirty and walked uptown. He paced the block on which the Brier Bush was situated until he began to feel conscious—then he walked around the block, always hurrying until he came in sight of the tea room. He felt that all the summer inhabitants of the city were drinking tea there that afternoon, and he began to curse them for their folly.

It was five-forty-five when Joan came down the steps.

Raymond knew her at once by her walk. He had always noted that swing of hers under her white robe. He did not believe another girl in the world moved in just that way—it was like the laugh that belonged with it. Indifferent, pleading, sweet, and brave—a bit daring, too. Joan was all in white now. A trim linen suit; white stockings and shoes; a white silk hat with a wide bow of white—Patricia kept her touch on Joan's wardrobe.

Raymond waited until the girl before him had pulled on her long gloves and reached the corner of Fifth Avenue, then he walked rapidly and overtook her. He feared that he was leaping; he felt crude and rough; but he had never been simpler and more sincere in his life. The elemental was overpowering him, that was all.

"Good afternoon!" he blurted into Joan's astonished ears; "where are you going?"

Joan turned and confronted him, not in alarm, but utter rout. Naturally there was but one course for a girl to take at such a juncture—but Joan did not take it. Her elementals were alert, too, and she, too, had reached the stage when sounds know shades, and above any cautious appeal was the fear of sending this man adrift again.

"I wonder"—Raymond spoke hurriedly; he wanted to drive that startled look out of the golden eyes—"I wonder if you're the sort that knows truth when she sees it—even if it has to cover itself with the rags of things that aren't truth?"

At this Joan laughed.

"I am afraid the heat has affected you," was what she said, gently.

"Well, anyway, you're not afraid of me!" Raymond saw that her eyes had grown steady.

"Oh! no. I'm not afraid of you. I'm not often afraid of anything."

"I thought that. You wouldn't be doing that stunt at the Brier Bush if you were the scary kind." Raymond accompanied his step to Joan's as naturally as if she had permitted him to do so.

"I don't see why you speak as you do of my business," Joan interjected. "It's how one interprets what one does that matters. I make a very good income of what you term my stunt. Perhaps you're accustomed to girls who use such means —wrongfully."

Joan felt quite proud of her small sting, but Raymond broke in joyously:

"You're mighty clever; you've struck on just what I mean. See here, you don't know me and I don't know you—" At this Joan turned her face away. "And I'm jolly glad we don't. It makes it all easier. I know very little about girls—I dance with them and things like that when I have to, but as a class I never cottoned to them much, nor they to me. I know the ugly names tacked to things that might be innocent and happy enough. Now your business—it could be a cover for something rather different—?"

"But it isn't!" Joan broke in, hotly.

"I'm sure of that, but hear me out. There's something about you that—that's got me. I can't forget you. I only want to know what you care to give—the part that escapes the disguise that you wear! I want to talk to you. I bet we have a lot to say to each other. Don't you see it would be like fencing behind a shield? But how can we make this out unless we utilize chances that might, if people were not decent and honest, be wrong? I know I'm getting all snarled up—but I'm trying to make you understand."

"You're not doing it very well." Joan was sweetly composed.

"Now suppose you and I were introduced—you with your veil off—that would be all right, wouldn't it?"

Raymond was collecting his scattered wits.

"Presumably. Yes—it would," Joan returned.

"And then we could have all the talks we wanted to, couldn't we?"

"Within proper limitations," Joan nodded, comically prim under the circumstances.

Harriet T. Comstock

"But for reasons best known to you," Raymond went on, slowly, "you want to keep the shield up? All right. But then if we want the talks—"

"I don't want them!" Joan's voice shook. Poor, lonely little thing, she wanted exactly that!

"I bet that's not true!" ventured Raymond. Then suddenly:

"Why do you laugh as you do?"

"What's the matter with my laugh?"

"I don't know. It's old and it's awfully kiddish—it's rather upsetting. I keep remembering it as I always shall your face now that I have seen it!"

Truth can take care of itself if it has half a chance. It was beginning to grip Joan through the mists that shrouded her— mists that life has evolved for the protection of those who might never be able to distinguish between the wolf in sheep's skin and sheep in wolf hide.

Joan knew the ancient code of propriety, but she knew, also, the ring of truth and she was young and lonely. She knew she ought not to be playing with wild animals, but she was also sure in the deepest and most sincere parts of her brain that the man beside her, strange as it might seem, was really a very nice and well-behaved domestic animal and was making rather a comical exhibition of himself in the skin of the beast of prey.

"You haven't told me where you are going," Raymond said, presently.

"Home!" The one word had the dreary, empty sound that it could not help having when Joan considered the studio with Sylvia gone and Patricia an uncertain element.

"Are you?" Raymond asked, lamely. One had to say something

or turn back. Joan felt like crying. Then suddenly Raymond said:

"I wish you'd come and have dinner with me, and I'm not going to excuse myself or explain anything. I know I'm using all the worn-out tricks of fellows that are anything but decent; but I know that you know—though how you do I'm blest if *I* know—but I know that you understand. The thing's too big for me. I've just got to risk it! I'm lonely and I bet you are; we've got to eat—why not eat together?"

The words sounded like explosives, and Joan mentally dodged, but at the end felt that she knew all there was to know and she caught her breath and said very slowly:

"I'm going to be quite as honest as you are. I will have dinner with you because I'm as lonely as can be; my people, like yours, are out of town, and I *do* understand though I cannot say just how I do. One thing I want you to promise: You will never, under any circumstances, try to find out more about me than I freely give. Now or—ever! When I disappear, I want really to be safe from intrusion."

Raymond promised, and so they set out on the Sun Road.

Harriet T. Comstock

CHAPTER XVII

"IT IS EASY IN THE WORLD TO LIVE AFTER THE WORLD'S OPINION; IT IS EASY IN SOLITUDE TO LIVE AFTER OUR OWN"

The trouble with the Sun Road is this: one is apt to be blinded by the glare.

In their solitude, the solitude of a big city, Raymond and Joan trod the shining way with high courage.

This was romance in an age when romance was supposed to be dead! Here they were, they two, nameless—for they decided upon remaining so—living according to their own codes; feeling more and more secure, as time passed, that they were safe and were wisely enjoying what so easily might have been lost had they been limited in faith.

"It's the line in our hands!" Raymond declared. "It means something, all right. Think what we must have missed had we been unjust to each other and ourselves."

Joan nodded.

The sun and the dust of the pleasant highway had blinded her completely by the end of a week.

Patricia was a missing quantity most of the time. Patricia had taken to the Sun Road, also, but with her eyes wide open. If

Patricia ever turned aside it would be because she knew the danger, not because she did not.

She never explained her absences nor her private affairs to Joan. When she did appear at Sylvia's studio she was quiet and nervous.

"It's the heat," she explained. "I'm not hot, but I cannot get enough air to breathe."

Meanwhile, Sylvia was basking in success and cool breezes on the Massachusetts coast. Her letters had the tang of the sea.

And Raymond was always on hand, now, at the dinner hour. He was like a boy, and took great pride in his knowledge of just the right places to eat. Quiet, but not too quiet; good food, and, occasionally, good music, and if the night was not too hot, a dance with Joan which set his very soul to keeping time.

"Gee!" he said, after their first dance; "I wonder what you are, anyway? Do you do everything—to perfection?"

Joan twinkled.

"Every man must decide that for himself," she replied with a charming turn of her head.

"Every—man?" Raymond's face fell.

"Certainly. You don't think you are the only man, do you?"

"Well, the only one left in town."

Raymond gave a little laugh and changed the subject. He had no intention of getting behind his companion's screen. With a wider conception of his path, he more diligently kept to the middle.

Harriet T. Comstock

After the first fortnight he even went so far as to arrange for business engagements, now and then, in order to keep his brain clear.

Joan always met these empty spaces in her days with a keen sense of loss which she hid completely from Raymond.

His business demands were offset by her skilfully timed escapes from the Brier Bush. She would either be too early or too late for Raymond, and so while he paid homage to his code, Joan appeared to make the code unnecessary.

And the weather became hotter and moister and the moral and physical fibre of the city-bound became limper.

After a week of not seeing each other Joan and Raymond made up for lost time by galloping instead of trotting along.

"Stevenson and O. Henry couldn't beat this adventure of ours," Raymond exclaimed one evening, wiping the moisture from his forehead. "And I bet thousands of folks would think better of one another if—"

"If—they had the line in their hands," Joan broke in; "but they haven't, you know!"

"Exactly."

Just then Raymond made a bad break. He asked Joan if she did not trust him well enough to give him her telephone number.

"Something might occur," he said, "business pops up unexpectedly. I hate to lose a chance of seeing you—and I hate to wait on street corners."

"I am sorry," Joan replied, "but that would spoil everything."

Raymond flushed. It was just such plunges as this that made

him recoil.

"I understand," he replied, coolly; "I had hoped that you could trust me."

"It is not a matter of trust. It's keeping to the bargain."

There was nothing more to say. But, quite naturally, several days elapsed before they saw each other again.

Fierce, broiling days without even the debilitating moisture to ease the suffering citizens.

Joan, alone in the dark, hot studio, thought of Doris and Nancy and wondered!

"Of course, what I am doing would be horrid if I didn't know all about *him*," and then Joan tossed about. "Some day—it will be such a lark to tell them—and think of his surprise when he—knows! I'll see him with all barriers down next winter," for at this time Joan had written and accepted all Doris's plans for her. She was to study music determinedly—she had a proud little bank account—and she would live at the old house and revel in Nancy's social triumphs.

And Raymond, in his shrouded house, had his restless hours and with greater reason, for he was playing utterly in the dark and had to acknowledge to his grim, off-standing self that, except for the fact that he was in the dark, he would not dare play the very amusing game he was playing.

"If she is masquerading," Raymond beat about with his conscience, "it's the biggest lark ever, and she and I will have many a good laugh over it."

"*But if she—isn't?*" demanded the shadowy self.

"Well, if she isn't, she jolly well knows how to take care of herself! Besides, I'm not going to hurt her. Why, in thunder,

Harriet T. Comstock

can't two fellow creatures enjoy innocent things without having evil suggestions?"

"*They can!*" thundered the Other Self, "*but this isn't innocent—at least it is dangerous.*"

"Oh! be hanged!" Raymond flung back and the Shadow sank into oblivion.

Left to himself—one of his selves—Raymond resorted to sentiment.

"Of course we both know—under what might be—what *is.* She's like Kipling's girl in the Brushwood Boy."

But that did not take in the Other Self in the least. It laughed.

When July came the heat settled down in earnest on the panting city.

"Aren't you going to take any vacation?" asked Raymond. He and Joan were sauntering up Fifth Avenue to a certain haven in a backyard where the fountain played and the birds sang.

"No. I'm going to stay in town and let Miss Gordon have her outing. The Brier Bush is too young to be left alone this year. Next year it will be my turn."

"I'm afraid you'll wilt," Raymond looked at the blooming creature beside him. "Funny, isn't it, how things turn out? I expected to go in August to—to that lady with whom you first saw me" (Joan looked divinely innocent); "but only yesterday she informed me that she had resolved to go abroad, and asked if it would make any difference to me. She's like that. Her procedure resembles jumping off a diving plank."

"Well, does it make any difference?" Joan asked.

"You bet it does! It makes me free to stay in town."

"I'm afraid you'll wilt," Joan twinkled.

"We must take precautions against that." Raymond looked deadly in earnest.

The meetings of these two were now set, like clear jewels in the round of common days. They were not too frequent and they were always managed like chance happenings. Always there was a sense of surprise, a thrill of unbelievable good luck attending them; but there was, also, a growing sense of assurance and understanding.

"I wonder," Joan said once, pressing hard against the shield that protected them, "I wonder if you and I would have played so delightfully had we been—well—introduced! Miss Jones and Mr. Black."

"No!" Raymond burst in positively. "Miss Jones would have been enveloped in the things expected of Miss Jones, and Mr. Black would have been kept busy—keeping off the grass!"

"Aren't you ever afraid," Joan mused on, "that some day we'll suddenly come across each other when our shields are left behind in—in the secret tower?"

"I try not to think of it," Raymond leaned toward the girl; "but if we did we'd know each other a lot better than most girls and fellows are ever allowed to know each other," he said.

"Do you think so?" Joan looked wistfully at him. "You see this isn't real; it's play, and I'm afraid Miss Jones and Mr. Black would be awfully suspicious of each other—just on account of the play."

"And so—we'll make sure that shields are always in commission," Raymond reassured her. "In this small world of ours we cannot run any risks with Miss Jones and Mr. Black. They have no part here."

"No, they haven't!" Joan leaned back. That subtle weakness was touching her; the aftermath of strained imagination. She was often homesick for Doris and Nancy—she was getting afraid that she might not be able to find her way back to them when the time came to go.

"Poor little girl!" Raymond was saying over the table, and his words fitted into the tune the fountain sang—it was the same tune the fountain sang in the sunken room of long ago; all fountains, Joan had grown to think, sang the same lovely, drippy song.

"I wonder just how brave and free a little girl it is?"

Joan screwed up her lips.

"Limitless," she whispered, daringly.

"You're played out, child!" Raymond went on; "there are blue shadows under your eyes. I wish you'd let me do something for you."

"You are doing something," the words came slowly, caressingly; "you're making a hard time very beautiful; you're making me believe—in—in fairies, or what stands for fairies, nowadays; you're making me trust myself and for ever after when—when I slip back where I belong—I'm going to remember, and be—so glad! You see, I know, now, that in the world of grown-ups you *can* make things come true."

"Where you belong?" Raymond gripped his hands close. "Just where do you belong? *Are* you Miss Jones or are you the sweet nameless thing that I am looking at?"

"Oh! I'm Miss Jones!" Joan sat up promptly, "and I'm going to make sure that Miss Jones doesn't get hurt while I play with her."

And as she spoke Joan was thinking of the ugly interpretation of this beautiful play which Patricia would give. Patricia couldn't make things come true because she never tried hard enough.

"I wonder"—and the fountain made Joan dizzy as she listened to Raymond—"I wonder, now since I'm to stay in town, if you'd let me bring my car in? We'd have some great old rides. We'd cool off and have picnics by roadsides and—and get the best of this blasted heat."

"I think it would be heavenly!" Joan saw, already, cool woods and felt the refreshing air on her face.

Raymond was taken aback. He had expected protest.

But the car materialized and so did the picnics and the cool breezes on young, unafraid faces.

At each new venture reassurance waxed stronger—things could be made true in the world; it was only children who failed, in spite of tradition.

Just at this time Sylvia came to town radiating success and happiness.

The result was disastrous. There are times when one cannot endure the prosperity of his friends! Had Sylvia come back with her banners trailing, Joan and Patricia would have rallied to her standard, but she was cool, crisp, and her eyes were fixed upon a successful future.

She was going to do, not only the frieze, but a dozen other things. People whom she had met had been impressed. Things were coming her way with a vengeance. One order was in the Far West—a glorified cabin in a canyon.

"I'm to do all the interior decorating," Sylvia bubbled; "a little out of my line, but they feel I can do it. And"—here the girl looked blissful—"it will be near enough for my John to come and take a vacation."

Patricia and Joan, at that moment, knew the resentment of the unattached woman for the protected one. Sylvia appeared the child of the gods while they were merely permitted to sit at the gates and envy her triumphs.

"I suppose," Patricia burst in, "that this means the end?"

"End?" Sylvia looked puzzled.

"Yes. Plain John will gobble you, Art and all. But your duties here—" Patricia with a tragic gesture pointed to Joan. "What of Miss Lamb, not to mention me?"

Sylvia looked serious.

"Joan is to study music next winter," she said; "haven't you told Pat, Joan?"

Joan shook her head. She had almost forgotten it herself.

"And live with her people," Sylvia went on and then, noticing Patricia's pale little face, she burst forth:

"Pat, take that offer from Chicago that you've been thinking about! It's a big thing—designing for that firm. It will make you independent, leave you time to scribble, and give you a change. Pat, do be sensible."

Patricia drew herself up. She felt that she was being disposed of simply to get her out of the way. She resented it and she was hurt.

"I do not have to decide just now," she said, coldly; "and don't fuss about me, Syl. Now that you and Joan are provided for I can jog along at my own free will, and no one will have to pay but me!"

"Pat!" Joan broke in, "you and I will stick together. And it's all right about Syl. What is this one life for, anyway, if it does not leave us free? Syl, marry your John—your art won't suffer! Pat, where I go you go next winter."

But Patricia lighted a cigarette, and while the smoke issued from her pretty little nose she sighed.

What happened was this: Patricia shopped and sewed for Sylvia and made her radiantly ready for her trip West. And Joan, feeling the break final, although she did not admit it, forsook her own pleasures while she helped Patricia and clung to Sylvia.

"Pat has sublet her rooms," she confided to Sylvia one day, "and is coming here until our lease is up; so you are foot-loose, my precious Syl, and God bless you!"

In August Sylvia departed and Joan and Patricia set up housekeeping together. But at the end of the first week, and the beginning of a new hot spell, Joan found a note on her pillow one night when she came in, exhausted:

Had to get cool somewhere. I'm not responsible for losing my breath. Take care of yourself.

"This seems the last straw!" sobbed Joan, for Raymond had told her that day at the Brier Bush that important business was taking him out of town.

"He has to catch his breath," poor Joan cried, miserably, quite as if her own background was eliminated; "but what of my breath? And to-day is Saturday, and—" The bleak emptiness of a hot Sunday in the stifling studio stretched ahead wretchedly, like a parched desert.

That night Joan pulled her shade down. She hated the stars. They looked complacent and distant. She pushed memories of Doris and Nancy resolutely from her. Her world was not their world—that was sure. If this desperate loneliness couldn't drive her to them, nothing could. She must make her own life! Lying on her hot bed, Joan thought and thought. Of what did she want to make her life?

"I only want a decent amount of fun," she cried, turning her pillow over, "and I will not have strings tied to all my fun, either."

This struck her as funny even in her misery. She sat up in bed and counted her losses—what were they?

Ridge House and that dear, sweet life—sheltered and safe. Yes; she was sure she had lost them, for she could not go back beaten before she had really tried her luck, and if she succeeded she could never have them in a sense of ownership.

"And I will succeed!" Even in that hard hour Joan rose up in arms.

"And I have earned enough to begin real work in the autumn." She counted her gains. "And I can live close to Aunt Dorrie's beautiful life even if I am not of it. And I *am* sure of myself as dear Nancy never could be—because I have proved myself in ways that girls like Nancy never can."

Toward morning Joan fell asleep. When she awoke it was nearly noon time and half the desert of Sunday was passed.

Then Joan, refreshed and comforted, planned a wholesome afternoon and evening.

"I'll go out and get a really sensible dinner; take a walk in the Park, and come home and practise. Monday will be here before I know it."

Joan carried out her programme, and it was five o'clock when she returned, at peace with the whole world.

She took off her pretty street gown and slipped into a thin, airy little dress and comfortable sandals. The sandals made her think of her dancing; she always wore them unless she danced shoeless.

"And before I go to bed," she promised her gay little self, "I'll have a dance to prove that nothing can down me—for long!

"I wonder—" here Joan looked serious as if a thought wave had struck her—"I wonder where Pat is?"

This seemed a futile conjecture. Patricia was too elusive to be followed, even mentally.

As a matter of fact, Patricia was, at that hour, confronting the biggest question of her life.

Heretofore she had always left her roads of retreat open, had, in fact, availed herself of them at critical periods; but this time she had, she believed, so cluttered them that they were practically impassable and she said she "didn't care."

The heat and her rudderless life had been too much for her; she had, too, been honestly stirred by beautiful things— although they were not hers nor could ever rightfully be hers. She had slipped into the danger, that seemed now about to engulf her, on a gradual decline.

Her connection with the Burke home life was, apparently, innocent enough at first. No one but Patricia herself sensed what really was threatening, but the conditions were ripe for what occurred.

Mrs. Burke, bent upon her own pleasure, utterly indifferent to the rights of others, was glad enough to leave her house and family to the charm of Patricia while she could, at the same time, as she smilingly declared, give a bit of happiness to that poor, gifted young creature.

Harriet T. Comstock

The gifted young creature responded with all the hunger of her empty heart—she played with the children, who adored her; there was safety with the eyes of housekeeper and governess upon her—but when the eyes of a tired, disillusioned, and lonely man became fixed upon her, it was time for Patricia to flee. But she did not. Instead she gripped her philosophy of "grab"—and really managed to justify it to a certain extent—while she grew thinner and paler.

On the Sunday when Joan stopped short and wondered where Patricia was, Patricia was up the Hudson awaiting, on a charming hotel piazza, the arrival of the Burke automobile.

It was sunset time and beautiful beyond words. Something in the peaceful loveliness stirred Patricia—she wished that the day were dark and grim. It seemed incongruous to take to the down path—Patricia was not blinded by her lure—while the whole world was flooded with gold and azure.

Then Patricia's angel had a word to say.

"Who would care, anyway?" the girl questioned her upstanding angel—"in all the world, who would care? Why shouldn't I have—what I can get?"

And then, quite forcibly, Patricia thought of Joan! Joan seemed calling, calling. The thought brought a passionate yearning. Joan had the look in her eyes that children and dogs had when they regarded Patricia—a look that cut under the superficial disguise without seeing it, and clung to what they knew was there! The something that they loved and trusted and played with.

In a moment Patricia felt herself growing cold and hard as if almost, but not quite, a power outside herself had threatened the one and only thing in life that she held sacred.

"That Look!" Full well Patricia knew that the Look would no longer be hers to command if she held to her course!

Then, her strength rising with her determination, she glanced back over her cluttered trail. She had written a letter to Joan— it would be delivered to-morrow. A black, scorching statement that would leave not a trace of beauty for the old friendship to rest upon. She had also written a letter to the firm in Chicago definitely refusing to accept its offer—but that letter was not yet mailed!

The Burke automobile, like a devastating flood, might at any moment tear down the hill to the left. With this fear growing in her a strange perverted sense of justice rose and combated it. She had deliberately put herself in the way of the flood; she knew all about the risks of floods, and it seemed knavish to promise and then—leave the field.

"Better an hour of raging against the absence of me," she said, pitifully, "than years of regretting my presence. He'll hate me a little sooner, that's all. So—good-bye!" Patricia almost ran inside; left a hasty, badly written note, and, metaphorically, scrambled over the disordered path of retreat; she seemed to be racing against that letter on its way to Joan. She would write later to the man who was drawing near. Only one thing did Patricia pause to do: It was like driving the last nail in the old life. She telegraphed to Chicago, accepting the position of designer!

CHAPTER XVIII

"OURS, IF WE BE STRONG"

Joan had sung herself into an exalted mood. She had floated along on the wings of music, touching happy memories and tender, nameless yearnings. Her loved ones seemed crowding about her—Doris, dear, sweet Nancy, and pretty Pat. They were pressing against her heart and calling to her.

She began to feel a dull ache for them, a growing impulse stirred deep in her unawakened nature such as always drives the Prodigal unto his Father! The superficial life of the past year seemed husks indeed. It was the beautiful music that mattered and that she could have had with her blessed, safe, loved ones. She need not have left them lonely; she had been shamelessly selfish. Freedom! What was her freedom? Just a tugging against the sweetest thing in life—the false against the true!

Joan felt the tears falling down her cheeks while she sang on— and suddenly it was Patricia who seemed closest to her.

"I will not desert Pat," she actually sang the words into her song fiercely, resolutely. "Patricia must come into safety with me."

With this vowed to her soul, Joan dried her tears and sprang to her feet. She had never felt so lonely, so happy, so free as she did that moment when her spirit turned homeward again.

She kicked off her sandals and began to dance about the studio, lightly, joyfully.

The late afternoon was fading into a sudden darkness—a storm was coming; black, copper-dashed clouds were rolling on rapidly, full of noise and electricity; in a short time they would break over the city—but Joan danced on and on!

In that hour not one thought of Kenneth Raymond disturbed her. He belonged to the time of mistaken freedom; he was one who had helped her to think she could make unreal things true. He had no place here and now. She somehow felt that he had passed from her life.

Joan was abnormally young and only superficially old; her experiences had but developed her spiritually—aroused her better self; and in that self lay her womanhood, her knowledge of sex relations; there it rested unharmed, unheeding.

And then came a knock on the door!

The whirling figure paused on the tips of its toes; the brooding face broke into smiles.

"It's Pat! Come!"

The word "come" was all that reached the waiting man outside—and when he entered he gathered to himself the glad, joyous welcome meant for Patricia, and smiled at the poised figure.

"Why!" gasped Joan, and in her excitement almost spoke Raymond's name.

"How—did you find your way here? How did you know?"

"Forgive me; I had to come. I telephoned to the Brier Bush—they gave me your number."

Harriet T. Comstock

Raymond closed the door behind him and came to the centre of the big room, and there he stood smiling at Joan.

"So your name is Sylvia?" he said.

Then Joan understood—Elspeth had respected her wish to be unknown outside her business, she had given Sylvia's name, had made Sylvia responsible.

"I tried to get you earlier by telephone."

"I was not home." Joan was thinking hard and fast. Something was very wrong, but she could not make out what it was.

"Forgive me for breaking rules: I wanted to see you so that rules did not seem to count. Go on with your dance. You look like the spirit of twilight. Dance. Dance."

Joan grew more and more perplexed. The anger she felt was less than the sense of unreality about it all. Raymond was a stranger; he repelled her; in a way, shocked her.

"I'm through dancing," she said. "Since you are here, sit down. I will turn on the lights."

"Please don't. And you are angry. I'm awfully sorry, but it was this way: I was having dinner with some friends and suddenly I seemed to hear you calling to me. It gave me quite a shock. I thought you might be in danger, might be needing me."

Joan kept her eyes on Raymond's face. She was trying to overcome the growing aversion which alarmed her.

"No, I was not calling to you," she said. "I was bidding you good-bye—really, though I did not know it myself."

"Oh! come now!" Raymond bent forward over his clasped hands; "you are peeved! Not a bit like the little sport with that line in her hand."

"I—I wish you wouldn't talk like that." Joan frowned. "And I know it will sound rude—but I—wish you would go."

"You are—surly!" Raymond laughed again, and just then a deep, rumbling note of thunder followed a vivid flash.

"Come," he went on; "dance for me. There's going to be a devil of a storm—keep time to it. I'm here—I ask pardon for being here—but you can't turn me out in the storm. Come, let us have another big memory for our adventure."

Still Joan sat contemplating the man near her, her hands lightly clasped on her lap, her slim feet crossed and at ease—little stocking-shod feet to which Raymond's eyes turned. She had never looked, to Raymond, so provoking and tempting.

"What's up, really?" he asked, "you're not going to spoil everything by a silly tantrum, are you?"

Joan hadn't the slightest appearance of temper—she was quite at ease, apparently, though her heart almost choked her by its beating.

"You have spoiled everything," she said, "not I. You somehow have made our play end abruptly by coming here. I don't think I ever can play again. It's like knowing there isn't—any—any Santa Claus; I can't explain. But something has happened. Something so awful that I cannot put it into words."

Raymond got up and stood before Joan. He looked down and smiled, and at that moment she knew that he was not his old self and she knew what had changed him! And yet with the understanding a deeper emotion swept over her, one of familiarity. It was like finding someone she had known long ago in Raymond's place; as if she had lived through this scene before.

She summoned a latent power to deal with the new conditions.

Harriet T. Comstock

"You pretty little thing!" Raymond whispered, and touched Joan's shoulder. She got up quickly and moved across the room.

"I always want light when there is a storm," she said, and touched the switch.

Raymond, in the glare, looked flushed and impatient. A crash of thunder shook the old house.

"Will you dance for me?" he said.

Joan stiffened—she was dealing with the strange personality, not the man who was part of the happy past.

"No," she said, evenly. "And you have no right to be here. I wish you would go at once."

"Out in this storm, you little pagan?"

"You could go downstairs and wait in the hall."

"You are afraid of me?"

"Not in the least."

"Afraid of yourself, then?"

"Certainly not. Why should I be afraid of myself?"

"Afraid *for* yourself, then?"

Raymond was enjoying himself hugely.

"No, but I'm a bit afraid—for you!" Joan was watching the stranger across the room, and she shivered as peal after peal of thunder tore the brief lulls in the storm.

"Oh! that's all right—about me!" Raymond said, mistaking the trembling that he saw; "you know, while I was at dinner to-day I got to thinking what fools we were—not to—to take what fun there is in life—and not count the costs like mean-spirited misers. You've got more dash and courage than I have—you must have thought me, many a time, a— What did you think me, little girl?"

With the overpowering new knowledge that was possessing her Joan spoke hesitatingly. It seemed pitifully futile and untruthful; but her own thought was to get this stranger from her presence.

"I thought you—well, I thought about you just as I thought about myself. Someone who was strong enough and splendid enough to make something we both wanted come true! It was believing that we two grown-up, lonely people could—play—without hurting—anything—or each other. I see, now, just as I used to see when I was a little girl—that one can never, never do that."

Tears dimmed Joan's eyes and she tried to smile.

The whole weird and unbelievable experience was making her distrust herself, and the storm was more and more unnerving her. She feared she could not hold out much longer.

"You're a—damned good little actress!" Raymond gave a hard, loud laugh so unlike his own wholesome laugh that Joan started back.

"I want you to go away at once!" her eyes flashed. "I think you must be mad."

"But—the storm." Raymond walked across the room.

"I do not care—about the storm. I want you to go!" and now Joan retreated and unconsciously took her stand behind a chair.

A sudden, blinding flash, a deafening crash and—the lights went out!

In the terrifying blackness Joan felt Raymond's arms about her.

So frightened was she now that for an instant the human touch was a blessing. She relaxed, panting and trembling. In that moment she felt kisses upon her lips, her eyes, her throat!

She sprang away, dashing against the furniture and then, as suddenly as they had failed, the lights were blazing and in the revealment Joan faced the man across the room.

Her face was flaming, but his was as white as if death had marked it.

"You—coward!" she flung out.

The words stung and hurt.

Raymond did not move bodily, but his eyes seemed to be coming nearer the girl.

"If you do not go at once," Joan said, slowly, "I will call for help."

"Oh! no, you won't, and I am not going to-night."

The beast in Raymond had never risen before, had never been suspected, never been trained: it was the more dangerous because of that.

"What?" Joan stared at him aghast.

"I said that I am not going to-night."

The awful feeling of familiarity again swept over Joan. She felt that she must have lived through the scene: had made a mistake that must not be made a second time.

"You have been drinking," she said, and her voice shook. She had hoped that she might save him the degradation of knowing that she understood.

"Well! Suppose I have? It has made me live. Set me free. I wonder if you have ever lived?"

"I am afraid not." Joan could not repress the sob that rose in her throat.

"We can live, I bet." Raymond gave his ugly laugh. "That line in our hands gives us the right."

For a moment Joan contemplated escape. Any escape open to her. The telephone, the door, even a call from the window in the heart of the storm. Then the desire was gone and with it all personal fear. She wanted again, in a vague way, to save this man who had once been her friend. She felt that she must save him.

Somehow, she had wronged him. She must find out just how, and then he might once more be as she had known him.

Presently it came to her. She should have known that he could not understand the past. He had pretended to, while they had played their foolish game, but when restraint was set aside he showed the deadly truth. She had cheapened herself, cheapened all women—she could not fly now, not until she had made him see the mistake.

Raymond was crossing the room. He laughed, and insanity flashed in his eyes.

"What shall I call you from now on?" he said: "Sylvia?—or shall we make up another name?"

"My name is not Sylvia. And there is to be no time ahead for us."

"You are mistaken. A girl has no right to lead a man on as you have led me, and then run. It isn't the game, my dear. You must not be afraid to play the game."

Raymond reached his hand toward her and said pleadingly:

"Don't be afraid. I hate to see you flinch."

"You must not touch me." Joan's eyes flashed.

"I see. You've raised the devil in me—and you do not want to pay?" The brute was rearing dangerously.

"I do not want to pay more than I owe."

"What do you mean by that?"

"I mean that as true as God hears me I meant no wrong. I've done things that girls should not do. I see that now. But I believed that you understood. I thought that, in a way, you were like me—you were so fine and happy. I still have faith that when you are yourself again you will realize this. Oh! it is horrible that drink can do such an awful thing to you."

"Whatever ideals I may have had," Raymond broke in, "you have destroyed. Perhaps you think men have no ideals? Some women do."

"Oh! I believe with all my soul that they have. It was because I did think that, that I dared to trust you." Joan was pleading; she could not own defeat; she was appealing to him for himself.

But Raymond gave a sneering laugh.

"You trusted so much," he said, "that you hid behind a veil and would not tell your name."

Raymond was hearing himself speak as if he were an

eavesdropper. He trembled and breathed hard as a runner does who is near the goal.

"What's one night in a life?" he asked, as if it were being dragged from him.

Again his voice startled him. He looked around, hoping he might discover who it was that spoke.

It was Joan now who was speaking:

"I think that in me as well as in you there is something that neither of us knew. I cannot explain it—but it was something that we should have known before—"

"Before what?" Raymond asked.

"Before I—anyway—was left to go free! It is the *knowing* that makes it safe, safe for such as you and me! I do not believe you ever knew what you could be—and neither did I."

Raymond gripped his hands together and his face was ghastly.

"My God!" he breathed, and sank on the couch covering his eyes from Joan's pitiful look. He was coming to himself, trying to realize what had occurred as one does who becomes conscious of having spoken in delirium.

Outside, the storm was dying down—it sounded tired and defeated.

Joan looked at the bent form near her and then went to a chair and leaned her head back. She knew the feeling of desperate exhaustion. She had never fainted, was not going to faint now, but she had come to the end of a dangerous stretch of road and there was no strength left in her. Surprise, shock, the storm— all had combined to bring her to where she was now. The tears rolled unheeded down her cheeks; all her hope and faith were gone—she had left them in the struggle and could not even

Harriet T. Comstock

estimate her loss.

The clock ticked away the minutes—who was there to notice or care? Joan was thankful to have nothing happen! She closed her eyes and waited.

Presently Raymond spoke. His hands dropped from his haggard face and his eyes were filled with shame and remorse.

"Will you listen to me?" he said.

"Yes." Joan looked at him—her eyes widened; she tried to smile. She longed to cry out at what she saw, wanted to say: "You have come back. Come back." Instead she said slowly:

"Yes."

"I can never expect to have your forgiveness. I thank God that it is possible for us to part and, alone, seek to forget this horror. I will never intrude. I promise you that. Back in my college days I found out that I could not drink. It did something to me that it does not do to others. I never quite knew what until to-day. When I saw you standing there—the devil got loose. I know now. My God! To think that all one's life does not count when the devil takes hold."

"Oh! Yes, it does, and it is the knowing that will help." Joan was crying softly. "You will have the right to trust yourself hereafter because you know."

"I will always think of women as I see you now." Raymond spoke reverently.

"You must not. Some women do not have to learn—I did. I think the best women know."

"You must not say that."

"Yes, I feel it. Had I shown you a better self while we played all would have been different. You would not have misunderstood. Women must not expect what they are not willing to give. I had done things that no girl can safely do and be understood and then—when you lost control—you thought of me as you really believed me. I can see it all now, see how I hurt you; hurt myself and hurt other girls; but it was because—not because I am a bad girl—but because I did not know myself any more than you knew yourself. How could we hope to know each other? I seem so old, now—so old! And I understand—at last."

Raymond looked at her and pity filled his eyes, for she looked so touchingly young.

"I think," he said, "that I shall see all girls for ever as I see you at this minute."

"Oh, you must not." Joan gave a sob. "They are not like me, really."

There was an awkward silence. Then:

"Will you tell me your name? Will you try to trust me—just a little? It would prove it, if you only would."

"I do not want you to know my name. You must promise to keep from knowing. It is all I ask."

"Will you let me tell you—mine?"

"No! no!" Joan put up her hands as if to ward off something tangible.

"I only meant"—Raymond dropped his eyes—"that there isn't anything under heaven I wouldn't do to prove to you my sense of remorse. I thought if you knew you might call upon me some day to prove myself. I'm bungling, I know, but I wish I could make you understand how I feel."

"I do." And now Joan got up rather unsteadily. "And some day—I—I may call upon you—for—for I have known your name—always!"

"What!"

"Please—forgive me. I was taking an advantage—but it did not seem to matter then, and I must keep the advantage now—for your sake as well as mine. And now, before we say good-bye, I want to tell you that I know you are going to have your ideals again. You will try to get them back, won't you?"

"I will get them back, yes! I only lost them when the devil in me drove me mad."

"And bye and bye, try to believe that although one cannot make the unreal real, still there are some foolish people that think they can—and be kind to such people. Help them, do not hurt them."

"Will you—take my hand?" Raymond stretched his own forth.

"Why—of course—and tell you that I am glad, oh, so glad because—you have come back! Glad because it was I not another who saw that other you—for I can forget it!"

"And—and we are—to see each other some day?" This came hopefully. "Some day—as we left ourselves—back before this?"

"Some day—some day? Perhaps. If we do—we will understand better than we did then."

"Yes. We'll understand some things."

Raymond bent and touched Joan's hand with his lips and went quickly from the room.

He was conscious of passing, on the stairs, a wet and draggled young woman, but he did not pause to see the frightened look she cast upon him.

A moment later Joan raised her head from the pillow on which she was weeping the weakest—and the strongest—tears of her life.

"Oh! Pat," she sobbed. "Oh! Pat."

Patricia came to the couch and sat down. She was thinking fast and hard. Life had not been make-believe to Patricia; she had builded whatever towers had been hers with hard facts.

She drew wrong and bitter conclusions now—but she dealt with them divinely.

"You poor kid," she whispered, "and I left you—to this. I! Joan, I told you not to trust men. It's when you trust them that you get hurt.

"Listen, you poor little lamb, I felt you calling me, tugging at me. The storm delayed me, or I would have been here sooner. Joan, I had nearly run off the track myself—it was the thought of you that got me. I kept remembering that night you made the little dinner for me—no one had ever taken care of me like that—and, child, I've accepted that job in Chicago. If I go alone, remembering that dinner you got for me, I don't know what I'll do. Come with me, Joan, will you? No man in the world is worth such tears as these. You don't have to tell *me* anything. We'll begin anew. You'll have your music—I'll have my work—and we'll have a dinner every night."

Patricia was shivering in her wet clothing.

Joan put her arms about her. At that moment nothing so much appealed to her as to get away—get away to think and make sure of herself. Get away from the place where her idols lay shattered.

"Yes, Pat. I will go. But"—and here she took Patricia's face in

Harriet T. Comstock

her hot palms—"don't you believe that any man can be trusted?"

"No, I don't. It isn't their fault. They are not made for trust—they're made to do things."

"Pat, you're all wrong. It's girls like you and me that cannot be trusted. I—I didn't know myself that was the trouble. Pat—you mustn't—think what you are thinking—you are mistaken."

"I saw him—on the stairs," gasped Patricia.

"Suppose you did?"

"Joan, do you know what time it is?"

"No. I do not care. It takes time to have the world tumble about your ears."

"You—you—do not—love him, do you?"

Joan paused and considered this as if it were a startlingly new idea.

"Love him?—why, no. I'm sure I don't. But, Pat, what is it that seems like love, but isn't—you're sure it isn't—but it hurts and almost kills you?"

The two young faces confronted each other blankly.

"I don't know," Patricia said.

"Nor I, Pat. But we've got to know. All women have unless they want to mess their own lives and the lives of men. They cannot be free until they do."

Then Joan took hold of Patricia and exclaimed:

"Pat, you are dripping wet. Come to bed." While helping Patricia to undress she talked excitedly of going away.

"It's the only thing to do. This silly life is a waste of time. Why, Pat, we have been making all kinds of locks to keep ourselves shut away from freedom and the things we want. Some day we would want to get out and we could not. I am going to be free, Pat—not smudgy."

Patricia paused in the act of getting into bed and remarked demurely:

"My God! Out of the mouths of babes and pet lambs— Come, child, shut your eyes. You make me crawl."

Harriet T. Comstock

CHAPTER XIX

"QUEER—TO THINK NO DAY IS LIKE
TO A DAY THAT IS PAST"

When Joan and Patricia arose the following day they confronted life as two criminals might who realized that their only safety lay in flight, and that they must escape without running risks.

Patricia shuddered when the first mail was delivered. She rescued her own letter—addressed to Joan—and raised her heart in gratitude that no letter of angered remonstrance came from Burke.

But he might *come*; he might telegraph!

"My God!" Patricia exclaimed at noon time, "I cannot stand this, Joan, we must vacate."

Joan was quivering with excitement, too—she was wild-eyed and shook with terror at every step on the stairs.

Her ordeal of the day before had not merely devastated her beautiful dreams, but it had, in a marvellous fashion, created an entirely new outlook on life. She felt that once she was safe from any possible chance of meeting Raymond, he might, spiritually, rise from the ashes and eventually overcome the impression that would cling in spite of all she could do. Intellectually she understood—but her hurt and shocked sensibilities shrank from bodily contact with one who had forced the fruit of knowledge so crudely upon her. The youth in her seemed to have died, and it held all the charm and delight. The *woman* of Joan made a plea for the man, but as yet he was a stranger. More strange, even, than the unnamable creature who had, for an hour, while the storm raged, stood in her imagination like some evil thing between the woman who had not fully understood and the woman who was never again to misunderstand.

While she feared and trembled Joan could, already, recall the moment when Raymond began to gain the victory over his fallen self. She knew that he was always to be the master in the future. How she knew this she could not have explained, but she knew! In all the years to come Raymond would be the better for that hour that proved to him his weakness. And with this knowledge, poor Joan found comfort in her own part. He and she had learned together the strength of their hidden foes. She realized with a sense of hot remorse that she had wanted freedom not so much for the opportunity of expressing that which was fine and worth while, but that which she, herself, had not been conscious of.

But she had been awakened in time. She, like Raymond, had faced her worst self, and now the most desirable thing to do was to get away. Anywhere, separated from all that had led to the shock, she would look back and forward and know herself well enough to make the next step a safer one.

To go with Patricia for a few months would not interfere with her winter plans; so she decided not to write fully to Doris, but to state merely that she was going to see Patricia settled in her new venture—or, should the business not appeal, bring Patricia back with her.

"But," she said to Patricia while they restlessly moved about the studio, "what can we do about—this," Joan spread her arms wide, "the furniture and all Syl's beloved things?"

Patricia sighed.

"Has it ever struck you, my lamb," she said, "that our dear Syl is a selfish pig?"

Joan started in surprise.

"Oh, I know," Patricia went on, "her respectability and genius protect her, but she is selfish. How long did she stop to consider us when her own plans loomed high? She dumped everything on us and went! It was business, pleasure, art, and John. For the rest—'poof!'" Patricia spoke the last sound like a knife cutting through something crisp and hard.

Joan continued to stare. Unformed impressions were taking shape—she felt disloyal, but she was not deceived.

"Syl brought you here," Patricia was going on, "because she was lonely and you fitted in; she never changed her own course. She has engaged herself to her John because *he* fits in and will never interfere. I've seen him—and I grieve over him. He'll think, bye and bye, that he's gone into partnership with God in giving Syl and her art to the world! But he'll never have any nice little fire to warm the empty corners of his life by. I hope he'll never discover them—poor chap! He's as good as gold and Syl has pulled it all over him without knowing it. She's made him believe that he was specially designed to further a good cause—she is the good cause.

"And the best, or the worst, of it is that Syl will make good. That kind does. It is such fools as you and I who fail because we have imagination and find ourselves at the crucial moment in the other fellow's shoes."

"Oh, Pat!" It was all that Joan could think of saying.

Patricia was rushing on.

"Very well, then! Now, listen, lamb, you and I are going to

skip and skip at once. I'm done up. A change is all that will save me—and you've got to go with me!"

"Yes, yes, Pat!"

"Why, child, a step on the stairs is giving us electric shocks. This lease is up in October. I'll telegraph Syl to-day. She can make her own arrangements after that—we'll leave things safe here and get out to-morrow!"

Suddenly Joan got up and threw her hands over her head.

"Thank heaven!" was what she cried aloud.

There was much rush and flurry after that, and in the excitement the nervous tension relaxed.

A note, a most bewildering one, was posted to Elspeth Gordon. It came at a moment when Miss Gordon greatly needed Joan and was most annoyed at her non-appearance. It simply stated:

Something has happened—I'm going at once to Chicago with Pat.

Now as Patricia had been an unknown quantity to Miss Gordon—her relations with Joan being purely those of business—she raised her brows with all the inherited conservatism of her churchly ancestors and steeled her heart—as they often had.

"Temperamental!" sniffed Miss Gordon, "utterly lacking in honour. Just as I might have expected. A poor prospect for—Pat! I do not envy the gentleman."

Miss Gordon had contempt instead of passion, but her resentment was none the less.

And it was at high tide when Raymond came in at four-thirty

for a cup of tea and what comfort he could obtain by seeing how Joan had survived the storm. He was met by blank absence and a secret and unchristian desire on Miss Gordon's part to hurt Joan.

Miss Gordon had not been entirely unobservant of all that had been going on. She had had her qualms, but business must be business, and so long as Joan did not interfere with that she had not felt called upon to remonstrate with her on her growing friendliness with the protege of Mrs. Tweksbury.

But now things were changed and by Joan's own bad behaviour.

Raymond looked sadly in need of tea and every other comfort available—he was positively haggard.

While he sipped his tea he was watching, watching. So was Miss Gordon. Finally, he could stand it no longer and he spoke to her as she was passing.

"Your little sibyl—she is not here? On a vacation, I suppose?"

This was futile and cheap and Raymond felt that he flushed.

Miss Gordon poised for action. Her face grew grave and hard—she believed she was quite within her just rights when she sought to protect this very handsome and worth-while young man. She really should have done it before! She was convinced of that now.

"My assistant," she said, "has left without giving the usual notice. She has left me in a most embarrassing position but I suppose she felt her own personal affairs were paramount.

"I—I think she has made a hasty marriage." On the whole, this seemed more kind than Joan deserved.

"A—what?" Raymond almost forgot himself. "A—what—did

you say?"

"Well, I presume it was marriage. She simply stated that something had occurred that was taking her to Chicago at once with a young man."

Elspeth Gordon watched the face of Mrs. Tweksbury's adopted son. She felt she was serving a righteous cause. If any worthy young man came to harm from the folly she had permitted she could never forgive herself! Miss Gordon had an elastic conscience.

Raymond's countenance grew suddenly blank. He had recovered his self-control. He laughed presently—it was a light, well-modulated laugh, not the laugh of a shocked or very much interested man.

Miss Gordon was relieved—but disappointed.

And then Raymond went out to do his thinking alone. He walked the streets as people often do who are lonely and can find relief in action.

He had never been so confused in his life, but then, he reflected, what did he really know about the girl with whom he had spent so many happy, sweet, unforgettable hours? The one black hour through which she had, somehow, stood as the only tangible safe thing he could recall, had shattered his faith in himself, in everything.

What was she? Who was she? And now she had gone—with some man! It sounded cruel and harsh—but it could not, it never could, blot out certain memories which lay deep in Raymond's mind. He was miserable beyond words. He deplored his own part in the unhappy affair; he could not adjust himself to the inevitable—the end of the amazing and romantic episode.

Of course he had always known that it must end some time,

but while he drifted damnably he had not given much thought to that. But now he had finished it by his own beastiality when, had he kept his head, it might have passed as it came—a thing undefiled; a beautiful, tender memory.

Perhaps—and at this Raymond shuddered—perhaps he had driven the girl upon a reef. He had heard of such things. In despair she had violently taken herself out of his reach. He could not believe she had been seriously involved while she played with him. Whatever she was, he could but believe that she was innocent in her regard for him—else why this mad flight? And he could not believe that her regard for him was serious. He was humble enough.

After leaving Joan the night before Raymond had met his Other Self squarely in the shrouded house. Toward morning he had come to a conclusion: he was prepared to pay to the uttermost for his folly, whatever the demand might be. She must be the judge.

He would go to the tea room—not to the house that he had so brutally invaded. He would again talk to the girl and watch her—he would make her understand that he was not as weak as he might seem. If he had misunderstood, that should not exempt him from responsibility. But if she should spurn any attempt of his to remedy the evil he could regard himself with a comparatively clean conscience.

Raymond could not get away from the idea that the girl was of his world—the world where he was supposed, by Mrs. Tweksbury and her kind, to constantly be.

But then the empty tea room—and how empty it was!—stared him blankly in the face. Miss Gordon's manner angered him beyond expression. Almost he felt he must tell her of his own low part in the tragedy in order to place her beside the girl he had insulted, instead of beside him, as he felt she was.

Raymond was hurt, disappointed, and disgusted; but as the

day wore on a grave and common-sense wave of relief flooded his consciousness. Bad as things had been, they might, God knows, have been worse. As it was, with the best of intentions, he was set aside by the girl's own conduct of her affairs.

To seek her further would be the greatest of folly and then, toward night, lonely, half ill, Raymond undertook that time-honoured custom of turning over a new leaf only to find that it stuck to the old persistently!

Then he resorted to a sensible alternative—he read and re-read the old page. He tried to understand it line by line. He was humbled; filled with shame at his meaningless attitude of the past, and acknowledged that the grit in him, that he had hoped was sand, was, after all, the dirt that could easily defile. He must begin anew and rebuild. He must take nothing for granted in himself. Having arrived at that conclusion, the leaf turned!

And Joan, in like manner, thrashed about. It was not so much her actions that caused her alarm—she had played most sincerely—but it was the power behind the play that caused her to tremble and grow hot and cold. What was it within her that had driven her where wiser girls would fear to stray? What was it that was not love in the least and yet had caused her heart to beat at Raymond's touch or glance? Whatever it was, Joan concluded, it could not be depended upon. It could lay waste every holy spot unless it were understood and controlled, and Joan set herself to the task.

The first step was to get away. That was inevitable.

After a few months—and Joan was sure Patricia could not run in harness longer than that—they could both come back, saner and better women. Then Doris would be called into action; no more butting against the pricks and calling it freedom!

In the meantime, Patricia and Joan worked madly to get away and still secure Sylvia's interests.

Harriet T. Comstock

Telegrams passed to and fro. Sylvia was fair enough to see both sides, and while she was irritated at being disturbed she did not resent it and even bade Patricia and Joan success with honest enthusiasm.

"I'll run back and see to things," she wrote; "I'm making a lot of money."

And then Patricia tucked Joan, so to speak, under her frail wing and took to flight.

Chicago was new territory to both the girls but Patricia, from the necessity, as she told Joan, of grubbing, had become an adept at finding shelter.

After a week at a hotel, while she settled herself in business, Patricia had free hours for home-hunting, and she and Joan made a lark of it.

Patricia had the enviable power of shutting business from her own time, and she quickly discerned that Joan needed prompt and definite interests to hold her to what they had undertaken.

And the venture had suddenly assumed gigantic proportions to Patricia. She feverishly desired it to be a success.

She realized that Joan was being torn by conflicting emotions while she was idle and alone. She asked no questions; appeared not to notice Joan's teary eyes and pensive mouth. Wisely she made Joan feel her own need of her—to that Joan responded at once.

"Joan, I never had a home in my life before," she confided while they flitted from one apartment to another. "I used to walk around in strange cities and peep in people's windows, just to see homes!

"After my father died, I rustled about on the little money he left, and I got to sneaking into other women's homes. I didn't mean harm at first, but after awhile it seemed so easy to sneak and so hard to—make good! But down in my heart, as truly as God hears me, I've been homesick for—what I never had."

"Pat! Of all things—you are crying!" Joan looked frightened.

"Well, let me cry!" sniveled Patricia. "I've never given myself that luxury, either."

For a moment there was silence broken only by Patricia's sniffs. Then:

"What do your folks say about it, Joan?"

"I haven't sent the big letter yet—it's written. I don't want them to say anything until I'm fixed. I only told them of our leaving New York."

"Whew!" ejaculated Patricia. "You certainly run your career free-handed."

"Aunt Dorrie will take it like the darling she is," Joan mused on, "and she'll make Nan and Doctor Martin see it. When she gave me my chance she did not tie a string to me—not even the string of her love. We understand each other perfectly."

"I suppose you know," Patricia gave a sigh, "but I don't think an explanation would hurt any and I don't want her to blame me more than I deserve, Joan."

"Blame you, Pat? Why, how could she?"

"Oh, I don't know. She might get to thinking on her own hook if you don't give her the facts. Joan, send the letter at once!"

So Joan dispatched the letter, and it had the effect of depressing Nancy to an alarming degree and, in consequence, of spurring Doris to renewed effort.

Harriet T. Comstock

She was perturbed by the lack of what she knew. She had her doubts of Patricia; the sudden flight had an aspect of rout—what did it mean?

Her reply to Joan, however, was much what Martin's would have been to his nephew.

She accepted and took on faith what Joan had explained—or failed to explain.

She laid emphasis on plans for the coming winter and referred to Joan's promise to give herself seriously to her music.

"Either in New York or there, my dear, begin your real work. It is all well enough to look about before you decide, but there is a time for decision."

This letter put Joan on her mettle.

"Pat, I'm going to begin as soon as we've settled," she declared, and her wet eyes shone. "Aunt Dorrie is quite right."

The girls finally secured four pretty, sunny rooms overlooking the lake, and reverently selected the furniture for them.

"Let's get things artistic," Patricia wisely explained, "we'll make the place unique and then"—for Patricia always left, if possible, a way open for retreat—"if we should ever want to dispose of it, we'd have a good market."

But as the days passed it looked as if the venture were turning out better than one could have hoped. Joan had never felt so important in her life, and, to her surprise, developed possibilities never suspected before. She prepared for Patricia's homecomings with the keenest delight. The cozy, charming little dinners, the evenings by the open fire—for they had selected the rooms largely on account of the fireplace—or the occasional theatre or concert grew in delight. Patricia was the merriest of comrades, the most appreciative of partners. She also, to her own surprise, became deeply interested in her work and, while the hours and confinement sometimes irritated her, her field of invention was wide enough to employ her real talent, and her success was assured from the first.

And when things were running smoothly and there were hours too empty for comfort in the lonely day, Joan discovered a professor of music who gave her much encouragement and some good advice.

After this interview she wrote to Doris more frankly than she had done for a long time. She explained her financial situation and quite simply asked for help:

> It's very expensive learning *not* to be a fool, Aunt Doris. I have proved that. I am very serious now and Chicago, with Pat, is better for me than New York with Sylvia.

> What I really want is to prove myself a bit before I come back to you. I'm sorry about this winter, dear, but a year more and I will be able to come to you not *on* my shield, I hope, but with it in fairly good condition.

"I think you ought to make her keep her promise about this winter," Nancy quivered; "she is always upsetting things."

"Why, my little Nan!" Doris drew the girl to her. Oddly enough, she felt as if Nancy was all that she was ever to have. Never before had Joan sounded so determined.

"Instead," Doris comforted, "I am going to help Joan prove herself and you and I, little girl, will go up to town and have a very happy, a very wonderful winter, and next summer, if Joan does not come to us, we will go to her. I think we all see things very clearly now."

Nancy was not so sure of this but she, like Joan and Patricia, had felt the lash upon her back and was chafing at delay.

Harriet T. Comstock

Mary worked early and late to hasten the departure from The Gap. Always in Mary's consciousness was that threatening old woman on Thunder Peak.

With care and comfort old Becky was more alert; more suspicious. She was wondering *why*. And Mary felt that at any time she might defeat what daily was gaining a hold on Mary's suspicions. The woman tried hard to shield the secret from her own curiosity, but under all else lay the conviction that it was Nancy's toys which were in peril. And gradually the love that the silent, morose woman felt for the girl absorbed all other emotions. It was like having banked everything on a desired hope she was prepared to defend it. If her suspicions were true, then all the more must the secret be hid.

And so in November Doris and Nancy went to New York and Mary, apparently unmoved, saw them depart while she counted anew her assumed duties.

There was The Peak—and with winter to complicate her duties, it loomed ominously.

"And I'll have to back letters for old Jed." Mary had promised to write for the old man and to read from the Bible to him, as Nancy had always done. "And keep the old man alive as well." Mary sighed wearily. "And when there's a minute to rest— keep my own place decent." The cabin was the one bright thought and, because of that which had made the cabin possible, Mary bowed her back to her burdens.

"A strange woman is Mary," Doris confided to Nancy; "nothing seems to make any impression upon her."

Nancy opened her lovely blue eyes wide at this.

"Why, Aunt Dorrie," she replied, "Mary would die for us— and never mention it. She's made that still, faithful way."

Doris smiled, but did not change her mind. The people of the

hills were never to be to her what they had been to Sister
Angela—her people.

Harriet T. Comstock

CHAPTER XX

"IT IS FELICITY ON HER WINGS"

The old New York house was once more opened and the fountain set free. Birds sang and flowers bloomed, but Joan was not there and for a blank but silent moment both Doris and Nancy wondered if the lack were to defeat them. The moment was appalling but it passed.

Felicity brooded over them and her wings did not droop.

Martin, with his sound common sense, came to the fore among the first. He was never more alert. His nephew, Clive Cameron, was entrenched in Martin's office and home—his name, alone, shone on the new sign.

"I've flung you in neck and crop, Bud, because I believe in you and have told my patients so. Sink or swim, but you've got clear water to do it in. I'll hang around—make my city headquarters with you; lend myself to you; but for the rest I'm going to do exactly what I want to do—for a time."

Cameron regarded his uncle as the young often do the older—yearningly, covetously, tenderly.

"I—I think I understand about Miss Fletcher, Uncle Dave," he said.

"I had hoped you did, boy. And remember this—it's only

when a woman gets so into your system that she cannot be purged out, that you dare to be sure."

"But, Uncle Dave, the knowledge—what has it done for you?"

"You'll never be able to understand that, Bud, until you're past the age of asking the question."

And having settled that to his satisfaction, Martin turned resolutely to what threatened Doris and Nancy.

He meant to see fair play. Doris could be depended upon for a few strenuous months if her friends turned to and helped her as they should.

Nancy must no longer be sacrificed!

"If there is any sense in this tomfoolery about Joan," Martin mused, "it must apply to Nancy also."

Martin was extremely fond of Nancy. He often wished she would not lean so heavily, but then his spiritual ideal of a woman was after Nancy's design. Of Joan he disapproved, and Doris was a type apart.

"If we can marry Nancy off," plotted Martin—and he had his mind's eye on his nephew—"I'll bring Sister on from the West and get Doris to share Ridge House with us. Queer combination, but safe!"

And then he saw, as in a vision, the peaceful years on ahead. He would hold Doris's hand down the westering way. Hold it close and warm; never looking for more than the blessed companionship. And his sister, happy and content, would share the way with them and Nancy's children—would they be Clive's also?—would gladden all their hearts. And Joan?—well, Martin did not feel that Joan needed his architectural aid—she was chopping and hacking her own design.

At this point Martin sought Emily Tweksbury and bullied her into action.

Mrs. Tweksbury had not unpacked her trunks yet and was sorely depressed about Raymond.

"I wish I had stuck to Maine," she deplored, "and devoted myself to the boy. He looks like a fallen angel.

"Ken, what have you been doing to yourself?" she had asked.

"Just pegging away, Aunt Emily."

"Ken," Mrs. Tweksbury had an awful habit of felling the obvious by a blow of her common-sense hatchet; "Ken, you've got to be married. You're not the kind to float around town and enjoy it—and you are the kind that would enjoy the other."

"Oh! I'm having a bully time, Aunt Emily."

"That's not true, Ken. Life lacks salt; you look the need of it and I blame myself for going abroad."

"I'm glad you went!" fervently said Raymond.

"You are, eh? Well, I'm not going again until you're safely married."

At this Raymond found that he could laugh, and just then the hatchet fell, for Doctor Martin had entered the arena and Mrs. Tweksbury had agreed to help.

"Do you remember my speaking of that niece of Miss Fletcher's last spring?" she asked.

"Yes. I do recall it. Wasn't she to come here—or something like that?"

"Yes, she was, but she isn't. Doris Fletcher has brought her girl up to town herself and the old house is opened. I called there the other day. Ken, that girl is the loveliest thing I ever saw!"

"Is she?" Raymond was sitting on the edge of the table in Mrs. Tweksbury's dressing room. When she got through talking he was going to bed. He had to stifle a yawn.

"Yes, she is. She's not only the prettiest girl I've seen for many a year, but she's *the girl*."

"For what?" Raymond swung his lifted foot while he balanced with the other.

"For you, Ken!" The crash unsettled Raymond and he brought his free foot to the floor.

"Oh! come," he blurted; "don't begin that sort of rubbish, Aunt Emily. I thought you were above that."

"I'm not, Ken. I would go slow if I dared, but this girl will be snapped up before we get in touch with her, unless we act quick."

"Aunt Emily! For heaven's sake, is the girl hanging about open-mouthed for the first hook tossed to her?"

"No. But, Ken, she is the kind that men want—the kind they hold sacred in their souls and hardly dare hope ever to see in the flesh. The girl made me want to grab her. I remember as a child she was charming—she's a perfect, but very human, woman now."

With this Mrs. Tweksbury dilated upon what Doris had confided of Nancy's loyal and devoted life.

"You see, Ken," Mrs. Tweksbury ran on, "the girl is like a rare thing that you cannot debate much about, and once lost, the opportunity will never come again. I've gone off about

Harriet T. Comstock

her, Ken."

"I should say you had! Will you smoke, Aunt Emily?"

"Yes!"

To see Emily Tweksbury smoke was about as incongruous as to see an antique remodelled to bring it up to date; but the smoke calmed her.

"You will call with me upon her, won't you, Ken?"

"With pleasure."

Raymond felt that any compromise would be well to offer.

"I'll do my best by her, too, Aunt Emily. I rather shy at perfect types; girls, at the best, make me skittish. They make me think of myself and then I get gawky."

"You'll forget yourself when you see Nancy Thornton."

"Nancy—queer old name for a modern girl!" The two puffed away like old cronies—Raymond had got into a chair now and Mrs. Tweksbury had relaxed, also.

"She isn't modern!"

"No? What then, Aunt Emily?"

"Ken, she's just woman. She appears just once so often, like a prophet or something, that keeps your faith alive. She's the kind that the Bible calls 'blessed,' and if she didn't reappear now and then I think the race would perish."

"Ugh!" grunted Raymond. Then added: "Calm down, Aunt Emily, go slow. When you lose your head you're apt to buck."

Mrs. Tweksbury laughed at this and helped herself to

another cigarette.

It was a week later that Raymond met Nancy at his aunt's dinner table. He knew she was coming. At least he thought he knew—but when he saw her he felt that he had not expected her at all.

It was a small party: Doris Fletcher, Doctor Martin, young Doctor Cameron, and Nancy.

Nancy came into the dim old drawing room behind young Cameron. It was that fact that attracted Raymond first. He recalled what Mrs. Tweksbury had said about the type being the ideal of man—or something like that—and Cameron, whom he had just met a few weeks before, had apparently got into action.

After Nancy came Doctor Martin—it was as if the male element surrounded the girl.

She was rather breath-taking and radiant. She wore a coral-pink satin gown, very short and narrow. Her pretty feet were shod in pink stockings and satin slippers. Her dainty arms and neck were white and smooth, and her glorious fair hair was held in place by a string of coral beads.

There are a good many platitudes that are really staggering facts.

"Caught on the rebound," is one.

Raymond was more open to certain emotions than he had ever been in his life. He was sore and bruised; he had lost several beliefs in himself—and was completely ignorant of the big thing that had given him new strength.

He had had the vision of passion through the wrong lens; he had been blinded by the close range, but he *knew* what the vision was. In that he had the advantage of poor Joan.

Harriet T. Comstock

His youth cried out for Youth; he wanted what he had all but lost the right to have. But he in no sense just then wanted Nancy; it was what she represented. She was what Mrs. Tweksbury had said, the kind of girl that men enshrine in their souls and never replace even when they gladly accept a substitute.

"If only—"and then Raymond's eyes looked queer. He was living over the black hour which he did not realize was the hour of his soul's birth. He'd never have that battle again, he inwardly swore, but that was poor comfort.

And then, while talking to Nancy, he grew very gay and light-hearted, like someone who had made a safe passage past the siren's rocks. Not that it mattered, except that one did not want to be shipwrecked. Of course, Raymond knew, he wouldn't forget while he lived, the other thing just past, but it had not wrecked him.

After that dinner nothing would have happened if all sorts of pressure had not been brought to bear. Raymond was affectionately inclined to be kind to Mrs. Tweksbury because he knew he had wronged her faith in him, though she would never know; so he accompanied her whenever she beckoned, and she beckoned frequently and always toward Nancy.

Then Clive Cameron happened, at the crucial moment, to be on the middle of the stage for the same reasons that Raymond was there. Cameron followed Martin's vigorous beckoning, although he was bored to the limit. He liked Nancy and thought her very beautiful, but Cameron had not enshrined any type of woman—a few men are like that. He knew, because he was young and vital and sane, that he had a shrine, or pedestal, in his make-up and if, at any time, he saw a girl that made him forget, for a moment, the profession that was absorbing him just then, he'd humbly implore her to fill the empty niche and after that he would do the glorifying. But if it pleased his uncle to trot him about, he went with charming grace; and because it did not affect him in the least, he played almost boisterously with Nancy and made her jollier than she had ever been in her life.

He made her forget things! Forget The Gap!

Cameron simply knocked unpleasant memories into limbo; he was like a fresh northwest wind—he revived everyone. He made Doris think of David Martin as she first knew him—and naturally Doris adored Cameron. She came near praying that Nancy might, after a fashion, pay her debts for her. But no! she would not influence Nancy—she must be respected in her beautiful freedom as Joan was in hers.

So Doris widened the field of Nancy's vision, and old friends came happily to the front.

It is not wholly ignoble, the marriage market. To understand the game of life is to be prepared, and women like Doris Fletcher were not entirely self-seeking when they presented their best to what they believed should be the best. Nancy was worthy, as Martin often said, to carry on the truest American tradition of womanhood, so it became a reverent concern to help this matter personally, and nationally, on its course.

Young men swarmed about Nancy because, as Mrs. Tweksbury truly said, the *ideal* was in their hearts and they were stirred by it.

And Nancy was radiant and lovely. She blossomed and throbbed—she was happy and appreciative. She was charming to everyone, but ran to Cameron for safety and kept her sweet eyes on Raymond.

So secretly did she do this that no one but Cameron suspected it. The perfectly serene atmosphere that surrounded him and Nancy permitted him to understand the state of affairs.

When a girl uses a man as a buffer between her and others he does not confuse things.

For a short time Cameron debated as to which particular man Nancy wanted him to save her for while he was preserving her from the mass. It did not take him long to decide. He grinned at the truth when it struck him. He was surprised, as men usually are, at a woman's choice of males. Cameron liked Raymond; thought him a good sort, but herd-bound.

"But Nancy's got the brand mark, too," he reflected. "They're both headed in the same direction, only Raymond doesn't know it—a woman always finds things out first, and it's up to me, I guess, to lasso Raymond for her."

So Cameron took up the "big brother" burden and steered the unsuspecting Raymond to his fate.

Cameron did this in a masterly way. He blinded everyone except Nancy.

Doris sighed with content, and Martin lifted his eyes in praise and gratitude. Mrs. Tweksbury, like a war-horse smelling powder, saw danger to her plans and quickened Raymond to what was going on.

At first Raymond was relieved—he wished Cameron good luck. Having done that, he began to wonder if he really did?

There was something unutterably sweet about Nancy: she was so purely the kind of woman that made life a success. Why should he play straight into Cameron's hand? If Nancy really preferred Cameron, why, then—but did she?

This was interesting. He took to watching; presently he concluded that Cameron was a conceited ass.

After a short time Raymond began to feel the pressure of Nancy's little body in his arms—when their dance was over. He began to resent other arms about her. Her eyes were lovely —so blue and sympathetic. She never set a man guessing. Raymond had had enough of guessing!

About that time Mrs. Tweksbury added an urge to her heart's desire that she little suspected.

"Ken," she remarked one morning, "I dropped into the Brier Tea Room yesterday." It was the *brier* that signified the meaning of the place to the old lady.

"Do you remember?"

Raymond nodded. Did he *not* remember!

"The place is quite ordinary now—but the food is still superior. Miss Gordon has come to her senses."

"Has she?" Raymond asked, lamely.

"Yes. And that girl—do you remember her, Ken?"

Raymond nodded again.

"Just as one might expect," Mrs. Tweksbury rattled on, keeping to her one-tracked idea of things, "the minx ran off with a man, never considering Miss Gordon at all."

"I doubt if Miss Gordon could see any one's side but her own," ventured Raymond.

"Ken, that's unjust. The girl was a little fraud, and I think Miss Gordon is heartily ashamed of herself for having resorted to such cheap methods to get trade. She has young Scotch girls helping her now. No more tricks, says Miss Gordon."

There was a pause.

"I thought for a time, Ken, that that girl was one of our kind—risking far too much. I'm not usually mistaken in blood, but—the creature was a good counterfeit; I'm glad she's gone. Say what you will, we older women know the young man needs protection as well as the young women."

"Oh! Aunt Emily, cut it out!"

Raymond got up and stalked about. This added to Mrs. Tweksbury's uneasiness.

For days after that talk Raymond had his uncomfortable hours. He wished he knew about the girl of the tea room. It was "the girl" now. If she were only unscathed the future would be safer for everyone.

But how could he—Raymond was getting into the meshes— how could he run to safety and happiness and forget, if he had really harmed, in any way, a girl who might have cared? The difference between playing with fire and being burned by fire was clear now.

Had that hour, when the beast in him rampaged, killed forever the ideal she had had? Was she saved by his madness? Or had she been driven on the rocks? If he only knew!

Raymond still had moments when he believed that the girl would materialize in his own safeguarded world. He had seen a resemblance now and then that turned him cold, but when all was said and done there was no reason, no unforgivable reason, for him to exile himself from life.

And when he was in this state of mind, Cameron was like vinegar on a raw wound to him. Cameron's joyousness, born of indifference, passed for assurance based, as Raymond believed, on his asinine conceit.

"He takes Nancy for granted," Raymond grumbled, "and he need not be too sure—why, only last night—"

Then Raymond recalled the look in Nancy's eyes.

As a matter of fact, while Raymond was no better nor worse than the average young man visiting the marriage market, Nancy had selected him for worship and glorification. He loomed high and then, suddenly, he loomed alone!

There is that in woman which selects for its own. It is not merely the instinct of mating, it is choice, in the main, and makes either for success or failure—but it always has its compensations in that vague, groping sense that calls for its own. The world may look on wondering or dismayed, but the woman, under the crude exterior, clings to the ideal she sought.

With Nancy and Raymond conditions favoured the moment. Nancy had a wide choice and she was radiantly happy. Doris saw to it that the girl should see and hear the best of everything and be free to live her days unfettered.

Raymond had inherited the purest desires for family and home—he had never seen them gratified in his parents' life, so they still lay dormant in his heart. Nancy presently awakened them and Cameron's mistaken attitude drove them into action.

Raymond counted Nancy's charms. Her devotion to her aunt, her unselfish service while her twin sister followed her own devices, Doctor Martin's very pronounced admiration, and Mrs. Tweksbury's ardent affection all carried him along like favouring winds. And presently the constant appearance of Cameron with Nancy lashed Raymond to the amazing conviction that he was in love!

He grew pale and abstracted; the revealment was pouring like light and sun into the depths of his nature. He wished that he was a better man; he thanked whatever god he reverenced that he was not a worse one. He recalled the one foolish episode of his youth with contempt for his weakness and gratitude for the escape—not only for himself but for the unknown girl.

As a proof of the sincerity of his present change of heart he wished above everything that he might find the girl and confess to her, for he felt, beyond doubt, that it would give

Harriet T. Comstock

her joy.

He believed this, not because he wanted to believe it, but because he felt the truth of it, and presently it gave him courage.

But there was Cameron!

Finally Raymond discovered that his business was suffering. He grew indifferent to the exact hour of leaving his office; took no pride in his well-regulated habits. He began to dislike Cameron and he dreamed of Nancy. Day and night he saw her as the safe and sweet solution of all that was best in him. She held sacred what his inheritance reverenced; she was human and divine; she was his salvation—or Cameron's.

At this point Mrs. Tweksbury gave him an unlooked-for stab.

"Well!" she remarked with a groan—she never sighed, "I guess Clive Cameron has got in at the death!"

She looked gruesome and defeated. Raymond grew hot and cold.

"What do you mean?" he asked, and glared shamelessly.

"I mean," Mrs. Tweksbury confronted Raymond as if repudiating him forever, "I mean that you've let the chance of your life slip through your fingers and fall into the gaping mouth of that Clive Cameron. It's disgusting, nothing less!"

"Aunt Emily! What in thunder do you mean? Nancy Thornton has only been here a month; if she's so easily gobbled"—the discussion waxed crude—"I'm sure I could not prevent it—I'm not a gobbler."

"No—you're a fool!"

"Come, come, Aunt Emily." Raymond flushed and Mrs.

Tweksbury grew mahogany-tinted.

"Oh! I know"—two tears—they were like solid balls—rolled down the deep red cheeks. Almost it seemed that they would make a noise when they landed on the expansive bosom.—"I sound brutal, but I'm the female of the species and it hurts to know defeat the—the second time."

"The—second—time?" gasped Raymond.

"Yes—your father! I could—oh! Ken, it is no shame to say it to you—but I could have made him happy, but it came, the chance, too late. Then when you came I pledged my soul that I would try to secure your happiness. I know what you want, need, and deserve, and here is this perfect child—the one woman for you, snatched from under your nose by Clive Cameron who will—" Emily Tweksbury sought for a figure of speech—"who will, without doubt, end in dissecting her!"

"Good Lord!" gasped Raymond. The dramatic choice of words was unnerving him.

"Oh! you men," spluttered Mrs. Tweksbury. "You make me weary—disgusted; you're no more fit to manage your affairs than babies, and your monumental conceit drives sensible women crazy. We ought to ask you to marry us. We ought not wait to see you ruin yourselves and us, too."

"But, Aunt Emily, why in thunder do you think Nancy Thornton cares for me? If she wants Cameron, why shouldn't she have him?"

At this Emily Tweksbury flung her head back and regarded Raymond with flaming eyes.

"You—well!—just what are you? Can't you see? Could you possibly believe any girl would take Cameron if she had you to choose?"

At this Raymond laughed. He laughed with abandon, going the gamut of emotions like a scale. But presently he became quiet, and a rare tenderness overspread his face. He went over to Mrs. Tweksbury and bent to kiss her.

"I never knew before, Aunt Emily," he said, "just what a mother meant. I'm sorry, dear. Upon my word, I'm deadly sorry, but I'm made slow and cautious and mechanical—I'm afraid of making mistakes—and if I have lost because of my weakness, why, you and I must cling the closer."

"Oh! Ken. When you talk like that I feel that I must go and have it out with Nancy!"

"Aunt Emily, hands off!"

Raymond was suddenly stern, and Mrs. Tweksbury bowed before the tone.

But Raymond meant to make sure before he accepted defeat. He spurred himself to the test with the name of Emily Tweksbury on his lips. That name seemed to hold all his responsibilities and hopes—his long-ago past; the only claim upon the future except—And in this Raymond was sincere. His own honest love for the girl who had entered his life so soon after his doubt of himself had had birth made him fear to put his feet upon the broad highway.

But he braced himself for effort and on a stormy, sleety January afternoon he telephoned to Nancy and asked her if she were to be free that evening.

She was. And—to his shame Raymond heard it gleefully—she had a "sniffy little cold" that made going out impossible.

"Are you afraid of sniffy colds?" asked Nancy, "they say they are catching!"

"I particularly like them," Raymond returned.

"We'll have a big fire in the sunken room and," here Nancy gurgled over the telephone, "we'll toast marshmallows."

Raymond presented himself as early as he dared and was told by the maid to go to the sunken room. Believing that Nancy was there awaiting him, he approached with a beaming countenance.

Cameron stood with his back to the roaring fire.

"Hello, Ken!" he blurted, cheerfully. "You look like a gargoyle."

"Thanks!" All the light and joy fled at the sight of the big fellow by the hearth. Dispiritedly, Raymond sat down and resigned himself to what he believed was the inevitable.

Cameron regarded him critically as he might have a puzzling case. Then, having made a diagnosis, he prescribed:

"Sorry to see me here, old chap?"

"Why in thunder should I be?" Raymond glared.

"No reason—but then reason isn't everything. Nancy's a bit off—I'd hate to have her confront that mug of yours, Ken, if I can soften it up any. I came to bring some medicine from Uncle David—he's worried about colds these days. Nancy told me you were coming, she went upstairs to take her dose in private—she told me to stay and give you the glad hand and explain. Somehow you don't look exactly appreciative."

"Sorry!" Raymond found himself relaxing. "Want me to kiss you?"

"Try it! I'd like to have a fling at you. What's up, anyway, Ken? See here, old man, you know there might be any one of twenty fellows here to-night—you ought to be on your knees thanking heaven that it's I—not one of the twenty."

"What the devil do you mean?" Raymond got up, tried to feel resentment but could not.

"Nothing, only I'm going and—well, Ken, don't be an ass. It don't pay."

Raymond tried to think of something to say, but before the right thing occurred he heard Cameron's cheerful whistle cut off by the closing of the heavy front door.

Then he sat down by the fire and did some thinking. It was the kind of concentrated thought that separates the chaff and wheat; foregoes the glitter of romance and reaches out for the guiding, unfailing light of reality.

How long he sat alone Raymond never realized. It seemed like years, then like a moment—but it brought him to Nancy as she stood at the top of the flight of steps leading to the warm, fire-lighted room while the fountain splashed cheerfully and a restless, curious little bird twittered in its cage.

Nancy wore the faintest of blue gowns; a cloudlike scarf fell from her shoulders; her eyes held the full confession of her love as they met the groping in Raymond's.

He opened his arms.

"My darling!" he said, "will you come?"

Slowly, radiantly, Nancy stepped down.

"It seems as if I'd always been coming," she was saying. "I—I don't want to hurry now that I—I see you."

"I—I think I've always been coming, too," Raymond would not take a step, "but I was walking in the dark."

"And I—" but Nancy did not finish her sentence—she had found her heart's desire.

"I'm not worthy," murmured Raymond, pressing the light hair with his lips.

"Neither am I. We'll grow worthy together. It's like finding a beautiful thing we both were seeking. It isn't you or I—alone—it is something outside us that we are going to make—ours."

Spiritually Raymond got upon his knees, humanly he pressed the girl close.

"It's—you—the Thing is—*you*" he whispered, and at that moment knew the last, definite difference between what he now felt and—all that had gone before.

Harriet T. Comstock

CHAPTER XXI

"TO SUFFER SETS A KEEN EDGE ON WHAT REMAINS OF THE AGREEABLE. THIS IS A GREAT TRUTH THAT HAS TO BE LEARNED IN THE FIRE"

It was all so exactly as it should be—the love affair of Nancy and Raymond—that it lacked excitement. There was a moment when Doris and David Martin looked into each other's eyes and sadly smiled; but that was past as it came.

"It's all right, Davey!"

"Of course, Doris, and Bud wasn't in it after all. It was our desire—not his. He seems to feel he ought to be cheered for whooping the thing on; making Raymond jealous, you know."

"Dear boy!"

"Thanks, Doris. He is something worth while."

Mrs. Tweksbury was so expansive in her happiness that she embarrassed Nancy. She fairly bounded over the fragrant garden of new love and scanned the wide pastures beyond.

"Ken, if I can see children in this old house, I'll thank God and depart in peace. Say that you will come here, boy. You know I'm always scuttling overseas. I won't be in the way—but it is the one desire of my shrivelled old heart."

"Aunt Emily, go slow and don't be ridiculous. The idea of your being in the way in your own house!"

"Ken, make Nancy love me. I know I'm gnarled and crusty, but I need what she has to give all the more because of that. I have no pride—I want that girl's love so—that I'd—I'd humble myself."

Raymond kissed her.

"Has she told you of her—her sister—yet?" Mrs. Tweksbury asked.

"Yes. Nancy says that until Joan, that's the name I believe, comes home she cannot leave Miss Fletcher. Nancy must not sacrifice herself."

Raymond was quickly assuming the charms of ownership.

"She always has been," snapped Mrs. Tweksbury, "an unconscious offering. Where is her gad-about sister?"

"I forget—out West somewhere, I believe."

"What is she doing?"

"The Lord knows. I got a very disagreeable impression of her. I didn't do much questioning—Nancy was on the defensive. She adores her sister."

"Bless the child! I have an unpleasant remembrance of the girl, too." Mrs. Tweksbury smiled grimly. "She was always a pert chit, and I believe she is like her disreputable father—you know about him, Ken?"

"Yes—something. Miss Fletcher mentioned him—she says she wants to have a talk later on. But what do I care, Aunt Emily?"

"I should rather like to know, myself." Mrs. Tweksbury sniffed scandal. "I never have been sure about him, but I know he was socially above reproach. If he personally went wrong it is deplorable, but, Ken, if he had his roots in good soil instead of mud, it isn't fatal."

"Bosh! Aunt Emily."

"Bosh! all you want to, boy. It's easy to bosh when you're on the safe side—but neither you nor I can afford to ignore the difference."

"Nancy speaks for herself, Aunt Emily."

"Yes, thank God, and redeems her father. Wait until you see the sister. She was a lovely, distracting imp—but with a queer twist. I shouldn't be surprised a bit if she needs a deal of explaining and excusing."

But when Nancy's wonderful news reached Joan in the tiny Chicago home it made her very tender and wistful.

"Think, Pat, of dear little Nan—going to be married. Married!"

Patricia, who shared all Joan's letters, lighted a cigarette and puffed for a moment, looking into the glowing grate, then she quoted eloquently:

"There was a little woman,
So I've heard tell,
Who went to market,
Her eggs for to sell!"

Joan stared.

"My lamb, for this cause came Nancy and her kind into the world."

"I don't understand, Pat." Joan's eyes were shining and misty.

"Well, what on earth would you do with Nancy if you didn't marry her off? If she were homely she'd have to fill in chinks in other people's lives, but with her nice little basket of eggs, good looks, money, not too much wit, and a desire to please, she just naturally is put up for sale and off she goes!"

"Pat, you are vulgar! Nancy is the finest, sweetest of girls. She would only marry for love."

"Sure thing, my lamb. And she could make love out of— anything."

Joan was thinking of Nancy's capacity for making truth.

"Dear, little, sweet Nan," she whispered.

"Just the right stuff out of which to make successful marriages. Who is the collector, Joan?"

"Pat, you make me angry!" Joan really was hurt.

"She doesn't tell me his name. She says—" here Joan referred to the letter; "'I am going to try and keep him until you come and see him. Joan, he is worth a trip from Chicago.'"

"You are—going?" asked Patricia.

"Pat—I am. Only for a visit, but suddenly I find myself crazy hungry for them all.

"I'll be back in a couple of weeks; I'll only lose three lessons and surely, Pat, you'll forgive me if I desert you for that one glimpse of my darling Nan and her man?"

"I suppose so. But, Joan, don't stay long. I know how the reformed drunkard feels when he's left to his lonesome. He doubts his reformation."

"Pat!" Joan felt the tug of responsibility.

Harriet T. Comstock

The next night Patricia came home with a bedraggled little dog in her arms.

"Where did you find that, Pat?" Joan paused in her task of getting dinner and fondled the absurd creature.

"Oh! he was browsing along like a lost soul, sniffing to find— not a scent, I wager he never had one of his own, but a possible one. Out of all the mob, Joan, he chose me! He came up, nosed around my feet, and then whined delightedly—the old fraud! I picked him up and looked in his eyes—I know the look, Joan. He might be my never-had-brother, there is a family resemblance."

"Pat, how silly."

"No joking, lamb. I couldn't ignore the appeal—besides, he'll keep me straight while you are away."

"Pat—come with me!" Joan bent over the dog, who already showed his preference for Patricia.

"I cannot, Joan. The trade is growing—I am planning an exhibition. I'm ashamed to say it, but the business is getting into my gray matter. No—go to your duty, lamb—the pup and I will get acquainted and make up for lost time."

And while Joan made preparations to go to New York, and while Doris and Nancy planned to make her visit a success, something occurred that changed all their lives. It was the epidemic of influenza. The shrouded and menacing Thing approached like the plague that it was to prove itself. It was no discerner of people; its area was limitless, it harvested whence it would and, while it was named, it was not understood.

David Martin ordered Doris and Nancy out of town at once.

"You may not escape," he said, "but your best chance is in the open. Besides, you'll leave us freer here."

"But Joan—David!"

"Joan be hanged! Can't she get to Ridge House?"

"Of course. But I wanted to have her here to—to justify herself. Emily Tweksbury is trying to make a tragedy of Joan. I'm afraid Ken suspects her—his awful silences are insulting— I wanted to—to show her off."

"Nonsense, Doris! But this is no time for squibbling. Scoot!"

"But—you, David!"

"I? Oh! I'm all right. Remember I have Bud. Why, the chap is pulling up his sleeves and baring his breast to the foe. I'm going to stand close by him."

Martin's eyes shone.

"David, if anything should happen to you—" Doris paused.

"I'll run down now and then," Martin took the thin, delicate hands in his. "I'll come—when I feel tired."

"You promise, David?"

"I—swear it."

So Doris took Nancy away. A tearful, woe-begone Nancy who clung to Raymond with the tenacity of a love that faces a desperate situation.

"Beloved," whispered Raymond, "I'm going to get Aunt Emily out of the danger zone and then I'll come to you. If this Joan of yours has arrived—we'll be married, you and I, at once. We don't care for the society fizz. This epidemic makes you think about—taking joy while you can."

"Yes, Ken—if—if Joan will stay with Aunt Dorrie."

Harriet T. Comstock

"Well, by heaven! She'll have to stay. I'm not going to let them cheat me!"

To this Nancy gave a look that thrilled Raymond as he had never been thrilled before—it was supreme surrender.

And presently in the stricken city gaiety and laughter seemed to die away in the black, swooping shadow.

"When you use up all you know," Clive Cameron said one night to David, "you still keep hunting about for something else, don't you?"

Martin nodded. Both men were worn and haggard. They were fighting in the front ranks with the men of their profession—fighting an unknown foe, but bravely gaining confidence.

"The death rate is lower to-day, Bud. Hang to that!"

"I do, Uncle Dave. If it still goes down, will you take a vacation?"

"You are willing to go it alone, boy?"

"Yes!" grimly. "I know I must."

The two men relaxed and smoked peacefully, their feet stretched out to the fire. Their long day warranted this pause. They were strangely alike; strangely unlike. Occasionally their eyes met and then their lips smiled.

They were friends. The blood tie was incidental.

"You ought to be married, Clive."

"Why, especially?"

"A man should; a doctor especially. A wife and children are better to come home to than a pipe—and a housekeeper."

"You managed to buck along, Uncle Dave."

"Yes—buck along! I couldn't make up my mind to—"

"I understand, Uncle Dave. Miss Fletcher is great stuff—she makes other women look cheap."

"Bud, some women are like that."

"I suppose so."

Both men shook the ashes from their pipes—there was a night's work ahead.

Martin stared at the young face opposite. It was a strong, kind face—a face waiting for the high waves to strike it. Martin seemed never to have known the boy, really, before.

"Bud, suppose you never find your woman?" he asked, huskily.

"All right, then I'll peg along with that much lacking. Oh! I know what you are thinking of, Uncle Dave. I've been through it—and turned it down! Ever since I can remember I've kept a grip on myself by remembering you!"

"Good God, boy!" Martin choked; "I'm a poor model. At the best I've been—neutral."

"Like hell you have!" irreverently ejaculated Cameron, pleasantly. "Why, Uncle Dave, you've got muscle all over you from fighting the demon in you, but you have no ugly scars. We can look each other in the eyes as we couldn't—if there were scars. It's all right, Uncle Dave. We'll get Mother here before long and have a bully time."

Martin could not speak for a moment; he was looking ahead to the time when he'd have only this boy and his mother!

"Well, what's up, Uncle Dave?"

Harriet T. Comstock

"Bud, have you suspected anything about Miss Fletcher? Her health, I mean?"

"Yes. I've studied about her, too."

"And kept quiet, eh?"

"Sure! But, Uncle Davie, if we—" Martin blessed him for that "we"—"if we could get her outside of herself, it would do a lot for her. I've a hunch that you have let her get on the shelf. I wouldn't if I were you! I know it may be necessary to keep her to rules, but she thinks too much about the rules; they cramp her. When Nancy marries—what then?"

"The Lord knows!"

"Where's that other girl—Joan?"

Martin's face hardened.

"Living her life. *Her* life," he said.

"Anything—dirty about it?" Cameron asked.

"No. So far as I can find out, she's just taking what she calls *her own.*"

"Well, why shouldn't she, Uncle Dave? By all that's holy why shouldn't a woman have her own as well as a fellow? Just because she was born to petticoats doesn't mean that she's born to all the jobs men don't want."

"There are certain things the world exacts of a woman, Bud."

"What, for instance, Uncle Dave?"

Martin considered. He was a just man, but he was prejudiced.

"Self-sacrifice, for one thing!"

"Who says so? Who benefits most by her self-sacrifice?" Cameron flushed as he rambled on. "We may split on this rock, Uncle," he blurted. "Think of my mother—I sort of resent it, because I *am* a man, that we idealize virtues and plaster them on women when we know jolly well, if we lathered them on ourselves, we'd cave in under them. It's up to the woman! That's what I say. Let her select her own little virtues and see to it that she squares it with her soul and then men—well, men keep to the right and keep moving!"

Having flared forth, Cameron laughed at his own fireworks.

"Joan is selfish, Nancy quite the reverse." Martin's brows drew together. "Don't be an ass, Bud!"

"What's this Joan doing?"

"Thinking she's gifted," snapped Martin.

"How is she to find out if she doesn't try? Is Miss Fletcher paying for the racket?"

"No. That's the rub. The girl's paying for it herself. Smudging herself doing it, too. A woman can't escape the smudge."

"Oh! well"—Cameron was tiring of it all—"it's when the smudge sticks that counts. If it is only skin deep, it doesn't matter."

"But—a woman, Bud—well, skin matters in a woman."

"Who says so? Oh! chuck it, Uncle Dave. Which shall it be— bed for an hour or a rarebit at Tumbles and then—on to the fight?"

"What time is it?"

"Eleven-thirty."

Harriet T. Comstock

"Bud, let us have another look at our salvage before we choose; if we find them sleeping, we'll take the rarebit as a recompense for a night's sleep."

And together they went out into the night. Two tired men who had done a stiff day's work—but felt that they must make sure before they sought rest for themselves.

*   *   *   *   *

And Joan and Patricia faced the epidemic as so many of the young did—nothing really *could* happen to them, they believed—and Chicago was not paying so heavy a toll.

"We'll take a little extra care with food and sleep and wet feet," Joan cautioned, "and I'll put off my visit, Pat, for awhile."

"And, Joan," Patricia said, laughingly, "keep your mouth shut in the street!"

The four little rooms were sunshiny and warm; Joan sang hour by hour; worked at her music and "made the home," while Patricia kept to her rigid hours and designed marvellous things in which other women revelled.

Since Nancy had gone South and her beloved was absent, Joan felt that her duty was to Patricia. Without being able to classify her feeling she clung to Patricia with a nameless anxiety.

She taught the little dog to fetch Patricia's slippers to the living-room fire; she always had dinner ready when, tired and frail, Patricia appeared with that glad light in her eyes.

"You act as if I, not you, were going away, my lamb," Patricia often said; "but you are a blessing! And Cuff"—she leaned down and gathered the small, quivering dog in her arms—"and Cuff runs you a close second."

Cuff wagged his stubby tail excitedly. He was a proud creature,

The Shield of Silence   285

a proof of what could be done with a bad job, and he had all the snobbishness that is acquired, not bred in the bone. He slept on the foot of Patricia's bed and forgot back alleys. He selected tidbits with the air of one who knew not garbage cans, but he redeemed all shortcomings by his faithful love to her who had rescued him. The melting brown eyes found their highest joy in Patricia's approval, and a harsh word from her brought his diminutive tail between his legs for an hour.

It was April when Patricia came up the stairs, one night, laggingly. Cuff was on the landing with his token of devotion. The girl picked him up, kissed his smooth body and went on, more slowly. Joan had the table set for the dainty dinner by the broad western window. She turned when Patricia entered.

"What's the matter, Pat?" she asked.

"Nothing, only Cuff is growing heavy."

"Are you tired?"

"Not a bit. What a wonder you are, Joan! That table is a dream with those daffodils in the green bowl. Old Syl was right—you put the punch in home!"

"There's chicken to-night, Pat. I plunged on the strength of what my Professor said to-day."

There were times when Joan wondered if Patricia was not insisting upon home more for her sake than her own.

"What did she say, Joan?"

"That next winter I might—sing!"

"Bully! But you sing now—like several kinds of seraphs. Warble while I make ready for dinner, Joan."

So Joan sang as she flitted from kitchen to dining room.

Harriet T. Comstock

"I'll take the high road and you take the low road
And I'll get to Scotland before you—"

she rippled, and Patricia joined in:

"I'll get to Scotland before you!"

Then she said, from the bedroom beyond:

"I know what it is in your singing that gets us, Joan. It's the whole lot more than words can express."

"Of course! That's high art, Pat! Come on, dearie-thing, you must carve."

"Now, Scotland"—Patricia issued forth in a lovely gown and Joan dropped her long apron and appeared a happy reflection of Patricia's magnificence—"Scotland stands for everything your soul wants when you sing. Not a place—but—everything."

"Yes. That's what I feel," Joan replied, quite seriously.

Patricia did not eat much that evening, but she gave the impression that she was doing so.

The girls always disposed of the dishes, after dinner, in a wizard-like manner. They disappeared until morning—and no questions were asked!

Then, when the meal was over this night, Patricia flung herself on the couch, clasped Cuff in her arms, and asked Joan to sing her to sleep.

"You *are* tired, Pat. Was it a hard day?"

Joan came wistfully to the couch.

"No, not hard, only bracing. They're going to raise me in the summer, Joan. We'll be fat and lazy next winter—and just think: the summer in The Gap lies between!" For that was what Joan's deferred visit had resolved itself into.

"Pat, your cheeks are—red!"

"Joan, don't be silly. I touched them up. I never could see the difference between rouge and dyes and powder and false teeth! They're all aimed at the same thing—and it isn't mastication, either. It's how you handle the aids to beauty."

"Dear, funny, pretty old Pat!"

"Joan, go and sing!"

That night Cuff was dreaming the old haunting dream about waking up in the gutter when something startled him. It was a very soft call.

"Come up here, Cuff, I want you—close!"

Cuff needed no second invitation! But the closer he got the more nervous he became.

"Cuff, look at me!"

Cuff looked.

"Cuff—once—you wouldn't have looked!"

Cuff denied this by a vigorous whack of his stumpy tail.

There were a few minutes more during which Patricia said some very remarkable things about being glad that children and dogs could look at her; and that Joan felt happy with her, and that love had something to say for itself if you didn't wrong it, and then Cuff voluntarily jumped from the bed and scampered into Joan's room. Joan was sleeping and Cuff had to tug rather savagely at her sleeve before he attracted her attention. But when Joan was awake every sense was alert.

"What's the matter?" she asked, but while she was speaking she was on her way to Patricia's room.

Patricia was tossing about and laughing gently; she was insisting that she was going up the Climbing Way and that the travelling was hard and the weather hot! For a moment Joan stood still. All her strength deserted her, but in that instant she knew the worst, as people do at times—when the end is near!

It was only three days for Patricia and she never realized the truth for herself. A nurse, a weary but faithful doctor, and Joan kept her company on the Climbing Way which got easier toward the top.

"You take the high road and I'll take the low road
But I'll get to Scotland before you—"

It was Patricia who sang, not Joan, and then she laughed gaily.

"I bet I will beat you out, Joan—but it wasn't—Scotland, you know it—was—home!"

Just before the top was reached Patricia grew quiet and grave. She clung to Joan with one hand and patted Cuff with the other.

"I think," she whispered, "that when dogs and little children can look you in the eye, God can!"

She did not speak much after that—but she sang in fragments, hummed when very tired, and murmured—"Nice little old Joan and Cuff," just before she reached—home!

It was all so crushingly sudden that Joan was dazed and could not feel at all. Fortunately, the nurse arranged to stay with her for a week, and the doctor acted, through all his burdened days, as if an extra load was really a comfort to him. He asked

Joan what steps he should take about Patricia, and Joan stared at him.

"You see, Pat just belonged to me," she explained; "and—and well! must I decide anything just now?"

"I think we must—about the body—you know!" The doctor felt his heart beat quicker as he gazed into the wide, tearless eyes.

"The—the body? Oh! I see what you mean. I—I was going to take Pat home next summer; this summer—but—"

"Perhaps we can arrange to have the body remain here in Chicago until you make plans."

"Oh! if you only could." Joan looked her gratitude.

And so Patricia Leigh was laid to rest in the vault of strangers until the girl who had loved her could realize the thing that had overtaken her.

In the lonely rooms the empty stillness acted like a drug upon Joan. She mechanically performed the small services she used to perform so gladly for Patricia. She held Cuff in her arms as she repeated:

"It cannot be, Cuff, dear, it cannot! Such a terrible thing couldn't happen—not without warning. She *will* come back; she will, Cuff—please don't look so sad!"

It was three weeks after Patricia went that Cuff met Joan as she entered the room—with Patricia's slippers which he had found where Joan had hidden them! The sight of the pathetic little figure touched something in Joan and it sprang to hurting, suffering life.

For hours the girl wept in the dark rooms. She begged for death; anything to dull forever the pain that she could not understand. But the grief saved her and she began to think for herself, since no one was there to think for her. The city was full of sickness and death. Those who could, must do for themselves. Joan had not written home; she wondered what she had done in all the ages since Pat went.

All Patricia's small affairs were in order. Her money and Joan's were banked under both names, and the dreary little home was but an empty shell.

"I've failed—utterly," the girl sobbed over Cuff in her arms; "I told Aunt Dorrie when I found that out—I would go to her."

So Joan sold the furniture and sublet the rooms; she paid her small debts and promised her music teacher that she would continue her work in New York. Then she turned wearily, aimlessly—homeward, with Cuff in her arms.

CHAPTER XXII

"LOVE, HOPE, FEAR, FAITH—
THESE MAKE HUMANITY!"

The trip to New York was always marked in later years, to Joan, by the most trivial occurrences.

The passing to and fro to the baggage car where Cuff, a crumpled and quivering mass, seemed to ask her what it all meant; the sense of eagerness to get to The Gap before it was too late; the determination not to frighten any one she meant to telegraph from New York; she would leave her trunks in the station and take a bag to a little hotel where she and Pat had stayed the night before they fled from New York. So far, all was clear.

So she planned; forgot, and planned again. Between these wanderings and the care of Cuff there were long hours of forgetfulness and a sound of rushing water—or was it the train plunging through the dark?

Once in New York, with Cuff trotting behind, Joan seemed to gather strength—but not clear vision. She went to the small hotel and secured a room. She meant to telegraph and buy her ticket South—but instead she fed Cuff, took a little food herself, and fell asleep. It was late when she awakened to a realization of acute suffering that seemed confused and spasmodic. It was like being partially conscious. She was fright-ened and tried to fix upon some direct and immediate means

Harriet T. Comstock

of securing help for herself. She did not want to call assistance from the office, so she got up and dressed and half staggered downstairs. It needed all her effort to hold to one thought long enough to accomplish anything.

First there was Cuff. She must get Cuff, quiet his nervousness, and feed him. Then with that in mind she took food herself—as much as she could swallow. It was while she was forcing herself to this task that Doctor Martin came, like an actual presence, to her consciousness.

Why had she not thought of him before?

"Uncle Davey!" she murmured and her eyes filled with tears. Of course! She would take a cab to Doctor Martin's office and then everything would be solved. He would take care of her; send word to The Gap; protect Aunt Doris and Nancy from shock. She began to laugh quietly, tremblingly—she was safe at last. Safe!

It was after ten o'clock when she paid her taxi driver in front of Martin's office and dismissed him. Gathering Cuff in one aching arm and clutching her bag she slowly, painfully mounted the steps without noticing the sign bearing a new name.

If anything were needed to prove how detached Joan had been for the past year or two it was this ignorance concerning the arrangement between Martin and his nephew. Had she not been on the border of delirium she would have recalled certain things which would have guided her; as it was she felt, dazedly, for the bell, pressed the button, and to the maid who responded she faintly said:

"I—I want the doctor." She looked, indeed, as if this were shockingly true.

"It's past office hours," stammered the girl, a little scared; "but perhaps if you come in—"

Joan staggered in and, seeing a door open at the end of the hall, reached it, entered, and sank down in a chair with the astonished eyes of Clive Cameron upon her!

He was ready for his rounds—was on the way, then, to his hospital; it was Martin's pet institution and Cameron's first care in the morning.

"I'm—tired," Joan informed him. "Please take care of—Cuff!"

And then everything went black and quiet.

Never in all his life had Cameron had anything so surprising happen to him. He looked at the girl, whom he managed to carry to the couch; he turned to the dog whose faithful eyes rather steadied him, then he applied all the remedies that one does at such times. Eventually Joan revived, but she stared vacantly at the face above her and did not attempt to speak.

Presently Cameron called in his nurse.

"I think it is brain fever," he explained to the cool, capable woman who asked naturally:

"Who is she?"

"The Lord knows."

"Where did she come from? Where does she belong?"

"The Lord knows. She just came in with the dog and then dropped after asking me to care for—for Cuff—yes, that's what she called him—then she went off."

"It's a duck of a dog," the nurse remarked as one does make inane remarks at a critical time. Then:

"Have you looked in her bag?"

Harriet T. Comstock

"Certainly not!"

"We had better." And they did.

There was a trunk key, seventy-five dollars, and a letter signed "Syl," and frivolously dilating upon a man named John and loads of love to Miss Lamb!

"Well!" said the nurse, "and as one might expect, no heading, date, or any sensible clue—and the envelope missing. We must label this patient, I suppose, as Miss Lamb. The articles of clothing are unmarked. Queer all around!"

"We must get her into the hospital at once," Cameron replied. The doctor in him was getting into action.

"Can we manage her in my car?"

"Yes, Doctor."

"Then get busy. Call her Miss Lamb when you have to answer questions. We can find out about her later. Where's that dog?"

Cuff was making himself invisible. He was under the couch.

"Have him fed and taken care of, Miss Brown—tell the maid."

Joan leaned against Cameron on the way to the hospital while Miss Brown kept a finger on her pulse. The girl's body acted mechanically, but the brain was clogged.

Day by day in the white, quiet hospital room the battle for her life went on; day by day outside effort was made to trace her and find her friends.

"You wise-looking brute," Cameron often thought as he regarded Cuff at the day's end; "why can't you tell what you know?"

But Cuff simply wagged his stump and slunk off. Life was becoming too puzzling for him.

Cameron studied advertisements and certain columns in the papers, but no one seemed to have missed the pretty young creature in the Martin Sanatorium.

"It's the very devil of a case!" Cameron declared, and set about erecting some sort of foundation upon which "Miss Lamb" might repose without causing too much unhealthy curiosity.

Eventually, Joan was simply a bad case of Doctor Cameron's. One from out of town. Her folks trusted him, but were too distant to visit the girl.

Cameron considered telegraphing for Martin, who was at The Gap, but he knew that sooner or later he must rely upon himself alone, and so he began with "Miss Lamb."

The days and weeks dragged on. There were ups and downs, hopes and discouragements, but through them all Joan looked dazedly at Cameron, and if she ever showed intelligence it was when he spoke to her in a perfectly new set of tones that were being incorporated into his voice and which seemed to disturb her. To all questions, as to names, the girl in the dim room returned a dull stare and silence, but there were times when she deliriously rambled intimate confidences. When these times occurred, Cameron, if he chanced to be present, ordered the nurse from the room and listened alone. He was relieved to hear that the patient rarely spoke when he was not with her.

Joan dwelt upon her failure—her longing to go to Pat.

These items Cameron recorded in a small red book, for his memory was none too good and he was busy to a dangerous degree.

Then, again, the sick girl depicted the night of the storm—the shock and consequent flight.

Harriet T. Comstock

"But," she pleaded piteously, holding the strong hand that anchored her to life, "he won! he won, and it is always going to be all right. Oh! if he could only know!"

There would be a pause always ending in: "I want Pat."

"Where is—Pat?" Cameron ventured.

"Home!" And then, weakly, but with a wrenching pathos, Joan sang—"*I'll get to—Scotland*—no! *home*—before you!"

"Come, come, now!" Cameron pressed the thin form down. "You know you've got to live—for Pat."

"Yes—for Pat." And then Joan would sleep.

It was a day in late May that Cameron noticed a change in his case. She was weaker, but steadier. She seemed to connect him with something in the recent past, and that encouraged him. All her previous conscious moments had been like detached flashes.

"What was it you said I must live for?" she asked Cameron. "I've forgotten."

"For everything," he replied, throwing off his coat and gripping the promising moment. "You're not the kind to slink out. Besides, you've got to tell me about your folks. Give them a chance to prove themselves and set things straight." Cameron watched the struggle on the thin face. "And there is—Pat!" he added.

Joan looked amazed and then quivered.

"Yes, Pat, of course!"

There was a long pause, the consciousness was seeking something to which it might cling. Something forever eluding it.

A day or two later Cameron brought the dog into the sick room. Joan turned as she heard steps.

"Cuff!" she cried and then, as the dog leaped on to her, she sobbed and murmured over and over: "Pat's little Cuff; Pat's little Cuff."

Her way on ahead was safer after that—safer but more secretive.

As Joan got control of her thoughts she became more silent and watchful. She questioned the nurse and found out where she was and how long she had been there; she smiled with her old touch of humour when she was called Miss Lamb but gave thanks that she had a name not her own!

She regarded Cameron with deep gratitude, but drove him to a corner by insisting that he tell her how much she owed him.

Cameron, having her purse under lock and key, at home, told her she owed the hospital fifty dollars.

At that Joan laughed, and the sound gave Cameron more hope than he had known for some time, but it seemed to mark, also, Joan's complete self-control.

Often she lay for hours with closed eyes and wondered with a bit of self-pity why she had not been discovered? Had she so completely dropped from the lives of those she loved that they had forgotten her? She did not know, for some time to come, of the letters to her that were returned to The Gap! She was never to know, fully, the anguish that Doris Fletcher was enduring in her mistaken determination not to hamper the girl who was testing her strength.

While David Martin rated her for ingratitude and carelessness; while Nancy's face set in resentment and disapproval, Doris smiled and insisted that she would not judge until Joan explained.

Harriet T. Comstock

"Of course," she added, "if anything were really wrong Joan or Patricia would write. They are probably away on business—and at the worst they will soon let me know when to expect them. Joan was always a poor correspondent."

"Would you like to have me go to Chicago?" Martin asked.

"David, would you go if—it were your boy?" Doris hung on his answer.

"I jolly well wouldn't! I'd let the scamp learn the whole lesson."

"Very well, then I do not want you to go to Chicago!"

Joan, slowly recovering, could hardly have explained to herself why she was so secretive, but more and more she determined not to go to The Gap and open her heart to Doris until she was able to command the situation. Since she had, for some reason, dropped from their lives, she would wait. Meanwhile, her heart ached with the pity of it all.

She wondered how the name of Lamb had ever been attached to her, and finally she decided to ask Cameron about it.

It was Cameron's custom, now, to delay his call upon Joan until late afternoon. When he was on his way to dinner he took a half hour or more to sit beside her bed and indulge in various emotions.

So long as Joan had been a desperate case she had no individuality at all, except scientifically.

She was bathed, and eventually her hair was cut, not shaved—the nurse put in a plea at the cutting point—and she was fed and made to sleep; but gradually, as she emerged from the shadowy boundary, she assumed different proportions.

Cameron concluded that her reticence, now her brain was

growing clearer, came from a determined effort to cover her tracks and perhaps those of a man—unworthy, undoubtedly, and Cameron believed this man to be the "Pat" to whom his patient had so frantically referred in her raving.

There had evidently been a strenuous scene in which Pat had figured and through which he and the girl had emerged rather deplorably.

Cameron also arrived at the conclusion that the young woman in his care must be made to take a keener interest in life than she seemed to be taking, or her recovery would be slower than it ought to be, according to physical indications. The growing silence worried him; he wished that he could gain her confidence, not in order to gratify curiosity, but to enable him to be of real service.

One afternoon he called at the hospital reinforced with a box of roses.

The flowers had an immediate effect upon Joan. She buried her face in them and closed her eyes, and then Cameron saw large, slow tears escaping the close-shut lids. He welcomed these. Presently Joan asked:

"How is—is—Cuff?"

"Oh! he's ripping," Cameron replied; "after seeing you he seemed to size up the situation and come to terms."

"How—how did you happen to know his name?" This had been a burning curiosity for the past week.

"You happened to mention it when you keeled over in my office. Cuff was apparently your one responsibility. We found your name in a letter—Miss Lamb."

The roses hid the quivering face while a new and hurting question for the first time entered in. Then:

"Did—did I go to your office? I thought I—was brought here from—"

"You were brought here, all right," Cameron felt his way slowly along the opening path; "Miss Brown and I had rather a vigorous trip with you—in my automobile."

"Cuff belonged to—to Pat!" Joan remarked, irrelevantly. She was forcing her thought back to the blank period lying between the hotel and the hospital. Gradually it brightened and a smothered sob found place in the roses.

"So that is why they have left me alone!" Joan reflected; "but oh! how frightened they must be!"

"I rather imagine Pat must be fairly well used up wondering about you," Cameron was saying as if the whole matter were an everyday affair, but rather annoying; "queer things happen in a big city. We've done our best to locate your friends; I think some of the officials I have consulted have their doubts as to my mental condition. I kept under cover as well as I could until you were well enough to act for yourself."

"Thank you—oh! thank you." This very faintly and brokenly.

"You see, you are one of the cases that prove that an impossibility is—possible. Truth-stronger-than-fiction idea. But if you would like me to communicate with Pat, I'll be glad to help you."

"No—I will wait now." Joan drew her lips close.

Cameron controlled his features while he listened, but he never referred to Pat again.

"I've sometimes thought," Cameron spoke calmly, "that you might have been looking for my uncle, Doctor Martin, when you stumbled into his old office. I could not flatter myself that you were bent upon obtaining my services."

At this Joan astonished Cameron almost as much as if she had sat up in her coffin.

She rose, as though propelled by a spring, she stared at him and then, as slowly, sank back, still holding him with her eyes that seemed preternaturally large.

"Oh! come now!" Cameron exclaimed. "What's up?" He took her hand and bent over her and to his amaze discovered that she was laughing! He touched the bell. Things were bewildering him—Miss Brown always managed trying situations by reducing them to normal. She responded at once; cool, serene, and capable.

"Nerves?" she asked. And then took command. She raised Joan and settled the pillows into new lines; she removed the roses almost sternly—she disliked the nuisance of flowers in a sick room.

"There, now!" she whispered to Joan, "take this drink and go to sleep like a good girl."

In the face of this sound common sense laughing was out of the question. Joan pretended sleep rather than risk another: "There, now!"

But her recovery was rapid after that day. Like a veil withdrawn she reflected upon the past as if it were, not a story that was told, but a preface to the real story that her life must be.

The folly, the irresponsibility, no longer dismayed her, but gave her reasons and arguments.

She wanted to live at last! She wanted to go home and separate herself forever from the cheap, theatrical thing she had believed was freedom! She saw the folly of it all; she seemed an old woman regarding the dangerous passage of a younger one.

She realized her own selfishness in her demand for

self-expression. What had she expressed while others fixed their faithful eyes on duty?

Nancy shone high and clear in those dull hospital days. Nancy who demanded so little, but who trod, with divine patience, the truer course.

"Well, Nan shall have her own!" Joan thought, and gripped her thin hands under the bedclothes. "I'll strive for Nan as I never have for myself."

Out of the debris of the feverish past Joan held alone to Patricia. Strange, it seemed to her, that the dead girl should have grown to such importance, but so it was. Patricia was the real, the sacred thing, and she planned the home-bringing of the dear body and the placing of it on the hillside in The Gap.

And through the convalescing days Cameron had his place, like a fixed star.

Often worn by the day's silent remorse and earnest promise as to the future, Joan looked to that hour when Cameron, calm, serious but cheerful, sat by her bedside—a strong link between the folly of the past and the hope of the times on ahead.

Vaguely she recalled the blurred weeks of fever and pain, and always his quiet voice and cool touch held part.

"And to think," Joan could but smile, "that he does not know me—but I know who he is just as I knew about—" She could not name Raymond yet—she could only think kindly of him when she held to the days before that last, tragic night.

And Cameron, meanwhile, was drawing wrong conclusions. Not that they changed his personal attitude toward the girl whose life he had helped save. To him she was a human creature whose faith in her future must be restored as her body was in the process of being. Cameron believed in stepping-stones and was utterly opposed to waste of any kind.

"She's paid her debt and his, too, I wager," Cameron often muttered; "that's the devil of it all, and she'll go on and perhaps down—if she doesn't get a start up. If I could only get hold of her folks—it would help!"

But Joan held him at bay when he ventured on that line.

"When I am quite well," she said with gentle dignity, "I am going home and do my own explaining."

"Are you considering—them?" Cameron frowned at her.

"I am—as I never have before!"

To this silence was the only reply.

Presently Joan made her first big stride toward complete recovery. She forsook her bed during the day and, in pink gown and dainty cap—procured by Miss Brown—she passed from a "case" to an individual.

The twilight hour now became something of a function and Cameron dropped his professional manner with his outdoor trappings and appeared, often, as a tired but very humanly interesting young man.

He talked of safe, ordinary things, he brought books and flowers, and while Miss Brown kept a rigid appearance, she inwardly sniffed—or the equivalent.

And then came the Sunday before Joan was to leave the hospital. It happened to be Easter, and a woman was singing in the little chapel down the hall. The room doors were open and the sweet words and melody floated in to the silent listeners— Joan pictured them as she sat and felt her tears roll down her cheeks.

"Some—are going out!" she thought, "and others, like me, must go on. And here we all are with walls between, but our doors open to:

> "He weaves the shining garments
> Unceasingly and still
> Along the quiet waters
> In niches of the hills."

The words seemed to paint, in the narrow room, the dim Gap. The sound of the river was in Joan's ears and she knew that the niches of the safe hills where her loved ones waited, were full of the spring blossoms.

> No leaf that dawns to petal,
> But hints the Angel-plan.

Joan looked up and saw Cameron at the doorway. He almost filled it, and his eyes grew troubled as he noted the thin, white, tear-wet face.

"Shall I close the door?" he asked.

"No. Please do not. I like to think that all the others, down the corridor, and I are together—listening, growing better!"

"Oh! I see." Cameron tossed aside his coat and sat down.

"I—I don't think you do," Joan smiled at him; "I think I puzzle you terribly, but some day I am going to explain every-thing. All my life I have been, as I am now, in a narrow little room—peeping out and never touching others any more than I am touching"—she pointed to the right and left—"my neighbours, here. But we were all listening to much the same thing then as now.

"I am going"—here Joan dashed her tears off—"I am going somehow to pull the walls down and know really!"

"Bully!" Cameron had a peculiar feeling in his throat. Then added: "I cut something out of a paper the other day that seemed to me to hold all the philosophy necessary for this tug-of-war we call life. Here it is!"

"Read it, please," Joan dropped her eyes.

"A shipwrecked sailor, buried here, bids you set sail. Full many a gallant bark, when he was lost, weathered the gale."

"Isn't that good, gripping stuff? I've caught the sense of it, and when I get to thinking—well, of such as lie in many of these little rooms, I'm glad—you're—setting sail!"

"Thank you, Doctor Cameron. I am setting sail! I thought I was before—I see the difference now. And to-morrow—"

"And to-morrow—where are you going—to-morrow?"

Cameron was ill at ease.

"To a little hotel—I will give you the address in the morning. It is from there that I will set sail."

CHAPTER XXIII

"NO ONE CAN TRAVEL THAT ROAD FOR YOU, YOU MUST TRAVEL IT FOR YOURSELF"

David Martin came into the living room of Ridge House bringing, as it seemed, the Spring with him. He left the door open and sat down. He was in rough clothes; he was brown and rugged. He was building, with his own hands, much of the cabin at Blowing Rock. He had never been more content in his life. He often paused, as he was now doing, and thought of it.

The hard winter's work was over and Martin felt the spring in his blood as he had not felt it in many a year.

Things were going to suit him—and they had had a way of eluding him in the past. Perhaps, he thought, because he had always wanted them just his way.

Somewhere, above stairs, Doris was singing, and Nancy from another part of the house was calling out little joyous remarks.

"Two telegrams in one day, Aunt Doris. Such riches!"

Doris paused in her song long enough to reply:

"Joan may come any day, Nan, dear. It is so like her to act, once she decides."

Martin, sitting by the hearth, reflected upon the injustice of

Prodigal Sons and Daughters—but he smiled.

"They don't deserve it—but it's damnably true that they get it," he mused, irrelevantly.

"Joan's room is a dream, Nan, come and see it!" called Doris, and Nancy could be heard running and laughing to inspect the Prodigal's quarters.

"It looks divine!" she ejaculated. "Push that pink dogwood back a little, Aunt Dorrie—make it like a frame around the mirror for the dear's face."

"How's that, Nan?"

"Exactly—right. Aunt Dorrie?"

"Yes, my dear girl."

"I have the dearest plan—I feel that Ken would love it, but I hate to be the one to propose it."

From his armchair Martin smiled more broadly.

"Perhaps I can do it for you, Nan." Doris spoke abstractedly— she was, apparently, giving more thought to the decorations for the returning wanderer than to the plans of the good child who had remained at her post.

"Well, Aunt Doris, I don't want to wait until next winter to be married. Ken writes that he will have Mrs. Tweksbury safely settled in New York by the first of June—" Emily Tweksbury had fled the influenza and gone to Bermuda only to fall victim to pneumonia. Kenneth Raymond had been summoned, to what was supposed to be her death-bed, but which she indignantly refused to accept as such.

"When women are as old as I, Ken," she had whispered as he bent over her, "they consign them to death-beds too easily.

Harriet T. Comstock

Give me a month, boy, and I'll go back with you."

Kenneth had given her a month, then two weeks extra; he was bringing her back now—a frail old woman, but one in whose heart the determination to live was yet strong.

"But, darling, we'd have to give up the beautiful wedding—Mrs. Tweksbury could never stand the excitement now, or even this summer."

Doris's voice was more suggestive of attention as she now spoke. Martin waited.

"I know, Aunt Dorrie, but I am sure she would rather have me and Ken married than come to our wedding. Listen, duckie! Suppose, after Joan comes, we plan the dearest little service in the Chapel—I'm sure we could snatch Father Noble as he flits by. There would be you and Uncle David and Joan, and perhaps Clive could wrench himself away, and Mary and Uncle Jed—and," a tender pause, "and—Ken and me! We could make the Chapel beautiful with flowers from The Gap—our flowers—and then I could help Ken with Mrs. Tweksbury—for you, Aunt Dorrie, will have Joan."

Martin blinked his eyes. He never admitted a mistiness to the extent of wiping them. He listened for Doris's next words.

"Childie, it sounds enticing and just like you. I will talk it over with Uncle David."

The voices upstairs fell into a silence and Martin got up and paced the room.

A few minutes later Doris came down the stairs and, singing softly, entered the living room.

There was welcome in her eyes; the languor and helpless expression had faded from her face.

"Davey," she said, "I felt the draught—you have left the door open—I knew you were here.

"Oh! Davey, to-day the twenty-year limit seems quite the possible thing. My dear, my dear, Joan is coming home!"

Martin met Doris midway of the big room. He was startled at the change in her.

"I heard that a telegram had come. It's great news, Doris."

"Queer, isn't it, Davey, how one can brace and bear a good deal while there is the necessity, and then realize the strain only when the need is past? Joan says only 'coming home,' but I know as surely as I ever knew anything that it has been for the best and she is coming gladly to me—coming home! I could not have endured the silence much longer."

Martin put his arm around Doris and led her to the hearth. A mild little fire was crackling cheerfully, rather shyly, between the tall jars of dogwood that seemed to question the necessity of the small blaze.

"Davey, I want to talk to you. There are so many things to say if you are absent twenty-four hours. How goes the cabin?"

"Like magic. It will be livable by June or before. The men like to have me pothering around, and I've discovered that one never really has a house unless he helps build it. I'm going to get Bud down the minute I can put a bed up. And, Doris—"

"Yes, Davey."

"I've been eavesdropping, I've been here a half hour. I heard what Nancy said—let the child have her wish!"

"You feel that way, David? I had hoped to have everything rather splendid—to make up for what I could not do for—Merry."

Harriet T. Comstock

"All stuff and nonsense! Give the girl her head. She knows her path and will not make mistakes. What she wants is Raymond and her own life. Nancy is simple and direct; no complications about her. Don't make any for her."

"David, her happiness and peace almost frighten me. You remember how she drooped last summer? Taking her to New York has done more than give her love and happiness. She is quite another girl, so resourceful and clear visioned."

"She's on her own trail, Doris, that's all. Things are right with Nancy. The rule holds."

"But, David, I have not told her yet—"

"Told her?—oh! I see—about the birth mix-up?"

Martin smiled—he always did when the subject was referred to. The humour and daring of it had never lost their zest.

"It is no laughing matter, Davey; as the time draws near when I must tell I am in a kind of panic. I always thought it would be easy; if it had been right why should I know this fear?"

Martin was serious enough now. He folded his arms and leaned back in his chair—he held Doris with his calm gray eyes.

"It seems to me," he spoke thoughtfully, "that you should stand by your guns. You did what you did from the highest motives; you have succeeded marvellously—why upset the kettle of fish, my dear?"

Doris's face softened.

"I think if I had committed murder," she said, "you would try to defend the deed."

"I certainly would!"

They smiled into each other's eyes at this.

"But, David, I am afraid to tell Nancy. Somehow I think the doubt would hurt her more cruelly than the real truth might have. It has always been the not knowing that mattered to Nan—unless what was to be known was a happy thing. Merry was like that, you remember."

"Then why run a risk with Nancy, Doris?"

Martin had the look in his eyes with which he scanned the face of a patient who could not be depended upon to describe his own symptoms.

"I—think—Ken should know."

"What?"

"Why—why—what there is to know!"

"Just muddle him. Nancy would be the same girl, but he'd get to puzzling over her and tagging ideas on her—and to what end, Doris? The girl has the right to her own path and you have, by the grace of God, pushed obstacles from before her, in heaven's name give her fair play and don't—flax out at this stage of the game."

"But, Davey, if in the future anything should disclose the truth, might Ken not resent?"

"I don't see why he should. When the hour struck you could call him into the family circle and share the news. By that time he'd feel secure in his own right about Nancy."

"I'm not afraid of, or for, Joan, Davey." Doris lifted her head proudly. "And, David, I want to tell you now that my coming to The Gap was more on the children's account than my own. I have always felt that here, if anywhere, the truth might be exposed. At first I was anxious; fearful yet hopeful. I know now that The Gap has no suspicions, and I am more and more confident that George Thornton has passed from our lives."

"Very good!" Martin sat up and bent forward in order to take Doris's hands in his own.

"My dear," he said, gently, "have you never thought that—Nancy is—your own?"

"Yes, Davey, I have grown to believe it. She is very like Meredith—not in looks, but in her character and habits. She is stronger, happier than Merry, and oh! Davey, for that very reason I hesitate to touch the beautiful faith and love of the child. I do not want her disillusioned. It would kill her as it did Merry."

"Then, again I caution against risks, especially when the odds are with Nancy, not against her."

The fire burned low—a mere twinkle in the white ashes, then David asked as one does ask a useless question:

"Are those words over the fireplace, Doris?" He puckered his near-sighted eyes.

"I think so. There are carvings and paintings everywhere through the house. One of the Sisters did them. This one is so blackened by smoke that it is all but destroyed—some day I will see what can be done to restore it."

"I like the idea," Martin said. "I mean to have something over my fireplace. It sort of strikes one in the face."

Presently Doris spoke, going back past the interruption:

"Davey, the wonderful thing to me is that while believing Nancy to be Merry's child I find my heart clinging passionately to Joan. I know how you disapprove of her—but I glory in her. Through this anxious time I have been able to follow her, understand her better, even, than I have Nan. Joan has often seemed like—well, like myself set free. I might have been like Joan in many ways. And, Davey, this could not have happened had I known the real truth concerning the girls."

"No, I do not think it could. And it goes to prove my theory that two thirds of the inherited traits are common to us all. The whole business lies in the handling of them by the one third that does come down the line. The thing we know as the ancient law of inheritance. Doris, take my advice and keep your hands off."

"Oh! Davey. To keep my hands off is so easy that it doesn't seem safe or right."

David smiled, then said:

"There are times, Doris, when I fear that you should be taken by the roots and—transplanted. The old soil is used up."

"I—I do not understand, David."

"Don't try! Come, now, I want you to take a rest. Go on the porch in the sun, I'll wrap you warm. I'm going to take Nancy over to the cabin for lunch and plan her wedding with her. This afternoon you and I are going for a drive—the roads have settled somewhat and I want your advice about things to put in my garden."

As he spoke Martin was leading Doris to the piazza, gathering rugs and pillows in one arm as he went.

"I am so happy, David, so unspeakably happy." Doris sank into her pillows and smiled up at the face bending over her. "It's beautiful, all this care and love, and I have a feeling that I will be able, soon, to really live. I have had so much without paying the price."

"And you'd mess it all, would you, Doris, when you don't

know what the price is?"

"No, David, I wouldn't."

Martin walked into the house and whistled to Nancy. She responded, so did the hounds and a new litter of long-eared pups.

Doris, with closed eyes, smiled and then she thought. She, too, was planning for Nancy's wedding—she saw the small altar in the Chapel flower-decked; they must have some music, perhaps Joan would sing one of her lovely, quaint songs—and then Doris slept while the sun lay on her peaceful face and the sound of the busy river soothed her.

*   *   *   *   *

It was like Joan to do exactly what she did.

After two deplorable days in the little hotel—days devoted to collecting her belongings and eating and sleeping—she suddenly found herself so strong that she sent the telegram to The Gap.

Having sent it, she meant to prepare carefully against shock at her appearance by buying a rather giddy hat and coat to offset her short hair and thin body. Cameron had insisted, at the last, that she reserve her cash for emergencies and repay him later.

Joan accepted this solution, and having arrayed herself frivolously she bought Cuff a most remarkable collar which embarrassed the dog considerably. In all the changing events of Cuff's life a collar had not figured, and it was harder to adjust himself to it than to foots of beds and meals served on plates. However, Cuff rose to the emergency and bore himself with credit.

Twice Cameron came to the hotel; twice he took Joan for a drive—"It will help you get on your feet," he explained.

"I—I don't quite see how," she faltered and, as they were driving where once she and Raymond had driven, her eyes were tear-filled. The old, dangerous, foolish past had a most depressing effect upon her.

At Cameron's second attempt to put her on her feet he succeeded, for when he paid his third call, a quaint little note greeted him at the office:

> Thank you—thank you for all that you have done. I will explain everything soon, in the meantime, morally and physically, I am wobbling home.

Cameron's jaw set as he read.

"I'll wait," was what he inwardly swore. And at that moment he was conscious that, for the first time in his career, a woman had got into his system!

When Joan reached Stone Hedgeton she feared that she and Cuff would have to overcome many obstacles before they reached The Gap, for no one was willing to travel the roads.

"There is holes in the river road mighty nigh a yard deep," one man confided. "I ain't going to risk my hoss, nor my mule, nuther!"

It was the mail man who, at last, solved the problem. He had a small car whose appearance was disreputable but whose record was marvellous.

"If you-all," he included Cuff in the general remark, "ain't sot 'bout reaching The Gap at any 'pinted time, I'll scrooge you in. There's a couple of stops to make, and I reckon I'll have to dig us-all out of holes now and then—that shovel ain't in yo' way, is it, Miss?" he asked.

For Joan and Cuff were already among the mail bags and merchandise.

"Nothing is in the way!" Joan replied, "and I'll help you dig us out."

It was just daylight when they started.

It was past noon when, stiff and rather shaken, Joan scrambled out of the old car and, followed by Cuff, noiselessly made her way over the lawn to Ridge House.

She went lightly up the steps, then stood still. Doris Fletcher lay sleeping in the full, warm glow. So quiet was she, so pale and delicate, that for a moment Joan knew a fear that had had its beginning when Patricia passed from life.

The awful uncertainty, the narrow pass over which all travel, were newly realized perils to Joan, and her breath came sharp and quick.

So this was what had happened while she was learning her lessons! She had not learned alone.

"Oh! Aunt Dorrie," she murmured. "You and I have paid and paid—but you never held me back!"

Joan sat down and waited. It was always to be so with her from now on. In that hour a great and tender patience was born that was to calm and guide her future life. She was given, then and there, to draw upon the strength and vision that do not err. And it may have been that in sleep Doris Fletcher, too, was prepared, for when suddenly she opened her eyes upon Joan she was not startled: a gladness that was almost painful overspread her face.

"My darling! You have come at last!" was what she said.

And, as on that night when she had come to plead for freedom, Joan did not, now, rush into human touch. She nodded and whispered:

"I've come as I promised to, Aunt Dorrie. It—it wasn't my chance! Not my big chance, anyhow, but I had to find out, dearie."

"My little girl!"

Joan went nearer; she bent and kissed again and again that radiant face; then, sitting on the floor by the couch, with Cuff huddled close, she touched lightly the high peaks that lay between the parting and this home-coming, but Doris, with that deep understanding, followed laboriously, silently, through the dark valleys.

"I'm rather battered and cropped, Aunt Dorrie—but here I am!"

With this Joan tossed off her hat and voluminous coat.

"Your—hair, Joan? Your beautiful hair!"

"I have been very sick, Aunt Dorrie, my hair and my fat had to go—just enough bones left to hold my soul. But I'm all right now."

"Don't be sorry for me," Joan was pleading, "I'm the gladdest thing alive to-day. I've dropped all the old husks; I've found out just what they are worth, but some of them that seem like husks, dear, are not—I've learned that, too."

"Yes, Joan—and now go on, in just your own way. For a little while I have you to myself. Nancy will take lunch at Uncle David's new bungalow."

There was a good deal of explanation necessary in dealing with Sylvia's part in the past—Doris had banked on Sylvia. The tea room was easier, but Joan slipped over that experience so glibly that Doris made a mental reservation concerning it.

Patricia was the critical test. At the mention of her name Cuff

Harriet T. Comstock

whined pathetically, and Joan bent and gathered him in her arms.

"I—I can't talk much about Pat, dearie, not now"; Joan bent her head; "she was so wonderful. Just a beautiful, lost spirit in the world—trying to find its way home. There was only one way for Pat—I shall always be glad that I could go part of it with her."

"Yes, yes—I am glad, too!" Doris whispered, for she had caught up with Joan now. She did not know all that lay in the valleys—but she felt the chill and darkness through which her child had come up to the light. Strange as it might seem, she was thinking of that time, long ago, when she had escaped from the Park and had touched life in the open.

The hospital experience Joan could describe with a touch of humour that eventually brought a smile to Doris's face. She took for granted that it had been in Chicago, and when Joan told of flitting away from the young doctor who had saved her, Doris laughingly said:

"Joan, that was cruel. You should have explained."

"No, Aunt Dorrie, it was wise. Of course I'm going to explain to him and send him the money, but I wanted to shut the door on my silly past first. I shall only let in, hereafter, that part of it that I choose. When I saw a man looking at me, Aunt Dorrie, where before I had been seeing a doctor, there was nothing to do but scamper. He hadn't the least idea what was happening—he saw only the bag of bones that he had rescued, but I wasn't going to let him run any risks. You see, I've learned more than some girls."

And then Joan, mentally, turned her back on the past. With that power she had for holding to the thing she desired, the thing she wanted to make true, she laughed her merry, carefree laugh—she recalled only the joyous, amusing incidents and she watched with hungry, loving eyes the effect she was creating.

It was while this was going on that Mary came upon the piazza to announce luncheon. There were days when no one saw Mary, when her cabin was closed and locked; but after such absences she came to Ridge House and worked with a fervour that flavoured of apology.

She gazed long upon Joan before she spoke. It was not surprise she showed, but a slow understanding.

"Miss Joan," she said at last, "seems like you ain't got the world by the tail like you uster have."

Joan threw her head back and laughed.

"No, Mary," she presently replied, "it swung so fast that I fell off—but I'll catch hold soon."

The quiet little luncheon in the quaint dining room did much to restore the long-past relations of Joan with the family. Uncle Jed came in and chuckled with delight. The old man lived mostly in the past now, and followed Mary like a poor crumpled shadow. What held the two together was difficult to understand—but it was the kinship of the hills, the stolid sense of familiarity.

After the meal was over Joan wandered about through the living rooms for a few moments, touching Nancy's loom, but speaking seldom of Nancy.

"I want to hear all about it from her," she explained; and Doris, with Joan's affairs chiefly in her thought, referred merely to Nancy's happiness, their perfect sympathy with it; and if Kenneth's name was mentioned, Joan did not notice it.

At last she went up to her room to rest.

"Quite as if I had never been away, Aunt Doris," she said, "and you don't mind if I take Cuff? The poor little chap has had so many changes that I fear for his nerves!"

Joan went upstairs to the west wing chamber singing a gay little song—her own voice seemed to hold her to the safe, happy present—so she sang.

She paused at the door of her room to read the words carved there long ago by Sister Constance:

=And the Hills Shall Bring Peace=

It was like someone speaking a welcome.

"Oh! it is all so dear," Joan murmured, "how could it ever have seemed dull!"

Flowers filled the vases, and there was a small, fragrant fire on the hearth—a mere thing of beauty, there was no need of it, for the windows were open to the gentle spring day.

Joan slipped into a loose gown and then stood in the middle of the room leisurely taking in the comfort and joy of every proof of love that she saw.

On the desk by the window lay a pile of unopened letters—she took them up. They were the letters from Doris and Nancy which had been returned from Chicago. Pitiful things that had been so hopefully sent forth only to come back like blighted hopes!

For a moment Joan contemplated throwing them all on the fire. She did not feel equal to re-living the past. It was only by laughing and singing that she could hold her own.

But on second thought she opened the first one—it was from Nancy.

"I better have all I can get to begin on," she reflected; "it will save time."

She sat down in a deep chair and presently she was aware of

combating something that was being impressed upon her; she was not conscious of reading it.

"Such things do not happen—not in life—" her sane, cautious self seemed to say. For a second Joan believed her tired brain was playing her false as it had during those awful weeks in the hospital. She closed her eyes; grew calm—then tried again:

> Since you are not coming to see Ken now, Joan, I will try to describe him. You remember old Mrs. Tweksbury? Well, my dear boy belongs, in a way, to her—

Again Joan closed her eyes while a faintness saved her from too acute shock. She felt the soft air upon her face; she was conscious of that bewildered whine of poor Cuff. Vaguely she thought that he must be hungry; thirsty—then there was a moment's blank and—the sickening weakness was gone!

With the strength and clarity that sometimes comes at a critical moment Joan's mind worked fast and carried her where hours of quiet thought could not have done.

It was natural, of course, that Nancy should meet Raymond— the most natural thing in the world.

His loving her—so soon after what had happened! That was the thing that gripped and hurt. Joan tried to connect the date of that night in the studio and the one on Nancy's letter. She seemed powerless to do so—the time between was a blank; there was no time! Everything belonged to a previous incarnation.

With a shudder, Joan presently realized the insignificant part she had borne in Kenneth Raymond's life.

The humiliation turned her hot and cold. He had always held but one opinion of her; his loss of self-control had simply torn down the defences behind which he had played with her, amused himself with her, during the dull summer.

She was, to him, one of the women not to be considered, while Nancy was—the other kind!

Joan regarded, as she never had before, the freedom and safety of such girls as Nancy. She could realize the pressure, the favouring environment that surrounded so desirable a thing as this coming together of Raymond and Nancy!

She knew how the same force could blot such as she was supposed to be from the inner circle! How little they counted!

Oh! the bitterness of the knowledge that it was such girls as Patricia—as Raymond believed her—who were not free; who must snatch what they can from life and not resent what goes with it. They must—not care! Outside the code there was no real freedom—because there was no choice! It was a place of chains and bars compared to the other.

The waves of humiliation and shame swept over Joan, but each time she emerged she held her head higher.

"And he left me—to go my way and he went—to Nancy! He did not care!" It was anger now; proud, life-saving anger. "If he had only cared!"

"And why—should he?" The thought was like a dash of cold water in her face.

After all, why should he? It *was* only play until that awful night! That was the revealing hour of real danger.

Clutching her hands, Joan went over every step of the way upon which Raymond had gone with her.

It had all been a mad escapade in that time of mistaken freedom. He and she had both been brought to the realization of the folly by a blow that had awakened them, not stunned them. They had been forced to acknowledge the danger hidden in themselves. It was in such whirlpools many were lost, but they—

And at this point Joan recalled, as if he were before her now, the look in Raymond's face when he gained control of himself!

Always, since that night, Joan had felt, when thinking of Raymond, that she never wanted to see him again. She knew that he had never held any real part in her life and he would always hold her back, as she might him—from proving the best that was in each other if they came into contact.

With this conclusion reached Joan had gained a secure footing. As a man, detached from herself and her past, she knew that Raymond was worthy of love and happiness, just as, in her heart, she knew that she herself was. But could others understand? Others, like Nancy?

While she had been buffeted on a rough sea, since that stormy night in the studio, Raymond had drifted into his safe harbour, sooner. There was nothing to hold him back—and here Joan began to sob in self-pity; in pity for all girls, like Patricia and her, who were so lightly considered.

"We do not matter!" she murmured. Then she dashed her tears away. "But we *must* matter!"

She sprang up. She flung the letters upon the embers; she gathered Cuff to her bosom and—laughed!

It was her old, old laugh. The laugh that held in its depth, not scorn of life, but an appreciation of it.

"It's how we take it all, Cuff, my dear, just how we take it! And, Cuff"—here Joan held the little animal off at arms' length and looked into his deep, serious eyes—"I'm going to get the world by the tail again—*you watch me!*"

　　　　Harriet T. Comstock

CHAPTER XXIV

"O, FRIEND NEVER STRIKE SAIL TO A FEAR"

Because the woman in Joan had not been hurt by her experiences, because it was only the wildness of youth that had carried her to the verge of making mistakes and then sent her reeling back, she reacted quickly. She was no longer the reckless, heedless Joan—the change made Martin frown. He put full value on her cropped hair and thin body—he had grappled with the scourge, and he knew!

He presently found himself in friendly sympathy with this new, patient, tender Joan—they had much to say to each other.

Nancy was not so keen about the change. Joan had come back—Joan was putting into life all that it lacked. This was enough for Nancy! The spring days were dreams of bliss and she radiated joy.

"Ken will adore you, Joan!" she confided. "You see, he has a twisted idea about you just because you weren't with us all, but when he sees you, darling, he'll be on his knees before you as we all are!"

"I'd love to get my first view of him in that attitude," Joan laughingly replied, "but on the whole, I'd rather take him standing."

During those waiting days, until Raymond came to marry Nancy, Ridge House quivered with excited preparation.

"Of course!" Joan had agreed to the quiet wedding idea, "we must have it as Nancy wishes, but it must be perfect."

So Joan sewed and designed—some of Patricia's gift was hers—and often her face fell into pensive lines as she worked, for she seemed to see Patricia as she used to sit, well into the night, planning and evolving the dainty garments that others were to wear.

"My turn!" Joan comforted herself with the thought; "my turn now, dear Pat."

And then the day came when Kenneth Raymond was to arrive. Mrs. Tweksbury could be safely left in New York. She was resigned to the wedding but deplored the necessity of being absent.

"I know something will go wrong," she said to Kenneth; "do be careful and make sure that you are really married, Ken! They are so sloppy in the South, and it would be quite like Doris Fletcher, if she couldn't get that candlestick preacher of hers, to let Dave Martin or any one else read the service. Doris never could put the emphasis of life where it belonged."

Kenneth laughed merrily.

"Nancy and I will see to it, Aunt Emily," he replied, "that we are tied up close. Just use your time, until I bring her back, in thinking of the good days on ahead—when we'll have her always, you and I."

Mrs. Tweksbury relaxed.

"She's a blessed child, Ken. She always was."

Raymond arrived late one May afternoon. Joan was dressing

Harriet T. Comstock

for dinner, dressing slowly, tremblingly—she did not mean to go downstairs until dinner was served if she could avoid it.

She had worked late, worked until she was weary enough to plead an hour's rest, and now she stood by the window overlooking The Gap.

"I've got the world in my grip," she thought, "but the whirl makes me dizzy."

Silver River was rushing along rather noisily—there had been a big storm the night before and the water had not yet calmed down; the rocks shone in the last rays of the sun, and just then Joan looked up at The Rock!

There it was—The Ship! Sails set and the western light full upon it.

For a moment Joan gazed, trying to remember the old superstition. Then her face grew tender.

"Whatever happens," she murmured, "it shall not happen to Nancy. I've spoiled enough of her plays—she shall not be hurt now."

The thought held all the essentials of a prayer and it gave an uplift.

Then Joan turned to her toilet. Recalling Patricia's theory about the artistic helps to one's appearance, she worked fervently with her slim little body and delicate face.

A bit of fluffing and the lovely hair rose like an aura about the smiling face. The eyes did not seem too large when one smiled—so Joan practised a smile! The gowns, one by one, were laid out upon the bed and regarded religiously; finally, one was chosen that Patricia had loved.

"My lamb," Joan recalled the words and look, "a true artist

knows her high marks. This gown is a revealment of my genius."

It was a pale blue crepe, silver-touched and graceful; a long, heavy, silver cord held it at the waistline, and the loose, lacy sleeves made the slim arms look very lovely.

"If ever I needed bucking, Pat, dear, I need it now!" whispered Joan, and her eyes dimmed.

She heard the pleasant bustle below; the light laughter, the cheery calls. She heard Raymond's voice when he greeted Nancy—it startled her by its familiarity and its strangeness.

"He sounds as if he were in church," mused Joan. She felt as the old do as they re-live their youth.

There was candlelight in the dining room when Joan entered. The family were all assembled, for Doris had sent for Joan only at the last moment.

"Ken, dear, this is Joan."

Nancy said it as if she were flouting all the foolish things any one had ever felt about Joan. Pride, deep affection, rang in her voice. "This is Joan!"

Joan went slowly, smilingly forward. She saw Raymond's knuckles grow white and hard as his hands gripped the back of his chair. His eyes dilated, and for a moment he could not speak. Finally he managed:

"So this—is Joan!" and went forward to greet her.

"I reckon they will all get this shock," thought Doris; "what they have thought about the child ought to shame them. Emily Tweksbury was always a snob."

Martin, from under his shaggy brows, watched the scene

curiously. He, like everyone else, was, unconsciously, on guard where Nancy was concerned. This frank surprise was gratifying for Joan, but it placed Nancy, for a moment, to one side.

Joan had never looked lovelier; never more self-controlled. She was holding herself, and Raymond, too, by firm will power. He must not betray anything—he owed her and Nancy that! There was no wrong. No suggestion of it must enter in.

In another moment the danger was over; the colour rose to Raymond's face.

"I—I hadn't expected anything quite so—splendid," he said.

"You are very kind," Joan had her hands in his, now; "you see—I've been wandering in strange places; I am rather an outlaw and the best any one could do for me was to wait and let me speak for myself. I'm glad you approve!"

"I certainly do!" Raymond said, and gratefully joined the circle as it sat down.

As the time passed the situation caught Joan's feverish imagination; she dared much; she was cruel but fascinating. She proposed, after dinner, to read palms—explaining that she and Pat had learned the tricks.

At the name of "Pat" Raymond's grave eyes fixed themselves upon her. Joan saw the firm lips draw together, and she paused in her gaiety, sensing something she did not quite understand.

In the living room by the fire Joan again grew witchy. She insisted upon proving her cleverness at palm-reading. Raymond dared not refuse, but he showed plain disapproval.

"It's rot!" Martin broke in, "but here goes, Joan!" And spread his honest hand upon the altar.

Joan had a good field now for her wit, and she set the

company in a merry mood. When she touched upon Martin's nephew, which, of course, she wickedly did, she made an impression.

"See here," Martin broke in, "this isn't palm-reading, you little fraud—you're trying to be funny trading on what you've heard but couldn't know for yourself."

"That's part of the trick, Uncle David. Now, Nan, dear, let me have that small paw of yours."

Frankly Nancy extended the left hand upon which glittered Raymond's diamond.

"The right one, too, Nan darling! What dear, soft, pink things!" Joan bent and kissed them. "Such happy hands; good, true hands. Every line—unbroken. Running from start to finish—as it should run."

"A stupid pair of hands, I call them." Nancy puckered her lips.

"They are blessed hands, Nan."

Raymond went behind Nancy's chair and fixed his eyes upon Joan—he was almost pleading with her to have done with the dangerous play.

"Aunt Dorrie?" Joan turned to her, ignoring Raymond.

"My hands can tell you nothing, Joan, dear," Doris said; "I've been a coward. See, my hands are flabby inside—the hands of a woman who has had much too easy a time. 'Who has reached forth—but never grasped.'"

At this Martin came and stood over Doris. Joan looked up and suddenly her eyes dimmed. She seemed alone. Alone among them all. There was no one beside her—they seemed, Martin and Raymond, to be defending their loved ones from her.

Harriet T. Comstock

"And now, my brother Ken!" The words were like a call.

"Oh, let me off!" Raymond tried to speak lightly.

"No, indeed! The safety of my family is at stake!"

Raymond was inwardly angry, but he sat down and defiantly spread his hands.

Joan regarded them silently for a dramatic moment, then she quietly opened her own.

"Isn't this odd," she said, "there is a line in your hand and mine—alike!"

Every eye was fixed on the four hands.

"Right here—" Joan traced it.

"What does it mean?" Martin asked.

"Capacity for friendship; that we are rather daring; not afraid of many things—but canny enough to know—"

"What, Joan?—out with it!" It was Doris who spoke.

"Canny enough—to distrust ourselves once in awhile."

Martin gave a guffaw.

"Joan," he said, "you ought to be sent to bed. Your eyes are too big and your colour too high. Stop this foolishness and let us take a turn on the river road. The moonlight is filling it—it's too rare to be overlooked."

So they went out, keeping together and talking happily until it was time to return to the house; there, Raymond managed to say to Joan, just as they were parting:

"This has been rather a shock, you know, I wish I could see you alone—for a moment."

She looked up at him, and all the mad daring was gone from her eyes.

"Is there anything to say?" she whispered. "Now or—ever?"

"Yes."

And Raymond knew that Joan would come back.

He sat on the broad porch, opening to The Gap, and smoked. The house grew still with that holy quietness that holds all love safe.

Then came a slight noise; someone was coming!

It was significant that Raymond should know at once who it was. All the love and yearning in the world would not have drawn Nancy through the sleeping house to him. The knowledge made him smile grimly, happily.

Doris, once having said good-night, meant it, and Martin had gone to his bungalow.

"Well—here I am." Joan appeared and sat down, looking as if she were doing the most commonplace thing in life. It was the old daring that had led to dangerous ways.

"Is it—safe?"

"Why not?" It was the same frank, childlike look.

"But—Nancy; your Aunt—"

Joan twisted her mouth humorously.

"We'll have to risk them—you said you had something to say."

"Joan! Good Lord! but it's great to have a name to call you by—you drove me pretty hard to-night. I make no complaint—except—" He paused.

"For Nancy?" Joan asked.

"Yes! Joan, she's wonderful. She's the sort that makes a man rather afraid until he realizes that he means to keep her as she is—forever." This was spoken with a definiteness of purpose that made Joan recoil. Again he was defending Nancy from what he had believed Joan to have been!

"I wonder"—she looked away—"I wonder if any one could do that? Or if it would be wise if he could?"

"Joan, when I saw you to-night, after the shock—I could have fallen on my knees in gratitude—there have been hours when the fear I had about you nearly drove me crazy; made me feel I had no right—to Nancy."

"So you—did remember, for a little time?"

"Yes. I went to the Brier Bush—Miss Gordon gave me to understand that you had gone away with someone—married, she thought.

"Joan—who was—Pat?"

For a moment Joan could not understand, then, as was the way with her, the whole truth flooded in.

Raymond had taken thought for her—Elspeth had deceived him—oh! how hard Elspeth could be. Joan recalled scenes behind closed doors when Elspeth Gordon dealt with her assistants!

"And when you thought—I had—gone away—you felt free?" Joan's face quivered. Raymond nodded. How easy it was to talk to Joan. How quick she was to comprehend and help one over a hard stretch!

"Joan—who was Pat?" That seemed to be the vital thing now. And then Joan told him. As she spoke in low, trembling tones, she saw his head bow in his hands; she knew that he was suffering with her, for her; as good men do for their women. Joan was conscious of this attitude of Raymond's—she was reinstated; fixed, at last, where she could be understood: she belonged to his world!

"Poor little girl! After the beast in me dashed your card house to atoms you made another try—alone!" Raymond raised his face.

"No—I had Pat." At that instant Patricia symbolized the link between the unreal and the real.

"Yes, for a little while—but, Joan, it didn't pay—the danger you ran and all that—did it? Such girls as you cannot afford such experiences."

"Yes. Having had Pat, I am able to see—wider."

Joan was thinking of the girls whom Raymond could *not* have understood or sympathized with! Girls such as she might so easily have been like—unless—Unless what?

"Joan, you and I always said we could speak plain truth, didn't we?" Kenneth's words brought her back.

"Of course!"

"Well," Raymond dropped his eyes and flushed, "you really didn't care—not in the one, particular way, did you? It was only play; you meant that?"

"It was only play, Ken. The suffering came because we did not know what we were playing with. It's the not knowing that matters."

"Joan, you have seen the worst in me—?"

"Yes, and the best, Ken. It was like seeing you come back from hell—unharmed."

"Do you think I should tell Nancy? Put her on her guard? There *is* something in me—"

At this Joan leaned forward with a new light on her face—it was the maternal taking shape.

"No, Ken, you must *not* tell Nan. With her it is the *not* knowing that matters. She must be guarded; not put on guard. I know now that Nan will be safe with you; I wasn't sure before; but if you raised a doubt in her mind all would go wrong. She was always like that."

"But—" for a moment a beaten terror rose in Raymond's eyes.

Joan nodded bravely to him.

"You and I, Ken, must never give fear a chance. Once we know, we must not turn back."

She stood up, looking tall and commanding.

Raymond rose also and took her hands.

"You're great, Joan," he said, "simply great. You understand—though how you do, the Lord only knows.

"Joan!" Raymond flung out the question that was tormenting him. "Joan, why didn't we—care the other way?"

"I think," Joan looked ancient, but pathetically young, "I think men and women don't, when they understand too well. And the line in our hands explains that, perhaps," she smiled wanly. "You see, Miss Jones and Mr. Black are—paying!"

"Joan, go now, dear. Others might not understand." Raymond at that moment grimly shut the door on his one playtime!

"And you—would hate to have them misunderstand about me—for Nancy's sake?"

"No, Joan, for your own. You're too big and fine—to have any more hurting things knock you. May I kiss—you good-night?"

For a moment something in Joan shrank, then she raised her face.

"Yes. Good-night—brother Ken."

For another moment they stood silent. Then:

"What was it that made you so hard at dinner, Joan, and makes you so sweet now?"

"Ken, I thought that you—had not tried to find out about me—after that night!"

"Did the mere going back really matter?"

"It meant everything, Ken."

"How?"

"Oh! can you not understand? If you had just—not cared I would have been afraid to-night for Nancy! Ken, I believe you went back to pay for all our folly—had I been willing to accept; had I—cared in the way—you suspected."

"Yes, Joan. I would have." Raymond said this solemnly. "That's what I went for."

"And you should not have paid! Girls—must not—let others pay more than is owed—I've learned that, Ken. But it was the going back that made it—right for you to—go on. Ken, for

Nancy's dear sake I am glad it was—you and I!"

"For that I thank God!" Again Raymond bent his head. This time his lips fell on the open palms of the hands with those lines in them—lines like his own!

"Some day you are going to be happy, Joan."

"I am happy now. I was never happy, really, before. You see, I was always looking for myself in the past; now I think I have found myself—rather a dilapidated self, but mine own. It's going to be very interesting, this getting acquainted, and"— here Joan was thinking of the last day in the hospital and the rooms opening to the sweet singer—"and I'm going to touch and feel life instead of merely looking out through my own small door. And so—good-night."

She was gone as she had come—not stealthily, but noiselessly; not afraid, but cautious.

CHAPTER XXV

"THIS SHALL BE THY REWARD—
THE IDEAL SHALL BE REAL TO THEE"

Doris and Joan were in the living room of Ridge House trying to make things look "as usual" in the pathetic way people do after a loved one has gone forth never to return in quite the same relation.

Doris paused by Nancy's loom and touched gently the unfinished pattern.

"Dear little Nan," she said; "she used to make such dreadful tangles, but she learned to do beautiful work. This is quite perfect—as far as the child has gone."

Joan was on her knees polishing away at the fireboard. The smoke-covered wood with its motto she meant to restore. She looked up brightly as Doris spoke. Joan was accepting many things besides Nancy's going away as Raymond's wife; accepting them without question, without explanation, but with perfect understanding. She understood fully about David Martin and Doris—her heart beat quick at Martin's lifelong devotion; at Doris's withholding. She understood, too, she believed, why the coming to the South had been necessary— the look in Doris's eyes was the same that had haunted Patricia's—the look that holds the unfailing message.

"Aunt Dorrie, Nancy is the belonging kind. No matter how

Harriet T. Comstock

many places and people share her she will always belong to us and the hills. She told me that before she went. She meant it, too. She'll finish the weaving quite naturally, soon—New York is not far."

Doris gave a soft laugh. Almost she resented the constant tone of comfort, Joan's attitude of authority.

"No; it seems nearer and nearer all the time—since my strength has returned. We will have part of the winter in New York and Nan and Ken will be coming here, and there is your music, Joan!" Doris assumed authority and Joan submitted sweetly.

"Yes, Aunt Dorrie, and you and I will scour these hills and get acquainted with our people and have trips abroad, perhaps. It is simply splendid—the stretch on ahead."

The sun-lighted room was still radiant with the decorations of Nancy's wedding. Tall jars of roses woodbine and "rhoder-deners," as old Jed called them, were everywhere. Nancy had only departed two days before.

"What a charming wedding it was!" Doris mused, patting the loom; "every time I think of it something new and unusual recurs."

Joan rubbed away and laughed gaily.

"Father Noble looked like a precious old saint," she said. "I declare when he told about Mary I was almost afraid he'd be translated before he had a chance to marry Nan."

How little Joan realized that she was touching upon a mighty thing; how little either she or Doris were really ever to know.

Doris came to the hearth and sat down in a deep chair, her face had suddenly grown serious.

"I was thinking of that incident," she said.

"Joan, I have always misjudged Mary. She has always puzzled me. I have thought her hard and selfish—the people here have thought her mean." Doris paused, and Joan looked around and remarked:

"She's a blessed trump. Nan always understood Mary better than I; Mary liked Nan the best of all, but I'm going to cultivate Mary. There is something about her like these hidden words—it must be brought out."

"To think of her caring for and loving that poor, deserted creature on that lonely peak all this time!" Doris went back to the story. "Father Noble says the trail up there is the worst on the mountain, yet Mary went every day. She mended the cabin and kept the old woman clean and clothed and happy—to the very end. Think of her alone in that cabin at night when the poor soul passed away! Mary was always so timid, too, and superstitious—and we never suspecting!"

"And then," Joan took up the thread, "those ten miles to get Father Noble so that there might be a proper funeral, and Nancy's wedding having to wait while they saw the thing properly through. Oh! Aunt Dorrie, it's like a glorious old comedy with so much humanity in it that it hurts. Can you not just *see* that funeral as Father Noble described it?"

Joan stood up, her eyes shining; the polishing cloth held out daintily from the pretty blue gown.

"'Twilight and evening star' effect, and those silent, amazed folks that Mary had compelled to come up the trail; the children and dogs and that comical boy tolling an old, cracked dinner bell; the procession to the clump of trees where the old women's children and grandchildren are buried—why, Aunt Doris, I see it all like a wonderful picture! There's no place on earth like these hills."

Doris saw it, too, as Joan graphically portrayed it—but she was thinking still of Mary; she was baffled.

"And yet," she said, thoughtfully, "you cannot get Mary to talk about it, and she turned quite fiercely upon poor old Jed when he asked his simple questions. She's hard as well as gentle."

"And old Jed"—Joan waved her cloth—"here's to him! Think of him crying because The Ship wouldn't sail off The Rock and insisting that the old woman on Thunder Peak had something in her arms—that ought to have gone on The Ship, not in the ground. The place and the people, Aunt Dorrie, are like a Grimm fairy tale. I'm going to have the time of my life reading them and playing with them."

Joan was thinking, as she often did now, of touching the lives of others—all others who pressed close to her. She had never been so keen or vivid before—the calls upon her were awakening the depths of her nature. She had travelled far only to come home to find Truth.

"I am afraid I shall never be able to understand these silent, unresponsive folk, Joan." Doris shook her head—she was realizing her own shortcomings; her incapacity for new undertakings; "they frighten me. I have always been able to make an ideal seem real, dear, but I am afraid I fail utterly when it comes to making the real seem ideal—particularly when it is not lovely."

"Well, then, duckie, just let me do the interpreting. Father Noble is going to take me under his big, flapping capes and speak a good word for me."

Doris smiled. In the growing conviction that Joan had indeed come back to her she was happy and content. She rarely rebelled now. Her one great adventure was turning out perfectly; she was thankful she had taken David Martin's advice and kept her secret. She had been fair; she had made no personal claims, but she had done what Martin had once suggested that all mothers should do—"point out the channel and keep the lights burning." There were moments when she wished that Joan were more communicative—but she must accept what was offered. Nancy had gone forth radiant to her chosen life and Joan had come back—not defeated but clearer of vision. What more could any woman ask of her children? Her children!

Doris bent and touched Joan's pretty hair.

"I love to think of the look on Ken's face and Nancy's," she said.

"Yes, Aunt Dorrie, it was wonderful. Your opening the window and letting the west light in did the trick. It was inspiration—nothing less."

Doris nodded, recalling why she had opened the window— Meredith had seemed nearer!

"You sang beautifully, Joan," for Joan had sung at Nancy's request a wedding hymn. "Your voice has gained a richness, dear. Next winter—"

"Yes—Aunt Dorrie!" Joan broke in nervously, then suddenly she dropped on her knees by Doris's chair and said softly:

"Aunt Dorrie, I'm going to ask some very—queer questions. You see, while I was away—I missed a lot—and I want to catch up.

"If—if—Nan hadn't loved Ken, wouldn't you and Uncle David have wanted her to care for Clive Cameron?"

Joan felt that Nancy had garnered all that she had sown during her learning time, and often the thought made her lonely, detached her from them. She believed that Cameron's absence from the wedding covered a hurt that her loved ones hid from her.

Harriet T. Comstock

"Yes, Joan," Doris replied very simply, "but—we feel now that it is best as it is."

"Why, Aunt Dorrie?"

"I cannot explain. When you meet Clive Cameron"—Joan winced—"you will understand."

"Did—did Clive Cameron—care?"

Doris laughed.

"No. It was quite comic, Joan, the whole proceeding. Mrs. Tweksbury, Uncle David, and I played matchmakers with a vengeance—but we bungled frightfully, and then Clive Cameron wedged his big body in between Nancy and several young men who might have made trouble, and—and—" Doris thought for an illuminating word. Then—"whistled Ken on!"

"Why, that's awfully funny, Aunt Dorrie—I rather imagined that Ken plunged!"

"No, he always felt attracted by Nancy—she was wonderfully attractive to men, Joan, but I honestly believe it was Clive who made Ken realize. Ken is the slow, sure sort; while Clive is rather devastating, you know. He doesn't waste time or energy—when he sees his way he goes! He is very like what his uncle was when I first knew him—only surer of himself." Doris's lips trembled.

"More bumptious, maybe!" Joan laughed. She was again in high spirits, though why she could hardly have told.

"No, he isn't, Joan!" Doris took up cudgels for the absent Cameron. "You mustn't get that idea. He's the most humble of fellows—but he has a vision. David says he plods along after his dreams and ideals, but when he grips them—well, he grips! I see now how right he was about Nancy and Ken. They are suited to each other."

"Yes—they're the carrying-on sort, Aunt Dorrie"; Joan looked wise and confident. "They're like their kind—Nan is like you. Away back in the Dondale days she used to gloat over all that went to your making, all your grandfathers and grandmothers. She was fore-ordained to carry on, and so was Ken. They'd be done for on paths without signboards. Aunt Dorrie—"

"Yes, dear."

"I wonder why it was in me to—to well, not to carry on?"

Doris bent and laid her thin, fair cheek against the short, bright hair again.

"Your way, little girl," she whispered, "was to fly. You had to try wings."

"Well, I'm a homing pigeon, I reckon." And Joan tossed her short hair back.

Just then there was the toot of a horn outside.

"Uncle David!" Joan exclaimed, jumping up; "and by the manner of his toot I get an impression of exhilaration.

"Hello, Uncle Davey!" For Martin was filling the long window with his big presence.

He smiled on Joan—he did it very naturally these days. The girl was becoming strangely dear and companionable; then he looked at Doris as he always did, eagerly, gratefully.

"Jump into your coat and hat," he said to her with a ring in his voice; "I've just had a telegram. Bud's coming!"

"Oh! David," Doris's face flushed rosily. "And you want me to go with you to meet him. I *am* glad."

Harriet T. Comstock

"Yes," Martin replied. Doris was already on her way from the room. Joan dropped to the hearth and resumed her rubbing.

So the inevitable was upon her! She must not flinch! She wondered if this was the last dropped stitch she must take up?

"Want me to go, too, Uncle David?" she asked, keeping her back rigid.

"No," Martin was regarding the straight set shoulders and the pretty cropped hair. "No! You have too shocking an effect upon young men. They look as if they had seen you before! They must take you gradually." Martin laughed and lighted a cigar. He was recalling Raymond's face the night Joan had first appeared before him.

Joan struggled to keep control of the situation—she suddenly smeared her face with her sooty fingers and turned with a grimace.

"Am I discovered even in this disguise?" she said. Then:

"Uncle Davey, I believe you have your private opinion of me still."

"I have. I'll tell you now what it is—your face needs washing."

"I mean—really!" the smudges acted as a mask and diverted attention. "I wager you think girls like me—the me that *was*, the working girls—are, generally speaking, hounding young men on the matrimonial trail."

"Not necessarily *that* trail," Martin was teasing.

"You're all wrong, Uncle Davey, as far as most of them are concerned. They're young and love a good time and some of them have to learn a lot—learn not to play on volcanoes. But for downright, running-to-earth methods, look to such girls as Nan. They have the tide with them. Men, unless they're there to be caught, better watch out!"

"Oh! come, child, don't be sinister."

"I'm not, Uncle David," Joan's eyes shone; she was thinking of Patricia; "but you, everybody, lose a lot if they do not really know the truth about women—the real truth."

"My dear," David was quite serious, "I'm no longer hard or misjudging—I was frightened at your aunt's methods with you, but you're proving me wrong every day."

"You should have trusted her more, Uncle David."

"Yes, you are right, in part. I should have trusted her less—in some ways."

"About me?"

"No. About herself." Martin flecked the ashes from his cigar. "And now," he said with a huge sigh that seemed to sweep all regrets before it, "go and wash your face!"

Joan ran away, and when she came back the room was empty and the *honk-honk* of Martin's horn sounded down the river road.

Then, as often happens when one stands in an empty room, Joan was conscious of a supersensitiveness. She, quite naturally, attributed it to the ordeal she was about to undergo—the meeting with Clive Cameron and her late talk with Martin. Must she always be on the defensive? Must she always feel that her volcano had blown her up when really she had escaped by its light?

While there was a certain amount of pleasurable excitement in the meeting with Cameron, while it lacked all that her meeting with Raymond had held, still her past experiences were of so uncommon a nature that she could not contemplate them without nervous strain, and she wished that she might have had a longer reprieve before Cameron came.

"With nothing really to be ashamed of," she thought, "I feel like a criminal dodging justice. I wish something so big would come that I could lose myself in it."

Then she walked to the window overlooking The Gap.

"It's no easy matter, Joan my lamb!" almost it seemed as if it were Patricia speaking, "to tie both ends of the rainbow together." Joan smiled at her thought.

"Dear, dear old Pat!" she spoke the words aloud. "The very thought of you—braces me."

Joan was still on the backward trail. She did not often tread it, but when she did she always returned starry-eyed and brave-hearted. That was her reward: the reward that she could share with no one—except as it helped her to live.

Presently she turned to her task of restoring the motto on the fireboard. She worked vigorously, intently, and then leaned back to get a better view.

Suddenly, as if they were alive, the words emerged from the last sweep of the cloth.

"Aha, I am warm. I have seen the fire."

The meaning broke like sunshine from the clouds. It made Joan laugh.

"Well, of all the funny things," she said aloud, "and from the Bible, too," for "Isaiah" was brought into evidence by another rub. "This house is certainly haunted."

Just then a sharp knock on the panels of the door, set wide to the sweet summer day, startled Joan and brought her to her feet, with that quivering of the nerves that betokened an almost psychic state.

A tall man stood in the doorway. His clothes—good ones, well fashioned—were wrinkled and travel stained. They gave the impression of having been slept in. The man was like his garments—the worse for wear but, originally, of good material.

Joan recognized that at once—after she got over the surprise of finding that he was not Clive Cameron.

"Good morning," she said, quietly, while a familiarity about the stranger puzzled her. "Come in and sit down, please."

The man came in, walking stiffly, his eyes fixed upon Joan in a way that confused her. She felt that she ought to remember him, but could not.

"I've tied my horse down by the road," the stranger said, sitting down by the long table, "I got the beast at the station. The distance was longer than I imagined and the roads are—to say the least—not oiled." He laughed and flecked the dust from his coat—still keeping his eyes on Joan.

"Is your aunt at home?" he continued. So then, the man should be recognized—but he still eluded Joan's memory.

"No, she is not. She will not be back for some time. I am sorry that I cannot recall you—I am sure I have seen you—but—"

"You'd have a remarkable memory if you did recall me," there was a sneer in the laugh that followed the words; "you were very young when you saw me before. Perhaps I can help you—you are—Joan, are you not?"

"Yes." Joan sat down opposite the man—her hands were clasped close.

"I'm George Thornton, formerly of the Philippines, later of

Harriet T. Comstock

South Africa, more recently of New York, where I stayed long enough to learn my way here. Incidentally, I am your father."

Had Joan been standing she would have fallen. As it was, she quickly overcame the dizziness that made the speaker seem to dance about and, by gripping her hands closer, she steadied herself.

"I suppose you have never heard of me before?"

"Oh! yes!" Joan listened to her own voice critically; "Aunt Doris told Nancy and me all about you."

"All, eh?" Thornton could barely keep the surprise and relief from his voice. This simplified matters and he could talk freely.

"What do you want?" The question as Joan spoke it sounded brutal. "I do not suppose you have come here, after all these years, for nothing."

Thornton flushed angrily, and his resentment of old flamed into speech.

"I've come to make your aunt—pay. When I saw you before— you and your supposed sister—your aunt had all the cards in her hands, but I told her then that murder would out—and by God! it has—and now it is pay day." The years had coarsened Thornton.

Joan stared at the man across the table as if he had suddenly gone mad before her eyes. She was frightened; she heard distant voices—the cook speaking to Jed—she wanted to call out; meant to—but instead she asked dully:

"What do you mean by—my supposed sister?"

Thornton shifted his position and leaned forward over the table.

"So—eh? She didn't tell you all? I see. She confined the story to—me. And—you've believed all your life—that—that the girl, Nancy, was your sister? Well—by heaven! Doris has taken a chance."

"You have got to tell me what you mean!"

Joan was no longer filled with personal fear—it was wider, deeper than that.

"And you must not lie," she added, fiercely—anger was giving her strength. Thornton regarded her through half-closed eyes.

"Lying isn't my big line," he said, roughly, "if it had seen, I might have escaped the infernal mess that I hatched by— telling the truth in the first place. Since your aunt has neglected her duty—I will tell you the truth!"

Thornton took small heed of the stricken girl near him. Hate and revenge for the moment swayed him, but not for an instant did Joan disbelieve what was burning into her consciousness. Truth rang in every word of the almost unbelievable story. And while she listened and shrank back she was conscious of inanimate things taking on human attributes that pleaded with her. The chair by the hearth where Doris had but recently sat smiling so happily because her ideals had been real to her! Nancy and she, Joan seemed to know, were the ideals— Nancy and she! For them Doris had done the one, big, daring thing in her life. The loom by the window suddenly cried out, too, as if Nancy were bending over it—working on her unfinished but perfect pattern.

"Oh!" The word escaped Joan and found its way to Thornton's sympathy at last. He paused as he watched the suffering his words were causing.

"It's a damned ugly thing she did to you," he said, "a damned ugly one. I warned her about the time when you would have to know. I've travelled a long distance to set you straight. She'll pay—now!"

Joan tried to speak—failed—then tried again.

"What are you going to do?" she asked, huskily, at last.

Thornton regarded her with a dark frown.

"Do?" he repeated, "claim my own—and let her pay."

"What good—would that do—now?"

Thornton stared. Where had he heard words like those before?
Why should they seem to defy him? defeat him?

"I'm going to have the truth known at last or—"

"Or—what?"

Shame held Thornton silent for a moment, but life had him at
close grip—he was beaten unless help were given.

"You think they will enjoy—the Tweksbury crowd—I mean—
to know the parentage or—lack of it—of—the girl just palmed
off on them as a Thornton? I may not be all that could be
desired, but such as I am—I'm the saving clause." Thornton's
coarseness was more and more evident. "I wonder if you can
justify this mess?" he asked, suddenly, with a new interest.

Joan was not trying to justify it—she was seeing it only as the
beautiful thing Doris had accomplished by that power of hers
to make real her ideal. It had been, still was, her one hold on
life.

"It's too late to talk about that now," she answered, slowly, and
thinking fast and far, far ahead.

"I imagine it will be expensive not to think of it; but she'll
pay!" Thornton was braced for definite action. The girl

opposite confused him. She looked so young; so agonized—so brave. She was so like—At this Thornton turned away his eyes. Only by so doing could he hold to his course.

Slowly, like one dragging a heavy load, Joan was reaching a place of clear understanding. Flashed upon her aching brain were blinding pictures.

"One child was a forsaken waif of these hills—" Thornton had said. "*Thunder Peak! The old woman! Mary's silent and secret mission!*" rang the echo. Joan's eyes widened; her breath caught in her throat while she compelled herself to weigh and consider—though she did it in the dark. Then suddenly Mary became a tower of strength. Mary!

Then Nancy's loveliness and charm gave their convincing evidence against Joan's own characteristics. At this she shuddered.

"Doris said she never knew which child was mine," Thornton's words still echoed.

"But she must have known!" Joan bowed her head, and all the loneliness of her life gathered in this moment of supreme acceptance. She knew, now, why she was, as she was; she knew why they could all cling together. There was something that could hold them together; something stronger than Doris could command. There *was* a pay day! It had come!

"I do not see," Joan spoke at last, and her voice was heavy and even, "why you should think you can harm Nancy. If what you have told is—I mean, *because* what you have told is true— Nancy cannot be hurt—Nancy is—is yours! You would never doubt that if you saw her. I suppose you think"—here Joan's eyes flamed—"you can get more by attacking Nancy."

At this Thornton startled Joan by throwing his head back and laughing aloud, fearlessly, roughly.

Harriet T. Comstock

She was alarmed. The servants—what would they think? Mary—suppose Mary should appear? But above all else Joan wanted to get this hideous thing over before Doris returned. Never for an instant did she falter there.

But the laugh continued, less noisy but more reckless.

"Well, by heaven, you are game!" Thornton managed to form the words, and in his eyes there was a glint of admiration. His old sporting spirit awakened—he knew the genuine ring of metal.

"Why, see here, my girl," he drew from his pocket a gold locket and an old daguerreotype; "you don't suppose I came without evidence, do you?"

Mechanically Joan reached across the table and took the articles—her fingers were stiff and cold, but she managed to unclasp the cases. Thornton was watching her; he had stopped laughing.

In the locket were two miniatures—one of Meredith Fletcher, one of Thornton painted just after their marriage—Doris had the duplicate of Meredith's.

"That," Thornton spoke deliberately, as Joan turned to the other, "is my mother! She and I were very like."

Joan drew her breath in sharp.

Once, back in the Dondale days, she had sung some of her old English ballads in costume—a quaint picture of her had been taken at the time and, for an instant, she thought this was it— she vaguely wondered how Thornton had got it—she could not think clearly—her brain was growing cloudy. Then she turned the old case over in her hand and looked at it mutely.

"They discounted your resemblance to my side of the house." There was something almost pathetic underlying the sneer in

Thornton's voice. "I did not know myself until I came in the door—but when I saw you, it was as if my mother stood here."

Joan could not speak, but, as a change of wind turned the mists in The Gap *to* the east instead of *from* the east, so her clouds were drifting; drifting, and a flood of light was blinding her. She looked up—her eyes were shining with tears that did not fall; her lips twitched nervously, but she was happy; happy. The sensation brought strength and purpose. She did not seem alone—she was close, close to them who, unseen, but vital, were pressing near; waiting for her decision—now that she understood! What had her unconscious preparation done for her?

Oh! she would not fail them. She was almost ready to prove herself. In a moment she could master her emotions and be worthy.

Then she looked at Thornton and throbbed with hate; but as she looked her mood again changed—she felt such pity as she had never known in her life before.

It repelled; it did not attract—but it was pity that called forth a desire to help. Clasping the silent witnesses of the truth in her cold hands Joan spoke:

"No! Aunt Doris and Nancy shall not pay," she said, quietly.

"Who—then?" Thornton felt the ground slipping from under him. The young creature opposite looked so old and hard that she impressed him in spite of himself.

"You and I—will pay!"

By those words Joan took her stand with Thornton, not against him. He winced.

"Think—think what all this means," she faltered.

Thornton did think. He thought back of the girl confronting him with his mother's eyes. The backward path was black and wreck-strewn; it led—where?

"Aunt Doris has told me of—of my mother! You and I owe my mother—" here Joan choked and Thornton burst in:

"But is it right and decent—that this imposition should be put upon innocent people? That girl—may turn out to be—"

But Joan was not heeding. She paused and looked at the unfinished but perfect work upon the loom!

"It is too late now to consider that," she whispered, brokenly. Then: "Aunt Doris has saved Nancy. You need have no fear.

"Oh! can you not see what a chance you have to—to help this wonderful thing Aunt Doris did?"

"Help? How?" Thornton sunk back in his chair. He was crushed—but in the depths of his soul something was stirring; something that he believed had died when he heard of the birth of the girl across the table who was pleading with him for those who had made her what she was!

"How?"

"Why—by simply—going away!"

Thornton almost broke again into that maddening laugh, but caught himself in time.

"That sounds—devilish easy!" he said, furiously, but the flare of passion died at birth, for Joan was saying:

"I have some money of my own—I will send it all to you. I will get money for you—as long as you need it—but after a time you will—not need it! And then"—here Joan stretched out her clasped hands—"I know it sounds almost impossible—

but it can be made true—you can come back to us all; help us keep the secret, and—watch with us. You and I owe this—to Aunt Doris; to my mother! It may be your—your—recompense."

Thornton got upon his feet. He held to the table to steady himself, and a subtle dignity grew upon him.

"I am going away," he said, slowly, "until I can think over this infernal business by myself. The time to act hasn't come yet—that's certain. I don't want—your money; not now. If I do, I'll send for it. If I ever come again it will be to—"he paused, flung his head up—"to see you; to look on at the working out of the damned mess."

He reached out for the locket and case.

"Good-bye," he said, gruffly. "You need not be afraid—not now."

"I am not afraid." Joan rose weakly. "I shall wait for you. I am sure you will come.

"Good-bye; good-bye!"

Outside Thornton stumbled against old Jed.

"The Ship's sailing!" the quavering, foolish words startled Thornton; "you best get aboard, sir, anchor's lifting!" Jed staggered away, grinning and muttering.

Thornton stared after the swaying figure. Then he thought of the Philippines, his old battle ground—he would go back! The idea caught and held him.

On the river road his horse stood nibbling the grass; a woman was beside it—a lean, stooping woman with a home-spun shawl clutched over her sunken breasts by one hand, in the other was a massive, rusty gun!

She turned and confronted Thornton. She knew him at once, but he merely frowned at her as he eyed the weapon uneasily.

"Who are you?" he asked. The place, the experience were getting to be too much for his shaken nerves.

"That don't matter," Mary raised her deep eyes, they were burning with superstitious intentness; "but I have a message for you—you best heed it. We don't stand for strangers hanging around here. See there!" Mary pointed to The Rock— Thornton's excited fancy caught the wavering outlines of The Ship.

"All that's wise—goes with that." Mary turned away. "You best heed!" she muttered as Jed had, and slunk off.

Thornton shivered. He had not eaten for many hours; he was weary and beaten.

"My God!" he muttered as he mounted the horse; "what—a conspiracy! What a hole to get away from. She thinks I'm looking for stills. Stills!" he gave a weak laugh.

Joan stood until she heard the sound of the horse's hoofs on the road, then she turned to the freshly brushed but empty hearth and knelt, shivering.

"Aha, I am warm. I have seen the fire." Her eyes clung to the words as if they were living flames. She was not conscious of thought, but she seemed to *know* that she had only *seen* the fire before but that now she was to feel it. A glow was stirring within her—a bright, flaming thing that lighted her way, on before—the long, long splendid way on which responsibility rested like a halo.

She held within her soul all that had gone into her making— she belonged, in a great and demanding significance, to— Doris and Doris's people. Doris's and her own! Her own! She must prove herself—behind the shield; she must make the *real* her ideal. She must not be afraid. Fear was the only thing that mattered.

Her whole life had been but an outline up to now; she must fill it in! She must not be afraid to set sail.

Who had said that to her?

"Set sail. Bids—you set sail!"

So engrossed was Joan in the flooding tide of thought, so entirely was she abandoning herself to it, that it was only when she heard Doris speak that she turned.

"Joan, we've brought Clive! We met him on the way."

Joan did not rise. With hands clasped in her lap she faced the little group in the doorway.

Her eyes were filled with the golden light of day—she waited; all her life, she knew, she had been preparing for this moment. She saw Cameron's start of surprise; his wonder and doubt. Then she saw him gathering strength as for the last lap of a hard race.

"So I have found you!" he said, and pushing past Martin and Doris he came across the room with outstretched hands.

Something was calling in the tone which words could not convey, and Joan could not answer. It was like hearing a voice where before there had been but echoes.

"I always knew that I would find you!"

Cameron had reached the girl on the floor; he bent and drew her to her feet. His eyes were laughing; he saw her effort to answer him; her seeking to—understand what *he* had already learned.

"It's—all right now," he comforted.

"Yes—of course!"

How futile were the words, but they opened the way for truth to flood in.

Joan, her hands still in Cameron's, her eyes clinging to his, murmured again, "Yes; of course—now!"

Then she turned to the two silent, amazed people in the doorway and, by some magic, they were making her realize that she was facing her Big Chance. Hers!

She must not be afraid. Fear was the only thing that could harm.

Where they had been weak, she must be strong; where they had been blinded, she must—see!

Why, that was what her life and Cameron's meant, and the two, standing apart, together—but alone—had made it possible.

She, like Nancy, must "carry on," not mistakenly, not held on leash, but with a freedom born of choice and understanding; of failures, and the learning of the true from the false.

To her—and again Joan turned to Cameron—and to him, was given the glorious opportunity of making the *real*, ideal.

It was then that Joan threw her head back and laughed that laugh of hers that meant but one thing: An acceptance of life; a faith in its freedom; a conviction that it could be lived gladly and without fear.

Choose from Thousands of 1stWorldLibrary Classics By

A. M. Barnard
Ada Leverson
Adolphus William Ward
Aesop
Agatha Christie
Alexander Aaronsohn
Alexander Kielland
Alexandre Dumas
Alfred Gatty
Alfred Ollivant
Alice Duer Miller
Alice Turner Curtis
Alice Dunbar
Allen Chapman
Alleyne Ireland
Ambrose Bierce
Amelia E. Barr
Amory H. Bradford
Andrew Lang
Andrew McFarland Davis
Andy Adams
Angela Brazil
Anna Alice Chapin
Anna Sewell
Annie Besant
Annie Hamilton Donnell
Annie Payson Call
Annie Roe Carr
Annonaymous
Anton Chekhov
Archibald Lee Fletcher
Arnold Bennett
Arthur C. Benson
Arthur Conan Doyle
Arthur M. Winfield
Arthur Ransome
Arthur Schnitzler
Arthur Train
Atticus
B.H. Baden-Powell
B. M. Bower
B. C. Chatterjee
Baroness Emmuska Orczy
Baroness Orczy
Basil King
Bayard Taylor
Ben Macomber
Bertha Muzzy Bower
Bjornstjerne Bjornson

Booth Tarkington
Boyd Cable
Bram Stoker
C. Collodi
C. E. Orr
C. M. Ingleby
Carolyn Wells
Catherine Parr Traill
Charles A. Eastman
Charles Amory Beach
Charles Dickens
Charles Dudley Warner
Charles Farrar Browne
Charles Ives
Charles Kingsley
Charles Klein
Charles Hanson Towne
Charles Lathrop Pack
Charles Romyn Dake
Charles Whibley
Charles Willing Beale
Charlotte M. Braeme
Charlotte M. Yonge
Charlotte Perkins Stetson
Clair W. Hayes
Clarence Day Jr.
Clarence E. Mulford
Clemence Housman
Confucius
Coningsby Dawson
Cornelis DeWitt Wilcox
Cyril Burleigh
D. H. Lawrence
Daniel Defoe
David Garnett
Dinah Craik
Don Carlos Janes
Donald Keyhoe
Dorothy Kilner
Dougan Clark
Douglas Fairbanks
E. Nesbit
E. P. Roe
E. Phillips Oppenheim
E. S. Brooks
Earl Barnes
Edgar Rice Burroughs
Edith Van Dyne
Edith Wharton

Edward Everett Hale
Edward J. O'Biren
Edward S. Ellis
Edwin L. Arnold
Eleanor Atkins
Eleanor Hallowell Abbott
Eliot Gregory
Elizabeth Gaskell
Elizabeth McCracken
Elizabeth Von Arnim
Ellem Key
Emerson Hough
Emilie F. Carlen
Emily Bronte
Emily Dickinson
Enid Bagnold
Enilor Macartney Lane
Erasmus W. Jones
Ernie Howard Pie
Ethel May Dell
Ethel Turner
Ethel Watts Mumford
Eugene Sue
Eugenie Foa
Eugene Wood
Eustace Hale Ball
Evelyn Everett-green
Everard Cotes
F. H. Cheley
F. J. Cross
F. Marion Crawford
Fannie E. Newberry
Federick Austin Ogg
Ferdinand Ossendowski
Fergus Hume
Florence A. Kilpatrick
Fremont B. Deering
Francis Bacon
Francis Darwin
Frances Hodgson Burnett
Frances Parkinson Keyes
Frank Gee Patchin
Frank Harris
Frank Jewett Mather
Frank L. Packard
Frank V. Webster
Frederic Stewart Isham
Frederick Trevor Hill
Frederick Winslow Taylor

Friedrich Kerst
Friedrich Nietzsche
Fyodor Dostoyevsky
G.A. Henty
G.K. Chesterton
Gabrielle E. Jackson
Garrett P. Serviss
Gaston Leroux
George A. Warren
George Ade
Geroge Bernard Shaw
George Cary Eggleston
George Durston
George Ebers
George Eliot
George Gissing
George MacDonald
George Meredith
George Orwell
George Sylvester Viereck
George Tucker
George W. Cable
George Wharton James
Gertrude Atherton
Gordon Casserly
Grace E. King
Grace Gallatin
Grace Greenwood
Grant Allen
Guillermo A. Sherwell
Gulielma Zollinger
Gustav Flaubert
H. A. Cody
H. B. Irving
H.C. Bailey
H. G. Wells
H. H. Munro
H. Irving Hancock
H. R. Naylor
H. Rider Haggard
H. W. C. Davis
Haldeman Julius
Hall Caine
Hamilton Wright Mabie
Hans Christian Andersen
Harold Avery
Harold McGrath
Harriet Beecher Stowe
Harry Castlemon
Harry Coghill
Harry Houidini

Hayden Carruth
Helent Hunt Jackson
Helen Nicolay
Hendrik Conscience
Hendy David Thoreau
Henri Barbusse
Henrik Ibsen
Henry Adams
Henry Ford
Henry Frost
Henry James
Henry Jones Ford
Henry Seton Merriman
Henry W Longfellow
Herbert A. Giles
Herbert Carter
Herbert N. Casson
Herman Hesse
Hildegard G. Frey
Homer
Honore De Balzac
Horace B. Day
Horace Walpole
Horatio Alger Jr.
Howard Pyle
Howard R. Garis
Hugh Lofting
Hugh Walpole
Humphry Ward
Ian Maclaren
Inez Haynes Gillmore
Irving Bacheller
Isabel Cecilia Williams
Isabel Hornibrook
Israel Abrahams
Ivan Turgenev
J.G.Austin
J. Henri Fabre
J. M. Barrie
J. M. Walsh
J. Macdonald Oxley
J. R. Miller
J. S. Fletcher
J. S. Knowles
J. Storer Clouston
J. W. Duffield
Jack London
Jacob Abbott
James Allen
James Andrews
James Baldwin

James Branch Cabell
James DeMille
James Joyce
James Lane Allen
James Lane Allen
James Oliver Curwood
James Oppenheim
James Otis
James R. Driscoll
Jane Abbott
Jane Austen
Jane L. Stewart
Janet Aldridge
Jens Peter Jacobsen
Jerome K. Jerome
Jessie Graham Flower
John Buchan
John Burroughs
John Cournos
John F. Kennedy
John Gay
John Glasworthy
John Habberton
John Joy Bell
John Kendrick Bangs
John Milton
John Philip Sousa
John Taintor Foote
Jonas Lauritz Idemil Lie
Jonathan Swift
Joseph A. Altsheler
Joseph Carey
Joseph Conrad
Joseph E. Badger Jr
Joseph Hergesheimer
Joseph Jacobs
Jules Vernes
Julian Hawthrone
Julie A Lippmann
Justin Huntly McCarthy
Kakuzo Okakura
Karle Wilson Baker
Kate Chopin
Kenneth Grahame
Kenneth McGaffey
Kate Langley Bosher
Kate Langley Bosher
Katherine Cecil Thurston
Katherine Stokes
L. A. Abbot
L. T. Meade

L. Frank Baum
Latta Griswold
Laura Dent Crane
Laura Lee Hope
Laurence Housman
Lawrence Beasley
Leo Tolstoy
Leonid Andreyev
Lewis Carroll
Lewis Sperry Chafer
Lilian Bell
Lloyd Osbourne
Louis Hughes
Louis Joseph Vance
Louis Tracy
Louisa May Alcott
Lucy Fitch Perkins
Lucy Maud Montgomery
Luther Benson
Lydia Miller Middleton
Lyndon Orr
M. Corvus
M. H. Adams
Margaret E. Sangster
Margret Howth
Margaret Vandercook
Margaret W. Hungerford
Margret Penrose
Maria Edgeworth
Maria Thompson Daviess
Mariano Azuela
Marion Polk Angellotti
Mark Overton
Mark Twain
Mary Austin
Mary Catherine Crowley
Mary Cole
Mary Hastings Bradley
Mary Roberts Rinehart
Mary Rowlandson
M. Wollstonecraft Shelley
Maud Lindsay
Max Beerbohm
Myra Kelly
Nathaniel Hawthrone
Nicolo Machiavelli
O. F. Walton
Oscar Wilde

Owen Johnson
P.G. Wodehouse
Paul and Mabel Thorne
Paul G. Tomlinson
Paul Severing
Percy Brebner
Percy Keese Fitzhugh
Peter B. Kyne
Plato
Quincy Allen
R. Derby Holmes
R. L. Stevenson
R. S. Ball
Rabindranath Tagore
Rahul Alvares
Ralph Bonehill
Ralph Henry Barbour
Ralph Victor
Ralph Waldo Emmerson
Rene Descartes
Ray Cummings
Rex Beach
Rex E. Beach
Richard Harding Davis
Richard Jefferies
Richard Le Gallienne
Robert Barr
Robert Frost
Robert Gordon Anderson
Robert L. Drake
Robert Lansing
Robert Lynd
Robert Michael Ballantyne
Robert W. Chambers
Rosa Nouchette Carey
Rudyard Kipling
Saint Augustine
Samuel B. Allison
Samuel Hopkins Adams
Sarah Bernhardt
Sarah C. Hallowell
Selma Lagerlof
Sherwood Anderson
Sigmund Freud
Standish O'Grady
Stanley Weyman
Stella Benson
Stella M. Francis

Stephen Crane
Stewart Edward White
Stijn Streuvels
Swami Abhedananda
Swami Parmananda
T. S. Ackland
T. S. Arthur
The Princess Der Ling
Thomas A. Janvier
Thomas A Kempis
Thomas Anderton
Thomas Bailey Aldrich
Thomas Bulfinch
Thomas De Quincey
Thomas Dixon
Thomas H. Huxley
Thomas Hardy
Thomas More
Thornton W. Burgess
U. S. Grant
Upton Sinclair
Valentine Williams
Various Authors
Vaughan Kester
Victor Appleton
Victor G. Durham
Victoria Cross
Virginia Woolf
Wadsworth Camp
Walter Camp
Walter Scott
Washington Irving
Wilbur Lawton
Wilkie Collins
Willa Cather
Willard F. Baker
William Dean Howells
William le Queux
W. Makepeace Thackeray
William W. Walter
William Shakespeare
Winston Churchill
Yei Theodora Ozaki
Yogi Ramacharaka
Young E. Allison
Zane Grey